ALL THE DAYS
AND NIGHTS

ALL THE DAYS AND NIGHTS

THE

COLLECTED

STORIES

OF

WILLIAM

MAXWELL

Alfred A. Knopf   New York   1995

THIS IS A BORZOI BOOK
PUBLISHED BY ALFRED A. KNOPF, INC.

Copyright © 1965, 1986, 1992, 1994 by William Maxwell
All rights reserved under International and Pan-American Copyright Conventions.
Published in the United States by Alfred A. Knopf, Inc., New York
and simultaneously in Canada by Random House of Canada Limited, Toronto.
Distributed by Random House, Inc., New York.

"A Game of Chess" (signed Gifford Brown) and "What He Was Like" were originally
published in *The New Yorker;* "A fable begotten of an echo of a line of verse by W. B. Yeats"
was originally published in *Antaeus;* "The Lily-White Boys" was originally published in
The Paris Review; "A mean and spiteful toad" and "The pessimistic fortune-teller"
were originally published in *Story* under the titles "Alice" and "The Fortune-teller."
Improvisations 1, 12, and 21 were originally published in a volume of five tales
privately printed in honor of the author's eightieth birthday.

Library of Congress Cataloging-in-Publication Data
Maxwell, William.
All the days and nights : the collected stories of William Maxwell.
p. cm.
ISBN 0-679-43829-7
1. City and town life — Illinois — Fiction. 2. Manhattan (New York,
N.Y.) — Fiction. 3. Americans — Travel — France —
Fiction. 4. Family — New York (N.Y.) — Fiction. I. Title.
PS3525.A9464A79 1995
813'.54 — dc20 94-27509
CIP

Manufactured in the United States of America
First Edition

For my one and only

CONTENTS

PREFACE

THE four-masted schooner lay at anchor in Gravesend Bay, not far from Coney Island. It belonged to J. P. Morgan, and I persuaded a man with a rowboat to take me out to it. In my coat pocket was a letter of introduction to the captain. The year was 1933, and I was twenty-five. I had started to become an English professor and changed my mind, and I had written a novel, as yet unpublished. I meant to go to sea, so that I would have something to write about. And because I was under the impression, gathered from the dust-jacket copy of various best-sellers, that it was something a writer did before he settled down and devoted his life to writing. While the captain was reading my letter I looked around. The crew consisted of one sailor, chipping rust, with a police dog at his side. It turned out that the schooner had been there for four years because Mr. Morgan couldn't afford to use it. The captain was tired of doing nothing and was expecting a replacement the next day and was therefore not in a position to take me on. He had no idea when the beautiful tall-masted ship would leave its berth. And I had no idea that three-quarters of the material I would need for the rest of my writing life was already at my disposal. My father and mother. My brothers. The cast of larger-than-life-size characters — affectionate aunts, friends of the family, neighbors white and black — that I was presented with when I came into the world. The look of things. The weather. Men and women long at rest in the cemetery but vividly remembered. The Natural History of home: the suede glove on the front-hall table, the unfinished game of solitaire, the oriole's nest suspended from the tip of the outermost branch of the elm tree, dandelions in the grass. All there, waiting for me to learn my trade and recognize instinctively what would make a story or sustain the complicated cross-weaving of longer fiction.

I think it is generally agreed that stories read better one at a time. They need air around them. And they need thinking about, since they tend to have both an explicit and an un-spelled-out meaning. Inevitably, some of the stories I wrote, especially when I was young, are stuck fast in their period — or to put it differently, the material was not as substantial as it ought to have been — and I see no reason to republish them. When I was working on the ninth version of "A Final Report" I came on the seventh, in a desk drawer, and saw that it was better than the one I was working on and that I must have been too tired when I finished it to realize that there was no need to pursue the idea any further. On the other hand, "Love" came right the first time, without a word having to be changed, and I thought — mistakenly — that I had had a breakthrough, and stories would be easier to write from that moment on; all I needed to do was just *say* it.

The stories I have called "improvisations" really are that. They were written for an occasion — for a birthday or to be rolled up inside a red ribbon and inserted among the ornaments on the Christmas tree. I wrote them to please my wife, over a great many years. When we were first married, after we had gone to bed I would tell her a story in the dark. They came from I had no idea where. Sometimes I fell asleep in the middle of a story and she would shake me and say "What happened next?" and I would struggle up through layers of oblivion and tell her.

ALL THE DAYS
AND NIGHTS

Over by the River

THE sun rose somewhere in the middle of Queens, the exact moment of its appearance shrouded in uncertainty because of a cloud bank. The lights on the bridges went off, and so did the red light in the lantern of the lighthouse at the north end of Welfare Island. Seagulls settled on the water. A newspaper truck went from building to building dropping off heavy bundles of, for the most part, bad news, which little boys carried inside on their shoulders. Doormen smoking a pipe and dressed for a walk in the country came to work after a long subway ride and disappeared into the service entrances. When they reappeared, by way of the front elevator, they had put on with their uniforms a false amiability and were prepared for eight solid hours to make conversation about the weather. With the morning sun on them, the apartment buildings far to the west, on Lexington Avenue, looked like an orange mesa. The pigeons made bubbling noises in their throats as they strutted on windowsills high above the street.

All night long, there had been plenty of time. Now suddenly there wasn't, and this touched off a chain explosion of alarm clocks, though in some instances the point was driven home without a sound: Time is interior to animals as well as exterior. A bare arm with a wristwatch on it emerged from under the covers and turned until the dial was toward the light from the windows.

"What time is it?"

"Ten after."

"It's always ten after," Iris Carrington said despairingly, and turned over in bed and shut her eyes against the light. Also against the clamor of her desk calendar: *Tuesday 11, L. 3:30 Dr. de Santillo . . . 5:30—7:30? . . . Wednesday 1:45, Mrs. McIntosh speaks on the changing status of women.*

3:30 Dr. F.... Friday 11 C. Get Andrea ... Saturday, call Mrs. Stokes. Ordering pads. L ballet 10:30. 2 Laurie to Sasha's. Remaining books due at library. Explore dentists. Supper at 5. Call Margot ...

Several minutes passed.

"Oh my God, I don't think I can make it," George Carrington said, and put his feet over the side of the bed, and found he could make it, after all. He could bend over and pick up his bathrobe from the floor, and put it on, and find his slippers, and close the window, and turn on the radiator valve. Each act was easier than the one before. He went back to the bed and drew the covers closer around his wife's shoulders.

Yawning, stretching, any number of people got up and started the business of the day. Turning on the shower. Dressing. Putting their hair up in plastic curlers. Squeezing toothpaste out of tubes that were all but empty. Squeezing orange juice. Separating strips of bacon.

The park keepers unlocked the big iron gates that closed the river walk off between Eighty-third and Eighty-fourth Streets. A taxi coming from Doctors Hospital was snagged by a doorman's whistle. The wind picked up the dry filth under the wheels of parked cars and blew it now this way, now that. A child got into an orange minibus and started on the long, devious ride to nursery school and social adjustment.

"Have you been a good girl?" George inquired lovingly, through the closed door of the unused extra maid's room, where the dog slept on a square of carpet. Puppy had not been a good girl. There was a puddle of urine — not on the open newspaper he had left for her, just in case, but two feet away from it, on the black-and-white plastic-tile floor. Her tail quivering with apology, she watched while he mopped the puddle up and disposed of the wet newspaper in the garbage can in the back hall. Then she followed him through the apartment to the foyer, and into the elevator when it came.

There were signs all along the river walk:

NO DOGS

NO BICYCLES

NO THIS

NO THAT

He ignored them with a clear conscience. If he curbed the dog beforehand, there was no reason not to turn her loose and let her run — except that sometimes she stopped and arched her back a second time. When shouting and waving his hands didn't discourage her from moving her bowels, he took some newspaper from a trash container and cleaned up after her.

At the flagpole, he stood looking out across the river. The lights went off all the way up the airplane beacon, producing an effect of silence — as if somebody had started to say something and then decided not to. The tidal current was flowing south. He raised his head and sniffed, hoping for a breath of the sea, and smelled gasoline fumes instead.

Coming back, the dog stopped to sniff at trash baskets, at cement copings, and had to be restrained from greeting the only other person on the river walk — a grey-haired man who jogged there every morning in a gym suit and was afraid of dogs. He smiled pleasantly at George, and watched Puppy out of the corner of his eyes, so as to be ready when she leapt at his throat.

A tanker, freshly painted, all yellow and white, and flying the flag of George had no idea what country until he read the lettering on the stern, overtook him, close in to shore — so close he could see the captain talking to a sailor in the wheelhouse. To be sailing down the East River on a ship that was headed for open water . . . He waved to them and they waved back, but they didn't call out to him *Come on, if you want to,* and it was too far to jump. It came to him with the seriousness of a discovery that there was no place in the world he would not like to see. Concealed in this statement was another that he had admitted to himself for the first time only recently. There were places he would never see, experiences of the first importance that he would never have. He might die without ever having heard a nightingale.

When they stepped out of the elevator, the dog hurried off to the kitchen to see if there was something in her dish she didn't know about, and George settled down in the living room with the *Times* on his lap and waited for a glass of orange juice to appear at his place at the dining-room table. The rushing sound inside the walls, as of an underground river, was Iris running her bath. The orange juice was in no hurry to get to the dining-room table. Iris had been on the phone daily with the employment agency and for the moment this was the best they could offer: twenty-seven years old, pale, with dirty blond hair, unmarried, overattached to her mother, and given to burning herself on the anti-quated gas stove. She lived on tea and cigarettes. Breakfast was all the cooking she was entrusted with; Iris did the rest. Morning after morning his boiled egg was hard enough to take on a picnic. A blind man could not have made a greater hash of half a grapefruit. The coffee was indescribable. After six weeks there was a film of grease over everything in the kitchen. Round, jolly, neat, professionally trained, a marvellous cook, the mother was everything that is desirable in a servant except that, alas, she worked for somebody else. She drifted in and out of the apartment at odd hours, deluding Iris with the hope that some of her accomplishments would, if one were only patient, rub off on her daughter.

"Read," a voice said, bringing him all the way back from Outer Mongolia.

"Tonight, Cindy."

"Read! Read!"

He put the paper down and picked her up, and when she had settled comfortably in his lap he began: " 'Emily was a guinea pig who loved to travel. Generally she stayed home and looked after her brother Arthur. But every so often she grew tired of cooking and mending and washing and ironing; the day would seem too dark, and the house too small, and she would have a great longing to set out into the distance. . . .' "

Looking down at the top of her head as he was reading, he felt an impulse to put his nose down and smell her hair. Born in a hurry she was. Born in one hell of a hurry, half an hour after her mother got to the hospital.

LAURIE Carrington said, "What is the difference, what is the difference between a barber and a woman with several children?" Nobody answered, so she asked the question again.

"I give up," Iris said.

"Do you know, Daddy?"

"I give up too, we all give up."

"A barber . . . has razors to shave. And the woman has shavers to raise."

He looked at her over the top of his half-glasses, wondering what ancestor was responsible for that reddish blond hair.

"That's a terribly funny one, Laurie," he said. "That's the best one yet," and his eyes reverted to the editorial page. A nagging voice inside his head informed him that a good father would be conversing intelligently with his children at the breakfast table. But about what? No intelligent subject of conversation occurred to him, perhaps because it was Iris's idea in the first place, not his.

He said, "Cindy, would you like a bacon sandwich?"

She thought, long enough for him to become immersed in the *Times* again, and then she said, "I would like a piece of bacon and a piece of toast. But not a bacon sandwich."

He dropped a slice of bread in the toaster and said, "Py-rozz-quozz-gill" — a magic word, from one of the Oz books. With a grinding noise the bread disappeared.

"Stupid Cindy," Laurie remarked, tossing her head. But Cindy wasn't fooled. Laurie used to be the baby and now she wasn't anymore. She was the oldest. And what she would have liked to be was the oldest *and* the baby. About lots of things she was very piggy. But she couldn't whistle. Try though she might, *whhih, whhih, whhih,* she couldn't. And Cindy could.

The toast emerged from the toaster and Iris said, "Not at the breakfast table, Cindy." The morning was difficult for her, clouded with amnesia, with the absence of energy, with the reluctance of her body to take on any action whatever. Straight lines curved unpleasantly, hard surfaces presented the look of softness. She saw George and the children and the dog lying at her feet under the table the way one sees rocks and trees and cottages at the seashore through the early morning fog; just barely recognizable they were.

"WHY is a church steeple — "

"My gloves," he said, standing in the front hall, with his coat on.

"They're in the drawer in the lowboy," Iris said.

"Why is a church steeple — "

"Not those," he said.

"Why is a — "

"Laurie, Daddy is talking. Look in the pocket of your chesterfield."

"I did."

"Yes, dear, why is a church steeple."

"Why is a church steeple like a maiden aunt?"

"I give up."

"Do you know, Daddy?"

"No. I've looked in every single one of my coats. They must be in my raincoat, because I can't find that either."

"Look in your closet."

"I did look there." But he went into the bedroom and looked again anyway. Then he looked all through the front-hall closet, including the mess on the top shelf.

Iris passed through the hall with her arms full of clothes for the washing machine. "Did you find your raincoat?" she asked.

"I must have left it somewhere," he said. "But where?"

He went back to the bedroom and looked in the engagement calendar on her desk, to see where they had been, and it appeared that they hadn't been anywhere.

"Where did we go when we had Andrea to baby-sit?"

"I don't remember."

"We had her two nights."

"Did we? I thought we only went out one night last week."

She began to make the bed. Beds — for it was not one large bed, as it appeared to be in the daytime, but twin beds placed against each other with a king-sized cotton spread covering them both. When they were first married they slept in a three-quarter bed from his bachelor apartment. In time this became a double bed, hard as a rock because of the horsehair mattress. Then it also proved to be too small. For he developed twitches. While he was falling asleep his body beside her would suddenly flail out, shaking the bed and waking her completely. Six or seven times this would happen. After which he would descend at last into a deep sleep and she would be left with insomnia. So now there were twin beds, and even then her bed registered the seismic disturbances in his, though nothing like so much.

"We went to that benefit. With Francis," she said.

"Oh . . . I think I did wear my raincoat that night. No, I wore the coat with the velvet collar."

"The cleaner's?"

"No."

"I don't see how you could have left your raincoat somewhere," she said. "I never see you in just a suit. Other men, yes, but never you."

He went into the hall and pulled open a drawer of the lowboy and took out a pair of grey gloves and drew them on. They had been his father's and they were good gloves but too small for him. His fingers had burst open the seams at the end of the fingers. Iris had mended them, but they would not stay sewed, and so he went to Brooks and bought a new pair — the pair he couldn't find.

"The Howards' dinner party?" he said.

"That was the week before. Don't worry about it," Iris said. "Cindy, what have you been doing?" — meaning hair full of snarls, teeth unbrushed, at twenty-five minutes past eight.

"It makes me feel queer not knowing where I've been," George said, and went out into the foyer and pressed the elevator button. From that moment, he was some other man. Their pictures were under his nose all day but he had stopped seeing them. He did not even remember that he had a family, until five o'clock, when he pushed his chair back from his desk, reached for his hat and coat, and came home, cheerfully unrepentant. She forgave him now because she did not want to deal with any failure, including his, until she had had her second cup of coffee. The coffee sat on the living-room mantelpiece, growing cold, while she brushed and braided Cindy's hair.

"Stand still! I'm not hurting you."

"You are too."

The arm would not go into the sweater, the leggings proved to be on backwards, one mitten was missing. And Laurie wild because she was going to be late for school.

The girls let the front door bang in spite of all that had been said on the subject, and in a moment the elevator doors opened to receive them. The quiet then was unbelievable. With the *Times* spread out on the coffee table in the living room, and holes in the Woman's Page where she had cut out recipes, she waited for her soul, which left her during the night, to return and take its place in her body. When this happened she got up suddenly and went into the bedroom and started telephoning: Bloomingdale's, Saks, the Maid-to-Order service, the children's school, the electrician, the pediatrician, the upholsterer — half the population of New York City.

OVER the side of the bed Cindy went, eyes open, wide awake. In her woolly pajamas with feet in them. Even though it was dark outside — the middle of the night — it was only half dark in the bedroom. There was a blue night-light in the wall plug by the doll's house, and a green night-light in the bathroom, beside the washbasin, and the door to the bathroom was partly open. The door to the hall was wide open and the hall light was on, but high up where it wasn't much comfort, and she had to pass the closed door of Laurie's room and the closed door to the front hall. Behind both these doors the dark was very dark, unfriendly, ready to spring out and grab her, and she would much rather have been back in her bed except it was not safe there either, so she was going for help.

When she got to the door at the end of the hall, she stood still, afraid to knock and afraid not to knock. Afraid to look behind her. Hoping the door would open by itself and it did. Her father — huge, in his pajamas, with his hair sticking up and his face puffy with sleep. "Bad dream?" he asked.

Behind him the room was all dark except for a little light from the hall. She could see the big windows — just barely — and the great big bed, and her mother asleep under a mound of covers. And if she ran past him and got into the bed she would be safe, but it was not allowed. Only when she was sick. She turned and went back down the hall, without speaking but knowing that he would pick up his bathrobe and follow her and she didn't have to be brave anymore.

"What's Teddy doing on the floor?" he said, and pulled the covers up around her chin, and put his warm hand on her cheek. So nice to have him do this — to have him there, sitting on the edge of her bed.

"Can you tell me what you were dreaming about?"

"Tiger."

"Yes? Well, that's too bad. Were you very frightened?"

"Yes."

"Was it a big tiger?"

"Yes."

"You know it was only a dream? It wasn't a real tiger. There aren't any tigers in New York City."

"In the zoo there are."

"Oh yes, but they're in cages and can't get out. Was this tiger out?"

"Yes."

"Then it couldn't have been a real tiger. Turn over and let me rub your back."

"If you rub my back I'll go to sleep."

"Good idea."

"If I go to sleep I'll dream about the tiger."

"I see. What do you want me to do?"

"Get in bed with me."

What with Teddy and Raggedy Ann and Baby Dear, and books to look at in the morning, and the big pillow and the little pillow, things were a bit crowded. He put his hand over his eyes to shut out the hall light and said, "Go to sleep," but she didn't, even though she was beginning to feel drowsy. She was afraid he was going to leave her — if not right this minute then pretty soon. He would sit up in bed and say *Are you all right now?* and she would have to say *Yes*, because that was what he wanted her to say. Sometimes she said no and they stayed a little longer, but they always went away in the end.

After a while, her eyes closed. After still another while, she felt the bed heave under her as he sat up. He got out of bed slowly and carefully and fixed the covers and put the little red chair by the bed so she wouldn't fall out. She tried to say *Don't go*, but nothing happened. The floorboards creaked under the carpeting as he crossed the room. In the doorway he turned and looked at her, one last look, and she opened her eyes wide so he would know she wasn't asleep, and he waved her a kiss, and that was the last of him, but it wasn't the last of her. Pretty soon, even though there wasn't a sound, she knew something was in the room. Hiding. It was either hiding behind the curtains or it was hiding in the toy closet or it was hiding behind the doll's house or it was behind the bathroom door or it was under the bed. But wherever it was it was being absolutely still, waiting for her to close her eyes and go to sleep. So she kept them open, even though her eyelids got heavier and heavier. She made them stay open. And when they closed she opened them again right afterward. She kept opening them as long as she could, and once she cried out *Laurie!* very loud, but in her mind only. There was no sound in the room.

The thing that was hiding didn't make any sound either, which made her think maybe it wasn't a tiger after all, because tigers have a terrible roar that they roar, but it couldn't have been anything else, for it had stripes and a tail and terrible teeth and eyes that were looking at her through the back of the little red chair. And her heart was pounding and the tiger knew this, and the only friend she had in the world was Teddy, and Teddy couldn't move, and neither could Raggy, and neither could she. But the tiger could move. He could do anything he wanted to except roar his terrible roar, because then the bedroom door would fly open and they would come running.

She looked at the tiger through the back of the little red chair, and the tiger looked at her, and finally it thrashed its tail once or twice and then went and put its head in the air conditioner.

That isn't possible. . . . But it was. More and more of his body disappeared into the air conditioner, and finally there was only his tail, and then only the tip of his tail, and when that was gone so was she.

THE young policeman who stood all night on the corner of East End Avenue and Gracie Square, eight stories below, was at the phone box, having a conversation with the sergeant on the desk. This did not prevent him from keeping his eyes on an emaciated junkie who stood peering through the window of the drugstore, past the ice-cream bin, the revolving display of paperbacks, the plastic toys, hair sprays, hand creams, cleansing lotions, etc., at the prescription counter. The door had a grating over it but the plate-glass window did not. One good kick would do it. It would also bring the policeman running.

The policeman would have been happy to turn the junkie in, but he didn't have anything on him. Vagrancy? But suppose he had a home? And suppose it brought the Civil Liberties Union running? The policeman turned his back for a minute and when he looked again the junkie was gone, vanished, nowhere.

Though it was between three and four in the morning, people were walking their dogs in Carl Schurz Park. Amazing. Dreamlike. And the sign on the farther shore of the river that changed back and forth continually was enough to unhinge the mind: PEARLWICK HAMPERS became BATHROOM HAMPERS, which in turn became PEARLWICK HAMPERS, and sometimes for a fraction of a second BATHWICK HAMPERS.

In the metal trash containers scattered here and there along the winding paths of the park were pieces of waxed paper that had been around food but nothing you could actually eat. The junkie didn't go into the playground because the gates were locked and it had a high iron fence around it. He could have managed this easily by climbing a tree and dropping to the cement on the other side. Small boys did it all the time. And maybe in there he would have found something — a half-eaten Milky Way or Mounds bar that a nursemaid had taken from a child with a finicky appetite — but then he would have been locked in instead of out, and he knew all there was to know about that: Rikers Island, Sing Sing, Auburn, Dannemora. His name is James Jackson, and he is a figure out of a nightmare — unless you happen to know what happened to him, the steady rain of blows about his unprotected head ever since he was born, in which case it is human life that seems like a nightmare. The dog walkers, supposing — correctly — that he had a switchblade in his pocket and a certain amount of experience in using it, chose a path that detoured around him. The wind was out of the southeast and smelled of the sea, fifteen miles away on the other side of Long Beach and Far Rockaway. The Hell Gate section of the Triborough Bridge was a necklace of sickly-green incandescent pearls. When the policeman left his post and took a turn through the south end of the park, the junkie was sitting innocently on a bench on the river walk. He was keeping the river company.

And when the policeman got back to his post a woman in a long red coat was going through the trash basket directly across the street from him. She was harmless. He saw her night after night. And in a minute she would cross over and tell him about the doctor at Bellevue who said she probably dreamed that somebody picked the lock of her door while she was out buying coffee and stole her mother's gold thimble.

The threads that bound the woman in the long red coat to a particular address, to the family she had been born into, her husband's grave in the Brooklyn cemetery, and the children who never wrote except to ask for money, had broken, and she was now free to wander along the street, scavenging from trash containers. She did not mind if people saw her, or feel that what she was doing was in any way exceptional. When she found something useful or valuable, she stuffed it in her dirty canvas bag, the richer by a pair of sandals with a broken strap or a perfectly clean copy of *Sartor Resartus*. What in the beginning was only an uncertainty, an uneasiness, a sense of the falsity of appearances, a suspicion that the completely friendly world she lived in was in fact secretly mocking and hostile, had proved to be true. Or rather, had become true — for it wasn't always. And meanwhile, in her mind, she was perpetually composing a statement for her own use and understanding, that would cover this situation.

Three colored lights passed overhead, very high up and in a cluster, blinking. There were also lights strung through the park at intervals, and on East End Avenue, where taxicabs cruised up and down with their roof-lights on. Nobody wanted them. As if they had never in their life shot through a red light, the taxis stopped at Eighty-third Street, and again at Eighty-fourth, and went on when the light turned green. East End Avenue was as quiet as the grave. So were the side streets.

With the first hint of morning, this beautiful quiet came to an end. Stopping and starting, making a noise like an electric toaster, a Department of Sanitation truck made its way down Eighty-fourth Street, murdering sleep. Crash. Tinkle. More grinding. Bump. Thump. Voices. A brief silence and then the whole thing started up again farther down the street. This was followed by other noises — a parked car being warmed up, a maniac in a sports car with no muffler. And then suddenly it was the policeman's turn to be gone. A squad car drove by, with the car radio playing an old Bing Crosby song, and picked him up.

Biding his time, the junkie managed to slip past the service entrance of one of the apartment buildings on East End Avenue without being seen. Around in back he saw an open window on the ground floor with no bars over it. On the other hand he didn't know who or what he would find when he climbed through it, and he shouldn't have waited till morning. He stood flattened against a brick wall while a handyman took in the empty garbage cans. The sound of retreating footsteps died away. The door to the service entrance was wide open. In a matter of seconds James Jackson was in and out again, wheeling a new ten-speed Peugeot. He straddled the bicycle as if he and not the overweight insurance broker in 7E had paid good money for it, and rode off down the street.

" 'CLOUDY with rain or showers . . .' Cindy, did you know you dreamt about a tiger last night?"

"Cindy dreamt about a tiger?" Iris said.

"Yes. What happened after I left?"

"Nothing."

"Congratulations. I dreamt the air conditioner in our room broke and we couldn't get anybody to come and fix it."

"Is it broken?" Iris asked.

"I don't know. We'll have to wait till next summer to find out."

"GOOD morning, Laurie. Good morning, Cindy," Jimmy the daytime elevator man said cheerfully. No answer. But no rudeness intended either. They did not know they were in the elevator.

The red-haired doorman at No. 7 Gracie Square stretched out his arms and pretended he was going to capture Cindy. This happened morning after morning, and she put up with it patiently.

"Taxi!" people wailed. "*Taxi!*" But there were no taxis. Or if one came along there was somebody in it. The doorman of No. 10 stood in the middle of East End Avenue and blew his whistle at nothing. On a balcony five stories above the street, a man lying on his back with his hips in the air was being put through his morning exercises by a Swedish masseur. The tired middle-aged legs went up and down like pistons. Like pistons, the elevators rose and fell in all the buildings overlooking the park, bringing the maids and laundresses up, taking men with briefcases down. The stationery store and the cleaners were now open. So was the luncheonette.

The two little girls stopped, took each other by the hand, and looked carefully both ways before they crossed the car tunnel at No. 10. On the river walk Laurie saw an acquaintance and ran on ahead. Poor Cindy! At her back was the park — very agreeable to play in when she went there with her mother or the kindergarten class, but also frequented by rough boys with water pistols and full of bushes it could be hiding in — and on her right was the deep pit alongside No. 10; it could be down there, below the sidewalk and waiting to spring out when she came along. She did not look to see if it was there but kept well over to the other side, next to the outer railing and the river. A tug with four empty barges was nosing its way upstream. The Simpsons' cook waved to Cindy from their kitchen window, which looked out on the river walk, and Cindy waved back.

In the days when George used to take Laurie to kindergarten because she was too small to walk to school by herself, he had noticed her — a big woman with blond braids in a crown around her head. And one day he said, "Shall we wave to her and see what happens?" Sometimes her back was turned to the window and she didn't know that Cindy and Laurie were there. They did not ever think of her except when they saw her, and if they had met her face to face she would have had to do all the talking.

Laurie was waiting at the Eighty-third Street gate. "Come on," she said.

"Stupid-head," Cindy said.

They went into the school building together, ignoring the big girls in camel's-hair coats who held the door open for them. But it wasn't like Jimmy the elevator man; they knew the big girls were there.

Sitting on the floor of her cubby, with her gym sneakers under her bottom and her cheek against her green plaid coat, Cindy felt safe. But Miss Nichols kept trying to get her to come out. The sandbox, the blocks, the crayons — Cindy said no to them all, and sucked her thumb. So Miss Nichols sat down on a little chair and took Cindy on her lap.

"If there was a (   )?" Cindy asked finally.

In a soft coaxing voice Miss Nichols said, "If there was a what?"

Cindy wouldn't say what.

THE fire engines raced down Eighty-sixth Street, sirens shrieking and horns blowing, swung south through a red light, and came to a stop by the alarm box on the corner of East End Avenue and Gracie Square. The firemen jumped down and stood talking in the middle of the street. The hoses remained neatly folded and the ladders horizontal. It was the second false alarm that night from this same box. A county fair wouldn't have made more commotion under their windows but it had happened too often and George and Iris Carrington went on sleeping peacefully, flat on their backs, like stone figures on a medieval tomb.

IN the trash basket on the corner by the park gates there was a copy of the *Daily News* which said, in big letters, "TIGER ESCAPES," but that was a different tiger; that tiger escaped from a circus in Jamestown, Rhode Island.

"WHAT *is* it?" Iris asked, in the flower shop. "Why are you pulling at my skirt?"

The flower-shop woman (pink-blond hair, Viennese accent) offered Cindy a green carnation, and she refused to take it. "You don't like flowers?" the woman asked, coyly, and the tiger kept on looking at Cindy from behind some big, wide rubbery green leaves. "She's shy," the flower-shop woman said.

"Not usually," Iris said. "I don't know what's got into her today."

She gave the woman some money, and the woman gave her some money and some flowers, and then she and Cindy went outside, but Cindy was afraid to look behind her. If the tiger was following them, it was better not to know. For half a block she had a tingling sensation in the center of her back, between her shoulder blades. But then, looking across the street, she saw that the tiger was not back there in the flower shop. It must have left when they did, and now it was looking at her from the round hole in a cement mixer.

The lights changed from red to green, and Iris took her hand and started to cross over.

"I want to go that way," Cindy said, holding back, until the light changed again. Since she was never allowed on the street alone, she was not really afraid of meeting the tiger all by herself. But what if some day it should walk into the elevator when Jimmy wasn't looking, and get off at their floor, and hide behind Laurie's bicycle and the scooters. And what if the front door opened and somebody came out and pressed the elevator button and the tiger got inside when they weren't looking. And what if—

"Oh, please don't hold back, Cindy! I'm late as anything!"

So, dangerous as it was, she allowed herself to be hurried along home.

TAP, tap, tap . . .

In the night this was, just after Iris and George had got to sleep.

"Oh, no!" Iris moaned.

But it was. When he opened the door, there she stood.

TAP, tap . . .

That same night, two hours later. Sound asleep but able to walk and talk, he put on his bathrobe and followed her down the hall. Stretched out beside her, he tried to go on sleeping but he couldn't. He said, "What were you dreaming about this time?"

"Sea-things."

"What kind of seethings?"

"Sea-things under the sea."

"Things that wiggled?"

"Yes."

"Something was after you?"

"Yes."

"Too bad. Go to sleep."

TAP, tap . . .

This time as he heaved himself up, Iris said to him, "*You* lie still."

She got up and opened the door to the hall and said, "Cindy, we're tired and we need our sleep. I want you to go back to your bed and stay there."

Then they both lay awake, listening to the silence at the other end of the hall.

"I CAME out of the building," Iris said, "and I had three letters that Jimmy had given me, and it was raining hard, and the wind whipped them right out of my hand."

He took a sip of his drink and then said, "Did you get them?"

"I got two of them. One was from the Richards children, thanking me for the toys I sent when Lonnie was in the hospital. And one was a note from Mrs. Mills. I never did find the third. It was a small envelope, and the handwriting was Society."

"A birthday party for Cindy."

"No. It was addressed to Mr. and Mrs. George Carrington. Cocktail party, probably."

He glanced at the windows. It was already dark. Then, the eternal optimist (also remembering the time he found the button that flew off her coat and rolled under a parked car on Eighty-fifth Street): "Which way did it blow? I'll look for it tomorrow."

"Oh, there's no use. You can see by the others. They were reduced to pulp by the rain, in just that minute. And anyway, I did look, this afternoon."

In the morning, he took the Seventy-ninth Street crosstown bus instead of the Eighty-sixth, so that he could look for the invitation that blew away. No luck. The invitation had already passed through a furnace in the Department of Sanitation building on Ninety-first Street and now, in the form of ashes, was floating down the East River on a garbage scow, on its way out to sea.

The sender, rebuffed in this first tentative effort to get to know the Carringtons better, did not try again. She had met them at a dinner party, and liked them both. She was old enough to be Iris's mother, and it puzzled her that a young woman who seemed to be well bred and was quite lovely looking and adored *Middlemarch* should turn out to have no manners, but she didn't brood about it. New York is full of pleasant young couples, and if one chooses to ignore your invitation the chances are another won't.

"DID you hear Laurie in the night?" Iris said.

"No. Did Laurie have a nightmare?"

"Yes. I thought you were awake."

"I don't think so."

He got up out of bed and went into the children's rooms and turned on the radiators so they wouldn't catch cold. Laurie was sitting up in bed reading.

"Mommy says you had a bad dream last night."

"There were three dreams," she said, in an overdistinct voice, as if she were a grown woman at a committee meeting. "The first dream was about Miss Stevenson. I dreamed she wasn't nice to me. She was like the wicked witch."

"Miss Stevenson loves you."

"And the second dream was about snakes. They were all over the floor. It was like a rug made up of snakes, and very icky, and there was a giant, and Cathy and I were against him, and he was trying to shut me in the room where the snakes were, and one of the snakes bit me, but he wasn't the kind of snake that kills you, he was just a mean snake, and so it didn't hurt. And the third dream was a happy dream. I was with Cathy and we were skating together and pulling our mommies by strings."

WITH his safety razor ready to begin a downward sweep, George Carrington studied the lathered face in the mirror of the medicine cabinet. He shook his head. There was a fatal flaw in his character: Nobody was ever as real to him as he was to himself. If people knew how little he cared whether they lived or died, they wouldn't want to have anything to do with him.

THE dog moved back and forth between the two ends of the apartment, on good terms with everybody. She was in the dining room at mealtimes, and in the kitchen when Iris was getting dinner (when quite often something tasty fell off the edge of the kitchen table), and she was there again just after dinner, in case the plates were put on the floor for her to lick before they went into the dishwasher. In the late afternoon, for an hour before it was time for her can of beef-and-beef-byproducts, she sat with her front paws crossed, facing the kitchen clock, a reminding statue. After she had been fed, she went to the living room and lay down before the unlit log fire in the fireplace and slept until bedtime. In the morning, she followed Iris back and forth through room after room, until Iris was dressed and ready to take her out. "Must you nag me so?" Iris cried, but the dog was not intimidated. There was something they were in agreement about, though only one of them could have put it in words: It is a crime against Nature to keep a hunting dog in the city. George sometimes gave her a slap on her haunches when she picked up food in the gutter or lunged at another dog. And if she jerked on her leash he jerked back, harder. But with Iris she could do anything — she could even stand under the canopy and refuse to go anywhere because it was raining.

Walking by the river, below Eightieth Street, it wasn't necessary to keep her on a leash, and while Iris went on ahead Puppy sniffed at the godforsaken grass and weeds that grew between the cement walk and the

East River Drive. Then she overtook Iris, at full speed, overshot the mark, and came charging back, showing her teeth in a grin. Three or four times she did this, as a rule — with Iris applauding and congratulating her and cheering her on. It may be a crime against Nature to keep a hunting dog in the city, but this one was happy anyway.

AFTER a series of dreams in which people started out as one person and ended up another and he found that there was no provision for getting from where he was to where he wanted to go and it grew later and later and even after the boat had left he still went on packing his clothes and what he thought was his topcoat turned out to belong to a friend he had not seen for seventeen years and naked strangers came and went, he woke and thought he heard a soft tapping on the bedroom door. But when he got up and opened it there was no one there.

"Was that Cindy?" Iris asked as he got back into bed.

"No. I thought I heard her, but I must have imagined it."

"I thought I heard her too," Iris said, and turned over.

At breakfast he said, "Did you have any bad dreams last night?" but Cindy was making a lake in the middle of her oatmeal and didn't answer.

"I thought I heard you tapping on our door," he said. "You didn't dream about a wolf, or a tiger, or a big black dog?"

"I don't remember," she said.

"YOU'LL never guess what I just saw from the bedroom window," Iris said.

He put down his book.

"A police wagon drove down Eighty-fourth Street and stopped, and two policemen with guns got out and went into a building and didn't come out. And after a long while two more policemen came and *they* went into the building and pretty soon they all came out with a big man with black hair, handcuffed. Right there on Eighty-fourth Street, two doors from the corner."

"Nice neighborhood we live in," he said.

"DADDY, Daddy, Daddy, Daddy!" came into his dreams without waking him, and what did wake him was the heaving of the other bed as Iris got up and hurried toward the bedroom door.

"It was Cindy," she said when she came back.

"Dream?" he asked.

"Yes."

"I heard her but went on dreaming myself."

"She doesn't usually cry out like that."

"Laurie used to."

Why all these dreams, he wondered, and drifted gently back to sleep, as if he already knew the answer. She turned and turned, and finally, after three-quarters of an hour, got up and filled the hot-water bottle. What for days had been merely a half-formed thought in the back of her mind was now suddenly, in the middle of the night, making her rigid with anxiety. She needed to talk, and couldn't bring herself to wake him. What she wanted to say was they were making a mistake in bringing the children up in New York City. Or even in America. There was too much that there was no way to protect them from, and the only sensible thing would be to pull up stakes now, before Laurie reached adolescence. They could sublet the apartment until the lease ran out, and take a house somewhere in the South of France, near Aix perhaps, and the children could go to a French school, and they could all go skiing in Switzerland in the winter, and Cindy could have her own horse, and they both would acquire a good French accent, and be allowed to grow up slowly, in the ordinary way, and not be jaded by one premature experience after another, before they were old enough to understand any of it.

With the warmth at her back, and the comforting feeling that she had found the hole in the net, gradually she fell asleep too.

But when she brought the matter up two days later he looked at her blankly. He did not oppose her idea but neither did he accept it, and so her hands were tied.

As usual, the fathers' part in the Christmas program had to be rehearsed beforehand. In the small practice room on the sixth floor of the school, their masculinity — their grey flannel or dark-blue pin-striped suits, their size 9, 10, 11, 11½, and 12 shoes, their gold cufflinks, the odor that emanated from their bodies and from their freshly shaved cheeks, their simple assurance, based on, among other things, the *Social Register* and the size of their income — was incongruous. They were handed sheets of music as they came in, and the room was crammed with folding chairs, all facing the ancient grand piano. With the two tall windows at their backs they were missing the snow, which was a pity. It went up, down, diagonally, and in centrifugal motion – all at once. The fact that no two of the star-shaped crystals were the same was a miracle, of course, but it was a miracle that everybody has long since grown accustomed to. The light outside the windows was cold and grey.

"Since there aren't very many of you," the music teacher said, "you'll have to make up for it by singing enthusiastically." She was young, in her late twenties, and had difficulty keeping discipline in the classroom; the girls took advantage of her good nature, and never stopped talking and gave her their complete attention. She sat down at the piano now and played the opening bars of "O come, O come, Emmanuel / And ransom captive I-i-i-zrah-el . . ."

Somebody in the second row exclaimed, "Oh God!" under his breath. The music was set too high for men's voices.

"The girls will sing the first stanza, you fathers the second – "

The door opened and two more fathers came in.

" – and all will sing the third."

With help from the piano (which they would not have downstairs in the school auditorium) they achieved an approximation of the tune, and the emphasis sometimes fell in the right place. They did their best, but the nineteenth-century words and the ninth-century plainsong did not go well together. Also, one of the fathers had a good strong clear voice, which only made the others more self-conscious and apologetic. They would have been happier without him.

The music teacher made a flip remark. They all laughed and began again. Their number was added to continually as the door opened and let in the sounds from the hall. Soon there were no more vacant chairs; the latecomers had to stand. The snow was now noticeably heavier, and the singing had more volume. Though they were at some pains to convey, by their remarks to one another and their easy laughter, that this was not an occasion to be taken seriously, nevertheless the fact that they were here was proof of the contrary; they all had offices where they should have been and salaries they were not at this moment doing anything to earn. Twenty-seven men with, at first glance, a look of sameness about them, a round, composite, youngish, unrevealing, New York face. Under closer inspection, this broke down. Not all the eyes were blue, nor were the fathers all in their middle and late thirties. The thin-faced man at the end of the second row could not have been a broker or a lawyer or in advertising. The man next to him had survived incarceration in a Nazi prison camp. There was one Negro. Here and there a head that was not thickly covered with hair. Their speaking voices varied, but not so much as they conceivably might have — no Texas drawl, for instance. And all the fingernails were clean, all the shoes were shined, all the linen was fresh.

Each time they went over the hymn it was better. They clearly needed more rehearsing, but the music teacher glanced nervously at the clock and said, "And now 'In Dulci Jubilo.' "

Those who had forgotten their Latin, or never had any, eavesdropped on those who knew how the words should be pronounced. The tune was powerful and swept everything before it, and in a flush of pleasure they finished together, on the beat, loudly, making the room echo. They had forgotten about the telephone messages piling up on their desks beside the unopened mail. They were enjoying themselves. They could have gone on singing for another hour. Instead, they had to get up and file out of the room and crowd into the elevators.

In spite of new costumes, new scenery, different music, and — naturally — a different cast, the Christmas play was always the same. Mary and Joseph proceeded to Bethlehem, where the inns were full, and found shelter in the merest suggestion of a stable. An immature angel announced to very unlikely shepherds the appearance of the Star. Wise Men came and knelt before the plastic Babe in Mary's arms. And then the finale: the Threes singing and dancing with heavenly joy.

"How did it sound?" George asked, in the crowd on the stairs.

"Fine," Iris said.

"Really? It didn't seem to me — maybe because we were under the balcony — it didn't seem as if we were making any sound at all."

"No, it was plenty loud enough. What was so nice was the two kinds of voices."

"High and low, you mean?"

"The fathers sounded like bears. Adorable."

IN theory, since it was the middle of the night, it was dark, but not the total suffocating darkness of a cloudy night in the country. The city, as usual, gave off light — enough so that you could see the island in the middle of the river, and the three bridges, and the outlines of the little houses on East End Avenue and the big apartment buildings on Eighty-sixth Street, and the trees and shrubs and lampposts and comfort station in the park. Also a woman standing by the railing of the river walk.

There was no wind. The river was flowing north and the air smelled of snow, which melted the moment it touched any solid object, and became the shine on iron balustrades and on the bark of trees.

The woman had been standing there a long time, looking out over the water, when she began awkwardly to pull herself up and over the curved iron spikes that were designed, by their size and shape, to prevent people from throwing themselves into the river. In this instance they were not enough. But it took some doing. There was a long tear in the woman's coat and she was gasping for breath as she let herself go backward into space.

THE sun enters Aquarius January 20th and remains until February 18th. *"An extremely good friend can today put into motion some operation that will be most helpful to your best interest, or else introduce you to some influential person. Go out socially in the evening on a grand scale. Be charming."*

THE cocktail party was in a penthouse. The elevator opened directly into the foyer of the apartment. And the woman he was talking to — or rather, who was talking to him — was dressed all in shades of brown.

"I tried to get you last summer," she said, "but your wife said you were busy that day."

"Yes," he said.

"I'll try you again."

"Please do," somebody said for him, using his mouth and tongue and vocal cords — because it was the last thing in the world he wanted, to drive halfway across Long Island to a lunch party. "We hardly ever go anywhere," he himself said, but too late, after the damage had been done.

His mind wandered for an instant as he took in — not the room, for he was facing the wrong way, but a small corner of it. And in that instant he lost the thread of the story she was telling him. She had taken her shoe off in a movie theater and put her purse down beside it, and the next thing he knew they refused to do anything, even after she had explained what happened and that she must get in. Who "they" were, get in where, he patiently waited to find out, while politely sharing her indignation.

"But imagine!" she exclaimed. "They said, 'How valuable was the ring?' "

He shook his head, commiserating with her.

"I suppose if it hadn't been worth a certain amount," she went on, "they wouldn't have done a thing about it."

The police, surely, he thought. Having thought at first it was the manager of the movie theater she was talking about.

"And while they were jimmying the door open, people were walking by, and nobody showed the slightest concern. Or interest."

So it wasn't the police. But who was it, then? He never found out, because they were joined by another woman, who smiled at him in such a way as to suggest that they knew each other. But though he searched his mind and her face — the plucked eyebrows, the reserved expression in the middle-aged eyes — and considered her tweed suit and her diamond pin and her square figure, he could not imagine who she was. Suppose somebody — suppose Iris came up and he had to introduce her?

The purse was recovered, with the valuable ring still in it, and he found himself talking about something that had occupied his thoughts lately. And in his effort to say what he meant, he failed to notice what happened to the first woman. Suddenly she was not there. Somebody must have carried her off, right in front of his unseeing eyes.

". . . but it isn't really distinguishable from what goes on in dreams," he said to the woman who seemed to know him and to assume that he knew her. "People you have known for twenty or thirty years, you suddenly discover you didn't really know how they felt about you, and in fact you don't know how anybody feels about anything — only what they *say* they feel. And suppose that isn't true at all? You decide that it is better to act as if it is true. And so does everybody else. But it is a kind of myth you are living in, wide awake, with your eyes open, in broad daylight."

He realized that the conversation had become not only personal but intimate. But it was too late to back out now.

To his surprise she seemed to understand, to have felt what he had felt. "And one chooses," she said, "between this myth and that."

"Exactly! If you live in the city and are bringing up children, you decide that this thing is not safe — and so you don't let them do it — and that thing *is* safe. When, actually, neither one is safe and everything is equally dangerous. But for the sake of convenience — "

"And also so that you won't go out of your mind," she said.

"And so you won't go out of your mind," he agreed. "Well," he said after a moment, "that makes two of us who are thinking about it."

"In one way or another, people live by myths," she said.

He racked his brain for something further to say on this or any other subject.

Glancing around at the windows which went from floor to ceiling, the woman in the tweed suit said, "These vistas you have here."

He then looked and saw black night, with lighted buildings far below and many blocks away. "From our living room," he said, "you can see all the way to the North Pole."

"We live close to the ground," she said.

But where? Cambridge? Princeton? Philadelphia?

"In the human scale," he said. "Like London and Paris. Once, on a beautiful spring day, four of us — we'd been having lunch with a visiting Englishman who was interested in architecture — went searching for the sky. Up one street and down the next."

She smiled.

"We had to look for it, the sky is so far away in New York."

They stood nursing their drinks, and a woman came up to them who seemed to know her intimately, and the two women started talking and he turned away.

ON her way into the school building, Laurie joined the flood from the school bus, and cried, "Hi, Janet . . . Hi, Connie . . . Hi, Elizabeth . . ." and seemed to be enveloped by her schoolmates, until suddenly, each girl having turned to some other girl, Laurie is left standing alone, her expression unchanged, still welcoming, but nobody having responded. If you collect reasons, this is the reason she behaved so badly at lunch, was impertinent to her mother, and hit her little sister.

HE woke with a mild pain in his stomach. It was high up, like an ulcer pain, and he lay there worrying about it. When he heard the sound of shattered glass, his half-awake, oversensible mind supplied both the explanation and the details: Two men, putting a large framed picture into the trunk compartment of a parked car, had dropped it, breaking the glass. Too bad . . . And with that thought he drifted gently off to sleep.

In the morning he looked out of the bedroom window and saw three squad cars in front of the drugstore. The window of the drugstore had a big star-shaped hole in it, and several policemen were standing around looking at the broken glass on the sidewalk.

THE sneeze was perfectly audible through two closed doors. He turned to Iris with a look of inquiry.

"Who sneezed? Was that you, Laurie?" she called.

"That was Cindy," Laurie said.

In principle, Iris would have liked to bring them up in a Spartan fashion, but both children caught cold easily and their colds were prolonged, and recurring, and overlapping, and endless. Whether they should or shouldn't be kept home from school took on the unsolvability of a moral dilemma — which George's worrying disposition did nothing to alleviate. The sound of a child coughing deep in the chest in the middle of the night would make him leap up out of a sound sleep.

She blamed herself when the children came down with a cold, and she blamed them. Possibly, also, the school was to blame, since the children played on the roof, twelve stories above the street, and up there the winds were often much rawer, and teachers cannot, of course, spend all their time going around buttoning up the coats of little girls who have got too hot from running.

She went and stood in the doorway of Cindy's room. "No sneezing," she said.

Sneeze, sneeze, sneeze.

"Cindy, if you are catching another cold, I'm going to shoot myself," Iris said, and gave her two baby-aspirin tablets to chew, and some Vitamin C drops, and put an extra blanket on her bed, and didn't open the window, and in the morning Cindy's nose was running.

"Shall I keep her home from school?" Iris asked, at the breakfast table.

Instead of answering, George got up and looked at the weather thermometer outside the west window of their bedroom. "Twenty-seven," he said, when he came back. But he still didn't answer her question. He was afraid to answer it, lest it be the wrong answer, and she blame him. Actually, there was no answer that was the right answer: They had tried sending Cindy to school and they had tried not sending her. This time, Iris kept her home from school — not because she thought it was going to make any difference but so the pediatrician, Dr. de Santillo, wouldn't blame her. Not that he ever said anything. And Cindy got to play with Laurie's things all morning. She played with Laurie's paper dolls until she was tired, and left them all over the floor, and then she colored in Laurie's coloring book, and Puppy chewed up one of the crayons but not one of Laurie's favorites — not the pink or the blue — and then Cindy rearranged the furniture in Laurie's doll house so it was much nicer, and then she lined up all Laurie's dolls in a row on her bed and played school. And when it was time for Laurie to come home from school she went out to the kitchen and played with the eggbeater. Laurie came in, letting the front door slam behind her, and dropped her mittens in the hall and her coat on the living-room rug and her knitted cap on top of her coat, and started for her room, and it sounded as if she had hurt herself. Iris came running. What a noise Laurie made. And stamping her foot, Cindy noted disapprovingly. And tears.

"Stop screaming and tell me what's the matter!" Iris said.

"Cindy, I hate you!" Laurie said. "I hate you, I hate you!"

Horrible old Laurie . . .

But in the morning when they first woke up it was different. She heard Laurie in the bathroom, and then she heard Laurie go back to her room. Lying in bed, Cindy couldn't suck her thumb because she couldn't breathe through her nose, so she got up and went into Laurie's room (entirely forgetting that her mother had said that in the morning she was to stay out of Laurie's room because she had a cold) and got in Laurie's bed and said, "Read, read." Laurie read her the story of "The Tinder Box," which has three dogs in it — a dog with eyes as big as saucers, and a dog with eyes as big as millwheels, and a third dog with eyes as big as the Round Tower of Copenhagen.

TAP, tap, tap on the bedroom door brought him entirely awake. "What's Laurie been reading to her?" he asked, turning over in bed. That meant it was Iris's turn to get up. While she was pulling herself together, they heard *tap, tap, tap* again. The bed heaved.

"What's Laurie been reading to you?" she asked as she and Cindy went off down the hall together. When she came back into the bedroom, the light was on and he was standing in front of his dresser, with the top drawer open, searching for Gelusil tablets.

"Trouble?" she said.

STANDING in the doorway of Cindy's room, in her blue dressing gown, with her hairbrush in her hand, Iris said, "Who sneezed? Was that you, Cindy?"

"That was Laurie," Cindy said.

So after that Laurie got to stay home from school too.

"I SAW Phyllis Simpson in Gristede's supermarket," Iris said. "Their cook committed suicide."

"How?"

"She threw herself in the river."

"No!"

"They think she must have done it sometime during the night, but they don't know exactly when. They just came down to breakfast and she wasn't there. They're still upset about it."

"When did it happen?"

"About a month ago. Her body was found way down the river."

"What a pity. She was a nice woman."

"You remember her?"

"Certainly. She always waved to the children when I used to walk them to school. She waved to me too, sometimes. From the kitchen window. What made her do such a thing?"

"They have no idea."

"She was a big woman," he said. "It must have been hard for her to pull herself up over that railing. It's quite high. No note or anything?"

"No."

"Terrible."

ON St. Valentine's Day, the young woman who lived on tea and cigarettes and was given to burning herself on the gas stove eloped to California with her mother, and now there was no one in the kitchen. From time to time, the employment agency went through the formality of sending someone for Iris to interview — though actually it was the other way round. And either the apartment was too large or they didn't care to work for a family with children or they were not accustomed to doing the cooking as well as the other housework. Sometimes they didn't give any reason at all.

A young woman from Haiti, who didn't speak English, was willing to give the job a try. It turned out that she had never seen a carpet sweeper before, and she asked for her money at the end of the day.

WALKING the dog at seven-fifteen on a winter morning, he suddenly
stopped and said to himself, "Oh God, somebody's been murdered!" On
the high stone stoop of one of the little houses on East End Avenue
facing the park. Somebody in a long red coat. By the curve of the hip he
could tell it was a woman, and with his heart racing he considered what
he ought to do. From where he stood on the sidewalk he couldn't see the
upper part of her body. One foot — the bare heel and the strap of her
shoe — was sticking out from under the hem of the coat. If she'd been
murdered, wouldn't she be sprawled out in an awkward position instead
of curled up and lying on her side as though she was in bed asleep? He
looked up at the house. Had they locked her out? After a scene? Or she
could have come home in the middle of the night and discovered that
she'd forgotten to take her key. But in that case she'd have spent the
night in a hotel or with a friend. Or called an all-night locksmith.

He went up three steps without managing to see any more than he had
already. The parapet offered some shelter from the wind, but even so,
how could she sleep on the cold stone, with nothing over her?

"Can I help you?"

His voice sounded strange and hollow. There was no answer. The red
coat did not stir. Then he saw the canvas bag crammed with the fruit of
her night's scavenging, and backed down the steps.

NOW it was his turn. The sore throat was gone in the morning, but it
came back during the day, and when he sat down to dinner he pulled the
extension out at his end and moved his mat, silver, and glass farther away
from the rest of them.

"If you aren't sneezing, I don't think you need to be in Isolation
Corner," Iris said, but he stayed there anyway. His colds were prolonged
and made worse by his efforts to treat them; made worse still by his trying
occasionally to disregard them, as he saw other people doing. In the end
he went through box after box of Kleenex, his nose white with Noxzema,
his eyelids inflamed, like a man in a subway poster advertising a cold
remedy that, as it turned out, did not work for him. And finally he took
to his bed, with a transistor radio for amusement and company. In his
childhood, being sick resulted in agreeable pampering, and now that he
was grown he preferred to be both parties to this pleasure. No one could

make him as comfortable as he could make himself, and Iris had all but given up trying.

ON a rainy Sunday afternoon in March, with every door in the school building locked and the corridor braced for the shock of Monday morning, the ancient piano demonstrated for the benefit of the empty practice room that it is one thing to fumble through the vocal line, guided by the chords that accompany it, and something else again to be genuinely musical, to know what the composer intended — the resolution of what cannot be left uncertain, the amorous flirtation of the treble and the bass, notes taking to the air like a flock of startled birds.

THE faint clicking sounds given off by the telephone in the pantry meant that Iris was dialing on the extension in the master bedroom. And at last there was somebody in the Carringtons' kitchen again — a black woman in her fifties. They were low on milk, and totally out of oatmeal, canned dog food, and coffee, but the memo pad that was magnetically attached to the side of the Frigidaire was blank. Writing down things they were out of was not something she considered part of her job. When an emergency arose, she put on her coat and went to the store, just as if she were still in North Carolina.

The sheet of paper that was attached to the clipboard hanging from a nail on the side of the kitchen cupboard had the menus for lunch and dinner all written out, but they were for yesterday's lunch and dinner. And though it was only nine-thirty, Bessie already felt a mounting indignation at being kept in ignorance about what most deeply concerned her. It was an old-fashioned apartment, with big rooms and high ceilings, and the kitchen was a considerable distance from the master bedroom; nevertheless, it was just barely possible for the two women to live there. Nature had designed them for mutual tormenting, the one with an exaggerated sense of time, always hurrying to meet a deadline that did not exist anywhere but in her own fancy, and calling upon the angels or whoever is in charge of amazing grace to take notice that she had put the food on the hot tray in the dining room at precisely one minute before the moment she had been told to have dinner ready; the other with not only a hatred of planning meals but also a childish reluctance to come to the table. When the minute hand of the electric clock in the kitchen arrived at seven or seven-fifteen or whatever, Bessie went into the dining room and announced in an inaudible voice that dinner was ready. Two rooms away, George heard her by extrasensory perception and leapt to his feet, and Iris, holding out her glass to him, said, "Am I not going to have a second vermouth?"

To his amazement, on Bessie's day off, having cooked dinner and put it on the hot plate, Iris drifted away to the front of the apartment and read a magazine, fixed her hair, God knows what, until he discovered the food sitting there and begged her to come to the table.

"THEY said they lived in Boys Town, and I thought Jimmy let them in because he's Irish and Catholic," Iris said. "There was nothing on the list I wanted, so I subscribed to *Vogue*, to help them out. When I spoke to Jimmy about it, he said he had no idea they were selling subscriptions, and he never lets solicitors get by him — not even nuns and priests. Much as he might want to. So I don't suppose it will come."

"It might," George said. "Maybe they were honest."

"He thought they were workmen because they asked for the eleventh floor. The tenants on the eleventh floor have moved out and Jimmy says the people who are moving in have a five years' lease and are spending fifty thousand dollars on the place, which they don't even *own*. But anyway, what they did was walk through the apartment and then down one floor and start ringing doorbells. The super took them down in the back elevator without asking what they were doing there, and off they went. They tried the same thing at No. 7 and the doorman threw them out."

WALKING the dog before breakfast, if he went by the river walk he saw in the Simpsons' window a black-haired woman who did not wave to him or even look up when he passed. That particular section of the river walk was haunted by an act of despair that nobody had been given a chance to understand. Nothing that he could think of — cancer, thwarted love, melancholia — seemed to fit. He had only spoken to her once, when he and Iris went to a dinner party at the Simpsons' and she smiled at him as she was helping the maid clear the table between courses. If she didn't look up when he passed under her window it was as though he had been overtaken by a cloud shadow — until he forgot all about it, a few seconds later. But he could have stopped just once, and he hadn't. When the window was open he could have called out to her, even if it was only "Good morning," or "Isn't it a beautiful day?"

He could have said, *Don't do it. . . .*

Sometimes he came back by the little house on East End Avenue where he had seen the woman in the red coat. He invariably glanced up, half expecting her to be lying there on the stoop. If she wasn't there, where was she?

In the psychiatric ward of Bellevue Hospital was the answer. But not for long. She and the doctor got it straightened out about her mother's gold thimble, and he gave her a prescription and told her where to go in the building to have it filled, and hoped for the best — which, after all, is all that anybody has to hope for.

THE weather thermometer blew away one stormy night and after a week or two George brought home a new one. It was round and encased in white plastic, and not meant to be screwed to the window frame but to be kept inside. It registered the temperature outside by means of a wire with what looked like a small bullet attached to the end of it. The directions said to drill a hole through the window frame, but George backed away from all that and, instead, hung the wire across the sill and closed the window on it. What the new thermometer said bore no relation to the actual temperature, and drilling the hole had a high priority on the list of things he meant to do.

There was also a racial barometer in the apartment that registered *Fair* or *Stormy*, according to whether Bessie had spent several days running in the apartment or had just come back from a weekend in her room in Harlem.

The laundress, so enormously fat that she had to maneuver her body around, as if she were the captain of an ocean liner, was a Muslim and hated all white people and most black people as well. She was never satisfied with the lunch Bessie cooked for her, and Bessie objected to having to get lunch for her, and the problem was solved temporarily by having her eat in the luncheonette across the street.

She quit. The new laundress was half the size of the old one, and sang alto in her church choir, and was good-tempered, and fussy about what she had for lunch. Bessie sometimes considered her a friend and sometimes an object of derision, because she believed in spirits.

So did Bessie, but not to the same extent or in the same way. Bessie's mother had appeared to her and her sister and brother, shortly after her death. They were quarreling together, and her mother's head and shoulders appeared up near the ceiling, and she said they were to love one another. And sometimes when Bessie was walking along the street she felt a coolness and knew that a spirit was beside her. But the laundress said, "All right, go ahead, then, if you want to," to the empty air and, since there wasn't room for both of them, let the spirit precede her through the pantry. She even knew who the spirit was.

IT was now spring on the river, and the river walk was a Chinese scroll which could be unrolled, by people who like to do things in the usual way, from right to left — starting at Gracie Square and walking north. Depicted were:

A hockey game between Loyola and St. Francis de Sales

Five boys shooting baskets on the basketball court

A seagull

An old man sitting on a bench doing columns of figures

A child drawing a track for his toy trains on the pavement with a piece of chalk

A paper drinking cup floating on the troubled surface of the water

A child in pink rompers pushing his own stroller

A woman sitting on a bench alone, with her face lifted to the sun

A Puerto Rican boy with a transistor radio

Two middle-aged women speaking German

A bored and fretful baby, too hot in his perambulator, with nothing to look at or play with, while his nurse reads

The tugboat *Chicago* pulling a long string of empty barges upstream

A little girl feeding her mother an apple

A helicopter

A kindergarten class, in two sections

Clouds in a blue sky

A flowering cherry tree

Seven freight cars moving imperceptibly, against the tidal current, in the wake of the *Herbert E. Smith*

A man with a pipe in his mouth and a can of Prince Albert smoking tobacco on the bench beside him

A man sorting his possessions into two canvas bags, one of which contains a concertina

Six very small children playing in the sandpile, under the watchful eyes of their mothers or nursemaids

An oil tanker

A red-haired priest reading a pocket-size New Testament

A man scattering bread crumbs for the pigeons

The Coast Guard cutter *CG 40435* turning around just north of the lighthouse and heading back toward Hell Gate Bridge

A sweeper with his bag and a ferruled stick

A little boy pointing a red plastic pistol at his father's head

A pleasure yacht

An airplane

A man and a woman speaking French

A child on a tricycle

A boy on roller skates

A reception under a striped tent on the lawn of the mayor's house

The fireboat station

The Franklin Delano Roosevelt Drive, a cinder path, a warehouse, seagulls, and so on

Who said *Happiness is the light shining on the water. The water is cold and dark and deep. . . .*

"IT'S perfectly insane," George said when he met Iris coming from Gristede's with a big brown-paper bag heavy as lead under each arm and relieved her of them. "Don't we still have that cart?"

"Nobody in the building uses them."

"But couldn't you?"

"No," Iris said.

"ALL children," Cindy said wisely, leaning against him, with her head in the hollow of his neck, "all children think their mommy and daddy are the nicest."

"And what about you? Are you satisfied?"

She gave him a hug and a kiss and said, "I think you and Mommy are the nicest mommy and daddy in the whole world."

"And I think you are the nicest Cindy," he said, his eyes moist with tears.

They sat and rocked each other gently.

AFTER Bessie had taken the breakfast dishes out of the dishwasher, she went into the front, dragging the vacuum cleaner, to do the children's rooms. She stood sometimes for five or ten minutes, looking down at East End Avenue — at the drugstore, the luncheonette, the rival cleaning establishments (side by side and, according to rumor, both owned by the same person), the hairstyling salon, and the branch office of the Chase Manhattan Bank. Together they made a canvas backdrop for a procession of people Bessie had never seen before, or would not recognize if she had, and so she couldn't say to herself, "There goes old Mrs. Maltby," but she looked anyway, she took it all in. The sight of other human beings nourished her mind. She read them as people read books. Pieces of toys, pieces of puzzles that she found on the floor she put on one shelf or another of the toy closet in Cindy's room, gradually introducing a disorder that Iris dealt with periodically, taking a whole day out of her life. But nobody told Bessie she was supposed to find the box the piece came out of, and it is questionable whether she could have anyway. The thickness of the lenses in her eyeglasses suggested that her eyesight was poorer than she let on.

She was an exile, far from home, among people who were not like the white people she knew and understood. She was here because down home she was getting forty dollars a week and she had her old age to think of. She and Iris alternated between irritation at one another and sudden acts of kindness. It was the situation that was at fault. Given halfway decent circumstances, men can work cheerfully and happily for other men, in offices, stores, and even factories. And so can women. But if Iris opened the cupboard or the icebox to see what they did or didn't contain, Bessie popped out of her room and said, "Did you want something?" And Iris withdrew, angry because she had been driven out of her own kitchen. In her mind, Bessie always thought of the Carringtons as "my people," but until she had taught them to think of themselves as her people her profound capacity for devotion would go unused; would not even be suspected.

You can say that life is a fountain if you want to, but what it more nearly resembles is a jack-in-the-box.

· · ·

HALF awake, he heard the soft whimpering that meant Iris was having a nightmare, and he shook her. "I dreamt you were having a heart attack," she said.

"Should you be dreaming that?" he said. But the dream was still too real to be joked about. They were in a public place. And he couldn't be moved. He didn't die, and she consulted with doctors. Though the dream did not progress, she could not extricate herself from it but went on and on, feeling the appropriate emotions but in a circular way. Till finally the sounds she made in her sleep brought about her deliverance.

THE conversation at the other end of the hall continued steadily — not loud but enough to keep them from sleeping, and he had already spoken to the children once. So he got up and went down the hall. Laurie and Cindy were both in their bathroom, and Cindy was sitting on the toilet. "I have a stomach ache," she said.

He started to say, "You need to do bizz," and then remembered that the time before she had been sitting on the toilet doing just that.

"And I feel dizzy," Laurie said.

"I heard it," Iris said as he got back into bed.

"That's why she was so pale yesterday."

And half an hour later, when he got up again, Iris did too. To his surprise. Looking as if she had lost her last friend. So he took her in his arms.

"I hate everything," she said.

ON the top shelf of his clothes closet he keeps all sorts of things — the overflow of phonograph records, and the photograph albums, which are too large for the bookcases in the living room. The snapshots show nothing but joy. Year after year of it.

ON the stage of the school auditorium, girls from Class Eight, in pastel-colored costumes and holding arches of crepe-paper flowers, made a tunnel from the front of the stage to the rear right-hand corner. The pianist took her hands from the keys, and the headmistress, in sensible navy blue, with her hair cut short like a man's, announced, "Class B becomes Class One."

Twenty very little girls in white dresses marched up on the stage two by two, holding hands.

George and Iris Carrington turned to each other and smiled, for Cindy was among them, looking proud and happy as she hurried through the tunnel of flowers and out of sight.

"Class One becomes Class Two." Another wave of little girls left their place in the audience and went up on the stage and disappeared into the wings.

"Class Two becomes Class Three."

Laurie Carrington, her red hair shining from the hairbrush, rose from her seat with the others and started up on the stage.

"It's too much!" George said, under his breath.

Class Three became Class Four, Class Four became Class Five, Class Five became Class Six, and George Carrington took a handkerchief out of his right hip pocket and wiped his eyes. It was their eagerness that undid him. Their absolute trust in the Arrangements. Class Six became Class Seven, Class Seven became Class Eight. The generations of man, growing up, growing old, dying in order to make room for more.

"Class Eight becomes Class Nine, and is now in the Upper School," the headmistress said, triumphantly. The two girls at the front ducked and went under the arches, taking their crepe-paper flowers with them. And then the next two, and the next, and finally the audience was left applauding an empty stage.

"COME here and sit on my lap," he said, by no means sure Laurie would think it worth the trouble. But she came. Folding her onto his lap, he was aware of the length of her legs, and the difference of her body; the babyness had departed forever, and when he was affectionate with her it was always as if the moment were slightly out of focus; he felt a restraint. He worried lest it be too close to making love to her. The difference was not great, and he was not sure whether it existed at all.

"Would you like to hear a riddle?" she asked.

"All right."

"Who was the fastest runner in history?"

"I don't know," he said, smiling at her. "Who was?"

"Adam. He was the first in the human race. . . . Teeheeheeheehee, wasn't that a good one?"

WAKING in the night, Cindy heard her mother and father laughing behind the closed door of their room. It was a sound she liked to hear, and she turned over and went right back to sleep.

"WHAT was that?"

He raised his head from the pillow and listened.

"Somebody crying 'Help!' " Iris said.

He got up and went to the window. There was no one in the street except a taxi driver brushing out the back seat of his hack. Again he heard it. Somebody being robbed. Or raped. Or murdered.

"Help . . ." Faintly this time. And not from the direction of the park. The taxi driver did not look up at the sound, which must be coming from inside a building somewhere. With his face to the window, George waited for the sound to come again and it didn't. Nothing but silence. If he called the police, what could he say? He got back into bed and lay there, sick with horror, his knees shaking. In the morning maybe the *Daily News* would have what happened.

But he forgot to buy a *News* on his way to work, and days passed, and he no longer was sure what night it was that they heard the voice crying "Help!" and felt that he ought to go through weeks of the *News* until he found out what happened. If it was in the *News*. And if something happened.

The Trojan Women

THE business district of Draperville, Illinois (population 12,000), was built around a neo-Roman courthouse and the courthouse square. Adjoining the railroad station, in the center of a small plot of ground, a bronze tablet marked the site of the Old Alton Depot where the first Latham County Volunteers entrained for the Civil War, and where the funeral train of Abraham Lincoln halted briefly at sunrise on May 3rd, 1865. Other towns within a radius of a hundred miles continued to prosper, but Draperville stopped growing. It was finished by 1900. The last civic accomplishment was the laying of the tracks for the Draperville Street Railway. The population stayed the same and the wide residential streets were lined with trees that every year grew larger and more beautiful, as if to conceal by a dense green shade the failure of men of enterprise and sound judgment to beget these same qualities in their sons.

The streetcar line started at the New Latham Hotel and ran past the baseball park and the county jail, past the state insane asylum, and on out to the cemetery and the lake. The lake was actually an abandoned gravel pit, half a mile long and a quarter of a mile wide, fed by underground springs. Its water was very deep and very cold. The shoreline was dotted with summer cottages and between the cottages and an expanse of cornfields was a thin grove of oak trees. Every summer two or three dozen families moved out here in June, to escape the heat, and stayed until the end of August, when the reopening of school forced them to return to town. After Labor Day, with the cottages boarded up and the children's voices stilled, the lake was washed in equinoctial rains, polished by the October sun, and became once more a part of the wide empty landscape.

On a brilliant September day in 1912 the streetcar stopped in front of the high school, and a large, tranquil colored woman got on. She was burdened with a shopping bag and several parcels, which she deposited on the seat beside her. There were two empty seats between the colored woman and the nearest white passengers, who nodded to her but did not include her in their conversation. The streetcar was open on the sides, with rattan seats. It rocked and swayed, and the passengers, as though they were riding on the back of an elephant, rocked and swayed with it. The people who had flowers — asters or chrysanthemums wrapped in damp newspaper — rode as far as the cemetery where, among acres of monuments and gravestones (Protestant on the right, Catholic on the left), faded American flags marked the final resting place of those who had fallen in the Civil or Spanish-American wars. It was a mile farther to the end of the line. There the conductor switched the trolley for the return trip, and the colored woman started off across an open field.

A winding path through the oak trees led her eventually to a cottage resting on concrete blocks, with a peaked roof and a porch across the front, facing the lake. Wide wooden shutters hinged at the top and propped up on poles gave the cottage a curious effect, as of a creosote-colored bird about to clap its wings and fly away.

The colored woman entered by the back door, into a kitchen so tiny that there was barely room for her to move between the kerosene stove and the table. She put her packages down and dipped a jelly glass into a bucket of water and drank. Through the thin partition came the sound of a child crying and then a woman's voice, high and clear and excitable.

"Is that you, Adah Belle?"

"Yes'm."

"I thought you'd never come."

The colored woman went into the front part of the cottage, a single disorderly room with magazine covers pasted on the walls, odds and ends of wicker furniture, a grass rug, and two cots. Japanese lanterns hung from the rafters, as if the cottage were in the throes of some shoddy celebration, and the aromatic wood smell from the fireplace was complicated by other odors, kerosene, camphor, and pennyroyal. A little boy a year and a half old was standing in a crib, his face screwed up and red with the exertion of crying. On his neck and arms and legs were the marks of mosquito bites.

"What's he crying about now?" the colored woman asked.

"I wish I knew." The woman's voice came from the porch. "I'll be glad when he can talk. Then we'll at least know what he's crying about."

"He's crying because he miss his Adah Belle," the colored woman said and lifted the little boy out of the crib. The crying subsided and the child's face, streaked with dirt and tears, took on a look of seriousness, of forced maturity. "Don't nobody love you like Adah Belle," she said, crooning over him.

"Virginia saw a snake," the voice called from the porch.

"You don't mean that?"

"A water moccasin. At least I think it was a water moccasin. Anyway it was huge. I threw a stick at it and it went under the porch and now I'm afraid to set foot out of the house."

"You leave that snake alone and he leave you alone," the colored woman said.

"Anything could happen out here," the voice said, "and we haven't a soul to turn to. There isn't even a place to telephone. . . . Was it hot in town?"

"I didn't have no time to notice."

"It was hot out here. I think it's going to storm. The flies have been biting like crazy all afternoon."

A moment later the woman appeared in the doorway. She was thirty years old, small-boned and slender, with dark hair piled on top of her head, and extraordinarily vivid blue eyes. Her pallor and her seriousness were like the little boy's. "Adah Belle," she said, putting her white hand on the solid black arm, "if it weren't for you—if you didn't come just when I think the whole world's against me, I don't know what I'd do. I think I'd just give up."

"I knows you need me," the colored woman said.

"Sometimes I look at the lake, and then I think of my two children and what would happen to them if I weren't here, and then I think, Adah Belle would look after them. And you would, Adah Belle."

The little boy, seeing his mother's eyes fill with tears, puckered his face up and began to cry again. She took him from the colored woman's arms and said, "Never you mind, my angel darling! Never you mind!" her voice rich with maternal consolation and pity for the lot of all children in a world where harshness and discipline prevail. "This has been going on all day."

"Don't you worry, honey," Adah Belle said. "I look after them and you, too. I got you some pork chops."

"Then you'll have to cook them tonight. They won't keep without ice. The first of the week I'm going in and have things out with the ice company." The white woman's face and manner had changed. She was in the outer office of the Draperville Ice & Coal Co., demanding that they listen to her, insisting on her rights.

"That flying squirrel been into the spaghetti again," Adah Belle said.

"You should have been here last night. Such a time as I had! I lit the lamp and there he was, up on the rafter — " The woman put her hands to her head, and for the moment it was night. The squirrel was there, ready to swoop down on them, and Adah Belle saw and was caught up in the scene that had taken place in her absence.

"I was terrified he'd get in my hair or knock the lamp over and set fire to the cottage."

"And then what?"

"I didn't know what to do. The children were sitting up in bed watching it. They weren't as frightened as I was, and I knew they oughtn't to be awake at that time of night, so I made them put their heads under the covers, and turned out the light — "

"That squirrel getting mighty bold. Some one of these days he come out in the daytime and I get him with a broom. That be the end of the squirrel. What happen when you turn out the light?"

"After that nothing happened. . . . Adah Belle, did you see Mr. Gellert?"

The colored woman shook her head. "I went to the back door and knock, like I ain't never work there, and after a while *she* come."

"Then she's still there?"

"Yes'm, she's there. She say, 'Adah Belle, is that you?' and I say, 'That's right, it's me. I come to get some things for Miz Gellert.' "

"And she let you in?"

"I march in before she could stop me."

"Weren't you afraid?"

"I march through the kitchen and into the front part of the house with her after me every step of the way."

"Oh, Adah Belle, you're wonderful!"

"I come to get them things for you and ain't no old woman going to stop me."

"She didn't dare not let you in, I guess. She knows I've been to see a lawyer. If I decide to take the case into court — "

With the single dramatic gesture that the white woman made with her bare arm, there was the crowded courtroom, the sea of faces, now friendly, now hostile to the colored woman on the witness stand.

"You going to do that, Miz Gellert?" she asked anxiously.

"I don't know, Adah Belle. I may. Sometimes I think it's the only solution."

From her voice it was clear that she also had reason to be afraid of what would happen in the courtroom. *If anybody is to blame, Mildred is,* her friends were saying over the bridge tables in town, women grown stout on their own accomplished cooking, wearing flowered dresses and the ample unwieldy straw hats of the period. Their faces flushed with the excitement of duplicate bridge and the combinations and permutations of gossip, they said, *If she can't stand to live with Harrison, then why doesn't she get a divorce?* Behind this attack was the voice of fear (in a high-keyed Middle Western accent), the voice of doubt.

They were not, like Mildred Gellert, having trouble with their husbands. Their marriages were successful, their children took music lessons and won prizes at commencement, and they had every reason in the world to be satisfied (new curtains for the living room, a glassed-in sun porch), every reason to be happy. It was only that sometimes when they woke in the middle of the night and couldn't get to sleep for a while, and so reviewed their lives, something (what, exactly, they couldn't say) seemed missing. The opportunity that they had always assumed would come to them hadn't come after all. *You mark my words,* the women said to each other (the words of fear, the counsel of doubt), *when cold weather comes, she'll go back to him.*

But could Mildred go back to him? After all, with his mother staying there keeping house for him, he might not want her back.

Oh he'll take her back, the women said, on the wide verandah of the brick mansion on College Avenue. *All you have to do is look at him to tell that. . . .*

The hangdog expression, they meant; the pale abject look of apology that didn't prevent him from nagging her about the grocery bills or from being insanely jealous whenever they were in mixed company and she showed the slightest sign of enjoying herself.

But it really was not fair to the friends who had stood by her again and again. The first two times Mildred Gellert left her husband, the women one and all stopped speaking to him, out of loyalty to her, they said. And then when she went back to him, it was very embarrassing to go to the house on Eighth Street and have to act as if nothing had happened. This time when he tipped his hat to them, they spoke. *There's no use fighting other people's battles,* they said, slipping their pumps off surreptitiously under the bridge table. *They never thank you for it. Besides, I like Harrison.*

I always have. I know he's difficult, but then Mildred isn't the easiest person in the world to get along with, either, and I think he tries to do what is right and she ought to take that into consideration.

The tragic heroine takes everything into consideration. That is her trouble, the thing that paralyzes her. While her lawyer is explaining to her the advantages of separate maintenance over an outright divorce, she considers the shape of his hands and how some people have nothing but happiness while they are young, and then, later, nothing but unhappiness.

Much as I like Mildred, the women said, driving back from the lake after listening to a three-hour monologue that had been every bit as good as a play, *I can't get worked up over it anymore. Besides, it's bad for the children. And if you ask me, I don't think she knows what she wants to do.*

This was quite right. Mildred Gellert left her husband and took a cottage out at the lake, in September, when all the other cottages were empty and boarded up, and this, of course, didn't solve anything but merely postponed the decision that could not be made until later in the fall, when some other postponement would have to be found, some new half measure.

Did you hear her ask me if I'd seen Harrison? the women said as the carriage reached the outskirts of town.

She wanted to know if he'd been at our house and I said right out that Ralph and I had been to call on his mother. She knows the old lady is there, and I thought I might as well be truthful with her because she might find it out some other way. I was all set to say, "Well, Mildred, if we all picked up our children and left our husbands every six months — " but she didn't say anything, so naturally I couldn't. But I know one thing. I'm not going all the way out there again in this heat just to hear the same old story about how Harrison wouldn't let her go to Peoria. And besides she did go, so what's there to get excited about? If she wants to see me, she can just get on the streetcar and come into town. After all, there's a limit.

The limit is boredom. Unless the tragic heroine can produce new stories, new black-and-blue marks, new threats and outrages that exceed in dramatic quality the old ones, it is better that she stay, no matter how unhappily, with her husband. So says the voice of doubt, the wisdom of fear.

IN the front room of the cottage out at the lake Adah Belle said, "She's been changing things around some."

"What?"

"She's got the sofa in the bay window where the table belong, and the table is out in the center of the room."

"I tried them that way but it doesn't work," Mildred Gellert said.

"It don't look natural," the colored woman agreed. "It was better the way you had it. She asked me did I know where to look for what I wanted and I said I could put my hands right on everything, so she sat down and commenced to read, and I took myself off upstairs."

"When Virginia was a baby, Mother Gellert came and stayed with her so Mr. Gellert and I could go to Chicago. When I got back she'd straightened all the dresser drawers and I thought I'd go out of my mind trying to figure out where she could have put things. She'd even got into the cedar chest and wrapped everything up in newspaper. She smiles at you and looks as though butter wouldn't melt in her mouth, and then the minute your back is turned — Did she ask for me?"

"No'm, I can't say she did."

"Or about the children?"

The colored woman shook her head.

"You'd think she might at least ask about her own grandchildren," Mildred Gellert said. Her eagerness gave way to disappointment. There was something that she had been expecting from this visit of Adah Belle's to the house on Eighth Street, something besides the woolens that Adah Belle had been instructed to get. "Was there any mail?"

"Well, they was this postcard for little Virginia. It was upstairs on the table beside the bed in her room. I don't know how that child's going to get it if she's out here. But anyway, I stick it inside my dress without asking."

"It's from her Sunday school teacher," Mildred Gellert said, and put the postcard — a view of stalagmites and stalactites in Mammoth Cave, Kentucky — on the mantel.

"While I was at it, I took a look around," Adah Belle said.

"Yes?"

"Judging from the guest-room closet, she's move in to stay."

"That's all right with me," Mildred Gellert said, her voice suddenly harsh with bitterness. "From now on it's her house. She can do anything she likes with it." As she put the little boy in the crib, her mind was filled with possibilities. She would force Harrison to give her the house on Eighth Street; or, if that proved too expensive for her to manage on the money the court allowed her, she could always rent those four upstairs rooms over old Mrs. Marshall. Adah Belle would look after the children in the daytime, and she could get a job in Lembach's selling dresses or teach domestic science in the high school.

"She save brown-paper bags. And string."

"Don't get me started on that," Mildred Gellert said. "Did she say anything when you left?"

"I call out to her I was leaving," Adah Belle said, "and when she come out of the library she had these two boxes in her hand."

"What two boxes?"

"I got them with me in the kitchen. 'Will you give these to the children,' she says. 'They're from Mr. Gellert. I don't know whether Mrs. Gellert will want them to have presents from their father or not, but you can ask her.' "

"As a matter of fact, I don't," Mildred Gellert said.

Out in the kitchen she broke the string on the larger package and opened it. "Building blocks," she said. The other box was flat and square and contained a children's handkerchief with a lavender butterfly embroidered in one corner. "I wish he wouldn't do things like that. With Edward it doesn't matter, but the sooner Virginia forgets her father, the better. He ought to realize that."

"He don't mean no harm by it," the colored woman said.

Mildred Gellert looked at her. "Are you going to turn against me, too?"

"No'm," Adah Belle said. "I ain't turning against you, honey. All I say is he don't mean no harm."

"Well, what he means is one thing," Mildred Gellert said, her eyes fever-bright. "And what he does is just exactly the opposite!" The next time they drove out, her intimate friends, to see her, she would have something to tell them that would make them sit up and take notice. It wasn't enough that Harrison had driven her from the house, forcing her to take refuge out here, in a place with no heat, and fall coming on; that didn't satisfy him. Now he was going to win the children away from her with expensive gifts, so that in the end he'd have everything and she'd be left stranded, with no place to go and no one to turn to. He'd planned it all out, from the very beginning. That would be his revenge.

"What you aim to do with them? Send them back?" Adah Belle asked, looking at the two boxes she had carried all the way out from town.

"Put this on the trash pile and burn it," Mildred Gellert said and left the kitchen.

Outside, under a large oak tree, a little girl of five, her hair in two blond braids, was playing with a strawberry box. She had lined the box with a piece of calico and in it lay a small rubber doll, naked, with a whistle in its stomach. "Now you be quiet," the little girl said to the doll, "and take your nap or I'll slap you."

From her place under the oak tree she watched the colored woman go out to the trash pile with the flat square box, set a match to the accumulation of paper and garbage, and return to the kitchen. The little girl waited a moment and then got up and ran to the fire. She found a stick, pulled the burning box onto the grass, and blew out the flames that were licking at it. Then she ran back to the oak tree with her prize. Part of the linen handkerchief was charred and fell apart in her hands, but the flames hadn't reached the lavender butterfly. The little girl hid the handkerchief under the piece of calico and looked around for a place to put the strawberry box.

When she came into the house, five minutes later, her eyes were blank and innocent. She had learned that much in a year and a half. Her eyes could keep any secret they wanted to. And the box was safe under the porch, where her mother wouldn't dare look for it, because of the snake.

The Pilgrimage

IN a rented Renault, with exactly as much luggage as the backseat would hold, Ray and Ellen Ormsby were making a little tour of France. It had so far included Vézelay, the mountain villages of Auvergne, the roses and Roman ruins of Provence, and the gorges of the Tarn. They were now on their way back to Paris by a route that was neither the most direct nor particularly scenic, and that had been chosen with one thing in mind— dinner at the Hôtel du Domino in Périgueux. The Richardsons, who were close friends of the Ormsbys in America, had insisted that they go there. "The best dinner I ever had in my entire life," Jerry Richardson had said. "Every course was something with truffles." "And the dessert," Anne Richardson had said, "was little balls of various kinds of ice cream in a beautiful basket of spun sugar with a spun-sugar bow." Putting the two statements together, Ray Ormsby had persisted in thinking that the ice cream also had truffles in it, and Ellen had given up trying to correct this impression.

At seven o'clock, they were still sixty-five kilometers from Périgueux, on a winding back-country road, and beginning to get hungry. The landscape was gilded with the evening light. Ray was driving. Ellen read aloud to him from the *Guide Gastronomique de la France* the paragraph on the Hôtel du Domino: "*Bel et confortable établissement à la renommée bien assise et que Mme. Lasgrezas dirige avec beaucoup de bonheur. Grâce à un maître queux qualifé, vous y ferez un repas de grande classe qui vous sera servi dans une élégante salle à manger ou dans un délicieux jardin d'été. . . .*"

As they drove through village after village, they saw, in addition to the usual painted Cinzano and Rasurel signs, announcements of the *spécialité* of the restaurant of this or that Hôtel des Sports or de la Poste or du Lion d'Or—always with truffles. In Montignac, there were so many of these signs that Ellen said anxiously, "Do you think we ought to eat *here?*"

"No," Ray said. "Périgueux is the place. It's the capital of Périgord, and so it's bound to have the best food."

Outside Thenon, they had a flat tire — the seventh in eight days of driving — and the casing of the spare tire was in such bad condition that Ray was afraid to drive on until the inner tube had been repaired and the regular tire put back on. It was five minutes of nine when they drove up before the Hôtel du Domino, and they were famished. Ray went inside and found that the hotel had accommodations for them. The car was driven into the hotel garage and emptied of its formidable luggage, and the Ormsbys were shown up to their third-floor room, which might have been in any plain hotel anywhere in France. "What I'd really like is the roast chicken stuffed with truffles," Ellen said from the washstand. "But probably it takes a long time."

"What if it does," Ray said. "We'll be eating other things first."

He threw open the shutters and discovered that their room looked out on a painting by Dufy — the large, bare, open square surrounded by stone buildings, with the tricolor for accent, and the sky a rich, stained-glass blue. From another window, at the turning of the stairs on their way down to dinner, they saw the delicious garden, but it was dark, and no one was eating there now. At the foot of the stairs, they paused.

"You wanted the restaurant?" the concierge asked, and when they nodded, she came out from behind her mahogany railing and led them importantly down a corridor. The maître d'hôtel, in a grey business suit, stood waiting at the door of the dining room, and put them at a table for two. Then he handed them the menu with a flourish. They saw at a glance how expensive the dinner was going to be. A waitress brought plates, glasses, napkins, knives, and forks.

While Ellen was reading the menu, Ray looked slowly around the room. The "*élégante salle à manger*" looked like a hotel coffee shop. There weren't even any tablecloths. The walls were painted a dismal shade of off-mustard. His eyes came to rest finally on the stippled brown dado a foot from his face. "It's a perfect room to commit suicide in," he said, and reached for the menu. A moment later he exclaimed, "I don't see the basket of ice cream!"

"It must be there," Ellen said. "Don't get so excited."

"Well, where? Just show me!"

Together they looked through the two columns of desserts, without finding the marvel in question. "Jerry and Anne were here several days," Ellen said. "They may have had it in some other restaurant."

This explanation Ray would not accept. "It was the same dinner, I remember distinctly." The full horror of their driving all the way to Périgueux in order to eat a very expensive meal at the wrong restaurant broke over him. In a cold sweat he got up from the table.

"Where are you going?" Ellen asked.

"I'll be right back," he said, and left the dining room. Upstairs in their room, he dug the *Guide Michelin* out of a duffel bag. He had lost all faith in the *Guide Gastronomique*, because of its description of the dining room; the person who wrote that had never set eyes on the Hôtel du Domino or, probably, on Périgueux. In the *Michelin*, the restaurant of the Hôtel du Domino rated one star and so did the restaurant Le Montaigne, but Le Montaigne also had three crossed forks and spoons, and suddenly it came to him, with the awful clarity of a long-submerged memory at last brought to the surface through layer after layer of consciousness, that it was at Le Montaigne and not at the Hôtel du Domino that the Richardsons had meant them to eat. He picked up Ellen's coat and, still carrying the *Michelin*, went back downstairs to the dining room.

"I've brought you your coat," he said to Ellen as he sat down opposite her. "We're in the wrong restaurant."

"We aren't either," Ellen said. "And even if we were, I've *got* to have something to eat. I'm starving, and it's much too late now to go looking for—"

"It won't be far," Ray said. "Come on." He looked up into the face of the maître d'hôtel, waiting with his pencil and pad to take their order.

"You speak English?" Ray asked.

The maître d'hôtel nodded, and Ray described the basket of spun sugar filled with different kinds of ice cream.

"And a spun-sugar bow," Ellen said.

The maître d'hôtel looked blank, and so Ray tried again, speaking slowly and distinctly.

"*Omelette?*" the maître d'hôtel said.

"No—ice cream!"

"*Glace,*" Ellen said.

"*Et du sucre,*" Ray said. "*Une—*" He and Ellen looked at each other. Neither of them could think of the word for "basket."

The maître d'hôtel went over to a sideboard and returned with another menu. "*Le menu des glaces,*" he said coldly.

"*Vanille*," they read, "*chocolat, pistache, framboise, fraise, tutti-frutti, praliné . . .*"

Even if the spun-sugar basket had been on the *menu des glaces* (which it wasn't), they were in too excited a state to have found it — Ray because of his fear that they were making an irremediable mistake in having dinner at this restaurant and Ellen because of the dreadful way he was acting.

"We came here on a pilgrimage," he said to the maître d'hôtel, in a tense, excited voice that carried all over the dining room. "We have these friends in America who ate in Périgueux, and it is absolutely necessary that we eat in the place they told us about."

"This is a very good restaurant," the maître d'hôtel said. "We have many *spécialités. Foie gras truffé, poulet du Périgord noir, truffes sous la cendre — *"

"I know," Ray said, "but apparently it isn't the right one." He got up from his chair, and Ellen, shaking her head — because there was no use arguing with him when he was like this — got up, too. The other diners had all turned around to watch.

"Come," the maître d'hôtel said, taking hold of Ray's elbow. "In the lobby is a lady who speaks English very well. She will understand what it is you want."

In the lobby, Ray told his story again — how they had come to Périgueux because their friends in America had told them about a certain restaurant here, and how it was this restaurant and no other that they must find. They had thought it was the restaurant in the Hôtel du Domino, but since the restaurant of the Hôtel du Domino did not have the dessert that their friends in America had particularly recommended, little balls of ice cream in —

The concierge, her eyes large with sudden comprehension, interrupted him. "You wanted truffles?"

OUT on the sidewalk, trying to read the *Michelin* map of Périgueux by the feeble light of a tall street lamp, Ray said, "Le Montaigne has a star just like the Hôtel du Domino, but it also has three crossed forks and spoons, so it must be better than the hotel."

"All those crossed forks and spoons mean is that it is a very comfortable place to eat in," Ellen said. "It has nothing to do with the quality of the food. I don't care where we eat, so long as I don't have to go back there."

There were circles of fatigue under her eyes. She was both exasperated with him and proud of him for insisting on getting what they had come here for, when most people would have given in and taken what there was. They walked on a couple of blocks and came to a second open square. Ray stopped a man and woman.

"*Pardon, m'sieur,*" he said, removing his hat. "*Le restaurant La Montagne, c'est par là*" — he pointed — "*ou par là?*"

"*La Montagne? Le restaurant La Montagne?*" the man said dubiously. "*Je regrette, mais je ne le connais pas.*"

Ray opened the *Michelin* and, by the light of the nearest neon sign, the man and woman read down the page.

"*Ooh, LE MonTAIGNE!*" the woman exclaimed suddenly.

"*LE MonTAIGNE!*" the man echoed.

"*Oui, Le Montaigne,*" Ray said, nodding.

The man pointed across the square.

STANDING in front of Le Montaigne, Ray again had doubts. It was much larger than the restaurant of the Hôtel du Domino, but it looked much more like a bar than a first-class restaurant. And again there were no tablecloths. A waiter approached them as they stood undecided on the sidewalk. Ray asked to see the menu, and the waiter disappeared into the building. A moment later, a second waiter appeared. "*Le menu,*" he said, pointing to a standard a few feet away. Le Montaigne offered many specialties, most of them *truffés*, but not the Richardsons' dessert.

"Couldn't we just go someplace and have an ordinary meal?" Ellen said. "I don't think I feel like eating anything elaborate any longer."

But Ray had made a discovery. "The restaurant is upstairs," he said. "What we've been looking at is the café, so naturally there aren't any tablecloths."

Taking Ellen by the hand, he started up what turned out to be a circular staircase. The second floor of the building was dark. Ellen, convinced that the restaurant had stopped serving dinner, objected to going any farther, but Ray went on, and protesting, she followed him. The third floor was brightly lighted — was, in fact, a restaurant, with white tablecloths, gleaming crystal, and the traditional dark-red plush upholstery, and two or three clients who were lingering over the end of dinner. The maître d'hôtel, in a black dinner jacket, led them to a table and handed them the same menu they had read downstairs.

"I don't see any roast chicken stuffed with truffles," Ellen said.

"Oh, I forgot that's what you wanted!" Ray said, conscience-stricken. "Did they have it at the Domino?"

"No, but they had *poulet noir* — and here they don't even have that."

"I'm so sorry," he said. "Are you sure they don't have it here?" He ran his eyes down the list of dishes with truffles and said suddenly. "There it is!"

"Where?" Ellen demanded. He pointed to "*Tournedos aux truffes du Périgord.*" "That's not chicken," Ellen said.

"Well, it's no good, then," Ray said.

"No good?" the maître d'hôtel said indignantly. "It's *very* good! *Le tournedos aux truffes du Périgord* is a *spécialité* of the restaurant!"

They were only partly successful in conveying to him that that was not what Ray had meant.

No, there was no roast chicken stuffed with truffles.

No chicken of any kind.

"I'm very sorry," Ray said, and got up from his chair.

HE was not at all sure that Ellen would go back to the restaurant in the Hôtel du Domino with him, but she did. Their table was just as they had left it. A waiter and a busboy, seeing them come in, exchanged startled whispers. The maître d'hôtel did not come near them for several minutes after they had sat down, and Ray carefully didn't look around for him.

"Do you think he is angry because we walked out?" Ellen asked.

Ray shook his head. "I think we hurt his feelings, though. I think he prides himself on speaking English, and now he will never again be sure that he does speak it, because of us."

Eventually, the maître d'hôtel appeared at their table. Sickly smiles were exchanged all around, and the menu was offered for the second time, without the flourish.

"What is *les truffes sous la cendre*?" Ellen asked.

"It takes forty-five minutes," the maître d'hôtel said.

"*Le foie gras truffé*," Ray said. "For two."

"*Le foi gras*, O.K.," the maître d'hôtel said. "*Et ensuite?*"

"*Œufs en gelée*," Ellen said.

"*Œufs en gelée*, O.K."

"*Le poulet noir*," Ray said.

"*Le poulet noir*, O.K."

"*Et deux Cinzano*," Ray said, on solid ground at last, "*avec un morceau de glace et un zeste de citron. S'il vous plaît.*"

The apéritif arrived, with ice and lemon peel, but the wine list was not presented, and Ray asked the waitress for it. She spoke to the maître d'hôtel, and that was the last the Ormsbys ever saw of her. The maître d'hôtel brought the wine list, they ordered the dry white *vin du pays* that he recommended, and their dinner was served to them by a waiter so young that Ray looked to see whether he was in knee pants.

The pâté was everything the Richardsons had said it would be, and Ray, to make up for all he had put his wife through in the course of the evening, gave her a small quantity of his, which, protesting, she accepted. The maître d'hôtel stopped at their table and said, "Is it good?"

"Very good," they said simultaneously.

The *œufs en gelée* arrived and were also very good, but were they any better than or even as good as the *œufs en gelée* the Ormsbys had had in the restaurant of a hotel on the outskirts of Aix-en-Provence was the question.

"Is it good?" the maître d'hôtel asked.

"Very good," they said. "So is the wine."

The boy waiter brought in the *poulet noir* — a chicken casserole with a dark-brown Madeira sauce full of chopped truffles.

"Is it good?" Ray asked when the waiter had finished serving them and Ellen had tasted the *pièce de résistance*.

"It's very good," she said. "But I'm not sure I can taste the truffles."

"I think I can," he said, a moment later.

"With the roast chicken, it probably would have been quite easy," Ellen said.

"Are you sure the Richardsons had roast chicken stuffed with truffles?" Ray asked.

"I think so," Ellen said. "Anyway, I know I've read about it."

"Is it good?" the maître d'hôtel, their waiter, and the waiter from a neighboring table asked in succession.

"Very good," the Ormsbys said.

Since they couldn't have the little balls of various kinds of ice cream in a basket of spun sugar with a spun-sugar bow for dessert, they decided not to have any dessert at all. The meal came to an abrupt end with *café filtre*.

Intending to take a short walk before going to bed, they heard dance music in the square in front of Le Montaigne, and found a large crowd there, celebrating the annual fair of Périgueux. There was a seven-piece orchestra on a raised platform under a canvas, and a few couples were dancing in the street. Soon there were more.

"Do you feel like dancing?" Ray asked.

The pavement was not as bad for dancing as he would have supposed, and something happened to them that had never happened to them anywhere in France before — something remarkable. In spite of their clothes and their faces and the *Michelin* he held in one hand, eyes constantly swept over them or past them without pausing. Dancing in the street, they aroused no curiosity and, in fact, no interest whatever.

AT midnight, standing on the balcony outside their room, they could still hear the music, a quarter of a mile away.

"Hasn't it been a lovely evening!" Ellen said. "I'll always remember dancing in the street in Périgueux."

Two people emerged from the cinema, a few doors from the Hôtel du Domino. And then a few more — a pair of lovers, a woman, a boy, a woman and a man carrying a sleeping child.

"The pâté was the best I ever ate," Ellen said.

"The Richardsons probably ate in the garden," Ray said. "I don't know that the dinner as a whole was all *that* good," he added thoughtfully. And then, "I don't know that we need tell them."

"The poor people who run the cinema," Ellen said.

"Why?"

"No one came to see the movie."

"I suppose Périgueux really isn't the kind of town that would support a movie theater," Ray said.

"That's it," Ellen said. "Here, when people want to relax and enjoy themselves, they have an apéritif, they walk up and down in the evening air, they dance in the street, the way people used to do before there were any movies. It's another civilization entirely from anything we're accustomed to. Another world."

They went back into the bedroom and closed the shutters. A few minutes later, some more people emerged from the movie theater, and some more, and some more, and then a great crowd came streaming out and, walking gravely, like people taking part in a religious procession, fanned out across the open square.

The Patterns of Love

KATE Talbot's bantam rooster, awakened by the sudden appearance of the moon from behind a cloud on a white June night, began to crow. There were three bantams — a cock and two hens — and their roost was in a tree just outside the guest-room windows. The guest room was on the first floor and the Talbots' guest that weekend was a young man by the name of Arnold, a rather light sleeper. He got up and closed the windows and went back to bed. In the sealed room he slept, but was awakened at frequent intervals until daylight Saturday morning.

Arnold had been coming to the Talbots' place in Wilton sometime during the spring or early summer for a number of years. His visits were, for the children, one of a thousand seasonal events that could be counted on, less exciting than the appearance of the first robin or the arrival of violets in the marsh at the foot of the Talbots' hill but akin to them. Sometimes Duncan, the Talbots' older boy, who for a long time was under the impression that Arnold came to see *him*, slept in the guest room when Arnold was there. Last year, George, Duncan's younger brother, had been given that privilege. This time, Mrs. Talbot, knowing how talkative the boys were when they awoke in the morning, had left Arnold to himself.

When he came out of his room, Mrs. Talbot and George, the apple of her eye, were still at breakfast. George was six, small and delicate and very blond, not really interested in food at any time, and certainly not now, when there was a guest in the house. He was in his pajamas and a pink quilted bathrobe. He smiled at Arnold with his large and very gentle eyes and said, "Did you miss me?"

"Yes, of course," Arnold said. "I woke up and there was the other bed, flat and empty. Nobody to talk to while I looked at the ceiling. Nobody to watch me shave."

George was very pleased that his absence had been felt. "What is your favorite color?" he asked.

"Red," Arnold said, without having to consider.

"Mine too," George said, and his face became so illuminated with pleasure at this coincidence that for a moment he looked angelic.

"No matter how much we disagree about other things," Arnold said, "we'll always have that in common, won't we?"

"Yes," George said.

"You'd both better eat your cereal," Mrs. Talbot said.

Arnold looked at her while she was pouring his coffee and wondered if there wasn't something back of her remark — jealousy, perhaps. Mrs. Talbot was a very soft-hearted woman, but for some reason she seemed to be ashamed — or perhaps afraid — to let other people know it. She took refuge continually behind a dry humor. There was probably very little likelihood that George would be as fond of anyone else as he was of his mother for many years to come. There was no real reason for her to be jealous.

"Did the bantams keep you awake?" she asked.

Arnold shook his head.

"Something tells me you're lying," Mrs. Talbot said. "John didn't wake up, but he felt his responsibilities as a host even so. He cried 'Oh!' in his sleep every time a bantam crowed. You'll have to put up with them on Kate's account. She loves them more than her life."

Excluded from the conversation of the grown-ups, George finished his cereal and ate part of a soft-boiled egg. Then he asked to be excused and, with pillows and pads which had been brought in from the garden furniture the night before, he made a train right across the dining-room floor. The cook had to step over it when she brought a fresh pot of coffee, and Mrs. Talbot and Arnold had to do likewise when they went out through the dining-room door to look at the bantams. There were only two — the cock and one hen — walking around under the Japanese cherry tree on the terrace. Kate was leaning out of an upstairs window, watching them fondly.

"Have you made your bed?" Mrs. Talbot asked.

The head withdrew.

"Kate is going to a house party," Mrs. Talbot said, looking at the bantams. "A sort of house party. She's going to stay all night at Mary

Sherman's house and there are going to be some boys and they're going to dance to the Victrola."

"How old is she, for heaven's sake?" Arnold asked.

"Thirteen," Mrs. Talbot said. "She had her hair cut yesterday and it's too short. It doesn't look right, so I have to do something about it."

"White of egg?" Arnold asked.

"How did you know that?" Mrs. Talbot asked in surprise.

"I remembered it from the last time," Arnold said. "I remembered it because it sounded so drastic."

"It only works with blonds," Mrs. Talbot said. "Will you be able to entertain yourself for a while?"

"Easily," Arnold said. "I saw *Anna Karenina* in the library and I think I'll take that and go up to the little house."

"Maybe I'd better come with you," Mrs. Talbot said.

The little house was a one-room studio halfway up the hill, about a hundred feet from the big house, with casement windows on two sides and a Franklin stove. It had been built several years before, after Mrs. Talbot had read *A Room of One's Own*, and by now it had a slightly musty odor which included lingering traces of wood smoke.

"Hear the wood thrush?" Arnold asked, as Mrs. Talbot threw open the windows for him. They both listened.

"No," she said. "All birds sound alike to me."

"Listen," he said.

This time there was no mistaking it—the liquid notes up and then down the same scale.

"Oh, that," she said. "Yes, I love that," and went off to wash Kate's hair.

FROM time to time Arnold raised his head from the book he was reading and heard not only the wood thrush but also Duncan and George, quarreling in the meadow. George's voice was shrill and unhappy and sounded as if he were on the verge of tears. Both boys appeared at the window eventually and asked for permission to come in. The little house was out of bounds to them. Arnold nodded. Duncan, who was nine, crawled in without much difficulty, but George had to be hoisted. No sooner were they inside than they began to fight over a wooden gun which had been broken and mended and was rightly George's, it seemed, though Duncan had it and refused to give it up. He refused to give it up one moment, and the next moment, after a sudden change of heart, pressed it upon George — *forced* George to take it, actually, for by that time George was more concerned about the Talbots' dog, who also wanted to come in.

The dog was a Great Dane, very mild but also very enormous. He answered to the name of Satan. Once Satan was admitted to the little house, it became quite full and rather noisy, but John Talbot appeared and sent the dog out and made the children leave Arnold in peace. They left as they had come, by the window. Arnold watched them and was touched by the way Duncan turned and helped George, who was too small to jump. Also by the way George accepted this help. It was as if their hostility had two faces and one of them was the face of love. Cain and Abel, Arnold thought, and the wood thrush. All immortal.

John Talbot lingered outside the little house. Something had been burrowing in the lily-of-the-valley bed, he said, and had also uprooted several lady's slippers. Arnold suggested that it might be moles.

"More likely a rat," John Talbot said, and his eyes wandered to a two-foot espaliered pear tree. "That pear tree," he said, "we put in over a year ago."

Mrs. Talbot joined them. She had shampooed not only Kate's hair but her own as well.

"It's still alive," John Talbot said, staring at the pear tree, "but it doesn't put out any leaves."

"I should think it would be a shock to a pear tree to be espaliered," Mrs. Talbot said. "Kate's ready to go."

They all piled into the station wagon and took Kate to her party. Her too short blond hair looked quite satisfactory after the egg shampoo, and Mrs. Talbot had made a boutonniere out of a pink geranium and some little blue and white flowers for Kate to wear on her coat. She got out of the car with her suitcase and waved at them from the front steps of the house.

"I hope she has a good time," John Talbot said uneasily as he shifted gears. "It's her first dance with boys. It would be terrible if she didn't have any partners." In his eyes there was a vague threat toward the boys who, in their young callowness, might not appreciate his daughter.

"Kate always has a good time," Mrs. Talbot said. "By the way, have you seen both of the bantam hens today?"

"No," John Talbot said.

"One of them is missing," Mrs. Talbot said.

ONE of the things that impressed Arnold whenever he stayed with the Talbots was the number and variety of animals they had. Their place was not a farm, after all, but merely a big white brick house in the country, and yet they usually had a dog and a cat, kittens, rabbits, and chickens, all actively involved in the family life. This summer the Talbots weren't able to go in and out by the front door, because a phoebe had built a nest in the porch light. They used the dining-room door instead, and were careful not to leave the porch light on more than a minute or two, lest the eggs be cooked. Arnold came upon some turtle food in his room, and when he asked about it, Mrs. Talbot informed him that there were turtles in the guest room, too. He never came upon the turtles.

The bantams were new this year, and so were the two very small ducklings that at night were put in a paper carton in the sewing room, with an electric-light bulb to keep them warm. In the daytime they hopped in and out of a saucer of milk on the terrace. One of them was called Mr. Rochester because of his distinguished air. The other had no name.

All the while that Mrs. Talbot was making conversation with Arnold, after lunch, she kept her eyes on the dog, who, she explained, was jealous of the ducklings. Once his great head swooped down and he pretended to take a nip at them. A nip would have been enough. Mrs. Talbot spoke to him sharply and he turned his head away in shame.

"They probably smell the way George did when he first came home from the hospital," she said.

"What did George smell like?" Arnold asked.

"Sweetish, actually. Actually awful."

"Was Satan jealous of George when he was a baby?"

"Frightfully," Mrs. Talbot said. "Call Satan!" she shouted to her husband, who was up by the little house. He had found a rat hole near the ravaged lady's slippers and was setting a trap. He called the dog, and the dog went bounding off, devotion in every leap.

While Mrs. Talbot was telling Arnold how they found Satan at the baby's crib one night, Duncan, who was playing only a few yards away with George, suddenly, and for no apparent reason, made his younger brother cry. Mrs. Talbot got up and separated them.

"I wouldn't be surprised if it wasn't time for your nap, George," she said, but he was not willing to let go of even a small part of the day. He wiped his tears away with his fist and ran from her. She ran after him, laughing, and caught him at the foot of the terrace.

Duncan wandered off into a solitary world of his own, and Arnold, after yawning twice, got up and went into the house. Stretched out on the bed in his room, with the Venetian blinds closed, he began to compare the life of the Talbots with his own well-ordered but childless and animalless life in town. Everywhere they go, he thought, they leave tracks behind them, like people walking in the snow. Paths crisscrossing, lines that are perpetually meeting: the mother's loving pursuit of her youngest, the man's love for his daughter, the dog's love for the man, and two boys' preoccupation with each other. Wheels and diagrams, Arnold said to himself. The patterns of love.

THAT night Arnold was much less bothered by the crowing, which came to him dimly, through dreams. When he awoke finally and was fully awake, he was conscious of the silence and the sun shining in his eyes. His watch had stopped and it was later than he thought. The Talbots had finished breakfast and the Sunday *Times* was waiting beside his place at the table. While he was eating, John Talbot came in and sat down for a minute, across the table. He had been out early that morning, he said, and had found a chipmunk in the rat trap and also a nest with three bantam eggs in it. The eggs were cold.

He was usually a very quiet, self-contained man. This was the first time Arnold had ever seen him disturbed about anything. "I don't know how we're going to tell Kate," he said. "She'll be very upset."

Kate came home sooner than they expected her, on the bus. She came up the driveway, lugging her suitcase.

"Did you have a good time?" Mrs. Talbot called to her from the terrace.

"Yes," she said, "I had a beautiful time."

Arnold looked at the two boys, expecting them to blurt out the tragedy as soon as Kate put down her suitcase, but they didn't. It was her father who told her, in such a roundabout way that she didn't seem to understand at all what he was saying. Mrs. Talbot interrupted him with the flat facts; the bantam hen was not on her nest and therefore, in all probability, had been killed, maybe by the rat.

Kate went into the house. The others remained on the terrace. The dog didn't snap at the ducklings, though his mind was on them still, and the two boys didn't quarrel. In spite of the patterns on which they seem so intent, Arnold thought, what happens to one of them happens to all. They are helplessly involved in Kate's loss.

At noon other guests arrived, two families with children. There was a picnic, with hot dogs and bowls of salad, cake, and wine, out under the grape arbor. When the guests departed, toward the end of the afternoon, the family came together again on the terrace. Kate was lying on the ground, on her stomach, with her face resting on her arms, her head practically in the ducklings' saucer of milk. Mrs. Talbot, who had stretched out on the garden chaise longue, discovered suddenly that Mr. Rochester was missing. She sat up in alarm and cried, "Where is he?"

"Down my neck," Kate said.

The duck emerged from her crossed arms. He crawled around them and climbed up on the back of her neck. Kate smiled. The sight of the duck's tiny downy head among her pale ash-blond curls made them all burst out laughing. The cloud that had been hanging over the household evaporated into bright sunshine, and Arnold seized that moment to glance at his watch.

They all went to the train with him, including the dog. At the last moment Mrs. Talbot, out of a sudden perception of his lonely life, tried to give him some radishes, but he refused them. When he stepped out of the car at the station, the boys were arguing and were with difficulty persuaded to say good-bye to him. He watched the station wagon drive away and then stood listening for the sound of the wood thrush. But, of course, in the center of South Norwalk there was no such sound.

What Every Boy Should Know

SHORTLY before his twelfth birthday, Edward Gellert's eyes were opened and he knew that he was naked. More subtle than any beast of the field, more rational than Adam, he did not hide himself from the presence of God or sew fig leaves together. The most he could hope for was to keep his father and mother, his teachers, people in general from knowing. He took elaborate precautions against being surprised, each time it was always the last time, and afterward he examined himself in the harsh light of the bathroom mirror. It did not show yet, but when the mark appeared it would be indelible and it would be his undoing.

People asked him, Who is your girl? And he said, I have no girl, and they laughed and his mother said, Edward doesn't care for girls, and they said, All that will change.

People said, Edward is a good boy, and that was because they didn't know.

He touched Darwin and got an electric shock: ". . . the hair is chiefly retained in the male sex on the chest and face, and in both sexes at the juncture of all four limbs with the trunk. . . ." There was more, but he heard someone coming and had to replace the book on the shelf.

He stopped asking questions, though his mind was teeming with them, lest someone question him. And because it was no use; the questions he wanted to ask were the questions grown people and even older boys did not want to answer. This did not interrupt the incessant kaleidoscopic patterns of ignorance and uncertainty: How did they know that people were really dead, that they wouldn't open their eyes suddenly and try to push their way out of the coffin? And how did the worms get to them if the casket was inside an outer casket that was metal? And when Mrs. Spelman died and Mr. Spelman married again, how was it arranged so that there was no embarrassment later on when he and the first Mrs. Spelman met in Heaven?

Harrison Gellert's boy, people said, seeing him go by on his way to school. To get to him, though, you had first to get past his one-tube radio, his experimental chemistry set, his growing ball of lead foil, his correspondence with the Scott Stamp & Coin Co., his automatically evasive answers.

Pure, self-centered, a moral outcast, he sat through church, in his blue serge Sunday suit, and heard the Reverend Harry Blair, who baptized him, say solemnly from the pulpit that he was conceived in sin. But afterward, at the church door, in the brilliant sunshine, he shook hands with Edward; he said he was happy to have Edward with them.

In the bookcase in the upstairs hall Edward found a book that seemed to have been put there by someone for his enlightenment. It was called *What Every Boy Should Know*, and it told him nothing that he didn't know already.

Arrived at the age of exploration, he charted his course by a map that showed India as an island. The Pacific Ocean was overlooked somehow. Greenland was attached to China, and rivers flowed into the wrong sea. The map enabled him to determine his latitude with a certain amount of accuracy, but for his longitude he was dependent on dead reckoning. In his search for an interior passage, he continually mistook inlets for estuaries. The Known World is not, of course, known. It probably never will be, because of those areas the mapmakers have very sensibly agreed to ignore, where the terrain is different for every traveler who crosses them. Or fails to cross them. The Unknown World, indicated by dotted lines or by no lines at all, was based on the reports of one or two boys in little better case than Edward and frightened like him by tales of sea monsters, of abysses at the world's end.

A savage ill at ease among the overcivilized, Edward remembered to wash his hands and face before he came to the table, and was sent away again because he forgot to put on a coat or a sweater. He slept with a stocking top on his head and left his roller skates where someone could fall over them. It was never wise to send him on any kind of involved errand.

He was sometimes a child, sometimes an adult in the uncomfortable small size. He had opinions but they were not listened to. He blushed easily and he had his feelings hurt. His jokes were not always successful, having a point that escaped most people, or that annoyed his father. His sister Virginia was real, but his father and mother he was aware of mostly as generalities, agents of authority or love or discipline, telling him to sit up straight in his chair, to stand with his shoulders back, to pick up his clothes, read in a better light, stop chewing his nails, stop sniffing and go upstairs and get a handkerchief. When his father asked some question at the dinner table and his mother didn't answer, or, looking down at her plate, answered inaudibly, and when his father then, in the face of these warnings, pursued the matter until she left the table and went upstairs, it didn't mean that his mother and father didn't love each other, or that Edward didn't have as happy a home as any other boy.

Meanwhile, his plans made, his blue eyes a facsimile of innocence, he waited for them all to go some place. Who then moved through the still house? No known Edward. A murderer with flowers in his hair. A male impersonator. A newt undergoing metamorphosis. Now this, now that mirror was his accomplice. The furniture was accessory to the fact. The house being old, he could count on the back stairs to cry out at the approach of discovery. When help came, it came from the outside as usual. Harrison Gellert, passing the door of his son's room one November night, seeing Edward with his hand at the knob of his radio and the headphones over his ears, reflected on Edward's thinness, his pallor, his poor posture, his moodiness of late, and concluded that he did not spend enough time out-of-doors. Edward was past the age when you could tell him to go outside and play, but if he had a job of some kind that would keep him out in the open air, like delivering papers . . . Too shocked to argue with his father (you don't ask someone to give you a job out of the kindness of their heart when they don't even know you and also when there may not even be any job or if there is they may have somebody else in mind who would be better at it and who deserves it more), Edward went downtown after school and stood beside the wooden railing in the front office of the Draperville *Evening Star*, waiting for someone to notice him. He expected to be sent away in disgrace, and instead he was given a canvas bag and a list of names and told to come around to the rear of the building.

FROM five o'clock on, all over town, all along College Avenue with its overarching elms, Eighth Street, Ninth Street, Fourth Street, in the block of two-story flats backed up against the railroad tracks, and on those unpaved, nameless streets out where the sidewalk ended and the sky took over, old men sitting by the front window and children at a loss for something to do waited and listened for the sound of the paper striking the porch, and the cry — disembodied and forlorn — of "Pay-er!" Women left their lighted kitchens or put down their sewing in upstairs rooms and went to the front door and looked to see if the evening paper had come. Sometimes spring had come instead, and they smelled the sweet syringa in the next yard. Or the smell was of burning leaves. Sometimes they saw their breath in the icy air. A few minutes later they went to the door and looked again. Left too long, the paper blew out into the yard, got rained on, was covered with snow. Their persistence rewarded at last, they bent down and picked up the paper, opened it, and read the headline, while the paper boy rode on rapidly over lawns he had been told not to ride over, as if he were bent on overtaking lost time or some other paper boy who was not there.

In a place where everybody could easily be traced back to his origin, people did not always know who the paper boy was or care what time he got home to supper. They assumed from a general knowledge of boys that if the paper was late it was because the paper boy dawdled some-where, shooting marbles, throwing snowballs, when he should have been delivering their paper.

Every afternoon after school the boys rode into the alley behind the *Star* Building, let their bicycles fall with a clatter, and gathered in the cage next to the pressroom. They were dirty-faced, argumentative, and as alike as sparrows. Their pockets sagged with pieces of chalk, balls of string, slingshots, marbles, jackknives, deified objects, trophies they traded. Boasting and being called on to produce evidence in support of what ought to have been true but wasn't, they bet large sums of unreal money or passed along items of misinformation that were gratefully re-ceived and stored away in a safe place. Easily deflated, they just as easily recovered their powers of pretending. With the press standing idle, the linotype machine clicking and lisping, the round clock on the wall a torment to them every time they glanced in that direction, they asked, What time is the press going to start? — knowing that the printing press of the Draperville *Evening Star* was all but done for, and that it was a question not of how soon it would start printing but of whether it could be prevailed upon to print at all. When the linotype machines stopped, there was a quarter of an hour of acute uncertainty, during which late-news bulletins were read in reverse, corrections were made in the price of laying mash and ladies' ready-to-wear, and the columns of type were locked in place. The boys waited. The pressroom waited. The front office waited and listened. And suddenly the clean white paper began to move, to flow like a waterfall. Words appeared on one side and then on the other. The clittering clattering discourse gained momentum. The paper was cut, the paper was folded. Smelling of damp ink, copies of the Draperville *Evening Star* slid down a chute and were scooped up and counted by a young man named Homer West, who never broke down or gave trouble to anyone. Cheerful, even-tempered, he handed the papers through a wicket to the seventeen boys who waited in line with their canvas bags slung over one shoulder and their bicycles in a tangle outside. One of them was Homer's brother Harold, but Homer was a brother to all of them. He teased them, eased the pressure of their high-pitched impatience with joking, kept them from fighting each other during that ominous quarter of an hour after the linotype machines fell silent, and listened for the first symptoms of disorder in the press. When it began chewing paper instead of printing, he pulled the switch, and a silence of a deeply discouraging import succeeded the whir and the clitter-clit-clatter. The boys who were left said, I can't wait around here all night, I have homework to do. And Homer, waiting also, for the long day to end and for the time still far in the future when he could afford to get married, said, Do your homework now, why don't you? They said, Here? and he said, Why not? What's the matter with this place? It's warm. You've got electric light. They said, I can't concentrate. And Homer said, Neither can I with you talking to me. He said, It won't be long now. And when they insisted on knowing how long, he said, Pretty soon.

The key to age is patience; and the key to patience is unfortunately age, which cannot be hurried, which takes time (in which to be disappointed); and time is measured by what happens; and what happens is printed (some of it) in the evening paper.

Just when it seemed certain that there would be no more copies of that evening's *Star*, the waterfall resumed its flowing — slowly at first, and then with a kind of frantic confidence. One after another the boys received their papers through the wicket, counted them, and, with their canvas bags weighted, ran out of the building to mount their bicycles and ride off to the part of town that depended on them for its knowledge of what was going on in the outside world in the year 1922.

After their first mild surprise at finding Eddie Gellert in the cage with them, the other boys accepted his presence there, serene in the knowledge that they could lick him if he started getting wise, and that they had

thirty-seven or forty-two or fifty-one customers in a good neighborhood
to his thirteen in the poorest-paying section of town. His route had been
broken off one of the larger ones, with no harm to the loser, who, that
first evening, went with him to point out the houses that took the *Star*,
and showed him how to fold the papers as he went along and how to
toss them so they landed safely on the porch. After that, Edward was on
his own.

The boys received their papers from Homer in rotation, and it was
better to be second or third or fourth or even fifth than it was to be first,
because if you were first it meant that the next night you would be last.
"Pay-er . . ." Edward called, like the others. "Pay-er?" — with his mind
on home. His last paper delivered, he turned toward the plate kept warm
for him in the oven, the place it would have been so pleasant to come to
straight from school. But he was twelve now, and out in the world. He
had put the unlimited leisure of childhood behind him. As his father said,
he was learning the value of money, his stomach empty, his nostrils
burning with the cold, his chin deep in the collar of his mackinaw.

How much money his father had, Edward did not know. It was one of
those interesting questions that grown people do not care to answer.
Since his mother was also kept in the dark about this, there was no reason
to assume he could find out by asking. But he knew he was expected to
do as well some day, and own a nice home and provide decently for the
wife and children it was as yet impossible for him to imagine. If all this
were easy to manage, then his father would not be upset about lights that
were left burning in empty rooms or mention the coal bill every time
somebody complained that the house was chilly. Life is serious and without adequate guarantees, whether your mother takes in washing or belongs to the Friday Bridge Club. Poverty is no joke — but neither is the
fear of poverty never experienced. Every evening Edward saw, like a
lantern slide of failure, the part of town he must never live in, streets that
weren't ever going to be paved, in all probability, houses that year
after year the banks or the coal company or old Mr. Ivens saw no need
for repainting or doing anything about, beyond seeing to it that the
people who lived in them paid their rent promptly on the first day of the
month.

On Saturday mornings he came with his metal collection book and
knocked and the door was opened by a solemn, filthy child or a woman
who had no corset on under her housedress and whose hair had not been
combed since she got out of bed. The women gave him a dime and took

the coupon he held out to them as if that were the commodity in question. If they asked him to step inside he held his breath, ignoring the bad air and an animal odor such as might have been left by foxes or raccoons or wolves in their lair. The women wadded the coupon into a ball or, if they were of a suspicious turn of mind, saved it for the day when he would try to cheat them, and they could triumphantly confront him with the proof of his dishonesty. If they didn't have a dime (often the case in that part of town) or were simply afraid, on principle, to part with money, they put him off with every appearance of not remembering that they had put him off the week before and the week before that. He turned away, disappointed but trying desperately to be polite, and the paper kept on coming.

Regardless of how many customers paid or put off paying the paper boy, the *Evening Star* claimed its percentage every Saturday morning. Any other arrangement would have complicated the bookkeeping, and the owners of the paper did not consider themselves responsible for the riot that broke out, one Friday afternoon, in the cage next to the press-room. The boys refused to take the papers Homer held out to them through the wicket, and nothing that he said to them had any effect, because their grievances were suddenly intolerable and they themselves were secure in the knowledge (why had they never thought of this before?) that the *Star* was helpless without them. The word "strike" was heard above the sound of the press, which had started on time, for once, and which went right on printing editorial after editorial advising the President of the United States to take over the coal mines — with troops if necessary, since the public welfare was threatened.

At quarter of five, home was not as Edward had remembered it. There was nothing to do, nobody to talk to except Old Mary, and she said, Now don't go spoiling your supper! when all in the world he wanted was company. He went back through the empty uneasy rooms and settled in a big chair in the library with a volume of *Battles and Leaders of the Civil War* on his lap. He didn't read; he only looked at the pictures (a farmhouse near Shiloh, the arsenal at Harpers Ferry) and listened for the sound of a step on the front porch. It was dark outside, and people all over town were beginning to look for the evening paper. His mind was still filled with remembered excitement, triumph that blurred and threatened to turn into worry. But then he turned a page. This had the same effect as when a dreamer, waking, escapes from the nightmare by changing his position in bed.

Virginia came in, and Edward called out to her, but she rushed upstairs, too absorbed in her own world of spit curls and charm bracelets, of what Ossie Dempsey said to Elsie McNish, of TL's and ukuleles, to answer her own brother. And where was his mother?

Mildred Gellert, unable to get along with her husband, unable to bear his bad temper, his nagging, had tried leaving him. Sometimes she took the children with her and sometimes, with her suitcases in the front hall, she clung to them and told them they mustn't forget her, and that when they were older they would understand. The trouble was, they did understand already. For a time it was very exciting, full of subtle moves (she communicated with Harrison through her lawyer) and countermoves (his mother came and kept house for him) like a chess game. The Gellerts' house, no matter who ordered the meals and sat at the opposite end of the dining-room table from Harrison Gellert, had a quality of sadness. This was partly architectural, having to do with the wide overhanging eaves, and partly because the shrubbery — the bridal wreath and barberry — had been allowed to become spindly and the trees kept the sunlight from the lawn. Neither surprised by its own prosperity, like the Tudor and Dutch Colonial houses in the new addition to Draperville, nor frankly shabby, like other old houses of its period, the Gellerts' house and yard were at a standstill, having reached their final look, which owed so much, apparently, to accident, and so little to design or intention or thought.

When Edward walked into Virginia's room she was lying on the bed reading a movie magazine, and she implied that she would just as soon he went somewhere else. Not that he cared. He sat slumped in a chair until she said, "Do you have to breathe like that?"

"Like what?"

"With your mouth open like a fish."

Nothing made him so uncomfortable as being reminded of some part of himself that there was no need to be reminded of. It took all the joy out of life. "This is the way you breathe," he said indignantly. "Just let me give you an imitation."

She laughed scornfully at his attempt to fasten on her a failing she did not have, and so he reminded her — a thing he had meant not to do — that she owed him thirty cents. This led to more insinuations and denials, in the heat of which he forgot he was home early until his mother, standing in the doorway with her hat on, said, "If you children don't stop this eternal arguing, I don't know what I will do!" Neither of them had heard her come upstairs. They looked at each other, conspirators, on the same side. "We're not arguing."

Convicted without a hearing (their mother went on to her own room), they drew apart from each other again. Virginia said, "That was all your fault. I didn't ask you in here, and you're not supposed to come in my room unless I ask you in." Which was a rule she made up, along with a lot of others.

Before they even realized they were arguing again, a voice called, "Children, please! please!" Their mother's voice, so nervous, unhappy, and remote after the Friday Bridge Club. It embarrassed them, reminding them of scenes at the dinner table and conversations between their mother and father that floated up the stairs late at night after they were in bed.

Edward went into the bathroom and ran lukewarm water into the washbasin. It takes patience and some native skill to make a pumice stone float. Absorbed in this delicate task, Edward forgot about his grimy hands and also about the hands of the clock. A warning from his mother as she started down the stairs (how did she know he was in the bathroom?) woke him from a dream of argosies, and the stone boat sank. He arrived in the dining room out of breath, his blond hair slicked down and wet, his hands clean but not his wrists, and an excuse ready on his tongue. He had decided not to mention the strike but it came out just the same. Halfway through dinner it burst out of him, and he felt better immediately.

"How did it start?" Harrison Gellert asked. The lamp that used to hang low over the dining-room table, with its red and green stained glass, its beaded glass fringe, had been replaced, in the last year or two, by glaring wall brackets, a white light in which nothing could be concealed.

"I don't know," Edward said. He passed his plate for a second helping. The plate was filled and passed back to him, and then his father said, "You were there, weren't you?"

"Yes."

"Well, all I'm asking you to tell me is what happened. Something must have happened. How did the strike get started in the first place?"

"I don't remember," Edward said.

He glanced at his sister, across the table. She had stopped eating and with a lurking smile, as if to say *You're going to catch it*, waited for him to flounder in deeper and deeper. He did not hold this against her. The shoe was often enough on the other foot.

"It seemed like it just happened," Edward said, hoping that this explanation, which satisfied him, was truthful and accurate, would also satisfy his father. "I left my arithmetic book in my desk at school and had to go back and get it."

Pleased to have recalled this detail, he stopped and then saw that his father was waiting for him to go on.

"When did the boys decide they weren't going to deliver their papers, before you got there or after?"

"After."

"But the trouble had already started?"

"Not exactly."

"You mean it was like any other evening."

Edward shook his head. What he could not explain was that the boys were always threatening to strike, to quit, to make trouble of one kind or another.

"What are you striking about?"

"The collection. We're supposed to go around collecting on Saturday morning. And people are supposed to pay us, and we're supposed to pay the *Star*. We pay Mrs. Sinclair seven cents and keep three. Only lots of times when we ask for the money, they— You want to see my collection book?"

"No. Just tell me about it."

There were times when, if it hadn't been for the reassurance of Edward's monthly report card, Harrison Gellert would have been forced to wonder if his son were a mental defective. No doubt he was passing through a stage, but it was a very tiresome one.

"Sometimes we have to wait five or six weeks for the money," Edward said.

"But you get it eventually?"

Edward nodded. "But she takes her share right away, out of whatever we do collect, and it's not fair."

"What's unfair about it?"

"She has lots of money and we don't."

"What else are the boys striking for?"

"When the press breaks down, sometimes we don't get home until after seven o'clock. One night it was nearly eight."

"It isn't Mrs. Sinclair's fault that the press breaks down."

To this Edward made no answer.

"What else?"

"We want more money."

"How much more?"

"Oh, let the poor child alone!" Mildred Gellert exclaimed, raising her wan, unhappy face from her salad and looking at her husband.

"He's not a child," Harrison Gellert said. "And I'm not picking on him. How much did you make this week?"

"Thirty-three cents," Edward said. "But some of it was back pay. I only have thirteen customers. Barney Lefferts has the most. He has fifty-two. He makes about a dollar and a half a week when he gets paid."

"That's very good, for a boy."

"I guess so," Edward said.

"Did anybody take the trouble to explain to Mrs. Sinclair why you were refusing to deliver the paper?"

"Oh, yes, but she didn't listen to us. She was awful mad. And Homer was standing there, too."

"What did she say to you?"

"She was inside, where the press and the linotype machines are."

"But what did she say?"

"She tried to get us to deliver the papers. So we all went outside and left her."

"And then what happened?"

"The other guys jumped on their bicycles and rode off."

"And what did you do?"

"I came on home."

"Who's going to deliver our paper?" Virginia asked.

"Nobody, I guess. They can't, if we're all on strike." Edward turned back to his father. "Do you think I did wrong?"

"It's something you're old enough to decide for yourself," Harrison Gellert said. Edward was relieved. On the other hand, it wasn't the same thing as being told that he had his father's complete and wholehearted approval to take part in a strike any time there was one. If he hadn't gone on strike with the others, it would have been uncomfortable. He would have had enemies. The school yard would not have been a very safe place for him, and neither would the alley in the back of the *Star* Building, but actually he had wanted to go out on strike and he had enjoyed the excitement.

"They'll have to take us all back, won't they?" he asked. "Since we all did it together?"

"Finish your potato, dear," Mildred Gellert said. "You're keeping Mary waiting." She was not young any more; she had given up searching for her destiny and had come home, for the sake of the children. Acceptance has its inevitable meager rewards. The side porch was now enclosed, and it was generally agreed that the new green brocade curtains in the living room had cost Harrison plenty.

During dessert, Edward remembered suddenly that he was saving his money to buy a bicycle, and the rice pudding stuck in his throat and would not for the longest time go down. When the others left the dining room, he lingered until Old Mary finished clearing the table and with her hand on the light switch said, "You figure on sitting here in the dark?"

Edward got up and went into the library, where his mother and Virginia were. His mother was sewing. She was changing the hem on Virginia's plaid skirt. Edward sat down, like a visitor waiting to be entertained. He heard the front door open and close, and then his father came in and sat down in his favorite chair and (quite as if he hadn't understood a word of all that Edward had been telling him) opened the evening paper.

WHEN the paper boys ran out of the building, Harold West got as far as the door when Homer called to him. Homer said, "You stay here, Harold," and Harold stayed. After he had delivered his own papers, he rode back downtown and with a list supplied by the front office, he and Homer had started out together. Ever so many houses had no street numbers beside the front steps or on the porch roof; or else the numbers, corroded, painted over five or six times, could not be seen in the dark. Not every subscriber to the Draperville *Evening Star* got a paper that night. The lists were incomplete, and there is no adequate substitution for habit. The office stayed open until ten, and there were a few telephone calls, but most people were not surprised that the evening paper, arriving at such different times every night, should finally have failed to arrive at all.

On Saturday morning, Edward went downtown. He saw a knot of boys standing on the sidewalk in front of the *Star* Building. The riot was over, the strike had collapsed, and though they had counted on him to act with them, they had not bothered to inform him of their surrender. If he hadn't been led there by curiosity, he would have been the only one not now apologizing and asking to have his route given back to him.

Riot, in the soul or in an alley, wears off. It is not self-sustaining.

Reason waits, worry bides its time. The recording angel assigned to mark the sparrow's fall took a little extra space in order to record the fact that George Gibbs, Harry Lathrop, John Weiner, Bert Savage, Dave O'Connell, Marvin Shapiro, Barney Lefferts, Edward Gellert, and nine other sparrows were flying and fluttering against a net of their own devising.

One at a time the boys were allowed to go inside. Through the plate-glass window Edward saw Barney Lefferts, sitting in a straight chair beside Mrs. Sinclair's desk, with his eyes lowered, anxiously twisting his dirty old cap while she talked on and on. Once, with an odd gesture of pleading, he interrupted her; he said something that she brushed aside. When Edward looked in the window again, Barney Lefferts was crying. While you are learning the value of money, you learn also — you can't, in fact, help learning — that whoever has it has the right to withhold it. Courage doesn't count, in these circumstances.

When Barney Lefferts came out of the building, all that was behind him and he was triumphant. He said, "Jesus, I got my route back!"

Edward's interview with Mrs. Sinclair was short, and the scolding he got from her was restrained, out of respect for his father's credit and certain social distinctions that both Edward and Mrs. Sinclair were aware of.

"I'm very disappointed in you, Edward," she said. "I know, of course, that you wouldn't have done what you did if you hadn't been led astray by the others. But there was somebody who didn't let himself be led astray. Harold West delivered papers until eleven o'clock last night, and Mr. Sinclair and I are very grateful to him." She played with a paper clip, and then said, "I know you are sorry, but that isn't the same as if you had behaved in an honorable way, is it? I've decided to let you have your route back, but I want you to promise me, on your word of honor, that if such a thing ever happens again around here, you will be on the side of the Newspaper."

Edward promised, conscious of the fact that her thin, flat chest would not be comforting to put his head on, in time of trouble. He was grateful, but not to her. While he was waiting his turn outside, he had made a bargain: He had offered to give up, from now on, for the rest of his life, the secret, sinful practices that would fill people with horror if they knew and that made God (who did know) sad, if God would give him back his paper route, and God had done it.

"We were thinking of giving you a larger route, Edward," Mrs. Sinclair said, "but I'm afraid, in the light of what happened yesterday . . . Well, we won't talk about it anymore. What's done is done. Suppose you go and do your Saturday-morning collecting."

THE promise to Mrs. Sinclair, Edward never had an opportunity to keep. The promise to God he broke, over and over and over. He prayed, he made new promises, he offered acts of kindness, acts of self-denial, in place of the one renunciation he could not manage. And though he knew it could not be so, it almost seemed at times as if God did not mind what he did as soon as he had the house all to himself; or else He was trying to make Edward feel worse, because he did get the larger paper route, with fifty-three customers, in a much better part of town, and the total in his bankbook rose higher and higher, with compound interest in red, and finally, on a clear bright windy day in September, Edward went to his father's office after school and a few minutes later they walked around the courthouse square to the bank, and from there they went to Kohler's bicycle shop, where Edward, with his father's solemn approval, parted gladly with his savings and rode off on his heart's delight. The new bicycle was blue and silver, and stood out conspicuously among all the other bicycles in the two long racks in the school yard. It had a headlight and a tool case. He adjusted the handlebars so they were low like the handlebars of a racing bike, and then rode without using them at all, unless it was a matter of keeping the front wheel out of the streetcar track. Boys asked to try his new bicycle out, and rather than get into a fight about it he let them have a brief ride, but it was agony to him until they jumped off and let him have his Blue Racer again. When the bicycle got rained on, he dried it with a rag he kept in his canvas bag. At night he stood it in the woodshed, out of the dew. He would have taken it into his bed if this had been at all practical.

The bicycle was still new, he had only had it a few weeks, when it was run over. It happened on a Saturday noon. Hungry, in a hurry to get home for lunch, he rode up in front of the *Star* Building. A voice in his head reminded him that the boys were not allowed to leave their bicycles in front of the building, and another voice said promptly, She won't see it, and even if she does, this once won't matter. . . . He leaned his bicycle carefully against the high curbing and went inside. There were two boys ahead of him. While he was counting the money in his change purse, a boy opened the street door and shouted, "You better come out here, Gellert! Somebody just ran over your new bicycle!"

Without any feeling whatever, as if he were dreaming, Edward went outside, and a man he'd never seen before said, "I didn't know it was there, and I backed over it."

Edward kept right on, without looking at the man, until he reached the edge of the sidewalk and could look down at what ought to have been somebody else's ruined bicycle, not (oh, please not) his.

His mouth began to quiver.

The man said, "I'm sorry," and Edward burst into tears. What had happened was so terrible, and he felt such pity for the mangled spokes, the tires torn from their rims.

Mrs. Sinclair, seeing that there was trouble of some kind in front of the building, left her desk and went to the door. She looked at the bicycle and then at Edward standing there blindly, with the tears streaming down his face. "You're not supposed to leave your wheels in front of the building," she said, and went inside. People gathered around Edward, trying to console him. The man who had run over Edward's bicycle got into his car and drove away. Someone told Edward his name, and where he lived.

That night Harrison Gellert backed the car out of the garage and, with Edward in the front seat beside him, drove out to the edge of town and stopped in front of a one-story frame house in a poor neighborhood. "You wait here," he said, and got out and went up the brick walk. A man came to the door, and Edward saw a lighted room. His father said something and the man said something. Then he held the screen door open, and his father stepped inside and the door closed. Edward waited in perfect confidence that his father would tell him that it was all settled and the man was going to buy him a new bicycle. Instead, his father came out, after about five minutes, and got in the car and started the engine without saying a word. They were halfway down the block before he turned to Edward and explained that the man didn't know anything about his bicycle.

"But they *said* it was him!"

"I know," Harrison Gellert said. "He may not have been telling the truth."

Conscious of how quiet it had become in the front seat, he added, "Would you like to drive downtown for an ice-cream soda?"

They parked in front of the ice-cream parlor, and his father honked and a high-school boy came out, with a white apron around his hips, and took their order. A few minutes later he reappeared with two tin trays and two tall chocolate sodas. The soda was as good a comfort as any, if

Edward had been allowed to eat it in silence, but Harrison Gellert was genuinely distressed and sorry for his son, and his sympathy took the form (as it had in the past when he tried to comfort his wife) of feeling sorry for himself. "As you get older," he said, "you will find that a great many things happen that aren't easy to bear. Things you can't change, no matter how you try. You have to accept them and go right on, doing the best you can."

"But it isn't right!" Edward burst out. "He ran over it. It's his fault!"

"I know all that."

"Then why doesn't he have to pay for it?"

"If it was his fault, he *ought* to pay for having your bicycle repaired. But you can't make him do it if he doesn't want to."

A year earlier, Edward would have cried out, "But *you* can!" He thought it now, but he didn't say it.

"We'll find out from Mr. Kohler how much it will cost to have your bicycle fixed, and I'll go fifty-fifty with you, when it comes to paying for it."

Edward thanked his father politely, but there was no use talking about having his bicycle fixed. It would never be the same. The frame was sprung, and you could always tell a repainted bike from one that was straight from the factory. His father could go to court if necessary, and the judge would make the man pay for ruining his bicycle, and maybe fine him besides.

"It may be cheaper in the end to get a secondhand bicycle," Mr. Gellert said.

With an effort Edward kept the tears from spilling over. He didn't want a secondhand bicycle. He wanted not to leave his new bicycle in front of the *Star* Building where it would be run over.

And Mr. Gellert wanted to say and didn't say, "I hope this will be a lesson to you."

It was a lesson, of course, in the sense that everything that happens, good or bad, is a lesson.

EDWARD Gellert was thirteen going on fourteen when the paper boys went on strike against the *Evening Star*, and he was fourteen going on fifteen when his bicycle was run over. One half the individual nature never seems any different, from the cradle to the grave; the other half is pathetically in step with the slightest physical change. Edward's voice had deepened, hairs had appeared on his body where Darwin said they should appear, his feet and hands were noticeably large for the rest of him, and something would not allow him to kneel in the dark beside his bed and ask God to give him back his new bicycle. People might be raised from the dead, as it said in the Bible, but a ruined bicycle could not by any power on earth or in heaven be made shining and whole again.

A Game of Chess

ON a mild evening in June, when the light in the sky, the softness of the air, the damp odors rising from the ground, and the roses everywhere all seemed to support the fiction that there is a natural harmony running through all natural things, Hugh and Laura Cahill came in from the country to have dinner with his older brother and sister-in-law, from Chicago. The train was crowded, and they had to sit across the aisle from each other. Hugh sat facing a little girl of two, who was dressed in white — starched white dress, white shoes and stockings, and a white piqué bonnet to show off her dark skin and immense dark Neapolitan eyes. She was restless. She bounced and jounced, she hung from her mother's neck, she got up and she got down, she flirted with the conductor, and from time to time, in spite of her mother's conscientious efforts to avoid this, the soles of her white kid shoes brushed against Hugh's light gabardine trousers. The smiles of apology that her mother and grandmother directed at him also asked him to tell them truthfully if there was ever since the beginning of time a more marvellously beautiful child. As the train plunged into the tunnel at Ninety-eighth Street, he leaned across the aisle and said, "I can hear Ellen saying to Amos, 'If we don't call them, they may find out we were in New York and be hurt.' "

"Would you have been hurt?" Laura asked.

He shook his head. "I'm not looking forward to the evening. Probably Ellen also had misgivings when she called us, but in the Middle West blood is thicker than water."

"Your trousers," Laura said.

"I know." He glanced down at the smudges. Ordinarily he wouldn't have cared, but it was the kind of thing Amos noticed, and Amos would much rather believe that Hugh had turned up at the Waldorf-Astoria with spots on his clothes than the truth, which was that his suit had just come back from the cleaner's. Aware that he would be made to feel the impassable gulf that exists between art and the automobile business, he had deliberately tried to avoid looking like a painter — or rather, like the popular conception of a painter. He was wearing a sober foulard tie, with a white shirt. His shoes were shined. He had just had a haircut. But of course he had overlooked something; his grey felt hat had seen better days.

Sitting in front of a mirror in the ladies' room of the Biltmore, Laura Cahill pinned the gardenia among the dark-brown curls on top of her head, was dissatisfied with the effect, took the bobby pin out and tried again, sighed over the impossibility of doing anything with her hair — which had no body to it — and would have walked off and left the gardenia on the dressing table except that Hugh had given it to her and wanted her to wear it. They had been married a little over two years, and she was considerably younger than he, and even less confident, but whereas his face announced with an almost comic facility any uncertainty or self-doubt, any unmanageable feeling, she was perfectly able to keep her feelings to herself. She had never met Amos and Ellen.

When she rejoined Hugh, it was six-forty-five. He gave up looking for a vacant taxi and they took the Madison Avenue bus as far as Fiftieth Street, walked east to the Waldorf, went through the lobby, and found the house phones.

"He says to tell you he's shaving for Laura, not you," Ellen Cahill said cheerfully. "You know your brother."

"How are you?" Hugh asked.

"Fine. The Murphys are with us. They came along to keep us company."

"Yes?"

"We'll be down in a minute."

Rather than wait for what (since he did know his brother) was going to be more than a minute, he took Laura's arm and guided her into the tropical cocktail lounge. Sitting at a little table in this almost empty room, with their drinks in front of them, they killed a quarter of an hour.

"You'll like the Murphys," Hugh said. "Pete's a doctor, and very easy-going and unworried and kind. He and Amos are inseparable. And I think you'll like his wife. She's thin and melancholy and intelligent. I liked her the best of any of their friends in Winnetka. I stopped in to see them once, on a Sunday morning, and Pete was out playing golf, and they'd had a party the night before, and she was tired and very funny. She kept finding pieces of spaghetti behind the sofa cushions and everywhere."

"Will Barbara be with them?" Laura asked.

"Probably. Unless she's tied up with commencement," he said, feeling a twinge of guilt. His niece had been here, in a convent school, since last fall, and they hadn't done anything about her. He worked at home, and the house was small, and company of any kind was a serious interruption. It affected his work. Ideas got away from him. Canvases that had started out well went bad or were only partly good. But they should have had her for a meal, or something. It was inexcusable. Tilting his glass this way and that, observing how the ice cubes remained serenely horizontal floating in Scotch and water, he said thoughtfully, "I love Amos, but I can't bear him. . . . Don't mind anything he says to you."

"I won't," Laura said.

"This time it's going to be different." He emptied his glass and picked up the check. "I have you. Always before, I've been outnumbered."

He didn't say, and was hardly aware that he thought, that it would *have* to be different, because whatever happened between Amos and him would take place in front of Laura.

They started through the lobby once more and discovered that, at the far end of a brown marble vista, they were being watched; they were the subject of a benign amusement. Even if Hugh hadn't stiffened, Laura would have known by the marked family resemblance that they were face-to-face with his older brother. Amos was broader in the shoulders, heavier, and older-looking, chiefly because he had less hair. His left arm, ending in a gloved hand, hung motionless at his side. He had lost his arm as the result of an accident with a shotgun; Amos and another boy were shooting at crows, and the gun (which they had been forbidden to touch) went off unexpectedly in the other boy's hands. The large woman with ash-blond hair and a black hat with pink roses on it — nothing to fear, nothing unfriendly in that direction.

Amos's greeting "Well, kid, it certainly is nice to see you," Hugh countered with a smile and an expression that was both alert and wary. *You're not going to fool me again?* he asked, with his eyes. *No monkey business, like the last time we met? . . .* Amos turned, his glance quickly took Laura in, and when his eyes met Hugh's again, he too was smiling. Amos approved. Amos had better approve, Hugh said to himself grimly.

An elevator took them all back upstairs to the fourteenth floor. They found the Murphys' room and knocked, and Pete came out carrying a bottle of whiskey. His hair was now partly grey, Hugh noticed, his face fuller than it had been thirty years ago when he wheeled his bicycle up the front walk and inquired, "Where's that Amos?" Aileen Murphy was still dressing, and so, instead of going in, they separated, the men taking the fire stairs, the two women the elevator, down to the thirteenth floor, to Barbara's room, which was much larger than her mother and father's and had a balcony and a view north over the city.

There was a profane squabble between Amos and Pete over whose liquor they were going to use, and Pete informed Amos that there was a men's bar in the hotel, very nice, where they put the whiskey bottle on the bar beside you.

"I've found it," Amos said.

Aileen Murphy came in and was introduced to Laura. Amos, offering Hugh a drink, said, "Hugh, do you count?" in the same stern tone of voice he had used long ago, checking up on whether Hugh had known enough to kiss the girl he took to the high-school fraternity dance when he said good night to her. He hadn't, but he did the next time, and she said, "Why did you do that?" and after that they didn't see each other except when they passed in the school corridors.

He stared at Amos now and said, "What do you mean?"

"One is not enough, two is plenty, three is you're drunk, and four there's no reason not to keep on going," Amos said, and burst out laughing.

Why make up jokes of your own was Amos's basic social principle, the idea that had always carried him along safely anywhere, in any company that he had ever wanted to find himself. Why avoid making the remarks that other people make, when the remarks are all there, ready to be used, and it's the surest way to make everybody like you? At thirteen, out of slavish admiration, Hugh had done his best to imitate Amos's jokes, his laugh, and never managed this successfully. On a raw November day, in the college stadium, he had humiliated Amos by cheering when there was nothing to cheer at. He saw Amos putting this new joke into his suitcase when he packed to come East.

They had a conversation about their younger brother, who had just finished college, after a period in the Army. "Rick never tells me anything," Hugh said. "Does he tell you?"

Amos shook his head solemnly. "No, Hugh, he doesn't."

When they couldn't get together on their own grounds, they could reach each other momentarily by talking about their younger brother.

"He's too anxious to prove that he's capable," Amos said, "and instead of asking for advice, he rushes in and announces how everything is going to be, and then it's too late to do anything. But he'll learn. I took him horseback riding and I told him off, right down the line, all the things that are wrong with him. He took it and went straight to work on them."

There was a knock on the door and Pete Murphy's brother Louis came in, with his wife. He and Pete met in the center of the room, after not seeing each other for two years. They shook hands, smiled, and turned away, leaving unfinished business (if there was any unfinished business between them) to be settled at some other time. With a fresh drink in his hand Hugh looked around the room and saw that there were no empty chairs. Laura had settled herself on one of the twin beds, with her back against the headboard, and was talking to Barbara, who, nearly Laura's age, was stretched out, leaning on her elbow, on the other bed, and telling her about her experiences as a practice teacher in a Puerto Rican neighborhood. "A friend of mine was teaching in the same school," she said, "and she got a letter from a little boy. 'Dear Teacher,' it said. 'You are very pretty, your friend is very pretty. I love you but you do not love me. I do not like Miss Worthing.' " Hugh sat down on the foot of Laura's bed, and then, aware that his back was turned to her and that the evening would probably seem interminable to her, among all these people she wasn't related to and didn't know, he reached behind him and took her high-heeled shoe in his hand.

THEY left the room finally, all nine of them. The Murphys went on up in the elevator to the Starlight Roof while Hugh was leaving his hat with the woman at the desk on the thirteenth floor. Amos, who had had four drinks, said, "Where did you get that hat? I'll give you five bucks so you can go and get yourself a good felt hat."

"That's a fine hat," Hugh said, his voice rising a little too sharp for banter — an effect that Amos never tired of producing. "It came from Tripler's. What more do you want?"

Amos was not impressed with Tripler's. His comment on Hugh's growing baldness, the circle on the crown of his head where the white scalp showed through his dark hair, Hugh was expecting. It was customary, both with Amos and with his father. He said, "I've got lots more hair than you had in 1960."

This counterattack Amos did not bother to understand, let alone guard against. It was too complicated to do any harm. It involved the recognition of the immutable difference between being six years old and being eleven, between being ten and being fifteen, between fourteen and nineteen, between thirty-eight and just arriving and forty-three arrived. Fairness compelled Hugh to compare not the present states of their respective baldnesses but his hair now with Amos's hair four years ago in Chicago. Fairness was a quality that Amos seemed to recognize and in general abide by, but somebody or something way back somewhere in the past had excused him from ever having to be fair with Hugh. As far as Hugh could make out, for Amos to be fair toward him would have been to say, *All right, I give up. I don't understand you and never will. If all you want is for me to treat you decently, I can easily enough. I can stop taking any interest in you — and will, from now on.*

Amos glanced at the light over the elevator doors, and then said to Laura, "Dad did the worst thing anybody can do."

Hugh waited for him to finish. Being older, Amos knew things — family history, old stories, old scandals — that he didn't. You never knew when something of this kind would burst out of him.

"He put water on his hair," Amos said. "And he still has some hair at seventy. I didn't used to have a stomach. I've put on twenty pounds since I stopped smoking. Hugh carries his weight well." And then Laura, whose brothers let each other alone, saw with astonishment that Amos was feeling Hugh's upper arm, the muscles of which Hugh obediently flexed. "Not bad," Amos said, and made Hugh feel how much bigger his own biceps were.

As they stepped into the elevator, Amos's attack shifted. "I was afraid you were going to marry a Jew," he said.

This was the fuse that had set off the fireworks the last time they saw each other, four years ago in Chicago. The argument, though bitter, got nowhere. Hugh grew red in the face, and then very pale. Amos dodged easily and expertly from one form of bigotry to the next, and brushed logic aside, cheerfully refusing to identify himself with anyone not in his rather pleasant economic circumstances.

"If he had," he said now, to Laura, "I'd never have had anything more to do with him."

Since childhood, Hugh reflected, looking at the floor of the ascending elevator, Amos had been threatening, continually threatening, to disown him.

SEATED at a big round table under the blue artificial stars, Barbara Cahill asked her New York (and therefore cosmopolitan, worldly) uncle to translate the French words on the menu.

" '*Escargots*' is snails," he said.

"Oh, I know I wouldn't like snails!" she exclaimed.

As she grew older, she would look like her mother, Hugh thought. She was sweet and young and unspoiled, and beyond that he had no idea what she was like. In the last ten years he hadn't stayed long enough in Illinois to find out.

"You ought to try them. They're very good. They're cooked in white wine and parsley," he said, and was aware of an unreasonable surprise as he heard Amos and Laura, side by side across the table, both order roast beef well done. At home it had always been rare, and he had assumed that Amos would go on to the end of his life ordering roast beef and steak rare, as he himself did. "I'll have eels," he said, daring Amos to appropriate that, as he had so many other things that didn't belong to him. Amos ordered a salad and then said, "I don't know about the rest of you but I'm ready for another drink."

During the long wait, Hugh talked first to Barbara and then, while she was telling Laura about going to Mass at St. Patrick's with her mother, he turned to Louis Murphy's wife, who was on his left. Louis had held her chair out for her as she sat down, and Hugh had caught a certain protective concern in his manner. It was none of his business, but now, having had three drinks — one in the cocktail lounge and two very much stronger ones upstairs — and being slightly drunk (otherwise he would never have ordered eels), he leaned toward her and said, "Your husband is still in love with you."

"Why shouldn't he be?" she said, smiling. "You don't remember me, but I remember you."

"Did you grow up in Winnetka?"

"I was Ruth Hayes," she said, nodding.

"You know how it is when you're growing up," he said. "Somebody four years older is in another world." He hesitated, wondering if he had been impolite — if he should have said "one or two years older."

"I know," she said. "Louis was in love with various girls while I watched him from afar."

"Did you really?" he asked, in all seriousness.

"No." She smiled again at him, this time as if she were talking to a child. "I was in love with Bruce Coddington." Then, extricating them both from the past: "I saw one of your pictures at the Whitney Museum."

Hugh nodded. He was trying to follow the conversation between Amos and Laura, across the table. He heard Amos say, "You must come out to Chicago. We've got a housing project with niggers and white people living together."

This remark, intended to beat Laura out of the bushes and perhaps test the timbre of her rising voice, she allowed to pass unchallenged. She was there to defend Hugh, not to argue.

A moment later, Hugh heard Amos say, "You must see that Hugh makes a lot of money."

"I'd rather he painted better and made less," Laura said.

"You don't know what you're talking about," Amos told her indignantly. "Wait till you have children and the doctors' bills start coming in. If I hadn't had Pete for a friend, I'd have been ruined."

Louis Murphy's wife was searching through her purse for a blank piece of paper. In the end she gave Hugh a credit slip from Lord & Taylor, so that he could write down for her the name and address of the gallery that handled his paintings. Ellen supplied him with a pencil, from her beaded evening purse.

"Deborah's more like you every day," she said, speaking of her youngest daughter. "She's even pigeon-toed — which is all right in a boy," she added hastily, lest this remark cause offense. "She even walks like you. I sometimes say to Amos, 'There goes Hughie across the lawn.' "

"Debbie's always the leader," Barbara said admiringly.

"She's in sixth grade," Ellen Cahill said, "believe it or not. They gave *Peter Pan* at school this year, and Debbie was Peter."

I was in a school play once, Hugh thought, and nobody came to see me. . . .

"Have you any children?" he asked, turning to Louis Murphy's wife.

"One. A girl seventeen."

Suddenly nervous lest she should ask him the same question, with Laura sitting directly across the table, he looked away and was grateful for the arrival of the waiter. Ellen Cahill offered her rare roast beef around the table to anyone who wanted it, just as an hour or two before she had offered Pete Murphy and his wife Barbara's spacious room. Her last anxious "Are you sure you wanted eels?" Hugh answered with "Yes. I've never had eels before," but he didn't want them and he wished he could put the queer white slices in his coat pocket. He looked up when Aileen Murphy was served a roast squab, and wondered, Should I have had that?

Amos passed his plate across to Ellen, so that she could cut his meat for him, and Hugh, noticing how quiet Barbara was, the only unmarried person at the table, said to her, "Just you wait. Your time is coming."

"But I'm enjoying myself, Uncle Hugh," she said earnestly.

And perhaps she is, he thought. Or perhaps she had not yet realized that she had a right to be bored in the company of older people.

The conversation took on an antiphonal quality. The remarks Amos made to Laura, a moment later Ellen made to Hugh. With his roast beef half eaten, Amos asked his wife to dance with him. At the age of ten, Hugh thought, he would not have done this. Nothing could have induced him to stop eating until his plate was empty, and then it would have been passed up the table for a second helping. Hugh looked at Ruth Murphy questioningly, and then they pushed their chairs back and went out on the dance floor, which was so crowded that dancing was impossible.

STANDING in front of a urinal in the men's room half an hour later, Hugh was startled by a hearty slap on the back. "I'm going to buy you a drink," Amos said. "You've been refusing drinks all evening, and now I'm going to buy you a drink you can't refuse."

They found a cocktail room, around the corner from the elevators, and Amos wanted to stand at the bar, but the bartender wouldn't serve them until they sat down at one of the tables.

"I want to talk to you, Hugh," Amos said. "I want to talk to you about your work. The time has come for you to take the bull by the horns." Hugh sat stiffly, unable to answer. He and Laura had got up from the table together and parted in the foyer with the understanding that he would wait there for her. He stood up, with his eyes on the people passing the door, and said, "I want to talk to you, too," and went outside. Laura was not there, so he went on into the dining room, intending to bend down and say to Barbara, "Will you come with me? I want you to wait for Laura outside." But to his surprise Laura was at the table with the others. She had not waited for him.

When he went back to the cocktail room, he found Amos sitting just as he had left him, heavy and solemn and larger than life-size — an epic figure waiting to give advice that was not asked for.

"What bull by what horns?" Hugh said as he sat down.

"I mean you've got to decide once and for all whether you're going to hold down a job or be an artist."

"But I have decided. I quit my job with Blake & Seymour last fall. I'm devoting all my time to painting."

"You've got to make up your mind," Amos said solemnly. "You can't work both sides of the street, no matter how smart you are."

He expatiated at some length on this dilemma that no longer existed. He questioned the wisdom of Hugh's living in the country. He insisted that Hugh needed more experience of the world. "You're leading too sheltered a life. You've always been on the defensive. At least you are with me, so I figure you are with other people."

"I know," Hugh said. "But now I want to be friends."

Amos's face was contorted by a look of disgust. This wasn't at all what he had meant; it was another instance of cheering when the other side scored a gain, of the joke with the painfully wrong inflection. "No . . . None of that. I'm hard," he said, and allowed Hugh to see, from the look in his eyes, just how hard he was. But there was something histrionic about that look, something that suggested that it had been practiced before a bathroom mirror while Amos was shaving. "I don't care about anybody but my family. They can hurt me, but nobody else."

"*I* can hurt you," Hugh said.

Amos shook his head. "No. Neither you or Dad."

The knight takes the pawn.

Hugh's expression was a mixture of bewilderment, hurt feelings, and the sense of loss. His offer had been sincere; he had been ready — at least he hoped he was ready — to be friends with Amos, and he had not counted on the possibility that this offer would not be acceptable. So he's done it at last, he thought; he's washed his hands of me.

Though Amos had never supported him in a moment of need, there had always been some slight comfort in the idea that Amos was there, loyal to his friends, and powerful; that his help, never asked for, would even so have been forthcoming at a word from Hugh, the word he had so far been too proud to speak. "If you don't care about anybody," he said, accepting his casting out, "why are you telling me what to do? And what do you mean 'hard'?"

Before Amos could explain, Pete Murphy appeared, out of nowhere.

"Sit down," Amos said. And then to Hugh, "*Pete* is my friend."

Pete refused the offer of a drink. Amos didn't resume. The three of them sat, silent. Realizing that the conversation could not proceed in the presence of an interested observer, Pete got up and left. It turned out then that Hugh was not rejected after all; the word "friends" was rejected. They were to be "brothers."

"Downstairs," Amos said, "you said Rick never tells you anything. Well, you never tell me anything."

"I'm ready now," Hugh said. "What do you want to know?"

Amos did not commit himself. It was still Hugh's move. There was one thing he could say that would make all the rest clear, but something warned him not to say it. Instead, he asked, "Do you remember a letter you wrote me after I got in a fight with the Chi Psis in my sophomore year and moved out of the fraternity house? It was a beautiful letter, and I'm sorry I never answered it."

The word "beautiful" made Amos wince. As for the letter, apparently he didn't remember ever having written it. Or *does* he remember, Hugh wondered. It was the only time that Amos had ever offered to help him or tried to understand him, and he could not imagine now why he hadn't answered it.

Amos wanted to know why Hugh didn't have a show every year, and Hugh explained that he worked slowly, that he didn't have that many canvases he was willing to have people see, that he had been, in effect, holding down two jobs.

"Don't give me that," Amos said. "I'm a salesman and a farmer." This meant that Amos managed Ellen's four hundred acres of farmland in central Illinois, not that he ever rode a tractor. "It's just as easy to fall in love with a girl with money," Amos used to say when he was twenty, but actually he had married for love, like everybody else.

Again Hugh felt the pull of the unsaid thing. To hold back something as important as that, he decided, was to be afraid. "A minute ago you were complaining that I never tell you anything. Do you understand the word 'neurotic'?"

"Yes."

"Well, I was."

"Are you still?" Amos demanded.

"I don't know," Hugh said, confused. This was not the question Amos should have asked. It was the last question he would have asked Amos, if the shoe had been on the other foot.

"What made you that way?"

"The usual reasons — what makes other people like that." Now that it was too late, he was cautious. "Their childhood, the past, something." His heart sank. All evening long he had been conscious of the approval of the figure in the chair at the head of the couch, the shadowy presence who listened, the patient, kind, supporting, encouraging, faceless father-substitute, whom he had found his way to when things finally came to a standstill and he was no longer able to work or to love any human being. . . . But he shouldn't have told Amos. In telling Amos he had behaved incorrectly; he had rejected the inner warning and failed to remember that confession can be a form of self-injury. And now he would have to go on without any encouragement and support.

"I have the same background as you," Amos was saying, "and I'm not neurotic."

What was so hard, Hugh thought was just to believe it — to believe that anything as terrible as that could happen: that she had died and left them. "You may have been stronger," he said.

This explanation Amos was willing to accept, in the literal as well as in the psychological sense.

"Sometimes I think Mother's death had a good deal to do with it," Hugh said.

"It was hard on me, too," Amos said.

The house was like a shell, and the food tasted of tears. And he and Amos undressed in the same room and got into their beds, and he never spoke to Amos under the cover of the dark about the terror that gripped him, and Amos never spoke to him. Neither of them tried to comfort the other.

"But I was all right," Hugh continued, "until I was twenty-five."

"You were nineteen when you tried to commit suicide."

"That was part of it," Hugh admitted. Without realizing it, he jerked his head up. His eyes went all around the room searching for help.

"That was something you had no right to do," Amos said sternly.

"No right to cut my wrists?"

"No right to disgrace your family. You didn't think of anybody but yourself. You're selfish, Hugh."

Again Pete Murphy appeared, though he didn't sit down this time; and again they waited until he went away.

"Barbie and I have been feuding," Amos said. "She almost flunked out of school last year. She didn't apply herself. That's why we sent her East to school."

"She thinks the world of you," Hugh said, by way of pouring oil on troubled waters. "I had such a nice conversation with her during dinner. . . . She says you never write to her; that she hasn't had a single letter from you since she's been here."

"I haven't written to her purposely. I don't want her to think she can get away with anything."

"She must have been pleased that you came to see her graduate."

Amos didn't answer. He was trying to get the attention of the bartender.

Hugh waited until Amos turned around, and then, leaning forward intently, with his elbows on the table, he said, "You said I was selfish. I want to know why."

"Also," Amos said, "she was running around with this guy twenty-eight years old. She's no judge of people, Hugh. She always picks out a lame duck. It's all right to be tenderhearted, but this guy had a nervous breakdown while he was in the Army—at least that's what *he* calls it. There's something creepy about him. I can't stay in the same room with him. I had to get out of the house when he was there. Ellen's forbidden her to see him or write to him, but she does anyway." His eyes filled with tears, which slowly overflowed the lids. "She wants to be a nun, Hugh, and I just don't know what to do."

There was nothing theatrical or rehearsed about this performance, and Hugh was moved by the tears, and by what Amos said, and by the fact that Amos was exposing his feelings to him. He waited while Amos unfolded a clean white handkerchief and blew his nose and regained his composure.

The bartender brought another round of drinks, and Amos took up finally the matter of Hugh's selfishness, which turned out to be nothing more (nor less) than the fact that they hadn't done anything about Barbara.

"Laura called her, but she — "

"You didn't ask her for Thanksgiving or Christmas," Amos said.

If they'd had Barbara for Thanksgiving and Christmas, they couldn't have had Laura's brother; the house was too small. But how to explain this to Amos, whose house was large, and whose hospitality was always being taken advantage of. They could have asked her out to the country some other time, and should have. But he'd been having difficulties with his work all through the fall and early winter. Lots of labor went into canvases which were eventually discarded. That seemed to have stopped, thank God.

"When I first came to New York," Hugh said. "I was always having to go someplace I didn't feel like going to, on holidays. Some family or business connection of Dad's trying to be kind. I used to dread it. From what Barbara told Laura over the phone, I gathered she had friends. In school, I mean. And some boy had been taking her to all the shows, she said. We just assumed she'd rather spend Christmas with Ellen's cousins on Long Island."

Amos was not interested in Hugh's excuses. Having made his accusation, though, he put it aside and began to talk about his younger daughter. "Debbie's got the same cockeyed brain you have," he said.

Hugh resented this at first, before he understood that it was half a criticism, half a grudging compliment. On the other hand, to have a brain at all, to be in any way brighter than or different from the average person was, so far as Amos was concerned, cockeyed. "You have a photographic mind," he said accusingly.

Hugh denied this.

"All you have to do is look at a book and get A," Amos said. "I never could do that. . . . Don't look at me like that. I'm not running you down. I think you're quite a classy guy. I'm trying to build you up."

"I don't need building up," Hugh said. As evidence that he was doing all right, he offered the recognition that, during the past five years, his work had received from various critics and museum curators. "It's quite an honor," he said, "to be in the annual show at the Whitney Museum. They don't bother with anybody who isn't good."

"I'm a big duck in a little pond; you're a little duck in a big pond," Amos said serenely. "Ellen knows a woman who studied at the Art Institute. She knows a lot about art. I mentioned that I had a brother who is a painter, and drew a blank. . . . You've got to keep your name before the public, Hugh."

"I'm after bigger game," Hugh said. "I'm competing with Eakins."

"How much does he make a year?"

"He's dead."

"Well, then," Amos said agreeably, "maybe you've got to die to be great. But you have to turn out more paintings than you have been doing these last few years." He went on to tell Hugh about Grandma Moses: "She did what was expected of her; she raised her family and didn't even begin to paint till she was past seventy — with barn paint. Maybe you take it a little too seriously, Hugh."

"Maybe."

"Another instance of your selfishness," Amos said, "is your unwillingness to have children."

"But I'm not unwilling!" Hugh exclaimed.

Amos pounced. "Is there something wrong with you?"

Hugh shook his head.

Pete Murphy was standing in the doorway, with Laura and Barbara. He borrowed a chair from a nearby table, and they all three sat down.

The oblique approach, Hugh thought. Why was it he could never remember to protect himself against the double move, in which his castle took Amos's castle and Amos's bishop then took his queen.

"Doc," Amos said loudly, "I want you to give Hugh the name of a good gynecologist. You must know one."

WHEN they were seated once more at the table in the dining room, Amos turned to Louis Murphy's wife and said belligerently, "What you need is a drink. You look too healthy."

"Oh, Amos!" Ellen Cahill exclaimed. "I hoped you'd criticize *me*!"

"There's nothing the matter with you," Amos said. "You're perfect." Then, to the table in general: "That's my wife. Beautiful woman."

I don't understand it, Hugh said to himself wearily. I don't understand why I didn't kill him. . . . And Laura had not blamed him with so much as a look for discussing the subject there was no reason or need to discuss, in such a place, and with Amos, of all people. Instead, she had turned to Pete, as if he were an old and trusted friend. No, he had told her, he didn't know any doctors in New York. But two years was not an extraordinary time to wait. He had friends who had waited seven years and then had three children in a row. Matter-of-factly, but with the most glowing kindness in his blue eyes, he had answered her questions and described his own treatment, while Amos and Hugh had an argument about the check and Amos won.

The waiter arrived with the dessert course. Hugh thought of asking Laura to dance with him, and then, seeing that she and Amos had met head-on in serious conversation, he decided that she would prefer not to be interrupted. He glanced around the table. No one was loud, no one was drunk, but Amos. Was he drunk because this evening was dedicated, whether the others enjoyed it or not, to his meeting with Hugh? Was Amos's loud voice a mark of his respect?

Louis Murphy and his wife got up to dance, and Hugh moved around the table and sat beside Aileen Murphy, his friend, whom he had had no chance to talk to. She touched his forehead with her fingers.

"Furrows," she said. "You're having a serious time."

"It *is* serious," Hugh admitted. "And when you get home, you'd better defend me, after the way I feel about you."

"Ellen defends you," Aileen Murphy said. "She takes your side against Amos — and besides, you don't need anybody to defend you."

Across the table, Amos said to Laura, "Take a look at him and decide what you want him to be. Hugh doesn't have much ability to get on with people. You have to be the one to do it — meet people and make contacts and smooth the way for him. I wouldn't be what I am if she" — his eyes found Ellen — "hadn't made me that."

"Amos is sensitive," Aileen Murphy said in a low voice to Hugh. "You get under his skin more than you realize."

"I don't mean to," Hugh said.

"Possibly not, but you do. You and Amos are both extremes. So is Rick. You're a family of individualists. I don't know anybody like you." She shook her head mournfully.

Hugh heard Amos say, "When are you coming out to the Middle West?"

"Our car is so old it would never stand the trip," Laura said.

"Get him to buy you a new one," Amos said.

Laura laughed.

"He can afford it," Amos said. "Or if he can't, he's a damn fool to have left his job."

Barbara leaned across her mother and said to Laura, "Dad isn't like this. You mustn't pay any attention to him. He's really very kind. And he and Uncle Hugh only seem different on the surface. Underneath, they're quite a lot alike."

"Tell me about your children," Hugh said, remembering suddenly a boy and a girl, three and four — somewhere about that age — tracking mud in and out of the Murphys' house in Winnetka. "Are they remarkable?"

"They're not handsome," Aileen Murphy said.

"I don't mean handsome. Are they intelligent?"

"No," she said, reflecting. "I wouldn't say they were."

"But I don't mean that kind of intelligent," Hugh persisted. He was dead tired, he realized, and his brain was befuddled. "I mean are they wise in a certain way, about the world?"

"You've got to come West and see us," she said.

"Do you have Russian blood in you?"

"A little Jewish." She pointed to her thin Roman nose. Actually, he knew, she was Irish on both sides of the family.

"I asked if you had Russian blood in you," he said, "because you like to talk about life. You have a feeling for — You're realistic about people." Then watching Pete and Laura leave the table and go toward the dance floor: "What about Pete? Is he realistic?"

"Doc loves everybody."

"You mean he has no shrewdness, where people are concerned."

"That's right."

"Does he lose by it?"

"Not a thing," Aileen Murphy said, smiling. And then, sadly: "He has fair-weather friends."

Dancing with Laura, Pete Murphy said, "Don't you pay any attention to Amos. Amos doesn't know anything about painting."

"I know that," Laura said.

"I wouldn't offer Hugh advice, any more than Hugh would try to tell Amos how to sell automobiles. . . . The thing is not to worry."

"I don't," Laura said, "but we're living on very little money. And Hugh likes to be extravagant."

"My family is taken care of," Pete said, "if anything happens to me. So what I make I spend — and a little more. It's what I enjoy, and what makes *me* happy. And if I lose five hundred dollars on the races, I don't tell Amos."

THE party broke up around a quarter of one. Hugh tried to pay for his share of the dinner check and Amos waved him aside indignantly. Barbara said good night and left them. There was talk of going on to someplace else — to the Copacabana. For Hugh the evening was finished; he was ready to go home. He invited Amos to come out to the country with Barbara and Ellen, any time during the remainder of their three-day visit. This invitation was left hanging. Amos wanted Pete to go with him to see the Mets play the Cardinals; Pete wanted to go to the races. They decided, while Amos was tipping the waiter, to go their own ways.

All eight of them crowded into one elevator, and the four Cahills got off at the thirteenth floor. Amos had decided that he was tired and wanted to go to bed. They wandered through the corridor, made a wrong turning, and retraced their steps. Amos, reverting to the age of eleven, began ringing the bells of all the doors that lined the corridor. Ellen tried to stop him. Loud, drunk, and not at all unpleasant, Amos was not to be stopped. "I'll tell them Hugh did it," he said.

They got Hugh's hat. The two brothers, the two sisters-in-law said good-bye, and five minutes later, as Laura and Hugh were trying to find their way out of the lobby to the Park Avenue entrance of the hotel, they ran into Amos and Ellen, on their way to join the others at the Copacabana. At this final parting, the handshake of Hugh and Amos was prolonged, the expression in Amos's eyes tender, misty, and only slightly histrionic.

"He's got a handshake like a gorilla," Amos said proudly, to Laura.

"I HAD a feeling he would notice," Laura said, going home on the train. "And sure enough, he did. He said, 'Where'd you get that ring?' and I said, 'Hugh gave it to me.'"

"That was smart of you," Hugh said. "To realize, I mean, before you met him, that he'd look to see whether I'd given you an engagement ring."

"I just had a feeling," she said, and settled into the seat contentedly, with her head on his shoulder. They were taking the last train. The coach was almost full. The passengers were tired, and many of them sat and dozed, with their heads drooping, their necks bent to one side. Hugh looked down at the ring on the fourth finger of Laura's left hand — the diamond between two smaller sapphires, in a gold setting. It had been her grandmother's. Next to the false engagement ring was the plain gold wedding band Hugh had given her.

"Do you wish I'd given you an engagement ring?" he asked suddenly.

"No."

"I don't like diamonds."

"Someday I'd like you to give me a ring."

"What kind of ring?"

"For a special reason," she said. "On a special occasion."

He waited, unable to imagine what she had in mind.

"I'd like you to give me an emerald ring when our first child is born."

"I don't know that I trust myself when it comes to choosing a ring," he said. "What if I got one and you don't like it?"

"We could go and pick it out together," she said. "When you reached out and took my shoe, Barbara was telling me that Amos never has eyes for any other woman but Ellen, and she thought you had overheard."

"No. I didn't."

"She said, 'I'd just love to have a husband who'd reach out and take my foot, to say that he was following the conversation and loved me.'"

The train drew to a stop at 125th Street. When it started up again, Laura said, "It must be terrifying to be an older brother and have a younger brother who shows a kind of early promise, and then nothing seems to come of it for a while, and then the predictions begin to come true. . . . And being helpless," she added.

Amos *helpless?* Hugh wondered. He was exhausted. He felt battered and bruised. The encounter had not come off as well as he had hoped, but at least Amos had not got through (and he always had in the past) his inmost defenses. The fight had been a draw.

"I thought you'd never come back to the table," Laura said. "When you and Amos weren't there, it left a vacuum. Nobody had anything to say."

"I was caught," Hugh said. "Very nice of him, wasn't it, to ask Pete to recommend a doctor. And in front of Barbara. How *can* he do things like that?"

"It didn't matter," Laura said.

"It mattered to me," Hugh said. "I don't understand it. I don't understand why I didn't pick up a chair and brain him with it. There was the chair, and there I was, and he deserved to be killed, and I couldn't lift my arms to do it. I couldn't move. You had to do everything."

"It wasn't important," Laura said. And then, slowly: "I have only one complaint against you." (She had several, as it turned out, all handed to her, all expertly put in her mind by Amos.) "You don't love me the way Amos loves Ellen."

Oh my God, he thought, he's got through to *her!*

"You didn't ask me to dance with you," Laura said.

He sat up in the seat indignantly. "I was dancing with you all evening," he said. "Everything I said and did was for you and on account of you."

Neither of them said anything more. He knew that, having said this, she would forgive him, she would never refer to it again. She didn't hold grudges or put things aside in order to bring them up against him later. He sat back in the seat and drew her head over against his shoulder once more. Looking down at her soft brown hair, at the gardenia now edged with ivory, a chilling idea occurred to him: What if she defended me from Amos cleverly and successfully but at the expense of her faith that *I* can defend *her?* Was that Amos's triumph for this evening?

He couldn't bear to go on thinking about this, and put it out of his mind, but Amos continued to occupy his thoughts. What had he ever done to Amos that Amos should want to destroy him or to destroy his marriage?

As he sat pondering this unsolvable question, he noticed his own hands, and then thoughtfully, as if he had never seen them before, moved the fingers of one hand back and forth, surprised at what a thing the human hand is, how many ways, and how marvellously, the fingers moved. And then, with no shudder or feeling of any kind, he had a momentary image of the immovable sleeve, the gloved facsimile of a hand that he had so long ago become accustomed to that when he was with Amos he never gave it a thought.

The French Scarecrow

DRIVING past the Fishers' house on his way out to the public road, Gerald Martin said to himself absentmindedly, "There's Edmund working in his garden," before he realized that it was a scarecrow. And two nights later he woke up sweating from a dream, a nightmare, which he related next day, lying tense on the analyst's couch.

"I was in this house, where I knew I oughtn't to be, and I looked around and saw there was a door, and in order to get to it I had to pass a dummy—a dressmaker's dummy without any head."

After a considerable silence the disembodied voice with a German accent said, "Any day remnants?"

"I can't think of any," Gerald Martin said, shifting his position on the couch. "We used to have a dressmaker's dummy in the sewing room when I was a child, but I haven't thought of it for years. The Fishers have a scarecrow in their garden, but I don't think it could be that. The scarecrow looks like Edmund. The same thin shoulders, and his clothes, of course, and the way it stands looking sadly down at the ground. It's a caricature of Edmund. One of those freak accidents. I wonder if they realize it. Edmund is not sad, exactly, but there was a period in his life when he was neither as happy or as hopeful as he is now. Dorothy is a very nice woman. Not at all maternal, I would say. At least, she doesn't mother Edmund. And when you see her with some woman with a baby, she always seems totally indifferent. Edmund was married before, and his first wife left him. Helena was selfish but likable, the way selfish people sometimes are. And where Edmund was concerned, completely heartless. I don't know why. She used to turn the radio on full blast at two o'clock in the morning, when he had to get up at six-thirty to catch a commuting train. And once she sewed a ruffle all the way around the bed he was trying to sleep in. Edmund told me that her mother preferred her older sister, and that Helena's whole childhood had been made miserable because of it. He tried every way he could think of to please her and make her happy, and with most women that would have been enough, I suppose, but it only increased her dissatisfaction. Maybe if there had been any children ... She used to walk up and down the road in a long red cloak, in the wintertime when there was snow on the ground. And she used to talk about New York. And it was as if she was under a spell and waiting to be delivered. Now she blames Edmund for the divorce. She tells everybody that he took advantage of her. Perhaps he did, unconsciously. Consciously, he wouldn't take advantage of a fly. I think he needs analysis, but he's very much opposed to it. Scared to death of it, in fact ..."

Step by step, Gerald Martin had managed to put a safe distance between himself and the dream, and he was beginning to breathe easier in the complacent viewing of someone else's failure to meet his problems squarely when the voice said, "Well — see you again?"

"I wish to Christ you wouldn't say that! As if I had any choice in the matter."

His sudden fury was ignored. A familiar hypnotic routine obliged him to sit up and put his feet over the side of the couch. The voice became attached to an elderly man with thick glasses and a round face that Gerald would never get used to. He got up unsteadily and walked toward the door. Only when he was outside, standing in front of the elevator shaft, did he remember that the sewing room had a door opening into his mother and father's bedroom, and at one period of his life he had slept there, in a bed with sides that could be let down, a child's bed. This information was safe from the man inside — unless he happened to think of it while he was lying on the couch next time.

That evening he stopped when he came to the Fishers' vegetable garden and turned the engine off and took a good look at the scarecrow. Then, after a minute or two, afraid that he would be seen from the house, he started the car and drove on.

THE Fishers' scarecrow was copied from a scarecrow in France. The summer before, they had spent two weeks as paying guests in a country house in the Touraine, in the hope that this would improve their French. The improvement was all but imperceptible to them afterward, but they did pick up a number of ideas about gardening. In the *potager*, fruit trees, tree roses, flowers, and vegetables were mingled in a way that aroused their admiration, and there was a more than ordinarily fanciful scarecrow, made out of a blue peasant's smock, striped morning trousers, and a straw hat. Under the hat the stuffed head had a face painted on it; and not simply two eyes, a nose, and a mouth but a face with a sly expression. The scarecrow stood with arms upraised, shaking its white-gloved fists at the sky. Indignant, self-centered, half crazy, it seemed to be saying: *This is what it means to be exposed to experience.* The crows were not taken in.

Effects that had needed generations of dedicated French gardeners to bring about were not, of course, to be imitated successfully by two amateur gardeners in Fairfield County in a single summer. The Fishers gave up the idea of marking off the paths of their vegetable garden with espaliered dwarf apple and pear trees, and they could see no way of having tree roses without also having to spray them, and afterward having to eat the spray. But they did plant zinnias, marigolds, and blue pansies in with the lettuce and the peas, and they made a very good scarecrow. Dorothy made it, actually. She was artistic by inclination, and threw herself into all such undertakings with a childish pleasure.

She made the head out of a dish towel stuffed with hay, and was delighted with the blue stripe running down the face. Then she got out her embroidery thread and embroidered a single eye, gathered the cloth in the middle of the face into a bulbous nose, made the mouth leering. For the body she used a torn pair of Edmund's blue jeans she was tired of mending, and a faded blue workshirt. When Edmund, who was attached to his old clothes, saw that she had also helped herself to an Army fatigue hat from the shelf in the hall closet, he exclaimed, "Hey, don't use that hat for the scarecrow! I wear it sometimes."

"*When* do you wear it?"

"I wear it to garden in."

"You can wear some other old hat to garden in. He's got to have something on his head," she said lightly, and made the hat brim dip down over the blank eye.

"When winter comes, I'll wear it again," Edmund said to himself, "if it doesn't shrink too much, or fall apart in the rain."

The scarecrow stood looking toward the house, with one arm limp and one arm extended stiffly, ending in a gloved hand holding a stick. After a few days the head sank and sank until it was resting on the straw breastbone, and the face was concealed by the brim of the hat. They tried to keep the head up with a collar of twisted grass, but the grass dried, and the head sank once more, and in that attitude it remained.

The scarecrow gave them an eerie feeling when they saw it from the bedroom window at twilight. A man standing in the vegetable garden would have looked like a scarecrow. If he didn't move. Dorothy had never lived in the country before she married Edmund, and at first she was afraid. The black windows at night made her nervous. She heard noises in the basement, caused by the steam circulating through the furnace pipes. And she would suddenly have the feeling — even though she knew it was only her imagination — that there was a man outside, looking through the windows at them. "Shouldn't we invite him in?" Edmund would say when her glance strayed for a second. "Offer him a drink and let him sit by the fire? It's not a very nice night out."

He assumed that The Man Outside represented for her all the childish fears — the fear of the dark, of the burglar on the stairs, of what else he had no way of knowing. Nor she either, probably. The Man Outside was simply there, night after night, for about six weeks, and then he lost his power to frighten, and finally went away entirely, leaving the dark outside as familiar and safe to her as the lighted living room. It was Edmund, strangely, who sometimes, as they were getting ready for bed, went to the front and back doors and locked them. For he was aware that the neighborhood was changing, and that things were happening — cars stolen, houses broken into in broad daylight — that never used to happen in this part of the world.

THE Fishers' white clapboard house was big and rambling, much added onto at one time or another, but in its final form still plain and pleasant-looking. The original house dated from around 1840. Edmund's father, who was a New York banker until he retired at the age of sixty-five, had bought it before the First World War. At that time there were only five houses on this winding country road, and two of them were farmhouses. When the Fishers came out from town for the summer, they were met at the railroad station by a man with a horse and carriage. The surrounding country was hilly and offered many handsome views, and most of the local names were to be found on old tombstones in the tiny Presbyterian churchyard. Edmund's mother was a passionate and scholarly gardener, the founder of the local garden club and its president for twenty-seven years. Her regal manner was quite unconscious, and based less on the usual foundations of family, money, etc., than on the authority with which she could speak about the culture of delphinium and lilies, or the pruning of roses. The house was set back from the road about three hundred yards, and behind it were the tennis courts, the big three-story barn, a guest house overlooking the pond where all the children in the neighborhood skated in winter, and, eventually, a five-car garage. Back of the pond, a wagon road went off into the woods and up onto higher ground. In the late twenties, when Edmund used to bring his school friends home for spring and fall weekends and the Easter vacation, the house seemed barely large enough to hold them all. During the last war, when the taxes began to be burdensome, Edmund's father sold off the back land, with the guest house, the barn, and the pond, to a Downtown lawyer, who shortly afterward sold it to a manufacturer of children's underwear. The elder Mr. and Mrs. Fisher started to follow the wagon road back into the woods one pleasant Sunday afternoon, and he ordered them off his property. He was quite within his rights, of course, but nevertheless it rankled. "In the old days," they would say whenever the man's name was mentioned, "you could go anywhere, on anybody's land, and no one ever thought of stopping you."

Edmund's father, working from his own rough plans and supervising the carpenters and plumbers and masons himself, had converted the stone garage into a house, and he had sold it to Gerald Martin, who was a bachelor. The elder Fishers were now living in the Virgin Islands the year round, because of Mrs. Fisher's health. Edmund and Dorothy still had ten acres, but they shared the cinder drive with Gerald and the clothing manufacturer, and, of course, had less privacy than before. The neighborhood itself was no longer the remote place it used to be. The Merritt Parkway had made all the difference. Instead of five houses on the two-and-a-half-mile stretch of dirt road, there were twenty-five, and the road was macadamized. Cars and delivery trucks cruised up and down it all day long.

In spite of all these changes, and in spite of the considerable difference between Edmund's scale of living and his father's — Dorothy had managed with a part-time cleaning woman where in the old days there had been a cook, a waitress, an upstairs maid, a chauffeur, and two gardeners — the big house still seemed to express the financial stability and social confidence and belief in good breeding of the Age of Trellises. Because he had lived in the neighborhood longer than anyone else, Edmund sometimes felt the impulses of a host, but he had learned not to act on them. His mother always used to pay a call on new people within a month of their settling in, and if she liked them, the call was followed by an invitation to the Fishers' for tea or cocktails, at which time she managed to bring up the subject of the garden club. But in the last year or so that she had lived there, she had all but given this up. Twice her call was not returned, and one terribly nice young couple accepted an invitation to tea and blithely forgot to come. Edmund was friendly when he met his neighbors on the road or on the station platform, but he let them go their own way, except for Gerald Martin, who was rather amusing, and obviously lonely, and glad of an invitation to the big house.

"I AM sewed to this couch," Gerald Martin said. "My sleeves are sewed to it, and my trousers. I could not move if I wanted to. Oedipus is on the wall over me, answering the spink-spank-sphinx, and those are pussy willows, and I do not like bookcases with glass sides that let down, and the scarecrow is gone. I don't know what they did with it, and I don't like to ask. And today *I* might as well be stuffed with straw. The dream I had last night did it. I broke two plates, and woke up unconfident and nervous and tired. I don't know what the dream means. I had three plates and I dropped two of them, and it was so vivid. It was a short dream but very vivid. I thought at first that the second plate — why *three* plates? — was all right, but while I was looking at it, the cracks appeared. When I picked it up, it gave; it came apart in my hands. It was painted with flowers, and it had openwork, and I was in a hurry, and in my hurry I dropped the plates. And I was upset. I hardly ever break anything. Last night while I was drying the glasses, I thought how I never break any of them. They're Swedish and very expensive. The plates I dreamed about were my mother's. Not actually; I *dreamed* that they were my mother's plates. I broke two things of hers when I was little. And both times it was something she had warned me about. I sat in the tea cart playing house, and forgot and raised my head suddenly, and it went right through the glass tray. And the other was an etched-glass hurricane lamp that she prized very highly. I climbed up on a chair to reach it. And after she died, I could have thought — I don't ever remember thinking this, but I could have thought that I did something I shouldn't have, and she died. . . . Thank you, I have matches. . . . I can raise my arm. I turned without thinking. I can't figure out that dream. My stepmother was there, washing dishes at the sink, and she turned into Helena Fisher, and I woke up thinking, Ah, that's it. They're *both* my stepmothers! My stepmother never broke anything that belonged to my mother, so she must have been fond of her. They knew each other as girls. And I never broke anything that belonged to my stepmother. I only broke something that belonged to my mother. . . . Did I tell you I saw her the other day?"

"You saw someone who reminded you of your mother?"

"No, I saw Helena Fisher. On Fifth Avenue. I crossed over to the other side of the street, even though I'm still fond of her, because she hasn't been very nice to Dorothy, and because it's all so complicated, and I really didn't have anything to say to her. She was very conspicuous in her country clothes." He lit another cigarette and then said, after a prolonged silence, "I don't seem to have anything to say now, either." The silence became unbearable, and he said, "I can't think of anything to talk about."

"Let's talk about you — about this dream you had," the voice said, kind and patient as always, the voice of his father (at $20 an hour).

THE scarecrow had remained in the Fishers' vegetable garden, with one arm limp and one arm stiffly extended, all summer. The corn and the tomato vines grew up around it, half obscuring it during the summer months, and then, in the fall, there was nothing whatever around it but the bare ground. The blue workshirt faded still more in the sun and rain. The figure grew frail, the straw chest settled and became a middle-aged thickening of the waist. The resemblance to Edmund disappeared. And on a Friday afternoon in October, with snow flurries predicted, Edmund Fisher went about the yard carrying in the outdoor picnic table and benches, picking up stray flowerpots, and taking one last look around for the pruning shears, the trowel, and the nest of screwdrivers that had all disappeared during the summer's gardening. There were still three or four storm windows to put up on the south side of the house, and he was about to bring them out and hang them when Dorothy, on her hands and knees in the iris bed, called to him.

"What about the scarecrow?"

"Do you want to save it?" he asked.

"I don't really care."

"We might as well," he said, and was struck once more by the lifelike quality of the scarecrow, as he lifted it out of the soil. It was almost weightless. "Did the doctor say it was all right for you to do that sort of thing?"

"I didn't ask him," Dorothy said.

"Oughtn't you to ask him?"

"No," she said, smiling at him. She was nearly three months pregnant. Moonfaced, serenely happy, and slow of movement (when she had all her life been so quick about everything), she went about now doing everything she had always done but like somebody in a dream, a sleepwalker. The clock had been replaced by the calendar. Like the gardeners in France, she was dedicated to making something grow. As Edmund carried the scarecrow across the lawn and around the corner of the house, she followed him with her eyes. Why is it, she wondered, that he can never bear to part with anything, even though it has ceased to serve its purpose and he no longer has any interest in it?

It was as if sometime or other in his life he had lost something, of such infinite value that he could never think of it without grieving, and never bear to part with anything worthless because of the thing he had had to part with that meant so much to him. But what? She had no idea, and she had given some thought to the matter. She was sure it was not Helena; he said (and she believed him) that he had long since got over any feeling he once had for her. His parents were both still living, he was an only child, and death seemed never to have touched him. Was it some early love, that he had never felt he dared speak to her about? Some deprivation? Some terrible injustice done to him? She had no way of telling. The attic and the basement testified to his inability to throw things away, and she had given up trying to do anything about either one. The same with people. At the end of a perfectly pleasant evening he would say "Oh no, it's early still. You mustn't go home!" with such fervor that even though it actually was time to go home and the guests wanted to, they would sit down, confused by him, and stay a while longer. And though the Fishers knew more people than they could manage to see, he would suddenly remember somebody he hadn't thought of or written to in a long time, and feel impelled to do something about them. Was it something that happened to him in his childhood, Dorothy asked herself. Or was it something in his temperament, born in him, a flaw in his horoscope, Mercury in an unsympathetic relation to the moon?

She resumed her weeding, conscious in a way that she hadn't been before of the autumn day, of the end of the summer's gardening, of the leaf-smoke smell and the smell of rotting apples, the hickory tree that lost its leaves before all the other trees, the grass so deceptively green, and the chill that had descended now that the sun had gone down behind the western hill.

Standing in the basement, looking at the hopeless disorder ("A place for everything," his father used to say, "and nothing in its place"), Edmund decided that it was more important to get at the storm windows than to find a place for the scarecrow. He laid it on one of the picnic-table benches, with the head toward the oil burner, and there it sprawled, like a man asleep or dead-drunk, with the line of the hipbone showing through the trousers, and one arm extended, resting on a slightly higher workbench, and one shoulder raised slightly, as if the man had started to turn in his sleep. In the dim light it could have been alive. I must remember to tell Dorothy, he thought. If she sees it like that, she'll be frightened.

The storm windows were washed and ready to hang. As Edmund came around the corner of the house, with IX in one hand and XI in the other, the telephone started to ring, and Dorothy went in by the back door to answer it, so he didn't have a chance to tell her about the scarecrow. When he went indoors, ten minutes later, she was still standing by the telephone, and from the fact that she was merely contributing a monosyllable now and then to the conversation, he knew she was talking to Gerald Martin. Gerald was as dear as the day was long — everybody liked him — but he had such a ready access to his own memories, which were so rich in narrative detail and associations that dovetailed into further narratives, that if you were busy it was a pure and simple misfortune to pick up the telephone and hear his cultivated, affectionate voice.

Edmund gave up the idea of hanging the rest of the storm windows, and instead he got in the car and drove to the village; he had remembered that they were out of cat food and whiskey. When he walked into the house, Dorothy said, "I've just had such a scare. I started to go down in the cellar — "

"I knew that would happen," he said, putting his hat and coat in the hall closet. "I meant to tell you."

"The basement light was burnt out," she said, "and so I took the flashlight. And when I saw the scarecrow I thought it was a man."

"Our old friend," he said, shaking his head. "The Man Outside."

"And you weren't here. I knew I was alone in the house . . ."

Her fright was still traceable in her face as she described it.

ON Saturday morning, Edmund dressed hurriedly, the alarm clock having failed to go off, and while Dorothy was getting breakfast, he went down to the basement, half asleep, to get the car out and drive to the village for the cleaning woman, and saw the scarecrow in the dim light, sprawling by the furnace, and a great clot of fear seized him and his heart almost stopped beating. It lay there like an awful idiot, the realistic effect accidentally encouraged by the pair of work shoes Edmund had taken off the night before and tossed carelessly down the cellar stairs. The scarecrow had no feet — only two stumps where the trouser legs were tied at the bottom — but the shoes were where, if it had been alive, they might have been dropped before the person lay down on the bench. I'll have to do something about it, Edmund thought. We can't go on frightening ourselves like this. . . . But the memory of the fright was so real that he felt unwilling to touch the scarecrow. Instead, he left it where it was, for the time being, and backed the car out of the garage.

On the way back from the village, Mrs. Ryan, riding beside him in the front seat of the car, had a story to tell. Among the various people she worked for was a family with three boys. The youngest was in the habit of following her from room to room, and ordinarily he was as good as gold, but yesterday he ran away, she told Edmund. His mother was in town, and the older boys, with some of the neighbors' children, were playing outside with a football, and Mrs. Ryan and the little boy were in the house. "Monroe asked if he could go outside, and I bundled him up and sent him out. I looked outside once, and saw that he was laying with the Bluestones' dog, and I said, 'Monroe, honey, don't pull that dog's tail. He might turn and bite you.' " While she was ironing, the oldest boy came inside for a drink of water, and she asked him where Monroe was, and he said, "Oh, he's outside." But when she went to the door, fifteen minutes later, the older boys were throwing the football again and Monroe was nowhere in sight. The boys didn't know what had happened to him. He disappeared. All around the house was woods, and Mrs. Ryan, in a panic, called and called.

"Usually when I call, he answers immediately, but this time there was no answer, and I went into the house and telephoned the Bluestones, and they hadn't seen him. And then I called the Hayeses and the Murphys, and they hadn't seen him either, and Mr. Hayes came down, and we all started looking for him. Mr. Hayes said only one car had passed in the last half hour — I was afraid he had been kidnapped, Mr. Fisher — and Monroe wasn't in it. And I thought, When his mother comes home and I have to tell her what I've done . . . And just about that time, he answered, from behind the hedge!"

"Was he there all the time?" Edmund asked, shifting into second as he turned in to his own driveway.

"I don't know where he was," Mrs. Ryan said. "But he did the same thing once before — he wandered off on me. Mr. Ryan thinks he followed the Bluestones' dog home. His mother called me up last night and said that he knew he'd done something wrong. He said, 'Mummy, I was bad today. I ran off on Sadie. . . .' But Mr. Fisher, I'm telling you, I was almost out of my mind."

"I don't wonder," Edmund said soberly.

"With woods all around the house, and as Mr. Hayes said, climbing over a stone wall a stone could fall on him and we wouldn't find him for days."

Ten minutes later, she went down to the basement for the scrub bucket, and left the door open at the head of the stairs. Edmund heard her exclaim, for their benefit, "God save us, I've just had the fright of my life!"

She had seen the scarecrow.

The tramp that ran off with the child, of course, Edmund thought. He went downstairs a few minutes later, and saw that Mrs. Ryan had picked the dummy up and stood it in a corner, with its degenerate face to the wall, where it no longer looked human or frightening.

Mrs. Ryan is frightened because of the nonexistent tramp. Dorothy is afraid of The Man Outside. What am I afraid of, he wondered. He stood there waiting for the oracle to answer, and it did, but not until five or six hours later. Poor Gerald Martin called, after lunch, to say that he had the German measles.

"I was sick as a dog all night," he said mournfully. "I thought I was dying. I wrote your telephone number on a slip of paper and put it beside the bed, in case I *did* die."

"Well, for God's sake, why didn't you call us?" Edmund exclaimed.

"What good would it have done?" Gerald said. "All you could have done was say you were sorry."

"Somebody could have come over and looked after you."

"No, somebody couldn't. It's very catching. I think I was exposed to it a week ago at a party in Westport."

"I had German measles when I was a kid," Edmund said. "We've both had it."

"You can get it again," Gerald said. "I still feel terrible. . . ."

When Edmund left the telephone, he made the mistake of mentioning Gerald's illness to Mrs. Ryan, forgetting that it was the kind of thing that was meat and drink to her.

"Has Mrs. Fisher been near him?" she asked, with quickened interest.

He shook his head.

"There's a great deal of it around," Mrs. Ryan said. "My daughter got German measles when she was carrying her first child, and she lost it."

He tried to ask if it was a miscarriage or if the child was born dead, and he couldn't speak; his throat was too dry.

"She was three months along when she had it," Mrs. Ryan went on, without noticing that he was getting paler and paler. "The baby was born alive, but it only lived three days. She's had two other children since. I feel it was a blessing the Lord took that one. If it had lived, it might have been an imbecile. You love them even so, because they belong to you, but it's better if they don't live, Mr. Fisher. We feel it was a blessing the child was taken."

Edmund decided that he wouldn't tell Dorothy, and then five minutes later he decided that he'd better tell her. He went upstairs and into the bedroom where she was resting, and sat down on the edge of the bed, and told her about Gerald's telephone call. "Mrs. Ryan says it's very bad if you catch it while you're pregnant. . . . And she said some more."

"I can see she did, by the look on your face. You shouldn't have mentioned it to her. What did she say?"

"She said—" He swallowed. "She said the child could be born an imbecile. She also said there was a lot of German measles around. You're not worried?"

"We all live in the hand of God."

"I tell myself that every time I'm really frightened. Unfortunately that's the only time I do think it."

"Yes, I know."

Five minutes later, he came back into the room and said, "Why don't you call the doctor? Maybe there's a shot you can take."

The doctor was out making calls, and when he telephoned back, Dorothy answered, on the upstairs extension. Edmund sat down on the bottom step of the stairs and listened to her half of the conversation. As soon as she had hung up, she came down to tell him what the doctor had said.

"The shot only lasts three weeks. He said he'd give it to me if I should be exposed to the measles anywhere."

"Did he say there was an epidemic of it?"

"I didn't ask him. He said that it was commonly supposed to be dangerous during the first three months, but that the statistics showed that it's only the first two months, while the child is being formed, that you have to worry." Moonfaced and serene again, she went to put the kettle on for tea.

Edmund got up and went down to the basement. He carried the dummy outside, removed the hat and then the head, unbuttoned the shirt, removed the straw that filled it and the trousers, and threw it on the compost pile. The hat, the head, the shirt and trousers, the gloves that were hands, he rolled into a bundle and put away on a basement shelf, in case Dorothy wanted to make the scarecrow next summer. The two crossed sticks reminded him of the comfort that Mrs. Ryan, who was a devout Catholic, had and that he did not have. The hum of the vacuum cleaner overhead in the living room, the sad song of a mechanical universe, was all the reassurance he could hope for, and it left so much (it left the scarecrow, for example) completely unexplained and unaccounted for.

Young Francis Whitehead

THE Whiteheads lived on the sheltered side of a New Hampshire hill, less than half a mile from town. Their house was set back from the road, and there were so many low-skirted pine trees on both sides of the drive that Miss Avery, who had a parcel under her arm and was coming to see Mrs. Whitehead, was almost up to the house before she could see the green shutters and the high New England roofline. The driveway went past the garage and up to the front door, then around and down again to the road. Both garage doors were open and the afternoon sun shone upon Mrs. Whitehead's Buick sedan and, beside it, a new and shiny blue convertible. While Miss Avery was admiring it, an Irish setter came bounding out of the shrubbery. The dog barked and whined and stepped on Miss Avery's feet and blocked her way no matter where she turned, so that in desperation she gave him a shove with the flat of her hand.

As soon as she did that, a window flew open upstairs and young Francis Whitehead put his head out. "Go on, beat it!" he said. Apparently he had no clothes on. His hair and his face and shoulders were dripping wet, and for a moment Miss Avery wasn't sure whether Francis was talking to her or to the dog. "You silly creature!" he said, and whistled and gave orders and made threats until finally the dog disappeared around the side of the house. Then for the first time Francis looked at Miss Avery. "Oh," he said. "It's you. Come on in, why don't you?"

"All right," she said. "I was going to."

"I'm in the shower," Francis explained, "but Mother's around somewhere. She'll be glad to see you." He drew his head in and closed the window.

Miss Avery had stood by, in one capacity or another, while Francis learned to walk and to talk, to cut out strings of paper dolls, and ride a bicycle but they had seen very little of each other the last two or three years. Francis had been away at school much of the time. He was at Cornell. And Miss Avery decided, as she raised the knocker on the big front door, that he probably wouldn't care to be reminded of the fact that she had once sewed buttons on his pantywaists. The knocker made a noise, but no one came. Miss Avery waited and waited, and finally she opened the door and walked in.

The house was dark after the spring sunlight outside. Miss Avery felt blind as a mole. The first thing she saw was herself — her coat with the worn fur at the collar and her thin, unromantic, middle-aged face — reflected in a mirror that ran from floor to ceiling. She turned her eyes away and walked on into the library. Bookcases went nearly around the room. A wood fire was burning in the fireplace and the clock on the mantel was ticking loudly. Over by the French windows a card table had been set up. There was a pile of little baskets on it, and a number of chocolate rabbits and little chickens made out of cotton, and quantities of green and yellow wax-paper straw.

Miss Avery put down her parcel, which contained some mending that Mrs. Whitehead had asked her to do, and stood looking at the confusion on the card table until a voice exclaimed, "Happy Easter!" She turned and found Mrs. Whitehead smiling at her. Mrs. Whitehead had a china dish in one hand and a paper bag in the other. She advanced upon Miss Avery, put both arms about her, and kissed her.

"Easter is still two days off," Miss Avery said. "This is only Good Friday."

"I know it is. I was just indulging myself," Mrs. Whitehead said, and she carried the dish over to the card table and poured out the sackful of Easter eggs. "I was just thinking about you and here you are." She drew Miss Avery down beside her on the sofa and took both of her hands. "How's your mother? I've been meaning to stop in and see how she was but we've had so much company lately — Mrs. Howard from Portsmouth and Cousin Ada Sheffield right after that, and I really haven't had a moment. And tell me how *you* are. That's what I really want to know."

"Well," Miss Avery began without enthusiasm, but Mrs. Whitehead had already got up and was searching everywhere for little dishes and jars, lifting the tops and peering into them hopefully.

"I had some ginger, but it looks as if I'd eaten every scrap of it," she said. "There isn't a thing to offer you but Easter eggs."

Miss Avery tried to explain that it was all right; she didn't like ginger any better than she liked Easter eggs, but Mrs. Whitehead paid no attention to her. "I was just going to fix some baskets. My only child is home for his spring vacation, and I'm having eight of his cronies to dinner tomorrow night. And they all have to have Easter baskets." She gave up looking among the dishes and jars and sat down again, at the card table this time. "Francis brought a dog home with him, too," she said as she took one of the baskets and began lining it with green straw. "A perfectly mammoth setter. You know how huge they are. And so beautiful and so dumb!"

Miss Avery nodded, out of politeness. One dog was much like another so far as she was concerned.

"The boy it belonged to got a job somewhere," Mrs. Whitehead said, choosing first a yellow chicken from the pile in front of her, then a rabbit, and then a white chicken small enough to fasten on the rim of the basket. "Boston, I think it was."

"Providence," Francis said from the doorway. He came in and sat down quietly and stretched his long legs out in front of him. His hair was still wet, but it was combed neatly back from his ears. He had flannel trousers on, and a white shirt, and an old tweed coat. He was also wearing heavy leather boots that were laced as far as his ankles and came halfway up his shins. Miss Avery let her eyes wander from boots to coat, to the right-hand pocket of the coat, which had been ripped open by accident last fall when Francis was home for Thanksgiving. The cloth had been torn a little, too, but it was all right now, Miss Avery decided. She had made it as good as new.

"Providence, then," Mrs. Whitehead was saying. "Anyway, they had the dog in their dormitory all year and this boy couldn't take it to work with him, so Francis brought it home, without saying a word to anybody. Red, his name is. And I give you my word, he's as big as a pony. All morning long he's been going around knocking things over, tracking dirt in and out, stealing meat off the kitchen table — all the things boys do in college, I'm sure." She looked at Francis slyly. "And then every time he does something wrong, he comes and apologizes with those great brown eyes of his until I really don't think I can stand it much longer."

Francis drew himself up into his chair. "You exaggerate something awful," he said.

Mrs. Whitehead looked at Miss Avery. "It isn't so," she said meekly. "Is it, Miss Avery? Francis is always saying that I exaggerate." She turned to Francis. "Miss Avery's mother exaggerates, too, Francis, even with her hardening of the arteries." Then back to Miss Avery: "Though I never heard her do it, you understand. I daresay all mothers exaggerate." She looked from one to the other of them and then burst into laughter. "Miss Avery takes me so seriously," she said. "She always did. She never changes a bit. We're the ones who have changed, Francis. There's not one piece of ginger in the house."

She held the Easter basket off, admiring it from this angle and that. Then she put it aside and began on another one, which she lined with yellow straw. Before she had finished the second basket, the maid appeared in the doorway, carrying a wide silver tea tray. The dog followed after her, sniffing. "Annie, how nice of you to think of tea," said Mrs. Whitehead. When Annie tried to put the tray down, the dog came forward, blocking her way completely. Mrs. Whitehead was plunged into despair. "You see, Francis?" she said.

Francis rose and took hold of the dog's collar. "Red," he exclaimed fondly, "did anyone ever tell you you were a nuisance?" and dragged the dog out of the room.

"Don't put him in the pantry," Mrs. Whitehead called. Then she turned to Miss Avery again. "He can open the swinging door with his paw. Besides, he'll just be there for Annie to fall over."

From where Miss Avery sat, she could see into the front hall. Francis was whirling the dog round and round by his front legs and saying "Swing, you crazy dog, swing, swing!"

"Francis is going to leave school," Mrs. Whitehead said. "Last summer nothing would do but he must learn to walk the tightrope. Now he wants to leave school." She began arranging the teacups absentmindedly in their saucers. "He intends to go back and take his examinations in June. Then he's going to stop. I've talked until I'm blue in the face and it makes no difference to him. Not the slightest. . . . What kind of sandwiches are there, Annie?"

"Cream cheese," Annie said, "and guava jelly, and hot cross buns."

"Hot cross buns!" Francis said, coming back into the room. "Do you hear that, Mother?"

Mrs. Whitehead looked at him disapprovingly as he sat down. "The way you twist Annie around your little finger! I don't know what I'll do when you come home to stay."

Francis bent over, and having folded the cuffs of his trousers inside his boots, continued lacing them. "I'm not coming home to stay," he said, with his chin between his knees.

For a moment the room was absolutely still. Without looking at her son, Mrs. Whitehead put the tea strainer on the tray where the plate of lemon had been, reflected, and changed them back again. "Sugar?" she said to Miss Avery.

"If you please," Miss Avery said.

Annie brought her tea and the plate of sandwiches, the plate of hot cross buns. When Francis also had been taken care of, Annie waited to see whether Mrs. Whitehead wanted anything else of her and then withdrew from the room. Francis went on lacing his boots. After he had finished, he adjusted his trousers so that they hung over like ski pants. Then, quite by accident, he discovered his cup of tea. Nobody spoke. The dog returned, making soft, padded noises on the hardwood floor. Miss Avery thought that Mrs. Whitehead would probably object and that Francis would have to take hold of Red and drag him out again, but it was not that way at all. The dog came and put his head on Mrs. Whitehead's lap and she began to stroke his long, red ears.

"If you're not coming here, Francis," she said suddenly, "where *do* you intend to go?"

"New York."

"Why New York?" Mrs. Whitehead asked.

"I want to get a job," Francis said, and pulled a hot cross bun to pieces and ate it.

Mrs. Whitehead watched him as if it were an altogether new sight. When he had finished, she said, "You can get a job right here. There are plenty of jobs. Your Uncle Frank will probably make a place for you."

"I don't wan't a job in the mill," Francis said.

In a spasm of exasperation, Mrs. Whitehead turned away from him and poured herself a second cup of tea. "Really, Francis," she said, "I don't know what's come over you."

Miss Avery was ready to get up as soon as she caught Mrs. Whitehead's eye, and go home. But when Mrs. Whitehead did glance in her direction, Miss Avery saw that she was more than exasperated — that she was frightened also. Her look said that, for a few minutes at least, Miss Avery was not to go; that she was to relax and sit back in her chair.

"You do what *you* want, Mother," Francis said reasonably. "You like to have breakfast in bed, so Annie brings it up to you. I want to do the things *I* like. I've had enough school. I want to begin living, like other people."

Mrs. Whitehead pushed the dog's head out of her lap. "Being grown up isn't as interesting as you think. Your father and I always hoped that you would study medicine. He talked so much about it during his last illness. But you don't seem to care for that sort of thing and I suppose there's no reason why you should be made to go on with your studies if you don't want to. There are other things to think of, however. I can't rent this house overnight. People don't want so large a place, you know. It may take all summer. And you may not like it in New York after you get there. You'll miss the country and you'll miss your home and your friends. You may not even be able to keep your car. Had you thought of that?" She waited for him to say something, but he went on intently balancing the heel of one boot on the toe of the other. "We'll have to take a little apartment somewhere," she said, "and it'll be cramped and uncomfortable — "

"I'm sorry, Moth!" He stood up suddenly, and his voice was strained and uncertain. "When I go to New York I'm going alone," he said. "I want to lead my own life." Then he turned and went out of the room, with the dog racing after him.

WHEN Mrs. Whitehead started talking again, it was not about Francis but something else entirely — a book she had read once long ago. The book was about New Orleans after the Civil War. She had forgotten the title of it, and she didn't suppose Miss Avery would remember it either, but it was about a little girl named Dea, who used to carry wax figurines around on a tray in the marketplace and sell them to people from the North.

Annie came in and carried the tea tray out to the kitchen. When they were alone again, Mrs. Whitehead seemed to have forgotten the book, or else she had said all there was to say about it. The moment had come for Miss Avery to bring forth her handiwork. She went and got the brown-paper parcel and sat down with it on her lap. Her fingers trembled slightly as she pulled the knot apart, and when the wrapping fell open she expected exclamations of approval. There were none. Mrs. Whitehead did not even see the mending. She was sitting straight up in her chair, and her eyes were quite blind and overflowing with tears.

"Francis is so young," she said. "Just twenty, you know. Just a boy. And there's really no reason why he should be in such a rush. Most people live a long time. Longer than they need to."

Miss Avery nodded. There was nothing that she could think of to say. She wanted to go home, but she waited until Mrs. Whitehead had found her handkerchief and wiped her eyes and given her nose a little blow and glanced surreptitiously at the clock.

A Final Report

IN *the matter of the estate of Pearl M. Donald, deceased,* who carried me on a pillow when I was a sickly baby, a little over fifty years ago, *Probate No. 2762,* for many years my mother's best friend and our next-door neighbor, a beautiful woman with a knife-edge to her voice and a grievance against her husband (What? What on earth could it have been? Everybody loved him): *Final report to the Honorable Frank Mattein, Judge of the County Court of Latham County, Illinois: The undersigned, Margaret Wilson, Executor of the Last Will of Pearl M. Donald, deceased, respectfully states: 1. That on or about the 17th day of June, 1961, Pearl M. Donald departed this life* . . . though it was far from easy. It took her almost twenty years of not wanting to live anymore. And if she had been left in her own house, in all that frightful squalor and filth and no air and the odor of cats' defecation, she might have needed still more time. But when she was carrying me on a pillow it was not a question of when she would die but of whether I would live.

It is safe to assume that she shared my mother's fears, comforted her, lied to her — comforting lies, about the way I looked today as compared with the way I looked yesterday; and that at some point she took my mother in her arms and let her cry. Though Aunty Donald lived to be so old, there was no question of her mental competence. She left a will, which was duly approved and admitted to probate. Letters testamentary were duly issued; the executor was duly qualified; an inventory of all estate assets, both real and personal, was filed and approved by the court; notices for the filing of claims were published, as provided by law; and proof of heirship was made, from which it appears *that the decedent left her surviving no husband* (there is nothing like the law for pointing out what everybody knows) *and the following named person as her only heir at law: Agnes Jones,* an adult cousin, whom I have never heard of.

I don't, of course, remember being carried on the pillow, but I remember the playhouse in Aunty Donald's back yard. It was made of two upright-piano boxes put together, in the fashion of that period, with windows and a door, and real shingles on the roof. It had belonged to a little girl named Mary King. The Donalds' house used to be the Kings'. And when I got to be five or six years old, my mother, seeing that I loved the playhouse, which was locked, which I never went in, and which I shouldn't have loved, since I was a little boy and playhouses are for little girls — my mother asked if she could buy the playhouse for me and Aunty Donald said no, she was keeping it for Bun. Bun was her dog — a bulldog. I don't know whether it was at that point that she stopped being my mother's best friend (my mother seldom took offense, but when she did it was usually permanent) or whether Aunty Donald said that because she had already stopped being my mother's best friend. There is so much that children are not told and that it never occurs to them to ask. Anyway, I went on peering through the windows of the locked playhouse at the things Mary King had left behind when the Kings moved away, and hoping that someday the playhouse would be unlocked and I could go inside. Once I heard my mother mention it to my Aunt Annette, and I realized from the tone of her voice that it was a mildly sore subject with her but not taken so seriously that — that what? That I didn't spend a great many hours in Aunty Donald's kitchen with the hired girl while my mother and Aunty Donald were talking in the front part of the house. I don't remember what they talked about. It didn't interest me, and so I went out to the kitchen, where I could do some of the talking. And in return I even listened. The hired girl's name was Mae, and she had a child in the state institution for the feeble-minded, on the outskirts of town. She was not feeble-minded herself, but neither was she terribly bright, I suppose. The men joked about her. My father had seen her leaving the Donalds' house all dressed up, on her afternoon off, and he had not recognized her. From the rear, the men agreed, she was some chicken. When you saw her face, it was a different story. She was about as homely as it is possible to be. Scraggly teeth, a complexion the color of putty, kinky hair, and a slight aura of silliness. What I talked to her about I don't know. Children never seem to suffer from a lack of things to say. What she talked to me about was the fact that Aunty Donald wouldn't let her have cream in her coffee. This was half a century ago, when hired girls got four or five dollars a week. At our house nobody ever told the hired girl she couldn't have what we had. So far as I know.

And I seem to remember telling my mother that Aunty wouldn't let Mae have cream in her coffee, but whether I remember or only think I remember, I undoubtedly did tell my mother this, because I told her everything. It was my way of dealing with facts and with life. The act of telling her made them manageable. I don't suppose I told her anything about Aunty Donald that she didn't know already. And she was a very good and loving mother, and didn't tell me everything by way of making her facts and her life manageable. She just shone on me like the sun, and in spite of my uncertain beginning I grew. I was not as strong as other children, but I came along. I stayed out of the cemetery.

OF all those times next door during my childhood, there are only four distinct memories. Two of them take place on the Donalds' front porch, in the summertime. It is almost dark, and my father is smoking a cigar, and the women are fanning themselves, and suddenly all this serenity vanishes because of a change in the color of the sky. The sunset is long past, and yet the sky above the houses on the other side of the street is growing pink. There is only one thing it could be. Aunty goes indoors and finds out from the telephone operator where the fire is, but they do not jump in the car, because there is no car, and if you are in your right mind you don't drive to a fire in a horse and buggy. Instead, my mother and Aunty Donald sit taking the catastrophe in from the porch swing. The whole sky is a frightening red now, and in their voices I hear something I have never heard before. It occurs to me that we might be witnessing The End of the World, so often mentioned in the Presbyterian Sunday school. In simple fact, it is the Orphans' Home burning down.

No. 2: One of the things that Aunty Donald held against her husband was that he spoke with a Scottish accent. He had every right to. (He always referred to Scotland as "the old country," and I thought as a child that it was the only place so called.) In the dusk, sitting on the porch steps, he suddenly exclaimed, "Pe'll, Pe'll, there's a speeder on you!" And though she had been married to him for I don't know how long — ten or fifteen years, I would guess — she affected not to understand that a "speeder" was a spider. She was from a little town nearby — Dover, Illinois — and according to the executor's report owned property there at the time of her death, a house that was sold for $1,600, for which somebody had been paying $22 a month rent.

The two other set pieces both happen upstairs. We — my mother and

I — are in Aunty's bedroom, and on the big brass double bed there are a great many Christmas presents, wrapped either in white paper with red ribbon or red paper with white ribbon. They are of all shapes and sizes, and interest me very much. Aunty is showing my mother something that still has to be wrapped — a bottle of cologne or some crocheted doilies, that sort of thing — and my mother is admiring whatever it is, and as I stand there, it is borne in on me, by intuition, that in all this collection of presents there is nothing for me.

The final memory is of a nightmare that I had when I was wide awake. I am in bed, in the Donalds' spare room, and the door is open, and I can see out into the hall. At the head of the stairs there is a large picture of a man in a nightshirt on a tumbled bed, by a brook, over which red-coated huntsmen are jumping their horses. The man is asleep and doesn't know the danger he is in. The horses' hoofs are going to come down on him and kill him, and there is nothing I can do to save him. Though it does not take very much to make me cry, this time I do not. I know that Aunty is just down the hall and would hear me and get up out of bed and come to me, and still I do not make a sound. I stare at the picture until I fall asleep and dream about it. What I was doing there I do not know. I had been left with Aunty for the night. My mother and father must have been away, and perhaps they took my brother with them.

Twenty-five or thirty years later, I spoke of the picture to Aunty Donald, and asked if I could see it. By that time, my mother was dead and we had moved away, like the Kings, and there was a layer of dust over everything. She was no longer the housekeeper that she used to be, but apart from this there was no change in her house, which pleased me, because there was nothing but change everywhere else. Our house, next door, had been sold to strangers and the furniture scattered. The house is still standing, but I have never been inside it since the day the moving men emptied it room by room. To come to see Dr. and Aunty Donald was to walk straight into the past. Ninth Street was lined with handsome shade trees that kept the houses from seeming ordinary, which they were, Aunty Donald's house no less than the others. But the inside of her house was not ordinary, it was amazing. When she was a young woman nobody thought her taste peculiar, for the simple reason that everyone else's taste was peculiar, too. It was an age that admired individuality, and in most cases individuality was arrived at through the marriage of Grand Rapids and *art nouveau*. Accident and sentiment also played a part. The total effect was usually homelike and comfortable, once the eye got over the shock. But a whole generation after all the other beaded portieres in Lincoln had been taken down, Aunty Donald's continued to divide the sitting room from the dark, gloomy dining room, and when you pushed your way through, it made an agreeable rattle. Along with the portiere, all sorts of things survived their period. For example, two long peacock feathers in a hand-painted vase on the upright piano that was never tuned and never played on. In an old snapshot that I came upon recently, I saw, to my surprise and pleasure, that most of my mother's friends were, as young women, beautiful. Some of them went on being beautiful, but Aunty Donald did not. The Donalds had no children. She lost both her parents. And Dr. Donald lost a good deal of money in a business venture that I never understood. Add to this those grotesque but common deprivations that people don't like to talk about, such as false teeth and bifocals and the fear of falling. Aunty Donald was sufficiently aware of all that she had lost, and did not want to add to it by throwing things away — even such things as the evening paper and second-class mail. Also clothes that were worn out or long out of fashion. Cups that had lost their handle, saucers that had no cup. The wallpaper had not even been changed, but was allowed to go on fading. In the sitting room, up next to the ceiling, at repeated intervals the same three knights rode up to the same castle that they used to ride up to when I was a small child. So it was reasonable to assume that the picture of the man sprawled out on the tumbled bed by a brook was still hanging at the head of the stairs, but it turned out that the picture was not there. Dr. Donald had taken it to Chicago, and it was hanging in a club near the stockyards. He had loaned it to them, Aunty said, but she would get it back. From that time on, she nagged him to bring the picture home so I could have it, and he promised to. Each time I went to see them he would say, "Billie, I haven't forgotten about your picture." And one night the club burned down, and then she had something else to blame him for. One more thing. The truth is, he — The truth is I have no idea what the truth is. Perhaps he gave the picture to the club, and would have been embarrassed to ask for it back, and so pretended that he kept forgetting to ask for it. Anyway, it is preserved forever, the way all lost things are. It is quite safe, from mildew and from the burning pile (*Nov. 19 Virgil Edmonds, George Colby, Roy Miller, Clarence Sylvester, labor for cleaning decedent's residence, $12, $16, $16,* and what a bonfire it must have been).

Whatever the picture was like, it wasn't the picture I remember; I know this much about pictures looked at in childhood. It was in color, perhaps hand-colored but more likely a lithograph. The man on the bed was not being trampled to death but dreaming of the hunt or steeplechase or whatever it was that was going on in the air above his bed. And I am glad I do not have it, because I cannot throw things away, either, and the attic is full of souvenirs of the past from which the magic has long since evaporated. The playhouse, strangely, I still regret. I find myself wondering if it is still there. The executor's report does not list it.

I ASSUMED that Aunty loved me, because of the way her face would light up when she opened the front door and saw me standing there. I know she loved my mother and father. And everybody loved my brother Edward, who was called "Happy." They loved him with a special love because when he was five years old he got his left leg caught in the wheel of a buggy and it had to be cut off above the knee. But they loved him before that, because he was a beautiful little boy, and because he was a handful. Being good, being well-behaved, simply didn't interest him. He did what he felt like doing, and spankings had no effect. Anything you didn't want him to investigate you had to keep locked up or on a shelf too high for him to reach. He gave up cigars when he was five. In the space of five minutes one afternoon, he turned the hose on my mother and my Aunt Edith and my father. The women retired shrieking into the house but my father walked right through the stream of water to the outside faucet and cut it off at the source. My Aunt Annette and Dr. Donald both worshiped the ground my brother walked on. The look in their eyes when they spoke to him or about him, the pleasure they took in telling stories about things he did when he was little, the way they said his name made this quite plain. As it happened, they were also devoted to each other. From the beginning of Time all these friendships were; from before I was born. And they lasted out the lifetime of all the people involved, and most of them lived to be very old. Dr. Donald was a small, compact man, in appearance and in character totally unlike anyone else in Lincoln. He was a horse dealer as well as a veterinary, and at one time he had a livery stable on the east side of the courthouse square. During the First World War, he supplied horses to the American Expeditionary Force. There is a picture of my brother in a pony cart alone and holding the reins. My father was earning a modest salary, and he was not extravagant by nature, and I rather think that the pony cart and the succession of ponies must have come from Dr. Donald's stable and were eventually returned to it. I was under the impression that I, too, would have a pony, when I was old enough. Perhaps I would have, except for the fact that the world was changing. My father sold the carriage horse when I was six years old, and bought a seven-passenger Chalmers. Where the barn had stood there was now a garage. The change from horses to cars cannot have made Dr. Donald any happier than it made me. It didn't affect Aunty Donald one way or the other, because she never went anywhere except to our house, and she didn't come there often. If you wanted to see her, you had to go to her house. She went to my mother's funeral, I have no doubt. And then, just before her own, she went to the hospital and to a nursing home. In between, for forty-one years, she never went out of her front door except to sweep the leaves off the front porch or to open the mailbox, or to pick up the *Evening Star*. The reason she gave for not going anywhere was that it was not suitable for the wife of a horse doctor to accept invitations. The horse doctor was universally loved and admired. People went to him for advice about financial matters and they also went to him when the time had come for them to open their hearts to somebody. In short, it was all in her head.

He lived to be almost ninety, and during his last illness, which went on for months, she took care of him herself. Often she was up all night with him. After he died, the change set in. She looked older, of course, but then she *was* old. In order to sit down, when you went to see her, you had to remove a pile of newspapers or a party hat with tired-looking cloth roses on it or a box of old letters or, sometimes, it was hard to say exactly what — an object. She would be pleased to see you, but you had the feeling as you were leaving that when the front door closed she would pick up the conversation with herself where it had left off and forget that you'd been there until she got a card from you at Christmastime. A cousin of mine who took care of her legal affairs for a time found that if he wanted to get her signature on a paper it was a good idea to telephone first, because she had stopped answering the door. She was deaf, but not that deaf; she just let the doorbell ring. I have tried this myself. In a little while, sometimes in a surprisingly little while, it stops ringing, leaving instead a silence that is full of obscure satisfaction. The same thing was true for the man who came to read the gas and electric-light meter, and for the salesman who was trying to interest her in a life-insurance policy, and for the minister who was concerned about her soul, and for the neighbors who wanted to bring some warm food over to her in a covered dish — they all took to telephoning first. Sometimes she let the telephone ring and ring.

A young woman turned up who had known Dr. Donald. I don't know her name or where she came from, but she was a businesswoman, energetic and capable, and with an understanding of financial affairs that most women did not have, and the patience to explain them. Her first visit was followed by others. It is easy to deduce from what happened what must have led up to it. The pleasure of finding a letter in the mailbox instead of the usual circulars, and of putting fresh sheets on the bed in the spare room because someone was coming on the six-fifteen train. What could it have been like except having the child, the affectionate daughter, that she had wanted and been denied? At last, someone was concerned about her. All sorts of people who actually were concerned about her — her husband's friends, the men at the bank, and the neighbors on Ninth Street — were satisfied that she was being taken care of and that they needn't worry about her anymore. So they weren't worried about her, until somebody gossiping over the back fence said that Mrs. Donald had said that the young woman wanted her to sign over to her everything she owned, with the understanding that she would take care of Mrs. Donald as long as she lived. In a small place, word always gets around — rather quickly, in fact. And small-town people are not in the habit of shrugging off responsibility. Two of Dr. Donald's friends — much younger men than he was, but he had a gift for friendship and it was not limited to his contemporaries — went to see Aunty Donald, and shortly afterward the young woman retired from the field.

Unfortunately, though they could protect her from being taken advantage of, they could not protect her from loneliness. She started feeding a stray cat, and then she let the cat into the house one cold night, and the cat had kittens. The dilemma is classical, and how you solve it depends on what kind of person you are. Between five-fifteen and five-thirty every morning, the back door opened and out came the cats. The smell of coffee drifted through the house, and another day was added to the long chain that went back, past the First World War and the Spanish-American War and the assassinations of Garfield and McKinley, to the eighteen-seventies, when things were so much pleasanter and quieter than they are now. The chain is not as strong as it seems: The beaded portiere fell down. All by itself. For no reason. In the middle of the night, she told me. It couldn't have been caused by a sudden stirring of air, because the windows were closed. When she came downstairs in the morning, the first thing she saw was the empty doorway, and then she saw the glass beads all over the sitting-room floor.

THE rest I know only from hearsay. I never saw her again after this visit. She fell and broke her hip. Out of the kindness of her heart, the woman who lived next door put food out for the cats, but no one expected Aunty Donald to come home from the hospital. She did come home, looking a lot thinner and older, and she went on as before, except that the experience had taught her something. If an accident could befall her, it could befall her cats. She found it harder and harder to let them out into a world full of vicious dogs, poisoned meat, boys with slingshots and BB guns, and people who don't like cats. She put down some shredded newspaper in a roasting pan in the back hall and showed it to the cats, and they quickly got the idea, and after that she didn't have to let them out of the house at all. At her age one doesn't go around opening windows recklessly in all kinds of weather, and so the house — to put it bluntly — smelled. Since she never went out of it, she had no idea how strong the smell really was. Sometimes when she had neglected to put down fresh paper, the cats retired to a corner somewhere, and this added to the unpleasantness. For she was half blind and could not be expected to go around on her hands and knees searching for the source of the smell. And if she had someone in to clean, as people often urged her to do, what was to prevent the cleaning woman from lifting the piano scarf or the corner of the bedroom rug and finding who knows how much money and putting it quietly in her apron pocket? No thank you.

One day she heard the doorbell ring, and this time it didn't stop ringing. It went on and on until finally, against her better judgment, she opened the door. The caller was not Death, but it might just as well have been. My brother is a forceful, decisive man, with a big heart and a loud, cheerful voice and enough courage for three people, but he had to excuse himself after five minutes and go to the front door for a breath of fresh air. By nightfall she was in bed in a nursing home. She lived on a few weeks, expecting that this time, too, she would go home, and instead she died in her sleep.

THE Donalds' house had too many trees around it, and so the grass was thin. The house was heated by hot-air registers, and had its own smell, as all houses did in those days. I don't remember ever having a meal in the dark dining room, though I must have, and I don't remember any flowers, inside or out, unless possibly iris around the foundations. No, I'm sure there weren't any. The flowers were on our side of the fence. Flower beds around a birdbath in the backyard, flower beds all along one side of the house, and vines on trellises — a trumpet vine, clematis, a grape arbor. What I remember cannot be true, if only because the climate of Illinois is not right for it, but the effect is of a full-blown lushness that I associate with Lake Como, which I have never seen, and old-fashioned vaudeville curtains. What can my mother and Aunty Donald have seen in each other? Something; otherwise the names of my older and younger brothers and my name would not have appeared in her will as beneficiaries — one-seventeenth of the estate each: $1,182.55, less Illinois inheritance tax amounting to $108.72. Or about twice her annual income. How did she live in the nineteen-fifties on $55 a month? On air; she must have subsisted on air and old memories and fear — the fear of something happening to her cats.

She did not ever say that she preferred me to my older brother, but when I was a child and cared one way or the other, I used to think that she would not have said so often that she carried me on a pillow if she hadn't meant that my brother was Dr. Donald's favorite and I was hers. I understood the principle of equity, even though I had not yet encountered the word. I know now that she loved my brother the way everyone else did — because of the terrible thing that had happened to him, and because of his pride, which kept him from feeling sorry for himself. And because he was so wicked when he was little, and so bold. How their faces shone with amusement when someone told the story of the hose, or how, totally unafraid, he said to the gypsy, "Mr. Gypsy, what have you got in your *bag*?"

Aunty Donald would not have let anyone but my brother remove her from her house to that nursing home, or have believed anyone else who told her, as he did, that it was only for a week or so. She believed him because he had had his leg cut off when he was five years old and still did everything that other boys could do. To see Dr. Donald with him when my brother was a grown man was to see, unforgettably, the image of love. We — my brother and his wife and I — went to the races with him in Chicago. Dr. Donald didn't touch my brother, but his hands fluttered around him. The expression on the old man's face was of someone looking into the sun.

. . .

THE balance transferred from the conservator's account to the executor's account was $2,073.04. In Aunty's bank account: $82.55. Half a year's interest on government bonds: $300. The rent from the house in Dover. On October 24th, the executor deposited the first collection of money found in the house: $293 in bills and $51.40 in coins. On November 3rd: $325 in gold pieces, which should have been turned in thirty years before. Thirty years before, Aunty was in her late fifties, and voted the straight Republican ticket, if she voted at all. She was, in any case, strong-minded. She did as she pleased, without regard for fiscal policies. On May 4th, these items: Proceeds from the sale of old car: $25, the standard price for junk. (I didn't know they had a car. I thought of Dr. Donald as loyal exclusively to horses.) A flower urn brought $15, which means that some woman in Lincoln had had her eye on it. $18 in gold, and $12.45 in cash. On June 29th, somebody made a down payment of $500 on the house on Ninth Street, the total sale price being $7,000. A big house for that, but it undoubtedly was run down. On August 7th: *liquidating dividend from German-American National Bank Stock owned by T. A. Donald,* but no mention of the stock, and the bank hasn't been called that since shortly after the sinking of the *Lusitania.* An uncashed dividend check turned up somewhere, in a book or in a box of old letters or God knows where. And then, oddly, jewelry not bequeathed in her will. A diamond ring: $175. An amethyst ring with a small pearl: $20. A small pocket watch: $5 (meaning it wouldn't run). A pearl and rhinestone (!) ring: $3. A small locket on a chain (which I have a feeling I remember, the only jewelry I remember her wearing, but perhaps this is imagination). A diamond ring: $150, and a dinner ring with small diamonds: $200. A down payment of $250 on the house in Dover. Proceeds from the sale of cufflinks, tiepins, collar buttons, etc.: $10. An imitation ruby ring: $7. All this in January and February. In March, a pin, another watch, and a ring: $25. They must have turned up in some hiding place, though the house had been cleaned, by four men, several months before. And probably these items were not mentioned in the will because Aunty had forgotten she had them.

The disbursements are less eccentric. It took $817.21 (the Abraham Lincoln Memorial Hospital, St. Joseph's Nursing Home) to help her out of this life. There is a charge for sewerage-system service — stopped-up drain or sink or toilet. And Ernest J. Gottlieb was paid $12 for opening a safe in the basement. Some of the money was probably there; or the jewelry. Or the safe could have been empty. Anything is possible. The spray of flowers for her own casket cost $34, and the funeral expenses were $1,470, so she was buried within the circumference of the middle class. She died in June, and the yard was mowed all through July, August, and September, and the water and gas were not turned off until the following February. The doctor bills were $150.50. In Lincoln, doctors still dispensed medicine. Apparently she had stopped taking the evening paper; there is no item for the paper boy. But from time to time during the settling of the estate, notices were run in the Lincoln *Evening Star* and the Dover *Times*. Carl Simmons was paid $3 for painting a "For Sale" sign. There is no telephone bill. In April the yard was raked, the porch and the windows were repaired. There are two items for real-estate taxes. The First Presbyterian Church received $500, according to the fifteenth clause of the will, and various sums of money were paid out for the recording of affidavits and for appraisals, broker's and auctioneer's commissions, and court costs. The executor's commission was $1,500, the attorney's fee $2,500.

In June the yard was mowed again, and on August 8th the house passed into the hands of somebody else and was no longer Aunty Donald's. The three knights that for so long rode up to that faded castle have no doubt been covered over. There is no mention in the final report of the peacock feathers or the piano that was never tuned and never played on. My cousin told me that the contents of the house were sold intact to someone from out of town, for $2,000; that the buyer wanted the clothes for theatrical purposes, and also thought they might be of interest to museums and historical societies. It was all carted off to a warehouse somewhere until he had a chance to go over everything and see what was there. It would have been a pleasure to go through Aunty Donald's things, up to a point, and after that probably nauseating. This is the past unillumined by memory or love. The sediment of days, what covered Troy and finally would have covered her if my brother hadn't come and taken her away.

Haller's Second Home

THE doorman, the two elevator men in the lobby all said "Good evening, Mr. Haller" to him and when he stepped off at the fourth floor he didn't ring the bell of the apartment directly in front of the elevator shaft but merely transferred the package he was carrying from his right arm to his left, opened the door, and walked in. A large grey cat was waiting just inside. "Well?" Haller said to it and the cat turned away in disappointment. There was only one human being the cat cared about and it was not Haller. He saw that the lights were on in the living room, but it was always empty at this time of evening. He put his hat and gloves on the front-hall table and, still wearing his raincoat, went in search of whoever he could find.

He had come here for the first time on a winter afternoon, when he was twenty-two years old. With a girl. Somebody else's girl, whom Mrs. Mendelsohn embraced and welcomed into the family. The girl was marrying Mrs. Mendelsohn's nephew, Dick Shields, who was Haller's best friend in high school in Chicago and on into college. And she and Haller were friends also. And she had asked him to come with her because he happened to be in New York—he had come down from Cambridge to go to the opera—and she was nervous about meeting these people who were about to become her relatives. The whole future course of her marriage and of her life might be affected favorably or unfavorably. And then what did she do but explain to them, before she had her coat off, that if she hadn't been marrying Dick she would have been marrying Haller. No one took this remark seriously, not even Haller. All in the world he wanted, behind those big horn-rimmed glasses, was to be loved, but he had his hands full with the Harvard Graduate School, and a wife would have been more than he could manage.

That first time, he rang the bell politely and, when the girl looked at herself in the round mirror of her compact, said, "Stop fussing. You look fine. You look like the Queen of the May." "I don't feel like the Queen of the May," she said, and they heard footsteps approaching and a woman's high, clear, beautiful voice finishing a remark that was addressed to someone in the apartment. Haller thought he was a spectator sitting on the sidelines, but in fact he was about to acquire a second home. This was eleven years ago: the winter of 1930–31. He was now thirty-three years old and still unmarried.

East Eighty-fourth Street was not noisy then, any more than it is now, and as always in New York a great deal depends on what floor you are on. The Mendelsohns' apartment was three stories above the street. Taxi horns, Department of Sanitation trucks, the air brakes of the Lexington Avenue buses—all such shattering sounds seemed to avoid the fourth floor and to choose a higher or lower level of the air to explode in. Even with the windows open, the Mendelsohns' living room was quiet. It was also rather dark in the daytime. Long folds of heavy red draperies shut out a good deal of the light that came from two big windows, and the glass curtains filtered out some more. These were never pulled back, and you had to part them if you wanted to see the brownstones across the way or the street below. It was hard to say whether the room was furnished with very bad taste or no taste at all. With time Haller had grown accustomed to the too bright reds and blues in the big Saruk rug, the queer statuary, the not quite comfortable and in some cases too ornate and in other cases downright rickety furniture. Though he was an aesthetic snob, there was nothing he would have changed. Not even a bronze nymph and satyr that would have been perfectly at home in the window of a Third Avenue thrift shop. What is a feeling for interior decoration compared to a front door that is never locked, day or night?

Through curtained French doors he saw a large female figure moving about the dining-room table and, being nearsighted, thought it was the Mendelsohns' cook. It turned out to be Mrs. Mendelsohn herself. "Hello, Haller darling," she said, and kissed him.

She was a stately woman, with blue eyes and black hair and a fine complexion. She was half Irish and a half English—that is, her grandparents were. She favored the Irish side. The small, oval, tinted photograph of her on the living-room table, taken when she was nineteen, suggested that she had always been beautiful and that the beauty had been improved rather than blurred by the years. The blue eyes were still clear, the black hair had becoming lines of grey in it. She flirted with her husband. Her children admired her appearance, made fun of her conversation, and were careful not to bring down on themselves the full force of her explosive character. Haller had the feeling that her kindness toward him was largely because of his connection with her sister's son. There were flowers on the table — sweet peas — and dubonnet candles in yellow holders, and little arsenic-green crepe-paper baskets filled with nuts. "Looks like a birthday," he said.

"I don't know whether it is or not," Mrs. Mendelsohn said. "I got home late and there were no preparations of any kind. Ab has forbidden Renée to bake a cake, and so I'm just trying to rustle something together before Father comes up and is angry because dinner isn't ready."

"Where'll I put the present?" Haller asked.

"Present?" Mrs. Mendelsohn said. "You dare to give her a present?"

"Certainly. What are birthdays for if not to get presents?"

"Put it on her chair, then," Mrs. Mendelsohn said with a sigh, "and take the consequences."

He did as she suggested and then left the dining room and walked along the hall, looking in one door after another. Renée was in the kitchen. She was a West Indian, from Barbados, and she had only been with the Mendelsohns a few months, but in this short time she had become the family clearinghouse for all secrets and private messages. Nathan was her favorite; he told her things he told no one else, and made her feel very special indeed, and so was slowly pushing her toward the precipice where the rights of the employer and the obligations of the employed give way, in a moment of too great clarity, to the obligations of the employer and the rights of the employed. But while she lasted, and especially in the beginning, she was a delight to everyone but Mrs. Mendelsohn, who did not like her all that much. The Doctor joked with Renée and praised her cooking. "Enjoy yourselves!" she called when Nathan and Leo and Abbie and their friends went out the front door together, on a Saturday afternoon. "We will, we will," they promised.

Haller was tempted to go in and tell her what he had up his sleeve, but her back was turned and she looked busy, so he went on to the boys' room. The light was on in there but it was empty, like the living room. He took his raincoat off and laid it on one of the beds. Then he walked out again, and down the hall to the next door on the right. It was closed. The door of Abbie Mendelsohn's room was always closed — against what went on in the rest of the apartment and what went on in the world. Her

brothers came and went without knocking, and Haller was permitted in
there, and one or two other friends. He knocked lightly, and a voice said,
"Come in."

The light went on as he pushed the door open and he saw that Nathan
was lying on one of the twin beds and Abbie on the other. She sat up and
looked at him. Then her blond head drooped. "Oh God," she said.
"There's no use trying to sleep. How are you, Haller, dear?"

"I'm fine. Happy birthday."

"Happy what?" she said, sinking back on the bed.

"Would you like me to go someplace else?"

"Don't pay any attention to her," Nathan said. "She's just being
difficult."

"I'm so tired my teeth water," Abbie said.

"Are you sure?" Haller asked. "I don't see how that's possible."

"It's what it feels like. I haven't slept for a week, on account of the
kittens. They crawl on my face all night long. Be careful you don't step
on them."

Haller made his way cautiously to the nearest chair and sat down. The
Victorian sofa and chairs had belonged to the great-aunt for whom Abbie
was named, and they gave this room an entirely different quality from
the family living room. There were flower prints on the walls, the window
looked out on a court, and the room was quiet as a tomb. "When are you
going to start giving them away?" he asked.

"We gave one of them away this afternoon," Nathan said. "To a
patient of Father's."

Officially the Mendelsohns had two cats — the altered male that was
waiting at the door and a recently acquired alley cat whose standing in
the family was doubtful. Dr. Mendelsohn did not like cats of any description and was convinced that they contributed to his asthma. "Two cats
are one more than there is room for in a city apartment," he announced
alarmingly from behind the *Evening Sun*, but so far he had done nothing
about it.

The cat yowled up at Nathan from the courtyard one snowy night, and
he went down in his bathrobe and slippers and rescued her. A month
later she had a litter of four, behind the closed door of Abbie's room, and
she was raising them without Dr. Mendelsohn's permission; without, in
fact, his knowing anything about it. She nursed her kittens in a grocery
carton on the floor between the twin beds, and now that they were able
to stagger around on their own feet an opening had been cut in the side

of the box for them to go in and out by. When they were not pushing at the mother cat's belly they clawed their way up the bedspreads, or collected in all but invisible groups on the mulberry-colored carpet, or went exploring. Except one, which Nathan now brought forth from the carton. This kitten could move, and it was apparently not in pain, but when he put his hand under it and tried to make it stand, the kitten collapsed and lay limp and miserable on the bedspread.

"The girl we gave the other kitten to is an orphan," he said. "First her mother died, and then she went to live with her grandfather and grandmother and *they* died."

"What a sad story," said Haller. "Do you believe it?"

Nathan was dark — dark hair, dark eyes, dark skin — and very handsome. Originally he had his mother's beautiful nose, but when he was a small child a dog bit him. He was playing with the dog, and teasing it, and it bit him on the nose. He had to have several stitches in it, and his nose was not the same shape afterward. His brother and sister mourned over this accident, as if it had been some tragic flaw in his destiny. He himself was resigned to his loss but did not minimize it.

"She's only eighteen," he said. "And her guardian was with her. A very nice woman. When I told her about the kittens she looked at the girl and said, 'Very well, we'll take the sick one.' But they took the one with the black mustache, instead. The one that looked like Hitler." He yawned.

"What you need is a change," Haller said, hanging over the arm of his chair to watch the kittens on the rug. "Why don't we all drive south into the spring. We could be as far south as Richmond, Virginia, the first night. We could see the tulips on the White House lawn."

"How do you know," Nathan asked, "how do you know there will be tulips on the White House lawn?"

"There will be something. If not tulips then there will be dandelions. When Moris Burge and I drove to Santa Fe last year we spent the first night in a wonderful tourist home in Richmond — "

"That Moris Burge," Nathan said.

" — and when we woke up the next morning we heard a cardinal singing in the backyard, and the lilacs were all in bloom. I'm not exaggerating. Why don't we drive south, the three of us, and go straight through the spring? We'll see iris in Alexandria, and in the southern part of New Jersey there will be pine forests with dogwood — white dogwood — all through them. Or we could go down the Shenandoah Valley and pick violets at Harpers Ferry, like I did when I was seventeen."

"You're such a traveler," Nathan said, but not unkindly.

"The West Indies when I was twenty-three. And Santa Fe, last summer. Where else have I been?"

"Boston."

"But you've all been to Europe."

"With Father."

"What were you doing in Harpers Ferry when you were seventeen?" Abbie asked, from her pillow.

"I went to Washington with a special train, from high school. We saw Mount Vernon, and Annapolis, and Fredericksburg, and Gettysburg. We saw George Washington's false teeth. And we had our picture taken in front of the Capitol Building. It was one of those moving cameras, on a track, and I was standing at one end of the group, and the boy who was standing next to me said, 'Come on!' and ran around in back, so I did too. We got in the picture twice. I had on an ice-cream suit. Twins is what it looked like. And perfectly plausible, except that I had one leg in the air because I'd just arrived. The next picture, everybody tried it and they had to give the whole thing up."

"Do you still have that picture?" Nathan asked. "I'd like to see it. I'd like to see what you'd be like if you were twins."

"It's somewhere. There isn't anything to look at in Gettysburg but wheat fields, but Harpers Ferry is remarkable. Three states meet there."

"Which three?" Nathan asked skeptically.

"West Virginia, Virginia, and I forget what the other is. But anyway, there are three states right in front of you—three mountains, green all the way to the top, with rivers between them, and the town is on a hill, and it's very old, and the streets are winding, and when I was seventeen I got off the train and ran all through the town and came back and picked violets by the tracks before the train started again. All this was in April."

"Haller, there's no such place, but I love you just the same." Abbie threw the quilt aside and sat up stretching.

"You haven't heard anything?" Nathan said. "No letter, I mean?"

"No," Haller said.

FOR three weeks, one of the people who was often in this unnaturally quiet room had been missing from it. A rubber stamp descending on a printed form separated Francis Whitehead from his civilian status. It was a grey day, and there was some snow mixed with rain. Governors Island offered a foretaste of things to come. Though now and then someone was sent back, the lines mostly moved one way. He was set down in a muddy Army camp, with a rifle and bayonet to take the place of his Leica and light meter, a footlocker for his earthly possessions — which, as it happened, he was indifferent to — and a serial number. He didn't really need a number to distinguish him from other soldiers, because he was the only one who could tell, in the dark, that the crease in the middle of the sheet he was lying on was not in the exact center of the bed.

There had been two letters from him since he went in the Army and they didn't say anything. He was not a letter writer, it seemed. He wrote notes, instead — on the backs of envelopes or other people's letters to him or laundry lists or old bank deposit slips. Not because of anything the messages were in themselves but because of something elusive in his character that made any clue seem interesting, Haller could never bear to throw these scraps of paper away. They drifted through his socks and handkerchiefs, in the top dresser drawer: *Why are you never home? If you want to lead a double life it's all right with me but I think you ought to live on the second floor. I'm tired of climbing these stairs. F. . . .* Or, *That new sport jacket is a mistake, you should have asked me to come with you. I can't make it tonight. What about Thursday? F. . . .* Or, *You are so pompous. F.*

When Francis Whitehead laughed his eyes filmed over with tears, but he kept his mouth closed, to cover his receding gums. This condition was apparent to his dentist and to him and to no one else. Like everything about him, his tight-lipped smile was charming. Before he went into the Army he was on the fringe of the world of fashion photography. Before that, he had been in the theater. His looks, the way he wore his clothes, his jokes, his talent for choosing just the present that would please above all other presents, his tormented smile enslaved people, but he himself did not quite know what he wanted, and so there was little prospect of his getting it.

Haller had written to remind him that today was Abbie's birthday. He didn't say — he didn't need to say — that if Francis could manage to call up from a pay station somewhere it would give her more pleasure than any present possibly could.

"Dinner's ready, children," Mrs. Mendelsohn said through the closed door. Abbie and Nathan scattered to wash. When Haller walked into the dining room, Dr. Mendelsohn was sitting down at the head of the table.

"Good evening, Haller," he said kindly and whisked his napkin into his lap. Mrs. Mendelsohn lit the candles, while Haller stood behind her chair. The others appeared one by one during the soup course. First Nathan. Then Leo, who had stayed at school for a meeting of the Geographical Society. He came into the dining room quietly, a tall thin youngster with the grey cat balancing serenely on his shoulders. Abbie was the last to turn up. She looked at the dining table and then said, "Mother, how could you?" but she was not really angry. The moroseness was overdone, and deliberately comic. It was true that she hadn't wanted any birthday celebration, but equally true that she was trying hard to grow up. And part of growing up was learning to accept the way her mother and father were, and not to hold it against them that they weren't the things she used to think they ought to be. If her mother wanted to decorate the table and bring home a birthday cake, it surely was possible to treat this as natural and not a crime, though silly.

She saw the package on her chair and said, "What's this?"

"It looks rather like a birthday present," Haller said.

"Do you mind if I don't open it until after dinner?" she said, and put the package on a chair at the far end of the room. And so indicated — rather too subtly for the people present to understand, but the guppies in the fish tank got it and so did the still life over the sideboard — that Haller had done something to her that, even if it was a long time ago, she had no intention ever of forgiving, though from time to time she forgot about it and from time to time she remembered and reminded him of it, and still he didn't understand. There was very little, as she observed to Nathan, that Haller did understand.

Haller didn't mind that his present had ended up in the far corner of the room. That is, he pretended that this, too, was funny and partially succeeded in believing that it was.

When Dr. Mendelsohn talked at the dinner table it was usually to one person only. Tonight it was Haller. He was telling Haller about one of his patients. "She's neurotic and self-pitying, you know what I mean? I gave the same treatment to somebody else that same afternoon and the whole thing was over in half an hour and the woman went home. But this patient was screaming before I ever got her on the table. Finally I had to say to her, 'Mrs. Weinstock,' I said, 'if you don't stop thrashing around, the instrument will pierce your bladder and you'll get peritonitis and die!' "

"Did she quiet down after that?" Haller asked politely.

"Yes, but she wouldn't go home. It was one-thirty and I was supposed to be at the hospital, so I . . ."

Haller didn't feel it was respectful to eat while Dr. Mendelsohn was addressing him, and his plate sat untouched in front of him. He compromised, however, by snitching cashew nuts out of the little crepe-paper basket. When he had eaten all there were, the two boys passed their paper cups around the table and Abbie slyly emptied them and finally her own into Haller's basket. He ate them all absentmindedly, and when Dr. Mendelsohn finished his story and took up his knife and fork, Haller saw that the crepe-paper basket at his place was empty and said indignantly, "Somebody's been stealing my cashew nuts!"

The boys leaned against each other with laughter.

"Mr. Napier called today, Father," Mrs. Mendelsohn said, and the Doctor quickly and furtively raised his napkin and wiped away the particle of food that was clinging to his mouth.

He had his office on the ground floor of the apartment building, and the waiting room, with dark-green walls and uncomfortable, turn-of-the-century oak furniture and dog-eared back numbers of *Time* and *Field and Stream* and the *Saturday Evening Post*, was always full. His working day began at seven and he had every excuse to be tired and cross by six-thirty at night. Actually, the practice of medicine was pure pleasure to him; it was his family, not his patients, that made him irritable. He had grown up on the Lower East Side, in extreme poverty — the oldest son of an immigrant couple who did not speak English. When there was nothing to eat he went through the neighborhood searching for food in the refuse cans. Certain storekeepers knew this and took to leaving something for him. Working at odd jobs before and after school, he earned what money a boy could. He got conspicuously high marks in school, and he cured himself of a speech impediment by imitating Demosthenes — that is to say, he took the Coney Island Express to the end of the line and walked up and down the deserted beach reciting the Gettysburg Address with pebbles in his mouth. The rabbi had no fault to find with him, and neither did his father and mother. But he had no childhood whatever. When his favorite sister died of tuberculosis, the direction of his future was fixed. By a long unbroken chain of miracles he put himself through medical school. And how, lacking the hardships that had shaped his character, his children's characters were to be shaped and made firm was a riddle he could not find the answer to. Abbie had an excellent mind, and she was an affectionate daughter, but she did not know how to cook and keep house and sew, the way his sisters had at her age. When she was just out of college she and a dancer in a Broadway musical stepped into a taxi and got out at the Municipal Building and went inside, to the chapel on the first floor. The marriage lasted ten days. All she ever said, in explanation, was that they couldn't talk to each other. She was now working in a public-relations firm. Nathan didn't finish school. He had a job but could not have lived on his salary. His father considered him immature for his age, and lazy. And Leo had a preference for low company. Loudmouthed roughnecks, and their vulgar girls. When Dr. Mendelsohn looked around the dinner table a spasm of irritation would come over him — at the thought of what his children might be making of themselves and all too obviously weren't — and he would put his napkin beside his plate and push his chair back and go off and eat by himself at Longchamps.

His children understood how he felt, but at the same time there was very little they could do about it. They couldn't very well go and live on the Lower East Side, in conditions of extreme poverty. No one would have taken them in. Their Hungarian grandparents were dead and their father's brothers and sisters had, through their own efforts and his, all risen in the world. And if Abbie and Nathan and Leo had tried to sleep in an areaway their father would have come and stood over them, impatient and scolding, and made them come home where they belonged.

Dr. Mendelsohn's irritability was, so far as Haller could see, a matter of pride to his family. It gave him an authority that his physical presence alone — he was smaller than his wife — would not have provided, and it made all their lives more interesting. They never hesitated to provoke him, while pretending to go to considerable lengths to avoid this. His explosions were brief and harmless. But Nathan said that his father didn't like Gentiles, and Haller didn't know whether he came under this proscription or not. On the other hand, Dr. Mendelsohn didn't like most Jews either. This much Haller knew: He was a wonderful doctor.

AFTER dinner, Abbie tore the wrapping off her present, which proved to be an album of Sibelius: "Night Ride and Sunrise" and "The Oceanides."

"I bought them on account of the titles," he said.

"The titles are beautiful," Abbie said. "And I'm sure they are too."

"I haven't the faintest idea what they're like," Haller said.

Unfortunately there was no way of finding out. When they went into the living room to play the records, they discovered that the machine wasn't working. It was connected to the amplifier and speaker of the radio, and where there should have been an empty space on the dial, free from broadcasting, three kinds of music were fighting for first place, none of them Sibelius.

Leo explained that it was a tube, and he and Nathan went out to buy a new one. Haller and Abbie sat down together on one of the beds in her room. He was expecting the telephone to ring, and his hand was ready to reach out for it as he watched her worrying over the sick kitten.

"You poor thing," she said, holding the kitten's head against her cheek. "Probably it's nothing but imagination — because he's only been this way since last night — but he seems thinner than the others, and his fur is dry and sickly looking."

"He doesn't look very happy," Haller agreed.

First she tried to make the kitten stand up, and then she took the others away and left the sick kitten with the mother cat. He soon lost interest, and Abbie tried to make him suck and found that it couldn't be done. She felt the kitten's vertebrae thoughtfully, and announced that its back was broken; there was a ridge that was definitely out of place. She made Haller feel it. When he said that if the kitten's back was broken oughtn't they to chloroform it, she decided that its back wasn't broken after all — though it was just possible that somebody had stepped on it. And moved by a sudden inspiration she gave the kitten cod-liver oil out of an eyedropper.

The boys came back with a new tube. When that didn't help, Leo sat down on the floor and began taking the radio apart with a screwdriver. Haller, with an unlit cigarette in his mouth, discovered that he had no matches.

"Leo, do you remember the time you soldered my glasses when they broke?" he asked fondly, going from table to table and not finding what he was looking for.

"Yes, I remember," Leo said.

"And do you remember how much it cost me afterward to have them fixed?" Haller said as he left the room and went down the hall. If he hadn't gone to the kitchen for matches he wouldn't have known about the plate that Renée was keeping warm in the oven. It was eight-thirty by the kitchen clock. Renée was sitting at the kitchen table. Her normally kinky hair was shining with pomade and hanging in straight bangs about her face. He saw the plate in the oven and said, "Who's *that* for?" She giggled mysteriously, and he opened his eyes wide in astonishment. "Tonight?" he exclaimed, and at that moment the doorbell rang.

By the time Haller got to the front hall, Francis Whitehead was inside, and Abbie and Nathan and Leo each had a piece of him, and were trying to go off somewhere with it. He put his little zipper bag down and then grinned at them. "A soldier," he said. And what a soldier. "Everything I've got on is several sizes too large for me," he said. "And I've lost ten pounds." With his hair clipped close to his skull he looked mistreated and ill. Haller was shocked.

"I've got till Tuesday," Francis said, rocking happily on his heels. "I've got thirty-six and a half more hours to do with exactly as I like. What do you think of my World War One pants?"

"They're lovely," Abbie said.

"Did you know he was coming?" Nathan and Leo were asking each other. "Did *you* know, Haller?"

"No," Haller said. "Renée is the only one who knew about it. All I was hoping for was that he'd call up."

"I called yesterday morning," Francis explained. "I picked a time when I was sure you'd all be out."

"That Renée," Abbie said, and began pulling him away from the others. "Have you eaten?"

Francis shook his head.

"Renée's got the whole dinner saved for you," Haller said.

Pushing and bumping into each other, they followed Francis Whitehead through the hall and the serving pantry into the kitchen. At the sight of them, the black woman turned her head away and laughed.

"Renée, you're wonderful!" Francis said, and threw his arms around her and hugged her. Then he sat down at the place she had just now set for him at the kitchen table. Abbie and Nathan drew up a stool and both of them perched on it, unsteadily. Leo sat on the kitchen stepladder. Haller paced back and forth, unable to settle anywhere, and asked questions that nobody paid any attention to. Francis looked at his plate heaped with chicken and creamed potatoes and asparagus and said, "I haven't seen food like this in so long. In the Army you never get a whole any-thing—just pieces of something. I dream about having a whole lamb chop." They were waiting to see him raise his fork to his mouth and he did, but then he put it down, with the food still on it. "I must go speak to your mother," he said, and got up and left the kitchen.

"How like him," Haller said, "to leave us all sitting here admiring his empty chair!"

. . .

WHEN they couldn't get Francis to eat any more they tried to put him to bed but he curled up on the sofa in Abbie's room, with the other boys sitting on the floor as close to him as they could get, and he talked till one o'clock in the morning. He began with the group that had left Grand Central Station together. He described their clothes, and what they said, and how they acted. How the boy from Brooklyn who sat opposite him on the train nearly drove him crazy by reading a furniture ad in the *Daily News* over and over. He told them about the induction center: about the psychological examination, which consisted of hitting you on the kneecap and asking, "Any nervous disorders in your family, buddy?"; about the medical examination, which was perfunctory but nevertheless took hours, in a place so jammed with naked inductees that there was nowhere to stand without touching somebody. And how, one by one and still naked, they were started down the length of a long room while voices called out the sizes of shoes, socks, shorts, shirts, trousers, and they found themselves at the other end, fully clothed and outfitted in four minutes.

He didn't really mind being continually pushed and shoved, herded from place to place, and sworn at. After all, it was the Army. It was not a school picnic. What he couldn't stand, as the day wore on, was the misery that he saw everywhere he looked. A great many of the men were younger than he was, and they became so worn out finally that they lost all hope and leaned against the wall in twos and threes, with the tears streaming down their faces. Eventually, he worked himself into such a fury that he began to shake all over, and a tough Irish sergeant came up to him and put both arms around him and said, "Wait a minute, buddy. You're all right. Take it easy, why don't you?" in the kindest voice Francis had ever heard in his life.

But the strangest thing was the continual pairing off, all day long — on the train, at the induction center, at the camp, where, long after midnight, you found yourself still instinctively looking around for somebody to cling to, and look after. Somebody you'd never laid eyes on before that day became, for two hours, closer than any friend you'd ever had. When you were separated, your whole concern was for him — for what might be happening to him. While you had one person to look after, among the crowd, you were not totally lost yourself. When the two of you were separated for good, you looked around and there was someone in obvious desperation, and so the whole thing happened all over again.

When they arrived in camp, somebody talked back to a sergeant who was not Irish, and he said, "All right, you sons of bitches, you can just wait." And they did, from midnight until one-thirty, when they were marched two miles in what proved to be the wrong direction and three miles back, before they sat down, at 2:15 a.m., in a mess hall, before a plate of food they couldn't look at, let alone eat. All through the next day it continued – the feeling that each thing was a little more than you could stand. And the pairing off. But the next day was better. And the third day they began to relax and settle into their ordinary selves. . . .

Of the three boys sitting on the floor in front of Francis Whitehead, listening to him gravely, Leo was still too young for military service, Nathan had drawn a high number and didn't expect to be called before September or October, and Haller was 4-F because of his bad eyes. Most of the things Francis told them they knew already, from what they had read in newspapers and magazines. It was his voice that made the experience real to them. The voice of the survivor. And here and there a detail that they couldn't have imagined. And because it happened to Francis, whom all three of them loved.

When Haller went home, Nathan and Leo put up the overflow cot in their room, and Abbie brought sheets from the linen closet, and a blanket and pillow from the other bed in her room. The boys knocked on the wall when they were in bed, and she came back to say good night. Nathan was sleeping on the cot, Francis was in Nathan's bed, and Leo in his own. After she had turned out the light and gone back to her own room she could hear them talking together, through the wall. The talking stopped while she was brushing her hair, and then there was no sound but Francis's coughing.

She was almost asleep when the kitten commenced complaining from the box on the floor. She had entirely forgotten about it in the excitement of Francis's homecoming. "A little chloroform for you, my pet," she said, "first thing in the morning," and rolled over on her back. I'm twenty-five, she thought. Finally. Thanks to one thing and another, including Haller and his "Oceanides."

Then she thought about Haller – about her grievance against him, which was that he went on courting her year after year, as if faithfulness, the *idea* of love, was the answer to everything, and had no instinct that told him when she was willing and when she couldn't bear to have him touch her. Why, when he was so intelligent, was he also so stupid – for she did like him, and sometimes even felt that she could love him.

As for Francis, it was as Haller had said. Nothing that happens over and over is pure accident; and what they (and God knows how many other people) were faced with, at the critical moment, was his empty chair.

Out of habit, her mother referred to them as "the children," and it was only too true. She and Nathan and Leo. And Haller. *And* Francis. They were all five aiming the croquet ball anywhere but at the wicket, and playing the darling game of being not quite old enough to button their overcoats and find their mittens. But for how long? *For ever*, the curtain said, blowing in from the open window. But what did the curtain know about it?

The kitten was quiet, but the coughing continued on the other side of the wall. Listening in the dark, she decided that Francis didn't have enough covers on. If he had another blanket, he'd stop coughing and go to sleep. She could not get to the extra covers without disturbing her mother and father, and so she took the blanket from her own bed, slipped a wrapper on, and went into the boys' room. All three of them were asleep, but Francis woke up when she put the blanket over him. He didn't seem to know where he was at first, and then she gathered from his sleepy mumbling that he didn't want her to go away. When she sat down, he wormed around in the bed until his thighs were against her back and his forehead touched her knee. There he stayed, without moving, without any pressure coming from his body at all. This time it was not the empty chair but a drowned man washed up against a rock in the sea.

The Gardens
of Mont-Saint-Michel

THE elephantine Volkswagen bus didn't belong to the French landscape. Compared to the Peugeots and Renaults and Citroëns that overtook it so casually, it seemed an oddity. So was the family riding in it. When they went through towns people turned and stared, but nothing smaller would have held the five of them and their luggage, and the middle-aged American who was driving was not happy at the wheel of any automobile. This particular automobile he loathed. There was no room beyond the clutch pedal. To push it down to the floor he had to turn his foot sidewise, and his knee ached all day long from this unnatural position. "Have I got enough room on my right?" he asked continually, though he had been driving the Volkswagen for two weeks now. "Oh God!" he would exclaim. "There's a man on a bicycle." For he was suffering from a recurring premonition: *In the narrow street of some village, though he was taking every human precaution, suddenly he heard a hideous crunch under the right rear wheel. He stopped the car and with a sinking heart got out and made himself look at the twisted bicycle frame and the body lying on the cobblestones.* . . . A dozen times a day John Reynolds could feel his face responding to the emotions of this disaster, which he was convinced was actually going to happen. It was only a matter of when. And where. Sometimes the gendarmes came and took him away, and at other times he managed to extricate himself by thinking of something else. At odds with all this, making his life bearable, was another scene — the moment in the airport at Dinard when he would turn the keys over to the man from the car-rental agency and be free of this particular nightmare forever.

Dorothy Reynolds, sitting on the front seat beside her husband, loved the car because she could see out of it in all directions. Right this minute she asked for nothing more than to be driving through the French countryside. Her worries, which were real and not, like his, imaginary, had been left behind, on the other side of the Atlantic Ocean. She could only vaguely remember what they were.

"In France," she said, "nothing is really ugly, because everything is so bare."

"In some ways I like England better," he said.

"It's more picturesque, but it isn't as beautiful. Look at that grey hill town with those dark clouds towering above it," she said, turning around to the two older girls in the seat directly behind her. And then silently scolded herself, because she was resolved not to say "Look!" all the time but to let the children use their own eyes to find what pleased them. The trouble was, their eyes did not see what hers did, or, it often seemed, anything at all.

This was not, strictly speaking, true. Reynolds's niece, Linda Porter, had 20/20 vision, but instead of scattering her attention on the landscape she saved it for what she had heard about — the Eiffel Tower, for example — and for the mirror when she was dressing. She was not vain, and neither was she interested in arousing the interest of any actual boy, though boys and men looked at her wherever she went. Her ash-blond hair had been washed and set the night before, her cuticles were flawless, her rose-pink nail polish was without a scratch, her skirt was arranged under her delightful young bottom in such a way that it would not wrinkle, her hand satchel was crammed with indispensable cosmetics, her charm bracelet was the equal of that of any of her contemporaries, but she was feeling forlorn. She had not wanted to leave the hotel in Concarneau, which was right on the water, and she could swim and then lie in the sun, when there was any, and she had considered the possibility of getting a job as a waitress so she could spend the rest of her life there, only her father would never let her do it. She had also considered whether or not she was in love with the waiter in charge of their table in the dining room, who was young and good-looking and from Marseilles; when a leaf of lettuce leaped out of the salad bowl, he said "*Zut!*" and kicked it under the table. He asked her to play tennis with him, but unfortunately she hadn't brought her own racquet and he didn't have an extra one. Also, it turned out he was married.

How strange that she should be sitting side by side with someone for whom mirrors did not reflect anything whatever. Alison Reynolds, who was eleven and a half, considered the hours when she was not reading largely wasted. "If Dantès has had lunch," she once confided to her father, "then I have had lunch. Otherwise I don't know whether I've eaten or not." With a note of sadness in her voice, because no matter how vivid and all-consuming the book was, or how long, sooner or later she finished it, and was stranded once more in ordinariness until she had started another. She couldn't read in the car because it made her feel queer. She was very nearsighted, and by the time she had found her glasses and put them on, the blur her mother and father wanted her to look at had been left behind. All châteaux interested her, and anything that had anything to do with Jeanne d'Arc, or with Marie Antoinette. Or Marguerite de Valois. Or Louise de La Vallière.

Because her mind and her cousin's were so differently occupied, they were able to let one another alone, except for some mild offensive and defensive belittling now and then, but Alison and her younger sister had to ride in separate seats or they quarreled. Trip was lying stretched out, unable to see anything but the car roof and hating every minute of the drive from Fougères, where they had spent the night. It didn't take much to make her happy — a stray dog or a cat, or a monkey chained to a post in a farmyard, or an old white horse in a pasture — but while they were driving she existed in a vacuum and exerted a monumental patience. At any moment she might have to sit up and put her head out of the car window and be sick.

They passed through Antrain without running over anybody on a bicycle, and shortly afterward something happened that made them all more cheerful. Another salmon-and-cream-colored Volkswagen bus, the first they had seen, drew up behind them and started to pass. In it were a man and a woman and two children and a great deal of luggage. The children waved to them from the rear window as the other Volkswagen sped on.

"Americans," Dorothy Reynolds said.

"And probably on their way to Mont-Saint-Michel," Reynolds said. "Wouldn't you know." They were no longer unique.

He saw a sign on their side of the road. She also noticed it, and they smiled at each other with their eyes, in the rearview mirror.

Eighteen years ago, they had arrived in Pontorson from Cherbourg, by train, by a series of trains, at five o'clock in the afternoon. They had a reservation at a hotel in Mont-Saint-Michel, but they had got up at daybreak and were too tired to go on, so they spent the night here in what the *Michelin* described as an "*hôtel simple, mais confortable,*" with "*une bonne table dans la localité.*" It was simple and bare and rather dark inside, and it smelled of roasting coffee beans. It was also very old; their guide-book said it had been the manor of the counts of Montgomery, though there was nothing about it now to indicate this. Their room was on the second floor and it was enormous. So was the bathroom. There was hot water. They had a bath, and then they came downstairs and had an apéritif sitting under a striped umbrella in front of the hotel. He remem-bered that there was a freshly painted wooden fence with flower boxes on it that separated the table from the street. What was in the flower boxes? Striped petunias? Geraniums? He did not remember, but there were heavenly blue morning glories climbing on strings beside the front door. Their dinner was too good to be true, and they drank a bottle of wine with it, and stumbled up the stairs to their room, and in the profound quiet got into the big double bed and slept like children. So long ago. And so uncritical they were. All open to delight.

In the morning they both woke at the same instant and sat up and looked out of the window. It was market day and the street in front of the hotel was full of people. The women wore long shapeless black cotton dresses and no makeup on their plain country faces. The men wore blue smocks, like the illustrations of Boutet de Monvel. And everybody was carrying long thin loaves of fresh bread. A man with a vegetable stand was yelling at the top of his lungs about his green beans. They saw an old woman leading a cow. And chickens and geese, and little black-and-white goats, and lots of bicycles, but no cars. It was right after the war, and gasoline was rationed, but it seemed more as if the automobile hadn't yet been heard of in this part of France.

They were the only guests at the hotel, the only tourists as far as the eye could see. It was the earthly paradise, and they had it all to them-selves. When they came in from cashing a traveler's check or reading the inscriptions on the tombstones in the cemetery, a sliding panel opened in the wall at the foot of the stairs and the cook asked how they enjoyed their walk. The waitress helped them make up their minds what they wanted to eat, and if they had any other problems they went to the concierge with them. The happier they became the happier he was for them, so how could they not love him, or he them? The same with the waitress and the chambermaid and the cook. They went right on drinking too much wine and eating seven-course meals for two more days, and if it hadn't been that they had not seen anything whatever of the rest of France, they might have stayed there, deep in the nineteenth century, forever.

REYNOLDS thought he remembered Pontorson perfectly, but something peculiar goes on in the memory. This experience is lovingly remembered and that one is, to one's everlasting shame, forgotten. Of the remembered experience a very great deal drops out, drops away, leaving only what is convenient, or what is emotionally useful, and this simplified version takes up much more room than it has any right to. The village of Pontorson in 1948 was larger than John Reynolds remembered it as being, but after eighteen years it was not even a village any longer; it was now a small town, thriving and prosperous, and one street looked so much like another that he had to stop in the middle of a busy intersection and ask a traffic policeman the way to the hotel they had been so happy in.

It was still there, but he wouldn't have recognized it without the sign. The fence was gone, and so were the morning glories twisting around their white strings, and the striped umbrellas. The sidewalk came right up to the door of the hotel, and it would not have been safe to drive a cow down the street it was situated on.

"It's all so changed," he said. "But flourishing, wouldn't you say? Would you like to go in and have a look around?"

"No," Dorothy said.

"They might remember us."

"It isn't likely the staff would be the same after all this time."

Somewhere deep inside he was surprised. He had expected everybody in France to stand right where they were (one, two, three, four, five, six, seven, eight, nine, *stillpost*) until he got back.

"I never thought about it before," he said, "but except for the cook there was nobody who was much older than we were. . . . So kind they all were. But there was also something sad about them. The war, I guess. Also, there's no place to park. Too bad." He drove on slowly, still looking.

"What's too bad?" Alison asked.

"Nothing," Dorothy said. "Your father doesn't like change."

"Do you?"

"Not particularly. But if you are going to live in the modern world — "

Alison stopped listening. Her mother could live in the modern world if she wanted to, but she had no intention of joining her there.

They circled around, and found the sign that said MONT-SAINT-MICHEL, and headed due north. In 1948 their friend the concierge, having found an aged taxi for them, stood in the doorway waving good-bye. Nine kilometers and not another car on the road the whole ride. Ancient farmhouses such as they had seen from the train window they could observe from close up: the weathered tile roofs, the pink rose cascading from its trellis, the stone watering trough for the animals; the beautiful man-made, almost mathematical orderliness of the woodpile, the vegetable garden, and the orchard. Suddenly they saw, glimmering in the distance, the abbey on its rock, with the pointed spire indicating the precise direction of a heaven nobody believed in anymore. The taxi driver said, "Le Mont-Saint-Michel," and they looked at each other and shook their heads. For reading about it was one thing and seeing it with their own eyes was another. The airiness, the visionary quality, the way it kept changing right in front of their eyes, as if it were some kind of heavenly vaudeville act.

After the fifth brand-new house, Reynolds said, massaging his knee, "Where are all the old farmhouses?"

"We must have come by a different road," Dorothy said.

"It has to be the same road," he said, and seeing how intently he peered ahead through the windshield she didn't argue. But surely if there were new houses there could be new roads.

Once more the abbey took them by surprise. This time the surprise was due to the fact they were already close upon it. There had been no distant view. New buildings, taller trees, something, had prevented their seeing it until now. The light was of the seacoast, dazzling and severe. Clouds funneled the radiance upward. It seemed that flocks of angels might be released into the sky at any moment.

"There it is!" Dorothy cried. "Look, children!"

Linda added the name Mont-Saint-Michel to the list of places she could tell people she had seen when she got home. Alison put her glasses on and dutifully looked. Mont-Saint-Michel was enough like a castle to strike her as interesting, but what she remembered afterward was not the thing itself but the excitement in her father's and mother's voices. Trip sat up, looked, and sank back again without a word and without the slightest change in her expression.

The abbey was immediately obscured by a big new hotel. Boys in white jackets stood in a line on the left-hand side of the road, and indicated with a gesture of the thumb that the Volkswagen was to swing in here.

"What an insane idea," Reynolds murmured. He had made a reservation at the hotel where they had stayed before, right in the shadow of the abbey.

At the beginning of the causeway, three or four cars were stopped and their occupants had got out with their cameras. He got out too, with the children's Hawkeye, and had to wait several minutes for an unobstructed view. Then he got back in the car and drove the rest of the way.

At the last turn in the road, he exclaimed, "Oh, *no!*" In a huge parking lot to the right of the causeway there were roughly a thousand cars shining in the sunlight. "It's just like the World's Fair," he said. "We'll probably have to stand in line an hour and forty minutes to see the tide come in."

A traffic policeman indicated with a movement of his arm that they were to swing off to the right and down into the parking lot. Reynolds stopped and explained that they were spending the night here and had been told they were to leave the car next to the outer gate. The policeman's arm made exactly the same gesture it had made before.

"He's a big help," Reynolds said as he drove on, and Trip said, "There's a car just like ours."

"Why, so it is," Dorothy said. "It must be the people who passed us."

"And there's another," Trip said.

"Where?" Alison said, and put on her glasses.

They left the luggage in the locked Volkswagen and joined the stream of pilgrims. Reynolds stopped and paid for the parking ticket. Looking back over his shoulder, he saw the sand flats extending out into the bay as far as the eye could see, wet, shining, and with long, thin, bright ribbons of water running through them, just as he remembered. The time before, there were nine sightseeing buses lined up on the causeway, from which he knew before he ever set foot in it, that Mont-Saint-Michel was not going to be the earthly paradise. This time he didn't even bother to count them. Thirty, forty, fifty, what difference did it make. But the little stream that flowed right past the outer gate? *Gone....* Was it perhaps not a stream at all but a ditch with tidal water in it? Anyway, it had been just too wide to jump over, and a big man in a porter's uniform had picked Dorothy up in his arms and, wading through the water, set her down on the other side. Then he came back for Reynolds. There was no indication now that there had ever been a stream here that you had to be carried across as if you were living in the time of Chaucer.

The hotels, restaurants, cafés, Quimper shops, and souvenir shops (the abbey on glass ashtrays, on cheap china, on armbands, on felt pennants;

the abbey in the form of lead paperweights three or four inches high) had survived. The winding street of stairs was noisier, perhaps, and more crowded, but not really any different. The hotel was expecting them. Reynolds left Dorothy and the children in the lobby and went back to the car with a porter, who was five foot three or four at the most and probably not old enough to vote. Sitting on the front seat of the Volkswagen, he indicated the road they were to take out of the big parking lot, up over the causeway and down into the smaller parking lot by the outer gate, where Reynolds had tried to go in the first place. The same policeman waved them on, consistency being not one of the things the French are nervous about. With the help of leather straps the porter draped the big suitcases and then the smaller ones here and there around his person, and would have added the hand luggage if Reynolds had let him. Together they staggered up the cobblestone street, and Reynolds saw to his surprise that Dorothy and the children were sitting at a café table across from the entrance to the hotel.

"It was too hot in there," she said, "and there was no place to sit down. I ordered an apéritif. Do you want one?"

And the luggage? What do I do with that? his eyebrows asked, for she was descended from the girl in the fairy tale who said, "Just bring me a rose, dear Father," and he was born in the dead center of the middle class, and they did not always immediately agree about what came before what. He followed the porter inside and up a flight of stairs. The second floor was just as he remembered it, and their room was right down there — where he started to go, until he saw that the porter was continuing up the stairs. On the floor above he went out through a door, with Reynolds following, to a wing of the hotel that didn't exist eighteen years before. It was three stories high and built in the style of an American motel, and the rooms that had been reserved for them were on the third floor — making four stories in all that they had climbed. The porter never paused for breath, possibly because any loss of momentum would have stopped him in his tracks. Reynolds went to a window and opened it. The view from this much higher position was of rooftops and the main parking lot and, like a line drawn with a ruler, the canal that divides Brittany and Normandy. He felt one of the twin beds (no sag in the middle) and then inspected the children's room and the bathroom. It was all very modern and comfortable. It was, in fact, a good deal more comfortable than their old room had been, though he had remembered that room with pleasure all these years. The flowered wallpaper and the flowered curtains had been simply god-awful together, and leaning out of the window they had looked straight down on the heads of the tourists coming and going in the Grande Rue — tourists from all over Europe, by their appearance, their clothes, and by the variety of languages they were speaking. There were even tourists from Brittany, in their *pardon* costumes. And they all seemed to have the same expression on their faces, as if it were an effect of the afternoon light. They looked as if they were soberly aware that they had come to a dividing place in their lives and nothing would be quite the same for them after this. And all afternoon and all evening there was the sound of the omelette whisk. In a room between the foyer of the hotel and the dining room, directly underneath them, a very tall man in a chef's cap and white apron stood beating eggs with a whisk and then cooking them in a long-handled skillet over a wood fire in an enormous open fireplace.

Reynolds listened. There was no *whisk, whisk, whisk* now. Too far away. A car came down the causeway and turned in to the parking lot. When night came, the buses would all be gone and the parking lot would be empty.

In this he was arguing from what had happened before. The tourists got back on the sightseeing buses, and the buses drove away. By the end of the afternoon he and Dorothy were the only ones left. After dinner they walked up to the abbey again, drawn there by some invisible force. It was closed for the night, but they noticed a gate and pushed it open a few inches and looked in. It was a walled garden from a fifteenth-century Book of Hours. There was nobody around, so they went in and closed the gate carefully behind them and started down the gravel path. The garden beds were outlined with bilateral dwarf fruit trees, their branches tied to a low wire and heavy with picture-book apples and pears. There was no snobbish distinction between flowers and vegetables. The weed was unknown. At the far end of this Eden there was a gate that led to another, and after that there were still others — a whole series of exquisite walled gardens hidden away behind the street of restaurants and hotels and souvenir shops. They visited them all. Lingering in the deep twilight, they stood looking up at the cliffs of masonry and were awed by the actual living presence of Time; for it must have been just like this for the last five or six hundred years and maybe longer. The swallows were slicing the air into convex curves, the tide had receded far out into the bay, leaving everywhere behind it the channels by which it would return at three in the morning, and the air was so pure it made them light-headed.

Before Reynolds turned away from the window, three more cars came down the causeway. Here and there in the parking lot a car was starting up and leaving. Though he did not know it, it was what they should have been doing; he should have rounded up Dorothy and the children and driven on to Dinan, where there was a nice well-run hotel with a good restaurant and no memories and a castle right down the street. But his clairvoyance was limited. He foresaw the accident that would never take place but not the disorderly reception that lay in wait for them downstairs.

ON the way into the dining room, half an hour later, they stopped to show the children how the omelettes were made. The very tall man in the white apron had been replaced by two young women in uniforms, but there was still a fire in the fireplace, Reynolds was glad to see; they weren't making the omelettes on a gas stove. The fire was quite a small one, though, and not the huge yellow flames he remembered.

"*Cinq*," he said to the maître d'hôtel, who replied in English, "Will you come this way?" and led them to a table in the center of the dining room. When he had passed out enormous printed menus, he said, "I think the little lady had better put her knitting away. One of the waiters might get jabbed by a needle." This request was accompanied by the smile of a man who knows what children are like, and whom children always find irresistible. Trip ignored the smile and looked at her mother inquiringly.

"I don't see how you could jab anybody, but put it away. I want an omelette *fines herbes*," Dorothy said.

The maître d'hôtel indicated the top of the menu with his gold pencil and said, "We have the famous omelette of Mont-Saint-Michel."

"But with herbs." Dorothy said.

"There is no omelette with herbs," the maître d'hôtel said.

"Why not?" Reynolds asked. "We had it here before."

The question went unanswered.

The two younger children did not care for omelette, famous or otherwise, and took an unconscionably long time making up their minds what they did want to eat for lunch. The maître d'hôtel came back twice before Reynolds was ready to give him their order. After he had left the table, Dorothy said, "I don't see why you can't have it *fines herbes*."

"Perhaps they don't have any herbs," Reynolds said.

"In *France*?"

"Here, I mean. It's an island, practically."

"All you need is parsley and chives. Surely they have that."

"Well maybe it's too much bother, then."

"It's no more trouble than a plain omelette. I don't like him."

"Yes? What's the matter with him?"

"He looks like a Yale man."

This was not intended as a funny remark, but Reynolds laughed anyway.

"And he's not a good headwaiter," she said.

The maître d'hôtel did not, in fact, get their order straight. Things came that they hadn't ordered, and Trip's sole didn't come with the omelettes, or at all. Since she had already filled up on bread, it was not serious. The service was elaborate but very slow.

"No dessert, thank you," Reynolds said when the waiter brought the enormous menus back.

"Just coffee," Dorothy said.

Reynolds looked at his watch. "It says in the green *Michelin* there's a tour of the abbey with an English-speaking guide at two o'clock. We just barely have time to make it. If we have coffee we'll be too late."

"Oh, let's have coffee," Dorothy said. "They won't start on time."

As they raced up the Grande Rue at five minutes after two, he noticed that it was different in one respect: The shops had been enlarged; they went back much deeper than they had before. The objects offered for sale were the same, and since he had examined them carefully eighteen years before, there was no need to do anything but avert his eyes from them now.

The English-speaking tour had already left the vaulted room it started from, and they ran up a long flight of stone steps and caught up with their party on the battlements. A young Frenchman with heavy black-rimmed glasses and a greenish complexion was lecturing to them about the part Mont-Saint-Michel played in the Hundred Years' War. There was a group just ahead of them, and another just behind. The guides manipulated their parties in and out of the same rooms and up and down the same stairs with military precision.

"There were dungeons," Alison Reynolds afterward wrote in her diary, "where you could not sit, lie, or stand and were not allowed to move. Some prisoners were eaten by rats! There were beautiful cloisters where the monks walked and watered their gardens. There was the knights' hall, where guests stayed. The monks ate and worked in the refectory. . . ."

"It's better managed than it used to be," Dorothy said. "I mean, when you think how many people have to be taken through."

The tour was also much shorter than Reynolds remembered it as being, but that could have been because this time they had an English-speaking guide. Or it could just be that what he suspected was true and they were being hurried through. He could not feel the same passionate interest in either the history or the architectural details of the abbey that he had the first time, but that was not the guide's fault. It was obvious that he cared very much about the evolution of the Gothic style and the various uses to which this immensely beautiful but now lifeless monument had been put, through the centuries. His accent made the children smile, but it was no farther from the mark than Reynolds's French, which the French did not smile at only because it didn't amuse them to hear their language badly spoken.

When the tour was over, the guide gathered the party around him and, standing in a doorway through which they would have to pass, informed them that he was a student in a university and that this was his only means of paying for his education. The intellectual tradition of France sat gracefully on his frail shoulders, Reynolds thought, and short or not his tour had been a model of clarity. And was ten francs enough for the five of them?

Traveling in France right after the war, when everybody was so poor, he had been struck by the way the French always tipped the guide generously and thanked him in a way that was never perfunctory. It seemed partly good manners and partly a universal respect for the details of French history. A considerable number of tourists slipped through the doorway now without putting anything in the waiting hand. Before, the guide stood out in the open, quite confident that no one would try to escape without giving him something.

At the sight of the ten-franc note, the young man's features underwent a slight change, by which Reynolds knew that it was sufficient, but money was not all the occasion called for, and there was a word he had been waiting for a chance to use. "*Votre tour est très sensible,*" he said, and the guide's face lit up with pleasure.

Only connect, Mr. E. M. Forster said, but he was not talking about John Reynolds, whose life's blood went into making incessant and vivid connections with all sorts of people he would never see again, and never forgot.

The wine at lunch had made him sleepy. He waited impatiently while

Dorothy and the children bought slides and postcards in the room where the tour ended. Outside, at the foot of the staircase, his plans for taking a nap were threatened when Dorothy was attracted to a museum of horrors having to do with the period when Mont-Saint-Michel was a state prison. But by applying delicate pressures at the right moment he got her to give up the museum, and they walked on down to their hotel. When he had undressed and pulled the covers back, he went to the window in his dressing gown. Some cars were just arriving. American cars. He looked at his watch. It was after four, and the parking lot was still more than half full. On the top floor of the hotel just below, and right next to an open window, he could see a girl of nineteen or twenty with long straight straw-blond hair, sitting on the side of a bed in an attitude of despondency. During the whole time he stood at the window, she didn't raise her head or move. He got into his own bed and was just falling asleep when somebody came into the courtyard with a transistor radio playing rock and roll. He got up and rummaged through his suitcase until he found the wax earplugs. When he woke an hour later, the court-yard was quiet. The girl was still there. He went to the window several times while he was running a bath and afterward while he was dressing. Though the girl left the bed and came back to it, there was no change in her dejection.

"That girl," he said finally.

"I've been watching her too," Dorothy said.

"She's in love. And something's gone wrong."

"They aren't married and she's having a baby," Dorothy said.

"And the man has left her."

"No, he's in the room," Dorothy said. "I saw him a minute ago, drinking out of a wine bottle."

The next time Reynolds looked he couldn't see anyone. The room looked empty, though you couldn't see all the way into it. Had the man and the girl left? Or were they down below somewhere? He looked one last time before they started down to the dining room. The shutters in the room across the court were closed. That was that.

AT dinner Reynolds got into a row with their waiter. For ten days in Paris and ten more days at a little seaside resort on the south coast of Brittany they had met with nothing but politeness and the desire to please. All the familiar complaints about France and the French were refuted, until this evening, when one thing after another went wrong. They were seated at a table that had been wedged into a far corner of the room, between a grotto for trout and goldfish and the foot of a stairway leading to the upper floors of the hotel. Reynolds started to protest and Dorothy stopped him.

"Trip wants to stay here so she can watch the fish," she explained.

"I know," he said as he unfolded his napkin, "but if anybody comes down those stairs they'll have to climb over my lap to get into the dining room."

"They won't," she said. "I'm sure it isn't used." Then to the children, "You pick out the one you want to eat and they take it out with a net and carry it to the kitchen."

"I have a feeling those trout are just for decoration," Reynolds said.

"No," Dorothy said. "I've seen it done. I forget where."

Nobody came down the stairs, and the trout, also undisturbed, circled round and round among the rocks and ferns. Though the room was only half full, the service was dreadfully slow. When they had finished the first course, the waiter, rather than go all the way around the table to where he could pick up Reynolds's plate, said curtly, "Hand me your plate," and Reynolds did. It would never have occurred to him to throw the plate at the waiter's head. His first reaction was always to be obliging. Anger came more slowly, usually with prodding.

The service got worse and worse.

"I think we ought to complain to the headwaiter," Dorothy said. Reynolds looked around. The maître d'hôtel was nowhere in sight. They went on eating their dinner.

"The food is just plain bad," Dorothy announced. "And he forgot to give us any cheese. I don't see how they can give this place a star in the *Michelin*."

When reminded of the fact that he had forgotten to give them any cheese, the waiter, instead of putting the cheese board on the table, cut off thin slices himself at the serving table and passed them. His manner was openly contemptuous. He also created a disturbance in the vicinity of their table by scolding his assistant, who had been courteous and friendly. In mounting anger Reynolds composed a speech to be delivered when the waiter brought the check. Of this withering eloquence all he actually got out was one sentence, ending with the words *"n'est plus un restaurant sérieux."* The waiter pretended not to understand Reynolds's French. Like a fool Reynolds fell into the trap and repeated what he had

said. It sounded much more feeble the second time. Smirking, the waiter
asked if there was something wrong with their dinner, and Reynolds said
that he was referring to the way it was served, whereupon the waiter went
over to the assistant and said, in English, "They don't like the way you
served them." It was his round, definitely.

REYNOLDS glanced at his wristwatch and then pushed his chair back
and hurried Dorothy and the three children out of the dining room and
through the lobby and down the street to the outer gate, and then along
a path to higher ground. They were in plenty of time. The sunset colors
lingered in the sky and in the ribbons of water. The children, happy to
have escaped from the atmosphere of eating, climbed over the rocks,
risking their lives. Dorothy sat with the sea wind blowing her hair back
from her face. He saw that she had entirely forgotten the unpleasantness
in the dining room. She responded to Nature the way he responded to
human beings. Presently he let go of his anger, too, and responded to the
evening instead.

"What if they fall?" she said. "It could be quicksand."

"If it's quicksand, I'll jump in after them. Isn't it lovely and quiet
here?"

For in spite of all those cars in the parking lot they had the evening to
themselves. Nobody had come down here to see the tide sweep in. At
first it was silent. They saw that the channels through the sandbars were
growing wider, but there was no visible movement of water. Then suddenly it began to move, everywhere, with a rushing sound that no river
ever makes on its way to the sea. It was less like a force of Nature than
like an emotion — like the disastrous happiness of a man who has fallen
in love at the wrong season of life.

When it was over, they walked up to the abbey in the dusk, by a back
way that was all stairs, and down again along the outer ramparts, looking
into the rear windows of houses and restaurants, and were just in time to
be startled by a blood-curdling scream. It came from a brightly lighted
room in a house that was across a courtyard and one story down from
where they were. It could have been a woman's scream, or a child's.
There was an outbreak of angry voices.

"What *is* it, Daddy?" the children asked. "What are they saying?"

"It's just a family argument," Reynolds said, making his voice sound
casual. His knees were shaking. Listening to the excited voices, he made

out only one word — "*idiot.*" Either the scream had come from a mental defective or somebody was being insulted. The voices subsided. The Americans walked on until they came to a flight of steps leading down to the street in front of their hotel.

When the children were in bed, Reynolds and Dorothy sat at the window of their room, looking out at the night. "The air is so soft," she said, and he said, "Ummm," not wanting to spoil her pleasure by saying what was really on his mind, which was that they should never have come here and that nothing on earth would make him come here again. In a place where things could easily have been kept as they were — where, one would have thought, it was to everybody's advantage to keep them that way — something had gone fatally wrong. Something had been allowed to happen that shouldn't have happened.

And it was not only here. The evening they arrived in Paris, the taxi driver who took them from the boat train to their hotel on the Left Bank said, "*Paris n'est plus Paris.*" And in the morning Madame said when she gave them their mail, "Paris is changed. It's so noisy now." "New York too," he said, to comfort her. But the truth was that nowhere in New York was the traffic like the Boulevard Saint-Germain. The cars drove at twice the speed of the cars at home, and when the lights changed there was always some side street from which cars kept on coming, and pedestrians ran for their lives. Like insects. The patrons who sat at the tables on the sidewalk in front of Lipp could no longer see their counterparts at the Deux Magots because of the river of cars that flowed between them. The soft summer air reeked of gasoline. And there was something he saw that he could not get out of his mind afterward: an old woman who had tried to cross against the light and was stranded in the middle of the street, her eyes wide with terror, like a living monument.

Reynolds was quite aware that to complain because things were not as agreeable as they used to be was one of the recognizable signs of growing old. And whether you accepted change or not, there was really no preventing it. But why, without exception, did something bad drive out something good? Why was the change always for the worse?

He had once asked his father-in-law, a man in his seventies, if there was a time — he didn't say whether he meant in history or a time that his father-in-law remembered, and, actually, he meant both — when the world seemed to be becoming a better place, little by little. And life everywhere more agreeable, more the way it ought to be. And then suddenly, after that, was there a noticeable shift in the pattern of events?

Some sort of dividing line that people were aware of, when everything started to go downhill? His father-in-law didn't answer, making Reynolds feel he had said something foolish or tactless. But his father-in-law didn't like to talk about his feelings, and it was just possible that he felt the same way Reynolds did.

Once in a while, some small detail represented an improvement on the past, and you could not be happy in the intellectual climate of any time but your own. But in general, so far as the way people lived, it was one loss after another, something hideous replacing something beautiful, the decay of manners, the lapse of pleasant customs, as by a blind increase in numbers the human race went about making the earth more and more unfit to live on.

IN the morning, Reynolds woke ready to pay the bill and leave as soon as possible, but it was only a short drive to Dinard, and their plane didn't leave until five o'clock in the afternoon, so after breakfast they climbed the steps of the Grande Rue once more, for a last look at the outside of the abbey, and found something they had overlooked before — an exhibition marking the thousandth year of the Abbey of Mont-Saint-Michel. There were illuminated manuscripts: St. Michael appearing to Aubert, Bishop of Avranches, in a dream and telling him to build a chapel on the Mount; St. Michael weighing souls, slaying dragons, vanquishing demons, separating the blessed from the damned; St. Michael between St. Benoît and the archbishop St. William; St. Michael presenting his arms to the Virgin; St. Michael the guardian of Paradise. There was a list of the Benedictine monks living and dead at the time of the abbot Mainard II, and an inventory of the relics of the monastery at the end of the fifteenth century. There was the royal seal of William the Conqueror, of Philip the Fair, of Philip the Bold, of Louis VIII, of Philip Augustus. There was an octagonal reliquary containing a fragment of the cranium of St. Suzanne the Virgin Martyr. There was a drawing, cut by some vandal from an illuminated manuscript, of Jeanne d'Arc, Alison's friend, with her banner and sword, corresponding exactly to a description given at her trial, and a letter from Charles VII reaffirming that Mont-Saint-Michel was part of the royal domain. There were maquettes of the abbey in the year 1000, in 1100, in 1701, and as it was now. There was an aquarelle by Viollet-le-Duc of the flying buttresses. There were suits of armor, harquebuses, a pistolet, and some cannonballs. There was far more than they could take in or do justice to. When they emerged from the exhibition rooms, dazed by all they had looked at, Reynolds remembered the little gardens. It would never do to go away without seeing them. He couldn't find the gate that opened into the first one, and he wasn't sure, after eighteen years, on which side of the Mount they were, but Dorothy had noticed a sign, down a flight of steps from the abbey, that said THE BISHOP'S GARDEN. They bought tickets from an old woman sitting at a table under a vaulted archway and passed into what was hardly more than a strip of grass with a few flowers and flowering shrubs, and could have been the terrace of a public park in some small provincial French town. Reynolds began to look for the medieval gardens in earnest, and in the end they found themselves in what must once have been the place they were looking for. It was overrun with weeds, and hardly recognizable as a garden, and there was only that one.

Later, after he had closed and locked his suitcase, he went to the window for the last time. The shutters of the room that had contained so much drama were still closed. Looking down on the courtyard between the new wing of their hotel and the hotel in front of it, he knew suddenly what had happened. The medieval gardens didn't exist any more. To accommodate an ever-increasing number of tourists, the hotels had been added on to. So that they could hold thousands of souvenirs instead of hundreds, the souvenir shops had been deepened, taking the only available land, which happened to be those enchanting walled gardens. The very building he was in at that moment, with its comfortable if anonymous rooms with adjoining bath, had obliterated some garden that had been here for perhaps five hundred years. One of the miracles of the modern world, and they did just what people everywhere else would have done — they cashed in on a good thing. And never mind about the past. The past is what filled the gigantic parking lot with cars all summer, but so long as you have the appearance you can sell that; you don't need the real thing. What's a garden that has come down intact through five hundred years compared to money in the bank? *This is something I will never get over*, he thought, feeling the anger go deeper and deeper. *I will never stop hating the people who did this. And I will never forgive them — or France for letting them do it. What's here now is no longer worth seeing or saving. If this could happen here, then there is no limit to what can happen everywhere else. It's all going down, and down. There's no stopping it. . . .*

In order to pay the bill, he had to go to the cashier's desk, which was at the far end of the dining room. As he started there, walking between the empty tables, he saw that the only maître d'hôtel in the whole of France who looked like a Yale man was avoiding his eyes — not because he felt any remorse for putting them next to the fish tank with a clown for a waiter, or because he was afraid of anything Reynolds might say or do. He didn't care if Reynolds dropped dead on the spot, so long as he didn't have to dispose of the body. He was a man without any feeling for his métier, *tout simplement*, and so the food and the service had gone to hell in a basket.

WHILE Reynolds was at the concierge's desk in the foyer, confirming their reservations at the airport by telephone, a gentle feminine voice said behind him, in English, "Monsieur, you left your traveler's checks," and he turned and thanked the cashier profusely.

He started up the stairs to see about the luggage and the concierge called after him, "Monsieur, your airplane tickets!"

They had banded together and were looking after him.

The same boy who carried the luggage up four flights of stairs now carried it down again and out through the medieval gate to the Volkswagen. "We were here eighteen years ago," Reynolds said to him as he took out his wallet. "You have no idea how different it was."

This was quite true. Eighteen years ago, the porter was not anywhere. Or if he was, he was only a babe in arms. But he was a Frenchman, and knew that a polite man doesn't sneer at emotions he doesn't feel or memories he cannot share. He insisted on packing the luggage for Reynolds, and tucked Dorothy and the children in, and closed the car doors, and then gave them a beautiful smile.

It's true that I overtipped him, Reynolds thought. But then, looking into the porter's alert, intelligent, doglike eyes, he knew that he was being unjust. The tip had nothing to do with it. It was because he was a harmless maniac and they all felt obliged to take care of him and see him on his way.

The Value of Money

"My son Ned, from New York," Mr. Ferrers said.

Why, he's proud of me, Edward Ferrers thought; he wouldn't be introducing me like this if he weren't.

He put his thin hand through the grilled window in the waiting room of the railway station and shook hands with the ticket agent, who said, "Glad to know you, Ned."

The ticket agent checked Edward's return ticket (the sleeping-car reservation needed to be confirmed in Chicago) and ignored the telegraph's urgent, lisping *click-click* . . . *click-click* . . . *click-click-click* . . . *click* . . . *click*. . . . The wall calendar, compliments of Orton Grain & Feed Co., was open to the month of June 1952.

Edward Ferrers came home to Draperville once every three years, for three or four days, which wasn't quite long enough for him to get used to the way the town looked, and so he was continually noting the things that had changed and the things that had not changed. He also had changed, of course, and not changed. He had acquired the tense, alert air of a city man, and his accent was no longer that of the Middle West but a mixture, showing traces of all the places he had lived in. On the other hand, people who had known him as a little boy on his way to the Presbyterian Sunday school or marching with the Boy Scouts on the Fourth of July had no trouble recognizing him, even though he was now forty-three years old and the crown of his head was quite bald.

"I want to stop at the bank for a minute," he said, as they were leaving the station.

"What for?" Mr. Ferrers demanded.

"I want to cash a check."

"How much do you need?"

"I just want to be sure I have enough for the diner and the porters and the taxi home," Edward said. "Ten dollars ought to do it, with what I have." His voice in speaking to his father was gentle but careful, as if he were piloting a riverboat upstream with due regard for submerged sandbars and dangerous snags under the smoothly flowing surface of the water.

Mr. Ferrers took out his billfold, which was as orderly as his person, and extracted two new ten-dollar bills. "Your Aunt Alice is expecting us at one," he said. "You don't want to keep her waiting."

Edward took the money and put it in his billfold, which was coming unsewed and was stuffed with he had no idea what. "I'll give you a check when we get home," he said.

"All right," Mr. Ferrers said.

Neither as a child nor as an adult had Edward ever lied to his father, but he did hold back information that he had reason to think his father would be troubled by. For example, he didn't tell his father what his salary as an associate professor was, or how much money he had. If his father knew, it would upset him, certainly. And what would upset him even more was that Edward had failed to put anything by. One of the primary rules of Mr. Ferrers's life was that a certain percentage of what he made should be saved for a rainy day.

As a sullen adolescent Edward had accused his father — often in his mind and once to his face — of caring about nothing but money. This was not true, of course. Mr. Ferrers never confused the making of money with a man's concern for his family or his own self-respect. But he took money seriously (who doesn't?) and to this day carried about with him, in his inside coat pocket, a little memorandum book containing an up-to-the-minute detailed statement of his assets. He took it out and showed it to Edward the day before, while they were admiring the roses in the backyard. What would have happened if Edward had asked to see what was written in the little book he didn't dare think. His father would probably have said that it wasn't any of his business, and in fact it wasn't.

They got in the front seat of the car and Mr. Ferrers rolled the window up on his side, though it was a warm day. He was past seventy, and the gradual refining and shrinking process of old age had begun, and with it had come a susceptibility to drafts.

"I can raise my window, too," Edward said.

Mr. Ferrers shook his head. "I'll tell you if I feel it."

The car was a Cadillac, five years old but without a scratch. It had been washed in honor of Edward's visit and looked brand-new.

"We ought to leave Alice's around three, if you want to see Dr. McBride," Mr. Ferrers said.

"I thought he was dead."

"Not at all. Old Doc goes his merry way at eighty-eight, spending his capital and thinking he can cure his ills and pains, which at his age is impossible. And Ruth hasn't had a new dress in many years. But he knows you're here, and he'll be hurt if you don't come to see him. . . . I tried to head your Aunt Alice off, but she wanted to do something for you."

"I know," Edward said.

"You'd think that by having people at the house where they could see you that that ought to satisfy them, but it doesn't. They all want to have you for cocktails or something, and the result is that I don't get any time with you — which I don't like. But there's nothing I can do about it."

"This evening we'll have some time," Edward said.

"Three days is not enough."

"I know it isn't."

Once they had left the business district there was no traffic whatever. As Edward drove, he continued to look both at the quiet empty street ahead of them and in the little oblong, bluish rearview mirror, at his father. Mr. Ferrers was aware that he was being studied, but what reasonable man is afraid of the scrutiny of his own child? Before he retired and moved back to Draperville, Illinois, Mr. Ferrers had been the vice-president in charge of the Chicago office of a large public-utility company. He was accustomed to speak with authority, and with confidence that his opinion, which had been arrived at cautiously and with due regard for the opinions of others, was the right one. He also came from a long line of positive people. Introspection was as foreign to his nature as dishonesty. Right was right and wrong was wrong, and to tell one from the other you had only to examine your own conscience. In general, Mr. Ferrers was on the side of the golden mean, or, as he would have put it, the middle of the road. When it came to politics, he threw moderation to the winds and was a fanatical Republican. Though he could not swallow the Book of Genesis, he believed every word that was printed in the Chicago *Tribune*. Also that Franklin Roosevelt had committed suicide. Fishing and golf were his two great pleasures. At the bridge table he deliberated, strumming his fingers, without realizing that he was holding up the game, and drove his wife, Edward's stepmother, to make remarks that she had meant to keep to herself. Now that his eyesight had begun to fail, he had trouble recognizing people at any distance, and so he spoke courteously to everyone he met on the street. He had no enemies. The younger men, Edward's contemporaries, looked up to him and came to him for advice. The older men, Mr. Ferrers's lifelong friends, considered it a privilege to be allowed to fasten the fly on the end of his fishing line, and loved him for his forthrightness, and saw to it that he did not lack company at five o'clock in the afternoon, when he got out the ice trays and the glasses and a bottle of very good Scotch.

"This part of town hasn't changed at all," Edward remarked.

He meant the houses. The look of things had changed drastically. The trees were gone. In a nightmare of three or four years' duration, the elm blight had put an end to the shade — to all those long, graceful, leafy branches that used to hang down over roofs and porches and reach out over the brick pavement toward the branches on the other side. Now everything looked uncomfortably exposed, as if standing on the sidewalk you could tell how much people owed at the bank. Not that there had ever been much privacy in Draperville, Edward thought; but now there was not even the appearance of privacy. . . . In the dark, cold, hungry, anxious to get home to his supper, he used to ride over these very lawns on his bicycle, and when he was close enough to the front porch he would reach backward into his canvas bag, take out a folded copy of the Draperville *Evening Star*, and let fly with it. That dead self, the boy he used to be. *The one you used to have such trouble with*, he wanted to say to his father, but Mr. Ferrers did not like talking about the past. "That's all water over the dam," he said once when Edward asked him a question about his mother. On the other hand, he did sometimes like to talk about local history — what the business district was like when he was a boy, where some long defunct dry goods store or shoe store or law office or livery stable used to be, and who the old families were. And gossip said that when he went to see old Dr. McBride, he talked about Edward's mother. So perhaps it's only that he doesn't like to talk about the past with me, Edward thought. Aloud, he said, "This car drives very easily, after our 1936 Ford."

"You ought to get a new car," Mr. Ferrers said.

"The old one runs. It runs very well."

"I know, but so does a new car. And Janet might enjoy having a car that isn't sixteen years old, did you ever stop to think of that?"

Edward smiled, without taking his eyes from the street, and did not commit himself. This was not the first time that his father had brought up the subject of their car, which had stopped being a joke and was now an affront to the whole family. Except possibly his Aunt Alice, who didn't have a car, because she had very little money—barely enough to live on. What she did have slipped through her fingers. This was equally true of Edward. When he was a little boy, his father made him lie stretched out on his hand in shallow water. "Don't be afraid, I won't take my hand away," he said, and when Edward stopped thrashing and looked back, his father was ten feet away from him and he had learned to swim. But learning the value of money was something else again.

On Edward's sixth birthday, Mr. Ferrers started his son off with a weekly allowance of ten cents—a sum so large in Edward's eyes that when Mrs. McBride gave him another dime for ice-cream cones, he wasn't sure whether it was morally right for him to take it. With advancing age, the ten cents became a quarter, all his own, to spend when and on what he pleased, and of course once it was spent there was no possibility of more until another week rolled around. In first-year high school, the quarter became fifty cents, and then, in Chicago, where he had lunch at school and carfare to consider, it jumped suddenly to three dollars. By walking to school, and a good deal of the time not eating any lunch, he could buy books, and did. Sometimes quite expensive ones. And in college he had sixty, then seventy-five, and then ninety dollars a month, with no questions asked, out of which he fed himself and paid for the roof over his head and bought still more books. If he ran short toward the end of the month, he lived on milk and graham crackers—which was not what his father had intended. And once when he ran out of money early in the month because he had shared what he had with a roommate whose check from home didn't come, he got a job waiting tables at a sorority house. What it amounted to was that he had learned when the money ran out not to ask for more.

When he finished college, he thought he wanted to teach English, but after three years of graduate work he threw up his part-time appointment with the university where he had been an undergraduate, took the hundred dollars that he had in a savings account, borrowed another hundred from his father, and went to New York on a Greyhound bus and got a job. After working three weeks, he paid his father back. A great load fell from Mr. Ferrers's shoulders with this act. He sat with Edward's letter and the check for a hundred dollars in his hand and wept. The only one of his three children who had ever given him cause for worry had demonstrated that he was responsible where money was concerned, and Mr. Ferrers felt that his work had been accomplished. It appeared to be so well accomplished that Edward, receiving raise after raise, in four years reached a point at which he must be making about as much income as his father. Since his father never revealed how much money he earned, this had to be concluded by inference, from his scale of living and his remarks about other people. Edward decided on ten thousand dollars a year as his mark, and when he reached it he rested there a few months, during the summer of 1939. His father and stepmother came East for the World's Fair in Flushing Meadow. Sitting in the Belgian Pavilion, with a clear view of the French Pavilion, where the food was better but notoriously expensive, Edward announced that he had resigned from his job in order to get a Ph.D. and go back to teaching. Mr. Ferrers took this decision calmly. Edward was a grown man now, he said, and he would not presume to tell him how to lead his life.

As Edward drove up in front of the place where his aunt lived, Mr. Ferrers said, "Don't get too close to the curbing—you'll scrape the whitewalls."

"How is that?" Edward asked.

Mr. Ferrers opened the door on his side and looked. "You're all right," he said.

Though now and then some old house would be divided into apartments, this was the only building in Draperville that had been originally designed for that purpose. It was two stories high, frame, with small porches both upstairs and down. It was painted a dreary shade of brown, and it backed on the railroad tracks. Mr. Ferrers's sister lived on the second floor, at the top of a rather steep flight of stairs.

"You go ahead, son," he said. "I have to take my time."

There were two doors at the top of the stairs. The one on the right opened and Edward's Aunt Alice said, "I've been watching for you. Come in, come in," and put her arms around him and gave him a hearty smack. Looking past her into the apartment, he saw that his stepmother had already come.

"What a pretty dress," he said.

"I put it on for you," his Aunt Alice said, and her face lit up with pleasure.

Edward loved her because his mother had loved her, and because she had been very good to him after his mother died—the one person who brought cheerfulness and jokes into a house where life had come to a standstill and people sat down to meals and went upstairs to bed and practiced the piano and read the evening paper and answered the telephone only because they didn't know what else to do. He always thought of her as she was then, and so it was a shock to find her with white hair, false teeth, wrinkles, rimless bifocals, and hands twisted out of shape by arthritis. And living alone for so many years had made her melancholy. Only her voice was not changed. Unlike most people of her generation, she could speak about her feelings. The night before, sitting off in a corner with him where nobody could hear what they were saying, she said, "I know I'm old, but my heart is young." During a long life, very little happiness had come her way and she had taken every bit of it, without a moment's fear or hesitation. And would again.

"Well, Alice," Mr. Ferrers said as he kissed her, "how are all your aches and pains today?"

"They're not imaginary, as you seem to think."

"Don't listen to him," Edward said.

"I know he just likes to get my goat," she said. "But even so."

"If you can't stand a little teasing," Mr. Ferrers said.

"I don't mind teasing, but sometimes your teasing hurts."

When they were children and he got into a fight on the way home from school, she dropped her books and sailed in and pulled his tormentors off him. Mr. Ferrers had had asthma as a boy and was not strong, but he outgrew it; the time came when he didn't need anybody to protect him. From the way she spoke his name, it was perfectly clear to Edward how much his aunt loved his father still.

The living room of the apartment was robbed of light by the porch. The deep shade that was lacking everywhere outside was here, softening the colors of Oriental rugs that were familiar to him from his childhood; like books that he had read over and over. His childhood was separated sharply from his adolescence by his mother's death, which occurred when he was ten. He was thirteen when his father remarried, and when he was fifteen they moved from Draperville to Chicago. He had known his stepmother since he was four years old. She had been his kindergarten teacher, and so it was not as if his father had married a stranger.

When Mr. and Mrs. Ferrers came East for a visit with Edward and his wife, the two couples played gin rummy with a good deal of gaiety and went for long drives. Edward's wife and his stepmother were comfortable together. If there was ever any strain, it was between father and son— because Edward had miscalculated the length of time it took to drive from the handsome street of old houses in Litchfield, Connecticut, to the inn where Mr. Ferrers could sit down to his evening drink; or because Mr. Ferrers could not keep off the subject of politics even though he knew what Edward thought of Senator McCarthy. But when Edward was going to high school in Chicago, it was different. He did not like to think of all that his stepmother had put up with — the sullenness; the refusal to admit her completely into his affections lest he be disloyal to his mother; the harsh judgments of adolescence; sand in the bathroom, tears at the dinner table, and implacable hostility toward his father. As if to make belated amends, he sat now holding her hand in his and reminding her of things that had happened when they were living in Chicago.

"Do you remember what a time you had teaching me to drive?" he said, and they both laughed. Streetcars had exerted a fatal attraction for him. He killed the engine on Sheridan Road. Returning to the garage where the car was kept, he couldn't decide between the entrance and the exit and almost drove up on a concrete post.

"I used to hear you coming home," Helen Ferrers said, "when we lived on Greenleaf Avenue, and your walk sounded so like your dad's that I couldn't tell which of you it was."

Edward also had put up with something. For the first few years, she suffered from homesickness and she and his father went home to Draperville as often as they could, and they had a good deal of company — mostly Helen's friends, who came up to Chicago for a few days to do some shopping. There was no guest room in the apartment, and when they had company Edward slept in the dining room, on a daybed that opened out. In his room there were twin beds with satin spreads on them, and before he got into bed at night, he folded the one on his bed carefully and put it on the other, but sometimes forgot to pin back the glass curtains so they wouldn't be rained on during the night. He studied at a card table, and in his closet, in a muslin bag, were Helen's evening dresses. The two pictures on the wall were colored French prints, from a series entitled *Les Confiances d'Amour*. By the light switch there was a small framed motto:

> *Hello, guest, and Howdy-do.*
> *This small room belongs to you.*
> *And our house and all that's in it.*
> *Make yourself at home each minute.*

Helen let go of his hand in order to go out to the kitchen and help put lunch on the table. Edward heard his Aunt Alice say, "I'm all ready. As soon as the ice tea is poured, we can sit down. I know Ed likes to have his meals on time."

"You shouldn't have gone to so much trouble," Helen said — meaning sweet corn and garden tomatoes and fried chicken and a huge strawberry shortcake.

"It wasn't any trouble," his aunt said, which was of course untrue; at her age everything was hard for her, and usually she was perfectly willing to admit it. When they pushed their chairs back from the table, an hour later, she said, "No, you can't help me, any of you. I won't hear of it. I don't have Ned with me very often, and we're going to talk, we're not going to stand around in the kitchen doing dishes. I don't mind doing them if I can take my time."

What they talked about, sitting in a circle in her small, dark living room, was her health. The doctor was trying cortisone, and she thought it had helped her. She had more movement in her fingers, and could put her hair up without feeling so much pain in her shoulder.

THEY were late getting away — it was after three-thirty when they said good-bye and got in the car and drove off to call on Dr. McBride, whom they found sitting up in bed in the downstairs room that used to be his den. "Sit right here on the bed where I can see you," he said.

"He won't be comfortable," Mrs. McBride objected.

"How do you know?" Dr. McBride said. He was born in Scotland and spoke with a noticeable burr. "Sit down, my boy. Don't pay any attention to your auntie. I've been expecting you. You have your mother's eyes. You remember her?"

Edward nodded.

"And you like living in New York?"

"Yes."

"And you're teaching. That's a fine profession for a man to be in. Very fine. You'll never have to worry for fear your life is being wasted. And how old are you now?"

Edward told him.

"I can recall very well the day you were born. Would you like to hear about it?"

"Yes, I would," Edward said.

"It was an extremely hot day, in the middle of August. . . . "

Looking into the old man's faded blue eyes, Edward thought, This is the first real conversation that we have ever had.

While Mrs. McBride and his father talked about the new road to Peoria and what a difference it would make, Dr. McBride held Edward's hand and told him things he had done and said when he was a little boy, and then he began to tell Edward about his own boyhood in Scotland. "My father was very strict," he said, "and by the time I was eleven years old I'd had enough of his heavy hand and I made up my mind to run away to America. I told my mother, because I couldn't bear not to, and because I knew she'd feel worse if I'd kept it from her. She gave me all the money there was in the teapot, and told me I mustn't leave without saying good-bye to my father. So I did. I edged my way all around the room until I arrived at the door, and then I said, 'Good-bye, Father, I'm leaving home,' and started running as fast as my legs would carry me. . . . "

He got a job on a tramp schooner that landed him eventually on the coast of California. He was homesick and couldn't find work, slept in doorways, and was half starved when he met up with a man whose name was also McBride, a well-to-do rancher who had recently lost his only son.

Somewhere, possibly during that far-off boyhood in Scotland, Dr. McBride had been exposed to the storyteller's art. He understood the use of the surprising juxtaposition, the impact of things left unsaid. Again and again there was a detail that couldn't not be true. He never relapsed into the pointless, never said "to make a long story short," and seemed not even to be aware that he was telling stories, and yet there was not one unnecessary word.

"Oh, but did that really happen?" Edward exclaimed. "How marvel-lous."

"It *was* marvellous," Dr. McBride agreed.

And a minute later Edward said, "But weren't you afraid of him?" He said, "He was still waiting, after all that time?" And "It's so beautiful — that it worked out that way." Looking altogether a different person — as if the essential part of him, his true self that could never show its face in Draperville because no child after he grows up can ever be wholly natural with his parents, had come and joined them on the bed — he asked, "And then what happened?" The old man's eyes lit up. He had found the perfect audience.

Mr. Ferrers consulted his wristwatch and then said, "Much as I hate to do this, Ruth, we've got to be moving on. We're due at the Franklins' at five."

Dr. McBride winked at Edward and said, "Your father is the slave of time," and went on telling the story of his life.

Edward got up from the bed only because it was the third time his father had spoken to him about leaving, and even then it was very hard to do. The stories he did not hear now he never would, and he had the feeling that he was depriving himself of his birthright.

"I thought you'd decided to spend the rest of your life there," Mr. Ferrers said crossly when they were in the car. "Do you have any idea what time it is?"

"I know, Dad," Edward said, "but I couldn't bear to leave. He's the most wonderful storyteller I ever heard, and I didn't even know it."

"I've heard Doc's stories," Mr. Ferrers said dryly. "He's always the hero."

What made Mr. Ferrers's anger so impressive was that it was never unleashed. The change in him now was less than it was in Edward, whose voice rose in pitch, in spite of his efforts to control it. He stammered as he defended himself from his father's remarks. The effect of this skirmish was to move them both back in time, to Edward's fifteenth year and Mr. Ferrers's forty-fifth — the difference being that Edward regarded it as a personal failure in steering the riverboat upstream, whereas Mr. Ferrers five minutes later had dismissed the incident from his mind.

AT the Franklins', Edward threw himself into one conversation after another, enjoying himself thoroughly, and trying, as always, to make sure that no one was skimped — as if the amount of attention he paid to each person who had known him since he came into the world was something that he must try to apportion justly and fairly. Why this should be, he had never asked himself.

From the Franklins' they drove downtown again, to join Helen's family in the cafeteria of the New Draperville Hotel. With several drinks under his belt, Edward looked around the noisy dining room. The faces he saw were full of character, as small-town faces tend to be, he thought, and lined with humor, and time had dealt gently with them. By virtue of having been born in this totally unremarkable place and of having lived out their lives here, they had something people elsewhere did not have. ... This opinion every person in the room agreed with, he knew, and no doubt it had been put into his mind when he was a child. For it was something that he never failed to be struck by — those sweeping statements in praise of Draperville that were almost an article of religious faith. They spoke about each other in much the same way. "There isn't a finer man anywhere on this earth," they would say, in a tone of absolute conviction, sometimes about somebody who was indeed admirable, but just as often it would be some local skinflint, some banker or lawyer who made a specialty of robbing widows and orphans and was just barely a member of the human race. A moment later, opposed to this falsehood and in fact utterly contradicting it, there was a more realistic appraisal, which to his surprise they did not hesitate to express. But it would be wrong to say that the second statement represented their true opinion; it was just their other one.

He saw that somebody was smiling at him from a nearby table, a soft-faced woman with blond hair, and he put his napkin down and crossed the room to speak to her. He even knew her name. She lived down the street from him, and when he was six years old he was hopelessly in love with her and she liked Johnny Miller instead.

When they walked into the house at ten o'clock, he was talked out, dead-tired, and sleepy, and aware that the one person who had been skimped was the person he had come to see in the first place, his father, and that he couldn't leave without a little time with his father, and that his father had no intention of permitting him to.

As they put their coats away in the hall closet, Helen said, 'Ned, dear, you must be dead. I know I am. What time do you want breakfast?"

"Eight-thirty or nine o'clock will be all right," Mr. Ferrers said. "His train doesn't leave till eleven. You go on up. Ned and I want to have a little visit."

"I think I will," Mrs. Ferrers said. But first she went around the room emptying ashtrays and puffing up satin pillows, until the room looked as if there had never been anybody in it. The two men walked through the sun parlor and out onto the screened porch. Mr. Ferrers sat down in the chair that was always referred to as his, and lit a cigar. Edward sat on a bamboo sofa. They did not turn the light on but sat in the dim light that came from the living room. Mr. Ferrers began by remarking upon the many changes he had seen in his lifetime — the telephone, electric light, the automobile, the airplane — and how these changes had totally changed the way people lived. "It's been a marvellous privilege," he said, drawing on his cigar, "to have lived in a time when all this was happening."

Edward managed not to say that he would gladly have dispensed with all of these inventions. He listened to his father's denunciation of the New Deal as he would have to some overfamiliar piece of music — "Fin-gal's Cave" or the overture to *Rosamunde* — aware that it was a necessary prelude to the more substantial part of the conversation, something uppermost in his father's mind that had to be said in order to get around to things that were deeper and more personal.

So long as Edward did not argue with his father or attempt to present the other side of the political picture, Mr. Ferrers did not investigate his son's opinions. As for converting Mr. Ferrers to the liberal point of view, history — the Depression, in particular — had done more than Edward could possibly have hoped to accomplish with rational arguments. Mr. Ferrers was aware that there is such a thing as social responsibility, and he merely complained that it had now gone far enough and any further effort in that direction would weaken the financial structure of the country. So far as Edward could make out, his father's financial structure had weathered the storm very well.

When Edward put his feet up and arranged the pillows comfortably behind his head, Mr. Ferrers said, "If you're too tired, son, go to bed." But kindly. There was no impatience in his voice.

"Oh, no," Edward said. "I just felt like stretching out."

"It's too bad it has to be this way. When we lived in Chicago, there was no one to consider but ourselves, and we could talk to our hearts' content."

Actually, in those days it was Mr. Ferrers who talked. Edward was full of secrets and couldn't have opened his mouth without putting his foot in it.

"Very nice," he said, when his father asked what he thought of his Aunt Alice's apartment. "She seemed very comfortable."

"She keeps very peculiar hours. She likes to read till two in the morning. But you can't tell other people how to lead their lives, and I guess she's happy doing that. And she's got all her things around her — all those old drop-leaf tables and china doodads she sets such store by and that no secondhand dealer would give you more than two dollars for, if that."

"Aunt Alice's things are better than you think," Edward said.

"If you like antiques," Mr. Ferrers said. "I used to argue with her, but I don't anymore. I've given up. There's a first-floor apartment coming vacant in the same building that she wants to move into. It's more expensive, but she complains about the stairs, and at her age they are a consideration. I'll probably have to help her with the rent. . . . She could have been in a very different situation today. I know of three very fine men who were crazy to marry her. She wouldn't have them. They've all done well for themselves."

They probably bored her, Edward said to himself in the dark.

"Father begged her with tears in his eyes not to marry Gene Hamilton," Mr. Ferrers said. "But she wouldn't listen to him."

"She's had lots of pleasure from her life, even so," Edward remarked.

"Now she wants to sell all her securities — she hasn't got very much: some Quaker Oats and some U.S. Gypsum and a few shares of General Motors — and buy an annuity, which at her age is the silliest thing you ever heard of."

Silly or not, she had his father to fall back on, Edward reflected philosophically. And then, less philosophically, he wondered what would happen if his Aunt Alice outlived his father. Who would look after her? Her only son was dead and she had no grandchildren. The question contained its own answer: Edward and his brothers would take on the responsibility that until now his father had shouldered alone.

"What was he like?"

"What was who like?"

"Grandfather Ferrers."

"He was as fine a man as you would ever want to know," Mr. Ferrers said soberly, and then he added to a long finished picture a new detail that changed everything. He said, "Father never saw me until my brother Will died."

Edward opened his eyes. His father very seldom ever said anything as revealing as this, and also it was in flat contradiction to the usual version, which was that his father and his grandfather had been extremely close.

The earliest surviving photographs of his father showed him playing the mandolin, with his cap on the back of his head and a big chrysanthemum in his buttonhole. His brother Will died at the age of twenty-five, leaving a wife and a child, and Grandfather Ferrers's health was poor, and so Edward's father, who had wanted to study medicine, dropped out of school instead and began to help support the family.

From where he lay stretched out on the sofa, Edward could see into the lighted living room of the house next door. The son-in-law sat reading a copy of *Life* under a bridge lamp. The two Scotties, whose barking Mr. Ferrers complained of, were quiet. There had been a divorce that had rocked the house next door to the foundations, but that, too, had quieted down. The whole neighborhood was still. Not even a television set. Just the insects of the summer night. His father would have been a good doctor, Edward thought, staring at the outlines of the house next door and the trees in the backyard, silhouetted against the night sky. He felt his eyelids growing heavier and heavier.

"But all that changed," Mr. Ferrers said. "Toward the end of his life we got to know each other."

Edward heard his stepmother moving about upstairs, and then without warning his mind darkened. When he came to, after he had no idea how long, Mr. Ferrers was discussing his will. Though Edward could hardly believe that this conversation was taking place at all, what made it seem even stranger was the fact that his father spoke without excitement of any kind, as if all his life he had been in the habit of discussing his financial arrangements with his children. The will was what Edward had assumed it would be. There was nothing that he could object to, nothing that was not usual. Everything was to go to his stepmother during her lifetime, and then the estate would be divided among Mr. Ferrers's three sons.

"I wanted very much to be able to leave you boys something at the time of my death," Mr. Ferrers said. "About fifteen thousand dollars is what I had planned. I wanted you to have a little present to remember me by. But with the state and federal inheritance tax, I don't see how this can be managed."

"It doesn't matter," Edward said.

"It matters to me," Mr. Ferrers said, and there they were, right back where they started.

Mr. Ferrers drew on his cigar and the porch was illuminated by a soft red glow. "When I was a young man," he said, "and just trying to get my feet on the ground, my father said to me, 'If you can just manage to save a thousand dollars, you'll never be in want, the whole rest of your life. . . .' " Though Edward had never heard Dr. McBride's stories, this story he knew by heart. His father had done it, had managed to save a thousand dollars, and his grandfather's words had proved true. As a young man, having been told the same thing by his father, Edward had put this theory to the test; he also had saved a thousand dollars, and then, gradually, unlike his father and his grandfather, he had spent it. Little by little, it went. But strangely enough, so far at least, the theory still held. He had never been in actual want, though the balance in their — his and Janet's — joint checking account at this moment his father would not have considered cause for congratulations.

It was an amusing thought that the same reticence that prevented his father from telling him just how much money he had would prevent him also from inquiring into Edward's financial circumstances. But it would not prevent him from asking if Edward was saving money. The conversation was clearly heading for this point, and so Edward braced himself and was ready when it arrived.

Mr. Ferrers said, "I assume you have managed to put something aside?"

Edward neither confirmed nor denied this.

"If you haven't, you should have," Mr. Ferrers said sternly. Then a long circuitous return to the same subject, this time in the guise of whether or not Edward had enough insurance, so that if anything happened to him Janet was taken care of.

Janet was taken care of. But not through Edward's foresight. She had money of her own, left her by her grandmother. They did not touch the principal but used the income.

"If anything happens to me, Janet is taken care of," Edward said. And it was all he said.

"That's fine," Mr. Ferrers said. "I'm very glad to hear it."

He passed on to the subject of Edward's two brothers, who were in business together, and, though very different, were adjusting to each other's personalities. His older brother had already done extremely well; his younger brother, just starting out after a two-year period in the Army, when his schooling was interrupted, had, of course, a long way to go, but he was showing such a determination to succeed that Mr. Ferrers could find nothing but satisfaction in contemplating his son's efforts.

"I know," Edward said, and "That's true," and "He certainly does," and his answers sounded so drowsy that at last Mr. Ferrers said with exasperation, "If you're so sleepy, why don't you go to bed?"

"Because I don't feel like it," Edward said. "I'm fine here on the sofa." Leaving the riverboat with nobody at the wheel, he began to talk about himself — a thing he did easily with other people but not with his father. He talked about his teaching — what he tried to put into it, and what he got from it. And about a very talented pupil, who showed signs of becoming a writer. And then about the book that he himself had been occupied with for the past five years — a study of changing social life in nineteenth-century England as reflected in the diaries of the Reverend John Skinner.

His older brother, it appeared, considered that Edward was a failure — not only financially but as a teacher. If he were a successful teacher he would be called to Harvard or Princeton or Yale.

"I don't know that I'd be happy teaching at Harvard or Princeton or Yale," Edward said. "And I am happy where I am. And valued."

"He doesn't understand," Mr. Ferrers said. "He lives very extravagantly — too much so, I think. They're flying very high these days. But he judges people by how much money they make. I explained to him when he was here that you care about money, too, but that you also care about other things, and that you are content to have a little less money and do the kind of work that interests you. . . . But, of course, you two boys have always been very different. And I don't interfere in your lives. I've given each of you a good education, the best I could manage, and from that time on you have been on your own. And you all made good. I'm proud of each of you. I have three fine boys."

Edward, floating, suspended, not quite anywhere, felt the safety in his father's voice, and a freedom in talking to him that he had never had before, not merely with his father but perhaps not even with anybody. In an unsafe world, he was safe only with one person. Which was so strange a thought — that his father, whom he had consistently opposed and resisted his whole life, and at one time even hated, should turn out to be the one person he felt utterly safe with — that he sat up and rearranged the pillows.

He would have gone on talking, half awake, drowsy but happy, for hours, and when Mr. Ferrers said, "Well, son, it's almost midnight, you'd better get some sleep," he got up from the sofa reluctantly. They went back through the sun parlor into the living room, and Edward blinked his eyes at the light, having been accustomed to darkness. He sat down at his stepmother's desk, took her pen, and wrote out a check for twenty dollars, and handed it to his father, who, smiling, tore the check up and dropped it in the wastebasket and went on talking about how much it meant to him to have Edward home.

The Thistles in Sweden

THE brownstone is on Murray Hill, facing south. The year is 1950. We have the top floor-through, and our windows are not as tall as the windows on the lower floors. They are deeply recessed, and almost square, and have divided panes. I know that beauty is in the eye of the beholder and all that, but even so, these windows are romantic. The apartment could be in Leningrad or Innsbruck or Dresden (before the bombs fell on it) or Parma or any place we have never been to. When I come home at night, I look forward to the moment when I turn the corner and raise my eyes to those three lighted windows. Since I was a child, no place has been quite so much home to me. The front windows look out on Thirty-sixth Street, the back windows on an unpainted brick wall (the side of a house on Lexington Avenue) with no break in it on our floor, but on the floor below there is a single window with a potted plant, and when we raise our eyes we see the sky, so the room is neither dark nor prisonlike.

Since we are bothered by street noises, the sensible thing would be to use this room to sleep in, but it seems to want to be our living room, and offers two irresistible arguments: (1) a Victorian white marble fireplace and (2) a stairway. If we have a fireplace it should be in the living room, even though the chimney is blocked up, so we can't have a fire in it. (I spend a good deal of time unblocking it, in my mind.) The stairs are the only access to the roof for the whole building. There is, of course, nothing up there, but it looks as if we are in a house and you can go upstairs to bed, and this is very cozy: a house on the top floor of a brownstone walk-up. I draw the bolt and push the trapdoor up with my shoulder, and Margaret and I stand together, holding the cat, Floribunda, in our arms so she will not escape, and see the stars (when there are any) or the winking lights of an airplane, or sometimes a hallucinatory effect brought about by fog or very fine rain and mist — the lighted windows of midtown skyscrapers set in space, without any surrounding masonry. The living room and the bedroom both have a door opening onto the outer hall, which, since we are on the top floor and nobody else in the building uses it, we regard as part of the apartment. We leave these doors open when we are at home, and the stair railing and the head of the stairs are blocked off with huge pieces of cardboard. The landlord says that this is a violation of the fire laws, but we cannot think of any other way to keep Floribunda from escaping down the stairs, and neither can he.

The living-room curtains are of heavy Swedish linen: life-sized thistles, printed in light blue and charcoal grey, on a white background. They are very beautiful (and so must the thistles in Sweden be) and they also have an emotional context; Margaret made them, and, when they did not hang properly, wept, and ripped them apart and remade them, and now they do hang properly. The bedroom curtains are of a soft ivory material, with seashells — cowries, scallops, sea urchins and sand dollars, turbinates, auriculae — drawn on them in brown indelible ink, with a flowpen. The bedroom floor is black, the walls are sandalwood, the woodwork is white. On the wall above the double bed is a mural in two sections — a hexagonal tower in an imaginary kingdom that resembles Persia. Children are flying kites from the roof. Inside the tower, another child is playing on a musical instrument that is cousin to the lute. The paperhanger hung the panels the wrong way, so the tower is even stranger architecturally than the artist intended. The parapet encloses outer instead of inner space — like a man talking to somebody who is standing behind him, facing the other way. And the fish-shaped kite, where is that being flown from? And by whom? Some other children are flying kites from the roof of the tower next to this one, perhaps, only there wasn't room to show it. (Lying in bed I often, in my mind, correct the paperhanger's mistake.) Next to the mural there is a projection made by a chimney that conducts sounds from the house next door. Or rather, a single sound: a baby crying in the night. The brownstone next door is not divided into apartments, and so much money has been spent on the outside (blue shutters, fresh paint, stucco, polished brass, etc.) that, for this neighborhood, the effect of chic is overdone. We assume there is a nurse, but nobody ever does anything when the baby cries, and the sound that comes through the wall is unbearably sad. (Unable to stand it any longer, Margaret gets up and goes through the brick chimney and picks the baby up and brings it back into our bedroom and rocks it.)

The double chest of drawers came from Macy's unfinished-furniture department, and Margaret gave it nine coats of enamel before she was satisfied with the way it looked. The black lacquered dining table (we have two dining tables and no dining room) is used as a desk. Over it hangs a large engraving of the Spanish Steps, which, two years ago, in the summer of 1948, for a brief time belonged to us — flower stands, big umbrellas, Bernini fountain, English Tea Room, Keats museum, children with no conception of bedtime, everything. At night we drape our clothes over two cheap rush-bottom chairs, from Italy. The mahogany dressing table, with an oval mirror in a lyre-shaped frame and turned legs such as one sees in English furniture of the late seventeenth century, came by express from the West Coast. The express company delivered it to the sidewalk in front of the building, and, notified by telephone that this was about to happen, I rushed home from the office to supervise the uncrating. As I stepped from the taxi, I saw the expressman with the mirror and half the lyre in his huge hands. He was looking at it thoughtfully. The rest of the dressing table was ten feet away, by the entrance to the building. The break does not show unless you look closely. And most old furniture has been mended at one time or another.

When we were shown the apartment for the first time, the outgoing tenant let us in and stood by pleasantly while we tried to imagine what the place would look like if it were not so crowded with his furniture. It was hardly possible to take a step for oak tables and chests and sofas and armoires and armchairs. Those ancestral portraits and Italian landscapes in heavy gilt frames that there was no room for on the walls were leaning against the furniture. To get from one room to the next we had to step over pyramids of books and scientific journals. An inventory of the miscellaneous objects and musical instruments in the living room would have taken days and been full of surprises. (Why did he keep that large soup tureen on the floor?) We thought at first he was packing, but he was not; this was the way he lived. If we had asked him to make a place in his life for us too, he would have. He was a very nice man. The disorder was dignified and somehow enviable, and the overfurnished apartment so remote from what went on down below in the street that it was like a cave deep in the forest.

Now it is underfurnished (we have just barely enough money to manage a small one-story house in the country and this apartment in town), instead, and all light and air. The living-room walls are a pale blue that changes according to the light and the time of day and the season of the year and the color of the sky. The walls are hardly there. The furniture is half old and half new, and there isn't much of it, considering the size of the room: a box couch, a cabinet with sliding doors, a small painted bookcase, an easy chair with its ottoman, a round fruitwood side table with long, thin, spidery legs and a glass tray that fits over the top, the table and chairs we eat on, a lowboy that serves as a sideboard, another chair, a wobbly tea cart, and a canvas stool. The couch has a high wooden back, L-shaped, painted black, with a thin gold line. It was made for an old house in Dover, New Hampshire, and after I don't know how many generations found itself in Minneapolis. I first saw it in Margaret's mother's bedroom in Seattle, and now it is here. It took two big men and a lot of patient maneuvering to get it four times past the turning of the stairs. The shawl that is draped over the back and the large tin tray that serves as a coffee table both came from Mexico — a country I do not regard as romantic, even though we have never been there. The lowboy made the trip from the West Coast with the dressing table, and one of its Chippendale legs got broken in transit, or by that same impetuous expressman. I suppose it is a hundred and fifty or two hundred years old. The man in the furniture-repair shop, after considering the broken leg, asked if we wanted the lowboy refinished. I asked why, and he said, "Because it's been painted." We looked, and sure enough it had. "They did that sometimes," he said. "It's painted to simulate mahogany." I asked what was under the paint, and he picked up a chisel and took a delicate gouge out of the underside. This time it was his turn to be surprised. "It's mahogany," he announced. The lowboy was painted to simulate what it actually was, it looks like what it is, so we let it be.

The gateleg table we eat on has four legs instead of the usual six. When the sides are extended, it looks as if the cabinetmaker had been studying Euclid's geometry. Margaret found it in an antique shop in Putnam Valley, and asked me to come look at it. I got out of the car and went in and saw the table and knew I could not live without it. The antique dealer said the table had an interesting history that she wasn't free to tell us. (Was it a real Hepplewhite and not just in the style of? Was it stolen?) She was a very old woman and lived alone. The shop was lined with bookshelves, and the books on the shelves and lying around on the tables were so uncommon I had trouble keeping my hands off them. They were not for sale, the old woman said. They had belonged to her husband, and she was keeping them for her grandchildren; she herself read nothing but murder mysteries.

Margaret wanted the table, but she wanted also to talk about whether or not we could afford it. I can always afford what I dearly want — or rather, when I want something very much I would rather not think about whether or not we can afford it. As we drove away without the table, I said coldly, "We won't talk about it." As if she were the kind of wife she isn't. And we did talk about it, all the way home. The next day we were back, nobody had bought the table in the meantime, I wrote out a check for two hundred dollars, and the old woman gave us a big rag rug to wrap around the marvel so it wouldn't be damaged on the drive home. Also heavy twine to tie it with. But then I asked for a knife, and this upset her, to my astonishment. I looked carefully and saw that the expression in her faded blue eyes was terror: She thought I wanted a knife so I could murder her and make off with the table *and* the check. It is disquieting to have one's intentions so misjudged. (Am I a murderer? And is it usual for the murderer to ask for his weapon?) "A pair of scissors will do just as well," I said, and the color came back into her face.

The rug the table now stands on is only slightly larger than the table-top. It is threadbare, but we cannot find another like it. For some reason, it is the last yellowish beige rug ever made. People with no children have perfectionism to fall back on.

The space between the fireplace and the door to the kitchen is filled by shelves and a shallow cupboard. The tea cart is kept under the stairs. Then comes the door to the coat closet, the inside of which is painted a particularly beautiful shade of Chinese red, and the door to the hall. On the sliding-door cabinet (we have turned the corner now and are moving toward the windows) there is a pottery lamp with a wide perforated grey paper shade and such a long thin neck that it seems to be trying to turn into a crane. Also a record player that plays only 78s and has to be wound after every record. The oil painting over the couch is of a rock quarry in Maine, and we have discovered that it changes according to the time of day and the color of the sky. It is particularly alive after a snowfall.

HERE we live, in our modest perfectionism, with two black cats. The one on the mantelpiece is Bastet, the Egyptian goddess of love and joy. The other is under the impression that she is our child. This is our fault, of course, not hers. Around her neck she wears a scarlet ribbon, or sometimes a turquoise ribbon, or a collar with little bells. Her toys dangle from the tea cart, her kitty litter is in a pan beside the bathtub, and she sleeps on the foot of our bed or curled against the back of Margaret's knees. When she is bored she asks us to remove a piece of the cardboard barricade so she can go tippeting down the stairs and pay a call on the landlord and his wife, Mr. and Mrs. Holmes, who live in the garden apartment and have the rear half of the second floor, with an inside stairs, so they really do go upstairs to bed. The front part of the second floor is the pied-à-terre of the artist who designed the wallpaper mural of the children flying kites from a hexagonal tower in an imaginary kingdom that resembles Persia. It is through the artist's influence (Mr. Holmes is intimidated by her) that we managed to get our rent-controlled apartment, for which we pay a hundred and thirteen dollars and some odd cents. The landlord wishes we paid more, and Mr. and Mrs. Venable, who live under us, wish we'd get a larger rug for the living room. Their bedroom is on the back, and Margaret's heels crossing the ceiling at night keep them awake. Also, in the early morning the Egyptian goddess leaves our bed and chases wooden spools and glass marbles from one end of the living room to the other. The Venables have mentioned this subject of the larger rug to the landlord and he has mentioned it to us. We do nothing about it, except that Margaret puts the spools and marbles out of Floribunda's reach when we go to bed at night, and walks around in her stocking feet after ten o'clock. Some day, when we are kept awake by footsteps crossing our bedroom ceiling, hammering, furniture being moved, and other idiot noises, we will remember the Venables and wish we had been more considerate.

The Venables leave their door open too, and on our way up the stairs I look back over my shoulder and see chintz-covered chairs and Oriental rugs and the lamplight falling discreetly on an Early American this and an Old English that. (No children here, either; Mrs. Venable works in a decorator's shop.) Mrs. Pickering, third floor, keeps her door closed. She is a sweet-faced woman who smiles when we meet her on the stairs. She has a grown son and daughter who come to see her regularly, but her life isn't the same as when they were growing up and Mr. Pickering was alive. (Did she tell us this or have I invented it?) If we met her anywhere but on the stairs we would have racked our brains to find something to say to her. The Holmeses' furniture is nondescript but comfortable. Mrs. Holmes has lovely brown eyes and the voice that goes with them, and it is no wonder that Floribunda likes to sit on her lap. *He* wants everybody to be happy, which is not exactly the way to be happy yourself, and he isn't. If we all paid a little more rent, it would make him happier, but we don't feel like it, any of us.

I am happy because we are in town: I don't have to commute in bad weather. I can walk to the office. And after the theater we jump in a cab and are home in five minutes. I stand at the front window listening to the weather report. It is snowing in Westchester, and the driving conditions are very bad. In Thirty-sixth Street it is raining. The middle-aged man who lives on the top floor of the brownstone directly across from us is in the habit of posing at the window with a curtain partly wrapped around his naked body. He keeps guppies or goldfish in a lighted tank, spends the whole day in a kimono ironing, and at odd moments goes to the front window and acts out somebody's sexual dream. If I could only marry him off to the old woman who goes through the trash baskets on Lexington Avenue, talking to herself. What pleasure she would have in showing him the things she has brought home in her string bag — treasures whose value nobody else realizes. And what satisfaction to him it would be to wrap himself in a curtain just for her.

The view to the south is cut off by a big apartment building on Thirty-fifth Street. The only one. If it were not there (I spend a good deal of time demolishing it, with my bare hands) we would have the whole of the sky to look at. Because I have not looked carefully enough at the expression in Margaret's eyes, I go on thinking that she is happy too. When I met her she was working in a publishing house. Shortly after we decided to get married she was offered a job with the *Partisan Review*. If she had taken it, it would have meant commuting with me or even commuting at different hours from when I did. When I was a little boy and came home from school and called out, "Is anybody home?" somebody nearly always was. I took it for granted that the same thing would be true when I married. We didn't talk about it, and should have. I didn't understand that in her mind it was the chance of a fulfilling experience. Because she saw that I could not even imagine her saying yes, she said no, and turned her attention to learning how to cook and keep house. If we had had children right away it would have been different; but then if we had had children we wouldn't have been living on the top floor of a brownstone on Thirty-sixth Street.

The days in town are long and empty for her. The telephone doesn't ring anything like as often as it does when we are in the country. There Hester Gale comes across the road to see how Margaret is, or because she is out of cake flour, and they have coffee together. Margaret sews with Olivia Bingham. There are conversations in the supermarket. And miles of woods to walk in. Old Mrs. Delano, whose front door on Thirty-sixth Street is ten feet west of ours, is no help whatever. Though she

knows Margaret's Aunt Caroline, she doesn't know that Margaret is her
niece, or even that she exists, probably, and Margaret has no intention of
telling her. Any more than she has any intention of telling me that in this
place where I am so happy she feels like a prisoner much of the time.

She is accustomed to space, to a part of the country where there is
more room than people and buildings to occupy it. In her childhood she
woke up in the morning in a big house set on a wide lawn, with towering
pine trees behind it, and a copper beech as big as two brownstones, and
a snow-capped mountain that mysteriously comes and goes, like an idea
in the mind. Every afternoon after school she went cantering through the
trees on horseback. Now she is confined to two rooms—the kitchen
cannot be called a room; it is hardly bigger than a handkerchief—and
these two rooms are not enough. This is a secret she manages to keep
from me so I can go on being happy.

There is another secret that cannot be kept from me because, with her
head in a frame made by my head, arms, and shoulder, I know when she
weeps. She weeps because her period was five days late and she thought
something had happened that she now knows is not going to happen.
The child is there, and could just as well as not decide to come to us, and
doesn't, month after month. Instead, we consult one gynecologist after
another, and take embarrassing tests (only they don't really embarrass
me, they just seem unreal). And what the doctors do not tell us is why,
when there is nothing wrong with either of us, nothing happens. Before
we can have a child we must solve a riddle, like Oedipus and the Sphinx.
On my forty-second birthday I go to the Spence-Chapin adoption service
and explain our situation to a woman who listens attentively. I like her
and feel that she understands how terribly much we want a child, and she
shocks me by reaching across the desk and taking the application blank
out of my hands: Forty-two is the age past which the agency will not
consider giving out a child for adoption.

MEANWHILE, Margaret herself has been adopted, by the Italian market
under the El at Third Avenue and Thirty-fourth Street. Four or five
whistling boys with white aprons wrapped around their skinny hips run
it. They also appear to own it, but what could be more unlikely? Their
faces light up when Margaret walks into the store. They drop what they
are doing and come to greet her as if she were their older sister. And
whatever she asks for, it turns out they have. Their meat is never tough,

their vegetables are not tarnished and limp, their sole is just as good as the fish market's and nothing like as expensive. Now one boy, now another arrives at our door with a carton of groceries balanced on his head, having taken the stairs two steps at a time. Four flights are nothing to them. They are in business for the pure pleasure of it. They don't think or talk about love, they just do it. Or perhaps it isn't love but joy. But over what? Over the fact that they are alive and so are we?

It occurs to the landlord that the tenants could carry their garbage down to the street and then he wouldn't have to. I prepare for a scene, compose angry speeches in the bath. Everybody knows what landlords are like — only he isn't like that. He isn't even a landlord, strictly speaking. He has a good job with an actuarial firm. The building is a hobby. It was very run down when he bought it, and he has had the pleasure of fixing it up. We meet on the front sidewalk as I am on my way to work. Looking up at him — he is a very tall man — I announce that I will not carry our garbage down. Looking down at me, he says that if we don't feel like carrying our garbage down he will go on doing it. What an unsatisfactory man to quarrel with.

I come home from the office and find that Margaret has spent the afternoon drawing: a pewter coffeepot (Nantucket), a Venetian-glass goblet, a white china serving dish with a handle and a cover, two eggs, a lemon, apples, a rumpled napkin with a blue border. Or the view from the living room all the way into the bedroom, through three doorways, involving the kind of foreshortened perspective Italian Renaissance artists were so fond of. Or the view from the bedroom windows (the apartment house on Thirty-fifth Street that I have so often taken down I now see is all right; it belongs there) in sepia wash. Or her own head and shoulders reflected in the dressing-table mirror. Or the goblet, the coffeepot, the lemon, a green pepper, and a brown luster bowl. The luster bowl has a chip in it, and so the old woman in the antique shop in Putnam Valley gave it to us for a dollar, after the table was safely stowed away in the backseat of the car. And some years later, her daughter, sitting next to me at a formal dinner party, said, "You're mistaken. Mother was absolutely fearless." She said it again, perceiving that I did not believe her. Somebody is mistaken, and it could just as well as not be me. Even though I looked quite carefully at the old woman's expression. In any case, there is something I didn't see. Her husband — the man whose books the old woman was unwilling to sell — committed suicide. "I was their only child, and had to deal with sadness all my life — sadness from within as well as from without." If the expression in the old woman's eyes was not terror, what was it?

FLORIBUNDA misses the country, and sits at the top of the living-room stairs, clawing at the trapdoor. She refuses to eat, is shedding. Her hairs are on everything. One night we take her across Park Avenue to the Morgan Library and push the big iron gate open like conspirators about to steal the forty-two-line Gutenberg Bible or the three folios of Redouté's roses. Floribunda leaps from Margaret's arms and runs across the sickly grass and climbs a small tree. Ecstatically she sharpens her claws on the bark. I know that we will be arrested, but it is worth it.

NEITHER the landlord and his wife, nor the artist and her husband, who is Dutch, nor Mrs. Pickering, nor the Venables ever entertain in their apartments, but we have a season of being sociable. We have the Fitzgeralds and Eileen Fitzgerald's father from Dublin for dinner. We celebrate Bastille Day with the Potters. We have Elinor Hinkley's mother to tea. She arrives at the head of the stairs, where she can see into the living room, and exclaims — before she has even caught her breath — "What beautiful horizontal surfaces!" She is incapable of small talk. Instead, she describes the spiritual emanations of a row of huge granite boulders lining the driveway of her house on Martha's Vineyard. And other phenomena that cannot be described very easily, or that, when described, cannot be appreciated by someone who isn't half mad or a Theosophist.

Dean Wilson brings one intelligent, pretty girl after another to meet us. Like the woman in Isak Dinesen's story who sailed the seas looking for the perfect blue, he is looking for a flawless girl. Flawless in whose eyes is the question. And isn't flawlessness itself a serious flaw? "What a charming girl," we say afterward, and he looks in our faces and is not satisfied, and brings still another girl, including, finally, Ivy Sérurier, who is half English and half French. When she was seven years old her nurse took her every day to the Jardin du Luxembourg and there she ran after a hoop. She is attracted to all forms of occult knowledge, and things happen to her that do not happen to anyone who does not have a destiny. The light bulbs respond to her amazing stories by giving off a higher voltage. The expression on our faces is satisfactory. Dean brings her again, and again. He asks Margaret if she thinks they should get married, but he cannot quite bring himself to ask Ivy this question.

On a night when we are expecting Henry Coddington to dinner, Hester and Nick Gale come up the stairs blithely at seven o'clock, having got the invitation wrong. Or perhaps it is our fault. There is plenty of food, and it turns out to be a pleasant evening. The guests get on well, but Henry must have thought we did not want to know why Louise left him and took their little girl, whom he idolizes — that we have insulated ourselves from his catastrophe by asking this couple from the country. Anyway, he never comes or calls again. But other people come. Melissa Lovejoy, from Montgomery, Alabama, comes for Sunday lunch, and her hilarious account of her skirmishes with her mother-in-law make the tears run down my cheeks. Melissa, who loves beautiful china, looks around the living room and sees what no one else has ever seen or commented on — a Meissen plate on the other end of the mantelpiece from the Egyptian cat. It is white, with very small green grape leaves and a wide filigree border. Margaret's brother John had it in his rucksack when he made his way from Geneva to Bordeaux in May 1940. As easily as the plate could have got broken, so he could have ended up in a detention camp and then what? But they are both safe, intact, here in New York. He has his own place, on Lexington Avenue in the Fifties. On Christmas Eve he bends down and selects a present for Margaret and another for me from the pile under the tree at the foot of the stair.

On New Year's Eve, John and Dean and Ivy and Margaret and I sit down to dinner. The champagne cork hits the ceiling. Between courses we take turns getting up and going into the bedroom and waiting behind a closed door until a voice calls "Ready!" If you were a school of Italian painting or a color of the spectrum or a character from fiction, what school of Italian painting or color or character would you be? John is Dostoevski's Idiot, Margaret is lavender blue. Elinor Hinkley joins us for dessert. Just before midnight a couple from the U.N., whom Dean has invited, come up the stairs and an hour later on the dot they leave for another party. It is daylight when we push our chairs back. We have not left the table (except to go into the front room while the questions are being framed) all night long. With our heads out of the window, Margaret and I wait for them to emerge from the building and then we call down to them, "Happy New Year!" But softly, so as not to wake up the neighbors.

Margaret's Uncle James, who is not her uncle but her mother's first cousin, comes to dinner, bringing long-stemmed red roses. He confesses that he has been waiting for this invitation ever since we were married — eight or nine years — and he thoroughly enjoys himself, though he is dying of cancer of the throat. Faced with extinction, you can't just stand and scream; it isn't good manners. And men and women of that generation do not discuss their feelings. Anyway he doesn't. Instead he says, "I like your curtains, Margaret," and we are filled with remorse that we didn't ask him sooner. But still, he did come to dinner. And satisfied his curiosity about the way we live. And we were surprised to discover that we were fond of him — as the rabbit is surprised to discover that he is what was concealed in the magician's hat. *I am not the person you thought I was,* Uncle James as much as says, sitting back in the easy chair but not using the ottoman lest he look ill.

I realize that the air is full of cigarette smoke, and prop the trapdoor open with a couple of books — but only a crack. At eleven-thirty Uncle James rises and puts his coat on and says good night, and tromps down the stairs, waking the Venables, and Mrs. Pickering, and the artist and her husband, and Mr. and Mrs. Holmes. And we lock the doors and say what a nice evening it was, and empty the ashtrays, and carry the liquor glasses out to the kitchen, and suddenly perceive an emptiness, an absence. "Floribunda? . . . Pussy?" She is nowhere. She has slipped through the crack that I thought was too small for her to get through. Fur is deceptive, her bone structure is not what I thought it was, and perhaps cats have something in common with cigarette smoke. I have often seen her attenuate herself alarmingly. Outside, on the roof, I call softly, but no little black cat comes. In the night we both wake and talk about her. The bottom of the bed feels strange when we put our feet out and there is nothing there, no weight. When morning comes I dress and go up to the roof again, and make my way toward Park Avenue, stepping over two-foot-high tile walls and making my way around projections and feeling giddy when I peer down into back gardens.

Margaret, meanwhile, has dressed and gone down the stairs. She rings the Delanos' bell, and the Irish maid opens the door. "A little cat came in through my bedroom window last night and the mistress said to put her on the street, so I did." *On the street* . . . when she could so easily have put her back on the roof she came from! "Here, Puss, Puss, Puss . . . here, Puss!" Up Thirty-sixth Street and down Thirty-fifth. All her life she has known nothing but love, and she is so timid. How will she survive with no home? What will the poor creature do? We meet Rose Bernstein, who has just moved into town from our country road, and just as I am saying "On the street. Did you ever hear of anything so heartless?" there is a faint miaow. Floribunda heard us calling and was too frightened to answer. I find her hiding in an areaway. Margaret gathers her up in her arms and we say good-bye to Rose Bernstein, and, unable to believe our good fortune, take her home. Our love and joy.

IN Chicago there is an adoption agency whose policy with respect to age is not so rigid as Spence-Chapin's. We pull strings. (Dean Wilson has a friend whose wife's mother is on the board.) Letters pass back and forth, and finally there we are, in Chicago, nervously waiting in the reception room. Miss Mattie Gessner is susceptible (or so I feel) to the masculine approach. It turns out that she voted for Truman too; and she doesn't reach across the desk and take the application from my hands. Instead she promises to help us. But it isn't as simple as the old song my mother used to sing: Today is not the day they give babies away with a half a pound of tay. The baby that is given to us for adoption must be the child of a couple reasonably like us — that is to say, a man and woman who, in the year 1952, would have a record player that plays only 78s and that you wind by hand; who draw seashells on their bedroom curtains and are made happy by a blocked-up fireplace and a stairway that leads nowhere. And this means we must wait God knows how long.

So we do wait, sometimes in rather odd places for a couple with no children. For example, by the carousel in Central Park. The plunging horses slowly come to a halt with their hoofs in midair. The children get off and more children climb up, take a firm grip on the pole, and look around for their mother or their nurse or their father, in the crowd standing in the open doorway. Slowly the cavalcade begins to move again, and I take the little boy in the plaid snowsuit, with half a pound of English Breakfast, and Margaret takes half a pound of Lipton's and the little girl with blue ribbons in her hair.

WE start going to the country weekends. And then we go for the summer, taking suitcases full of clothes, boxes of unread books, drawing materials, the sewing machine, the typewriter. And in September all this is carried up four flights of stairs. And more: flowers, vegetables from the garden, plants we could not bear to have the frost put an end to, even though we know they will not live long in town. And one by one we take up our winter habits. When Saturday night comes around we put on our coats at ten o'clock and go out to buy the Sunday *Times* at the newspaper stand under the El. We rattle the door of the antique shop on Third Avenue that always has something interesting in the window but has never been known to be open at any hour of any day of the week. On three successive nights we go to *Ring Round the Moon*, *King Lear*, and *An Enemy of the People*, after which it seems strange to sit home reading a book. I am so in love with Adlai Stevenson's speeches that, though I am afraid of driving in ordinary traffic in New York City, I get the car out of the garage and we drive right down the center of 125th Street, in a torchlight parade, hemmed in by a flowing river of people, all of whom feel the way we do.

HOW many years did we live in that apartment on Thirty-sixth Street? From 1950 to — The mere dates are misleading, even if I could get them right, because time was not progressive or in sequence, it was one of Mrs. Hinkley's horizontal surfaces divided into squares. On one square an old woman waters a houseplant in the window of an otherwise blank wall. On another, Albertha, who is black, comes to clean. When she leaves, the apartment looks as if an angel had walked through it. She is the oldest of eleven children. And what she and Margaret say, over a cup of coffee, makes Margaret more able to deal with her solitary life. On another square, we go to the Huguenot Church on Sunday morning, expecting something new and strange, and instead the hymns are perfectly familiar to us from our Presbyterian childhoods: In French they have become more elegant and rhetorical, and it occurs to me that they may not reach all the way to the ear of Heaven. But the old man who then mounts the stairs to the pulpit addresses Seigneur Dieu in a confident voice, as if they are extremely well acquainted, the two of them. On another square we go to Berlitz, and the instructor, a White Russian named Mikhael Milora-dovitch, sits by blandly while Margaret and I say things to each other in French that we have managed not to say in English. I am upset when I discover that she prefers the country to the city. The discussion becomes heated, but because it is in French nothing comes of it. We go on living in the city. Until another summer comes and we fill the car, which is now nearly twenty years old, to the canvas top with our possessions; then, locking the doors of the apartment, we drive off to our other life. At which point the shine goes out of this one. The slipcovers fade and so do the seashells and thistles that are exposed to the direct light of the summer sun. Dust gathers on the books, the lampshades, the record player. In the middle of the night, a hand pries at the trapdoor and, finding it securely locked, tries somewhere else. The man out of Krafft-Ebing shows himself seductively to our blank windows. And the intense heat builds up to a violent thunderstorm. After which there is a spell of cooler weather. And a tragedy. For two days there has been no garbage outside Mrs. Pickering's door in the morning. She does not answer her telephone or the landlord's knocking, and she has not said she was going away. The first floor extends farther back than the rest of the house, and he is able to place a ladder on the roof of this extension. From the top of the ladder he stares into the third-floor bedroom at a terrible sight: Mrs. Pickering, sitting in a wing chair, naked. He thinks it is death he is staring at, but he is mistaken; she has had a stroke. He breaks the door down, and she is taken to the hospital in an ambulance. She does not die, but neither does she ever come back to this apartment. Passing her door on our way up the stairs, we are aware of the silence inside, and think uneasily of those two days and nights of helpless waiting. Along with the silence there is the sense of something malign, of trouble of a very serious kind that could spread all through the house. To ward it off, we draw closer to the other tenants, linger talking on the stairs, and speak to them in a more intimate tone of voice. We have the Holmeses and the Venables and the artist and her husband up for a drink. It doesn't do the trick. There *was* something behind Mrs. Pickering's door. My sister's only son turns up and, since we are in the country, we offer him the apartment to live in until he finds a job. He leads a life there that the books and furniture do not approve of. He brings girls home and makes love to them in our bed, under the very eyes of the children flying kites. He borrows fifty bucks from me, to eat on, and to get some shirts, so he won't look like a bum when he goes job hunting. He has a check coming from his previous job, in Florida, and will pay me back next week. The check doesn't come, and he borrows some more money, and then some more, and it begins to mount up. Jobs that were as good as promised to him vanish into thin air, and meanwhile we are his sole means of support. I listen attentively to what I more and more suspect are inventions, but his footwork is fast, and what he says could be true; it just isn't what he said before, quite. My bones inform me that I am not the first person these excuses and appeals have been tried out on. He comes to my office to tell me that he has given up the idea of staying in New York and can I let him have the fare home, and I dial my sister's number in Evansville, Indiana, and hand the receiver to him and leave the room.

I give up smoking on one square, and on another I go through all the variant pages of a book I have been writing for four and a half years and reduce it to a single pile of manuscript. This I put in a blue canvas duffel bag that can absentmindedly be left behind on the curbing when we drive off to the country at eleven o'clock of a spring night. At midnight, driving up the Taconic Parkway, I suddenly see in my mind's eye the backseat of the car: The blue duffel bag is not there. Nor, when we come to a stop in front of our house on Thirty-sixth Street at one o'clock in the morning, is it on the sidewalk where I left it. With a dry mouth I describe it to the desk sergeant in the police station, and he gets up and goes into the back room. "No, nothing," he calls. And then, as we are almost at the door, "Wait a minute."

On another square Margaret starts behaving in a way that is not at all like her. Sleepy at ten o'clock in the evening, and when I open my eyes in the morning she is already awake and looking at me. Her face is somehow different. Can it be that she is . . . that we are going to . . . that . . . I study her when she is not aware that I am looking at her, and find in her behavior the answer to that riddle: If we are so longing for a child that we are willing to bring up somebody else's child — anybody's child whatever — then we may as well be allowed to have our own. Margaret comes home from the doctor bringing the news to me that I have not dared break to her.

After boning up on the subject, in a book, she shows me, on her finger, just how long the child in her womb now is. And it is growing larger, very slowly. And so is she. The child is safe inside her, and she is safe so long as she remains a prisoner in this top-floor apartment. The doctor has forbidden her to use the stairs. Everybody comes to see her, instead — including an emanation from the silent apartment two floors below. A black man, a stranger, suddenly appears at the top of the stairs. His intention, unclear but frightening, shows in his face, in his eyes. But the goddess Bastet is at work again, and the man comes on Albertha's day, and she, with a stream of such foulmouthed cursing as Margaret has never heard in her life, sends him running down the stairs. If he had come on a day that was not Albertha's day, when Margaret was there alone — But this holds true for everything, good or bad.

MARGARET'S face grows rounder, and she no longer has a secret that must be kept from me. The days while I am at the office are not lonely, and time is an unbroken landscape of daydreaming. When I get home at six o'clock, I creep in under the roof of the spell she is under, and am allowed into the daydream. But what shall we tell Miss Mattie Gessner when she comes to investigate the way we live?

The apartment, feeling our inattention, begins to withdraw from us sadly. And then something else unexpected happens. The landlord, having achieved perfection, having created the Peaceable Kingdom on Thirty-sixth Street, is restless and wants to begin all over again. "You'll be sorry," his wife tells him, stroking Floribunda's ear, and he is. But by that time they are living uptown, in a much less handsome house in the Nineties — a house that needs fixing from top to bottom. But it will never have any style, and it is filled with disagreeable tenants who do not pay their rent on time. On Thirty-sixth Street we have a new landlord, and in no time his hand is on everything. He hangs a cheap print of van Gogh's *The Drawbridge* in the downstairs foyer. We are obliged to take down the cardboard barricade and keep our doors closed. Hardly a day passes without some maddening new improvement. The artist is the first to go. Then we give notice; how is Margaret to carry the baby, the stroller, the package from the drugstore, etc., up four flights of stairs? *What better place can there be to bring up a child in?* the marble fireplace asks, remembering the eighteen-eighties, when this was a one-family house and our top-floor living room was the nursery. The stairway to the roof was devoted to the previous tenant (the man who lived in the midst of a monumental clutter) and says bitterly, in the night, when we are not awake to hear, *They seem as much a part of your life as the doors and windows, and then it turns out that they are not a part of your life at all. The moving men come and cart all the furniture away, and the people go down to the street, and that's the last you see of them. . . .*

What will the fireplace and the stairway to the roof say when they discover that they are about to be shut off forever from the front room? The landlord is planning to divide our apartment into two apartments and charge the same for each that he is now getting for the floor-through. For every evil under the sun there is a remedy or there is none. I soak the mural of the children flying kites, hoping to remove it intact and put it up somewhere in the house in the country. The paper tears no matter how gently I pull it loose from the wall, and comes off in little pieces, which end up in the wastebasket.

Now when I walk past that house I look up at the windows that could be in Leningrad or Innsbruck or Dresden or Parma, and I think of the stairway that led only to the trapdoor in the roof, and of the marble fireplace, the bathroom skylight, and the tiny kitchen, and of what school of Italian painting we would have been if we had been a school of Italian painting, and poor Mrs. Pickering sitting in her bedroom chair with her eyes wide open, waiting for help, and the rainy nights on Thirty-sixth Street, and the grey-and-blue thistles, the brown seashells, the Mills Brothers singing *Shine, little glowworm, glimmer, glimmer,* and the guests who came the wrong night, the guest who was going to die and knew it, the sound of my typewriter, and of a paintbrush clinking in a glass of cloudy water, and Floribunda's adventure, and Margaret's empty days, and how it was settled that, although I wanted to put my head on her breast as I was falling asleep, she needed even more (at that point) to put her head on mine. And of our child's coming, at last, and the black cat who thought *she* was our child, and of the two friends who didn't after all get married, and the old woman who found one treasure after another in the trash baskets all up and down Lexington Avenue, and that other old woman, now dead, who was so driven by the need to describe the inner life of very large granite boulders. I think of how Miss Mattie Gessner's face fell and how she closed her notebook and became a stranger to us, who had been so deeply our friend. I think of the oversexed ironer, and the Holmeses, and the Venables, and the stranger who meant nobody good and was frightened away by Albertha's cursing, and the hissing of the air brakes of the Lexington Avenue bus, and the curtains moving at the open window, and the baby crying on the other side of the wall. I think of that happy grocery store run by boys, and the horse-drawn flower cart that sometimes waited on the corner, and the sound of footsteps in the night, and the sudden no-sound that meant it was snowing, and I think of the unknown man or woman who found the blue duffel bag with the manuscript of my novel in it and took it to the police station, and the musical instrument (not a lute, but that's what the artist must have had in mind, only she no longer bothers to look at objects and draws what she remembers them as being like) played in the dark, over our sleeping bodies, while the children flew their kites, and I think if it is true that we are all in the hands of God, what a capacious hand it must be.

The Poor Orphan Girl

THE poor orphan girl had no mother and no father and was raised by her grandmother on one of the wind-swept islands of the Outer Hebrides. When she began running after the boys, her grandmother shipped her off to a cousin in Glasgow. At first the girl was well behaved and lent a hand wherever it was needed, and the cousin thought the grandmother just didn't understand the younger generation. But then she started staying out late at night and keeping bad company, and the cousin saw what the grandmother was up against. So she had a serious talk with the girl, and the girl made all sorts of promises, which she didn't keep, and the cousin didn't want to be blamed if the girl got in the family way, so she took her to an employment agency that specialized in sending servants to America.

"Mercy!" exclaimed the head of the most dependable domestic employment agency in New York City, when she looked at the girl's folder. "An unspoiled country girl, willing and strong, and with a heart of gold!" The folder was shown to a Class A client with a Fifth Avenue address, who snapped her up. The immigration papers were filled out, and the deposit paid, and the girl found herself on a boat going to America. What she was expecting was, naturally, what she had seen in the flicks. What she got was a six-by-eleven bedroom looking out on the back of another building, with a closet six inches deep, and the customary dwarf's bathtub that you find in servants' bathrooms in old apartment buildings. On the other hand, the girl had never before had a bed all to herself and a toilet that wasn't either outdoors or on the landing and shared by several large families. She wrote home to her grandmother that she was in luck.

She got on all right with the cook, and there was no heavy work, because a cleaning woman came in twice a week and a laundress two days, and the windows were done by a window-washing company, and all the girl had to do was remember what she was told. Unfortunately, this was more than she could manage. During dinner parties she couldn't decide whether you serve from the right and clear from the left or serve from the left and clear from the right, so she did both, and when she made the beds the top sheet was not securely fastened, and she used the master's washcloth to clean the tub, and what with one thing and another, including the state of her room, she received notice after two weeks and returned to the employment office looking only a little less fresh than when she arrived from Scotland. The head of the agency said, "This time suppose we don't aim quite so high. You don't mind children?" The girl said no, she liked children — which was true, she did — and off she went to an address on Park Avenue. The interview was successful, and she found herself in the exact same bedroom with the shallow closet and the little bath, only the room looked out on a blank wall instead of the back of another building. The work was harder than before and the hours much longer, but at least there were no dinner parties. She was supposed to have breakfast ready by quarter of eight, which was impossible, but she tried. Then she walked the children to the corner where they took the school bus, and made the children's beds, and picked up the toys, and ran the vacuum, and stuffed the clothes into the washing machine and the dryer, and so on.

In the afternoon she walked the dog and went to the supermarket, where she soon knew everybody, and Joe, who weighed the vegetables and was old enough to be her father, said, "Here comes my sweetheart," and Arthur the butcher said, "Tell me — where'd you get those beautyful eyes?" Then she took the children to the Park, and got their supper, and so on. She was supposed to baby-sit when the master and mistress went out, but they didn't very often go out. Once in a blue moon, to an early movie, was about the extent of it. If she had been in Glasgow, she would have known what to do with her evenings. Here she didn't know anybody, so she went to bed.

ONE day when she was with the children in the Park, she met a girl named Cathleen, who asked her to go with her to a dance hall on Eighty-sixth Street. This turned out to be very different from the Outer Hebrides, and just like the flicks. The next morning, her head was full of impressions, mostly of a sad young man who said he was in love with her and almost persuaded her to go home with him, and she was simultaneously pleased with herself for resisting temptation and sorry she hadn't done it. She burned the bacon, and the master wrinkled his nose over the coffee, but by that time she was stretched out on her bed getting forty winks. As the day wore on, a number of things went wrong; the dishwasher foamed all over the kitchen floor, because she had used the washing-machine detergent, and she broke a cup, and put a pair of red corduroy overalls in the washing machine in the same load with some pillowcases and the mistress's blouses and the children's underwear. They all were stained a permanent pink, but the mistress forgave her, because anyone can make a mistake now and then, and the cup was too small a matter to make a thing of. During dinner, the telephone rang, and it was for her. Though she had intended to fall into bed as soon as she finished the dinner dishes, she got dressed instead and met Cathleen at a bar on Second Avenue where they fed dimes into a jukebox, and another boy wanted her to go home with him, and she was so tired she almost did, but instead she left before Cathleen was ready, and was home in bed by two o'clock. She overslept, and there wasn't even time to comb her hair. She managed to stay out of sight until the master had left for his office, but then she forgot, so the mistress did catch her looking like I don't know what. A queer expression passed over her face, but she didn't say anything, and the girl realized that the mistress wasn't ever going to say anything *no matter what happened.*

The telephone always seemed to ring during dinner, and though there was an extension in the kitchen, the girl didn't think it was polite for her to answer it, so she let the master get up from the table and go to the phone in the bedroom. Sometimes, after the third or fourth call, she thought she could detect a note of irritation in his voice when he said, "It's for you." But she had the tray ready with the whiskey and the ice cubes and the jigger and all when he got home at night, and that he liked. As for the children, at first they didn't want to have anything to do with her. The mistress explained that they were very attached to the previous mother's helper — a German girl who had left to get married — and she was not to mind. She didn't. That is, she didn't mind anything but the fact they were being brought up as heathens. So she told them about how the Jews crucified Our Lord, and about the Blessed Saints, and Mary and Joseph, and promised to take them to Mass, and in no time they were eating out of her hand.

She found out there were more bars and dance halls than you could shake a stick at, and she was in one or another of them five nights out of seven. The other two nights she went straight to bed as soon as she had pressed the button on the dishwashing machine. In a hamburger bar she met a boy with blond wavy hair who was an orphan like her, only he had been raised in a Home. Though he didn't say he was in love with her, still and all she liked him. He was interesting to talk to, because so many things seemed to have happened to him, and he didn't ask her to go home with him, so she had no chance to refuse. She didn't really expect to hear from him again, but he called the very next night. She met him in front of the movie house, and during the movie she could feel his arm resting lightly on the back of her seat, and once or twice he gave her shoulder a squeeze, but she didn't have to move her leg away or say "Don't." Afterward, they went to a bar on First Avenue. She told him all about her cousin's family in Glasgow, and about coming over on the boat, and the things she liked about Cathleen and the things she didn't like, and about the way it used to be at home before her mother died and she went to live with her grandmother. Finally she was all talked out, and she just sat there, feeling happy and peaceful. He said, "Another beer?" and she said no, and he had one last one, which he didn't spend any time over, and then he put his hand on the back of her neck and said, "Come on, baby, I'll walk you to your domicile." And that was what she thought they were doing, only when she looked up they were standing in front of the building where *he* lived. He said, "I just want to get a coat, I'm chilly," and she said, "I'll wait here," and he said, "At this time of night, in this neighborhood? Are you out of your mind?" So she followed him up six flights of stairs, and the first thing she knew she was having her clothes torn off her, and the rest she didn't remember. It was daylight when she got home, and she had to wake the night elevator man, who was married and cranky, and he made a fresh remark, which she ignored.

SHE went to church but she was afraid to go to confession, for fear the priest would find out she was an orphan and put her in a Home. If she had only saved her money, she could have got on the boat and gone back to Scotland, but she had bought clothes instead. Lots of clothes. The children's closets were full of them. She could hear her grandmother's voice saying, "You're going to the dogs," and it was true, she was. She also had a stomach-ache, and it didn't go away. For three days she went around doubled up with the pain, and then the mistress noticed it and made her go to a doctor. They paid her wages while she was in the hospital having her appendix out, and for two weeks afterward, but they didn't want her to come back, because they had this colored woman, so she went to see the lady at the employment agency who had been so nice to her, only this time she was busy and somebody else gave her an address on Lexington Avenue, and on the way there she passed a bar-and-grill she liked the looks of. It was called Home on the Range, and it was pitch dark even in the daytime. Maybe I ought to start a New Life, the girl thought, and it turned out they did need a waitress, so that was that. Except that she wasn't forgotten. The children remembered her. Of all the maids, they liked her the best, and never forgot what she told them. And one night about a year after she left, the master was awakened out of a sound sleep by the ringing of the telephone, and a sad-voiced young man asked to speak to her. "No, you can't speak to her!" the master said indignantly. "Do you realize what time it is?" The sad voice seemed surprised to learn that it was the middle of the night, and unable to understand why anybody should mind being called at that hour, and unwilling to believe that the girl wasn't there.

The Lily-White Boys

THE Follansbees' Christmas party was at teatime on Christmas Day, and it was for all ages. Ignoring the fire laws, the big Christmas tree standing between the two front windows in the living room of the Park Avenue apartment had candles on it. When the last one was lit, somebody flipped a light switch, and in the hush that fell over the room the soft yellow candlelight fell on the upturned faces of the children sitting on the floor in a ring around the base of the tree, bringing tears to the eyes of the susceptible. The tree was strung with loops of gold and silver tinsel and popcorn and colored paper, and some of the glass ornaments — the hardy tin soldier, the drum, the nutmeg, and the Man in the Moon — went all the way back to Beth Follansbee's childhood. While the presents were being distributed, Mark Follansbee stood by with a bucket of water and a broom. The room smelled of warm wax and balsam.

The big red candles on the mantelpiece burned down slowly in their nest of holly. In the dining room, presiding over the cut-glass punch bowl, Beth Follansbee said, "You let the peaches sit all day in a quart of vodka, and then you add two bottles of white wine and a bottle of champagne — be a little careful, it isn't as innocuous as you might think," and with her eyebrows she signaled to the maid that the plate of watercress sandwiches needed refilling. Those that liked to sing had gathered around the piano in the living room and, having done justice to all the familiar carols, were singing with gusto, "Seven for the seven stars in the sky and six for the six proud walkers. Five for the symbols at your door and four for the Gospel makers, Three, three, the rivals, Two, two, the lily-white boys, clothèd all in green-ho. One is one and all alone and evermore shall *be* so." And an overexcited little boy with a plastic spaceship was running up and down the hall and shouting "Blast off!"

The farewells at the elevator door were followed by a second round down below on the sidewalk while the doorman was blowing his whistle for cabs.

"Can we drop you?" Ellen Hunter called.

"No. You're going downtown, and it would be out of your way," Celia Coleman said.

The Colemans walked two blocks north on Park and then east. The sidewalks of Manhattan were bare, the snow the weatherman promised having failed to come. There were no stars, and the night sky had a brownish cast. From a speaker placed over the doorway of a darkened storefront human voices sang "O Little Town of Bethlehem." The drug-store on the corner was brightly lighted but locked, with the iron grating pulled down and no customers inquiring about cosmetics at the cash register or standing in front of the revolving Timex display unable to make up their minds.

The Venetian-red door of the Colemans' house was level with the sidewalk and had a Christmas wreath on it. In an eerie fashion it swung open when Dan Coleman tried to fit his key in the lock.

"Did we forget to close it?" Celia said and he shook his head. The lock had been jimmied.

"I guess it's our turn," he said grimly as they walked in. At the foot of the stairs they stood still and listened. Nothing on the first floor was disturbed. There was even a silver spoon and a small silver tray on the dining-room sideboard. Looking at each other they half managed to believe that everything was all right; the burglars had been frightened by somebody coming down the street, or a squad car perhaps, and had cleared out without taking anything. But the house felt queer, not right somehow, not the way it usually felt, and they saw why when they got to the top of the first flight of stairs.

"Sweet Jesus!" he exclaimed softly, and she thought of her jewelry.

The shades were drawn to the sills, so that people on the sidewalk or in the apartments across the way could not see in the windows. One small detail caught his eye in the midst of the general destruction. A Limoges jar that held potpourri lay in fragments on the hearth and a faint odor of rose petals hung on the air.

With her heart beating faster than usual and her mouth as dry as cotton she said, "I can understand why they might want to look behind the pictures, but why walk on them?"

"Saves time," he said.

"And why break the lamps?"

"I don't know," he said. "I have never gone in for housebreaking."

A cigarette had been placed at the edge of a tabletop, right next to an ashtray, and allowed to burn all the way down. The liquor cupboard was untouched. In the study, on that same floor at the back of the house, where the hi-fi, the tape deck, and the TV should have been there was a blank space. Rather than bother to unscrew the cable, the burglars had snipped it with wire cutters. All the books had been pulled from the shelves and lay in mounds on the floor.

"Evidently they are not readers," he said, and picked up volume seven of *Hakluyt's Voyages* and stood it on an empty shelf.

She tried to think of a reason for not going up the next flight to the bedrooms, to make the uncertainty last a little longer. Rather than leave her jewelry in the bank and never have the pleasure of wearing it, she had hidden it in a place that seemed to her very clever.

It was not clever enough. The star ruby ring, the cabochon emeralds, the gold bracelets, the moonstones, the garnet necklace that had been her father's wedding present to her mother, the peridot-and-tourmaline pin that she found in an antique shop on a back street in Toulon, the diamond earrings — gone. All gone. Except for the things Dan had given her they were all inherited and irreplaceable, and so what would be the point of insuring them.

"In a way it's a relief," she said, in what sounded to her, though not to him, like her normal voice.

"Meaning?"

"Meaning that you can't worry about possessions you no longer have."

She opened the top right-hand drawer of her dressing table and saw that the junk jewelry was still there. As she pushed the drawer shut he said, "The standard procedure," and took her in his arms.

The rest was also pretty much the standard procedure. Mattresses were pulled half off the beds and ripped open with a razor blade, drawers turned upside down, and his clothes closet completely empty, which meant his wardrobe now consisted of the dark-blue suit he had put on earlier this evening to go to the Follansbees' Christmas party. Her dresses lay in a colored confusion that spilled out into the room from the floor of her walk-in closet. Boxes from the upper shelves had been pulled down and ransacked — boxes containing hats, evening purses, evening dresses she no longer had occasion to wear, since they seldom went out at night except to go to the theater or dine with friends.

When the police came she let him do the talking. Christmas Eve, Christmas Day were the prime moments for break-ins, they said. The house had probably been watched. They made a list of the more important things and suggested that Dan send them an inventory. They were pleasant and held out no hope. There were places they could watch, they said, to see if anything belonging to the Colemans turned up, but chances were that . . . When they left he put the back of a chair against the doorknob of the street door and started up the stairs.

From the stairs he could see into their bedroom. To his astonishment Celia had on an evening dress he hadn't seen for twenty years. Turning this way and that, she studied her reflection in the full-length mirror on the back of a closet door. Off the dress came, over her head, and she worked her way into a scarlet chiffon sheath that had a sooty footprint on it. Her hair had turned from dark brown to grey and when she woke up in the morning her back was as stiff as a board, but the dress fit her perfectly. While he stood there, watching, and unseen, she tried them on, one after another — the black taffeta with the bouffant skirt, the pale sea-green silk with bands of matching silk fringe — all her favorite dresses that she had been too fond of to take to a thrift shop, and that had been languishing on the top shelf of her closet. As she stepped back to consider critically the effect of a white silk evening suit, her high heels ground splinters of glass into the bedroom rug.

ITS load lightened by a brief stop in the Bronx at a two-story warehouse that was filled from floor to ceiling with hi-fi sets and color TVs, the Chrysler sedan proceeded along the Bruckner Elevated Expressway to Route 95. When the car slowed down for the tollgate at the Connecticut state line, the sandy-haired recidivist, slouched down in the right-hand front seat, opened his eyes. The false license plates aroused no interest whatever as the car came to a stop and then drove on.

IN the middle of the night, the material witnesses to the breaking and entering communicated with one another, a remark at a time. A small spotlight up near the ceiling that was trained on an area over the living-room sofa said, *When I saw the pictures being ripped from the walls I was afraid. I thought I was going to go the same way.*

So fortunate, they were, the red stair-carpet said, and the stair-rail said, *Fortunate? How?*

The intruders were gone when they came home.

I had a good look at them, said the mirror over the lowboy in the downstairs hall. *They were not at all like the Colemans' friends or the delivery boys from Gristede's and the fish market.*

The Colemans' friends don't break in the front door, the Sheraton sideboard said. *They ring and then wait for somebody to come and open it.*

She will have my top refinished, said the table with the cigarette scar. *The number is in the telephone turnaround. She knows about that sort of thing and he doesn't. But it will take a while. And the room will look odd without me.*

It took a long time to make that star ruby, said a small seashell on the mantelpiece.

Precious stones you can buy, said the classified directory. *Van Cleef & Arpels. Harry Winston. And auctions at Christie's and Sotheby Parke Bernet. It is the Victorian and Edwardian settings that were unusual. I don't suppose the thieves will know enough to value them.*

They will be melted down, said the brass fire irons, *into unidentifiability. It happens every day.*

Antique jewelry too can be picked up at auction places. Still, it is disagreeable to lose things that have come down in the family. It isn't something one would choose to have happen.

There are lots of things one would not choose to have happen that do happen, said the fire irons.

With any unpleasantness, said the orange plastic Design Research kitchen wall clock, *it is better to take the long view.*

Very sensible of them to fall asleep the minute their heads hit the pillow, said the full-length mirror in the master bedroom. *Instead of turning and tossing and going over in their minds the things they have lost, that are gone forever.*

They have each other, a small bottle of Elizabeth Arden perfume spray said. *They will forget about what happened this evening. Or, if they remember, it will be something they have ceased to have much feeling about, a story they tell sometimes at dinner parties, when the subject of robberies comes up. He will tell how they walked home from the Follansbees' on Christmas night and found the front door ajar, and she will tell about the spoon and the silver tray the thieves didn't take, and he will tell how he stood on the stairs watching while she tried on all her favorite evening dresses.*

Billie Dyer

I

IF you were to draw a diagonal line down the state of Illinois from Chicago to St. Louis, the halfway point would be somewhere in Logan County. The county seat is Lincoln, which prides itself on being the only place named for the Great Emancipator before he became President. Until the elm blight reduced it in a few months to nakedness, it was a pretty late-Victorian and turn-of-the-century town of twelve thousand inhabitants. It had coal mines but no factories of any size. "Downtown" was, and still is, the courthouse square and stores that after a block or two in every direction give way to grass and houses. Which in turn give way to dark-green or yellowing fields that stretch all the way to the edge of the sky.

When Illinois was admitted into the Union there was not a single white man living within the confines of what is now the county line. That flat farmland was prairie grass, the hunting ground of the Kickapoo Indians. By 1833, under coercion, the chiefs of all the Illinois Indians had signed treaties ceding their territories to the United States. The treaties stipulated that they were to move their people west of the Mississippi River. In my childhood — that is to say, shortly before the First World War — arrowheads were turned up occasionally during spring plowing.

The town of Lincoln was laid out in 1853, and for more than a decade only white people lived there. The first Negroes were brought from the South by soldiers returning from the Civil War. They were carried into town rolled in a blanket so they would not be seen. They stayed indoors during the daytime and waited until dark for a breath of fresh air.

Muddy water doesn't always clear overnight. In the running conversation that went on above my head, from time to time a voice no longer identifiable would say, "So long as they know their place." A colored man who tried to attend the service at one of the Protestant churches was politely turned away at the door.

The men cleaned out stables and chicken houses, kept furnaces going in the wintertime, mowed lawns and raked leaves and did odd jobs. The women took in washing or cooked for some white family and now and then carried home a bundle of clothes that had become shabby from wear or that the children of the family had outgrown. I have been told by someone of the older generation that on summer evenings they would sit on their porches and sing, and that the white people would drive their carriages down the street where these houses were in order to hear them.

I am aware that "blacks" is now the acceptable form, but when I was a little boy the polite form was "colored people"; it was how they spoke of themselves. In speaking of things that happened long ago, to be insensitive to the language of the period is to be, in effect, an unreliable witness.

In 1953, Lincoln celebrated the hundredth anniversary of its founding with a pageant and a parade that outdid all other parades within living memory. The *Evening Courier* brought out a special edition largely devoted to old photographs and sketches of local figures, past and present, and the recollections of elderly people. A committee came up with a list of the ten most distinguished men that the town had produced. One was a Negro, William Holmes Dyer. He was then sixty-seven years old and living in Kansas City, and the head surgeon for all the Negro employees of the Santa Fe line. He was invited to attend the celebration, and did. There was a grand historical pageant with a cast of four hundred, and the Ten Most Distinguished Men figured in it. Nine of them were stand-ins with false chin whiskers, stovepipe hats, frock coats, and trousers that fastened under the instep. Dr. Dyer stood among them dressed in a dark-blue business suit, and four nights running accepted the honor that was due him.

Two years later, he was invited back again for a banquet of the Lincoln College Alumni Association, where he was given a citation for outstanding accomplishment in the field of medicine. While he was in town he called on the president of the college, who was a childhood friend of mine. "What did you talk about?" I asked, many years later, regretting the fact that so far as I knew I had never laid eyes on William Dyer. My friend couldn't remember. It was too long ago. "What was he like?" I persisted, and my friend, thinking carefully, said, "Except for the color of his skin he could have been your uncle. Or mine."

I HAVE been looking at an old photograph of six boys playing soldier. They are somewhere between ten and twelve years old. There are trees behind them and grass; it is somebody's backyard. Judging by their clothes (high-buttoned double-breasted jackets, trousers cut off at the knee, long black stockings, high-button shoes), the photograph was taken around 1900. One soldier has little flowers in his buttonhole. He and four of the others are standing at attention with their swords resting on their right shoulders. They can't have been real swords, but neither are they made of wood. The sixth soldier is partly turned but still facing the camera. As soon as the bulb is pressed he will lead the attack on Missionary Ridge. I assume they are soldiers in the Union Army, but who knows? Boys have a romantic love of lost causes. They must have had to stand unblinking for several minutes while the photographer busied himself under his black cloth. One of them, though I do not know which one, is Hugh Davis, whose mother was my Grandmother Blinn's sister. And one is Billie Dyer. His paternal grandmother was the child of a Cherokee Indian and a white woman who came from North Carolina in the covered-wagon days.

Billie Dyer's grandfather, Aaron Dyer, was born a slave in Richmond, Virginia, and given his freedom when he turned twenty-one. He made his way north to Springfield, Illinois, because it was a station of the Underground Railroad. It is thirty miles to the southwest of Lincoln, and the state capital. In Springfield, the feeling against slavery was strong; a runaway slave would be hidden sometimes for weeks until the owner who had traced him that far gave up and went home. Then Aaron Dyer would hitch up the horse and wagon he had been provided with, and at night the fugitive, covered with gunnysacks or an old horse blanket, would be driven along some winding wagon trail that led through the prairie. Clop, clop, clopty clop. Past farm buildings that were all dark and ominous. Fording shallow streams and crossing bridges with loose wooden floorboards that rumbled. Arousing the comment of owls. Sometimes Aaron Dyer sang softly to himself. Uppermost in his mind, who can doubt, was the thought of a hand pulling back those gunnysacks to see what was under them.

As for the fugitive concealed under the gunnysacks in the back of Aaron

Dyer's wagon, whose heart beat wildly at the sound of a dog barking half a mile away, what he (or she) was escaping from couldn't have been better conveyed than in these complacent paragraphs from the Vicksburg, Mississippi, *Sun* of May 21, 1856:

> Any person, by visiting the slave depot on Mulberry Street, in this city, can get a sight of some of the latest importations of Congo negroes.
>
> We visited them yesterday and were surprised to see them looking so well, and possessing such intelligent countenances. They were very much like the common plantation negro — the only difference observable being the hair not kinking after the manner of the Southern darkey, while their feet, comparatively speaking, being very small, having a higher instep, and well-shaped in every respect.
>
> Some of the younger of these negroes are very large of their age, and are destined to attain a large growth. They all will make first-rate field hands, being easily taught to perform any kind of manual service. Their docility is remarkable, and their aptitude in imitating the manners and customs of those among whom they are thrown, is equally so.

On Decoration Day I saw, marching at the head of the parade, two or three frail old men who had fought in the war that freed them.

Two families lived in our house before my father bought it, in the early nineteen-hundreds. It had been there long enough for shade trees to grow around and over it. The ceilings were high, after the fashion of late-Victorian houses, and the downstairs rooms could not be closed off. My father complained, with feeling, about the coal bill. Like all old houses, it gave off sounds. The stairs creaked when there was no one on them, the fireplace chimneys sighed when the wind was from the east, and the sound, coming through the living-room floor, of coal being shoveled meant that Alfred Dyer was minding the furnace. Sometimes I went into the pantry and opened the cellar door and listened. The cellar stairs had no railing and the half-light was filtered through cobwebs and asbestos-covered heating pipes, and I never went down there. Sitting in the window seat in the library I would look out and see Mr. Dyer coming up the driveway to the cellar door. If he saw me playing outside he would say "Evening," in a voice much lower than any white man's. His walk was slow, as if he were dragging an invisible heaviness after him. It did not occur to me that the heaviness was simply that he was old and tired. Or even that he might have other, more presentable clothes than the shape-less sweater and baggy trousers I saw him in. I was not much better informed about the grown people around me than a dog or a cat would have been. I know now that he was born in Springfield, and could remember soldiers tramping the streets there with orders to shoot anybody who appeared to rejoice in the assassination of Abraham Lincoln. I have been told that for many years he took care of my Grandfather Blinn's horses and drove the family carriage. The horses and carriage were sold when my Uncle Ted persuaded my grandfather to buy a motorcar, and Mr. Dyer went to work for the lumber company.

Whoever it was that tried to worship where he wasn't wanted, it was not Alfred Dyer. He was for decades the superintendent of the African Methodist Episcopal Sunday school and led the choir. He knew the Bible so well, his daughter said, that on hearing any scriptural quotation he could instantly tell where it came from. As he was shaking the grates and setting the damper of our furnace, it seems likely that the Three Holy Children, Shadrach, Meshach, and Abednego, were more present to the eye of his mind than the little boy listening at the head of the cellar stairs.

After our house there were two more, and then Ninth Street dipped downhill, and at the intersection with Elm Street the brick pavement ended and the neighborhood took on an altogether different character. The houses after the intersection were not shacks, but they were not a great deal more. Grass did not grow in their yards, only weeds. There was usually a certain amount of flotsam and jetsam, whatever somebody more well-to-do didn't want and had found a way to get rid of. The Dyers' house was just around the corner on Elm Street. It was shaped like a shoebox and covered with green roofing paper. Elm Street was the dividing line between the two worlds. On either side of this line there were families who had trouble making both ends meet, but those who lived below the intersection didn't bother to conceal it.

As I sorted out the conversation of the grown people in my effort to get a clearer idea of the way things were, I could not help picking up how they felt, along with how they said they felt. While they agreed it was quite remarkable that Alfred Dyer's son William had got through medical school, at the same time they appeared to feel that in becoming a doctor he had imitated the ways of white people, as darkies were inclined to do, and done something that was not really necessary or called for, since there were, after all, plenty of white doctors. Apart from the doctors, the only things I can think of that the white people of Lincoln were at that

time willing to share with the colored people were the drinking water
and the cemetery.

BILLIE Dyer's mother was born in Sedalia, Missouri, the legal property
of the wife of a general in the Union Army. Her father and mother ran
away and were caught and returned, and the general put her father on
the block and he was sold to someone in the South and never heard of
again. When her children asked what the place where she was born was
like, she told them she couldn't remember. And that nobody could come
and take her away because the slaves were freed, all of them, a long time
ago, and there would never be slaves again.

For things that are not known — at least not anymore — and that there
is now no way of finding out about, one has to fall back on imagination.
This is not the same thing as the truth, but neither is it necessarily a
falsehood. Why not begin with the white lady? When he took the clean
washing in his express wagon and knocked on her back door, she called
him by his brother's name. She couldn't tell them apart. He didn't let on
he wasn't Clarence.

The smell of laundry soap was the smell of home. With steam on the
inside of the windows you couldn't always see out.

It was raining hard when school let out. Some children had raincoats
and rubbers they put on. He ran all the way home, to keep from getting
wet. He threw open the front door and fought his way through drying
laundry to get to the kitchen, where his mother was, and said, "Mama,
I'm starving," and she gave him a piece of bread and butter to tide him
over.

With his hands folded and resting on the edge of the kitchen table, he
waited for his father to say, "O Lord, we thank Thee for this bountiful
sustenance. . . ." Pork chops. Bacon and greens. Sausages. Fried cornmeal
mush. In summer coleslaw, and sweet corn and beets from the garden.

Saturday night his mother took the washtub down from its nail in the
kitchen and made him stand in it while she poured soapy water over his
head and scrubbed his back and arms. When she said, "Now that's what
I call one clean boy!" he stepped out of the tub, his eyes still shut tight,
and she threw a towel around him, and then it was Clarence's turn to
have the inside of his ears dug at with a washrag.

In Sunday school, making the announcements and leading the singing,
his father seemed twice as big as he did at home. Preacher told them

about the hand: "Think of it, brothers and sisters and all you children, a hand — just a hand all by itself, no arm — *writing on the wall!*" For Sunday dinner they had chicken and dumplings, and sometimes there were little round egg yolks in the gravy.

He said, "Mama, I don't feel good," and her hand flew to his forehead. Then she went and got the bottle of castor oil and a big spoon, and said, "Don't argue with me, just open your mouth." Lying in bed with a fever, he listened to the old mahogany wall clock. Tick . . . and then tock . . . and then tick . . . and then tock . . . If he told his mother a lie she looked into his eyes and knew. Nothing bad could happen to them, because his father wouldn't let it happen. But if any of them talked back to him he got a switch from outside and whupped them. It wasn't even safe to say "Do I have to?"

His sister Mary didn't want to go to school, because the teacher made fun of her and said mean things. The teacher didn't like colored children. "Why can't I stay here and help you with the washing and ironing?" Mary said, and his mother said, "You'll be bending over a washtub soon enough. Go to school and show that white woman you aren't the stupid person she takes you for." After he finished his homework he helped Mary with hers. It was hard to get her to stop thinking about the teacher and listen to what he was telling her. "Nine and seven is not eighteen," he said patiently.

He fell asleep to the sound of his father's voice in the next room reading from the Bible. The patchwork quilts were old and thin, and in the middle of the night, when the fire in the kitchen stove died down, it was very cold in the house. One night when he went to bed it was December 31, 1899, and when he woke up he was living in a new century.

When he brought his monthly report card home from school his mother went and got her glasses and held it out in front of her and said, "Is that the best you can do?" Then she put the report card where they could all see it and follow his example.

IF my Great-Aunt Ev's name was mentioned, my mother or my Aunt Annette would usually tell, with an affectionate smile, how she cooked with a book in her hand. They didn't mean a cookbook, and the implication was that her cooking suffered from it. She had graduated from the Cincinnati Conservatory of Music, and spoke several languages — which people in the Middle West at that time did not commonly do. The question "What will people think?" hardly ever crossed her mind. I have been told that my grandmother was jealous of her sister because my grandfather found her conversation so interesting. When her son Hugh Davis brought Billie Dyer home to play and they sat with their heads over the checkerboard until it was dark outside, she set an extra place at the table and sent one of the other children to ask Billie Dyer's mother if it was all right for him to stay for supper. Before long he was just one more child underfoot.

When he was alone with Hugh he thought only about what they were making or doing, but he never became so accustomed to the others that he failed to be alert to what they said. The eternal outsider, he watched how they ate and imitated it, and was aware of their moods. He learned to eat oysters and kohlrabi.

The first time they played hearts he left the hand that was dealt him face-down on the table. "Pick up your cards," Hugh said. "You're hold-ing up the game." The cards remained on the table. Mr. Davis said, "When your father told you you must never play cards, this isn't the kind of card-playing he meant. He meant playing for money. Gambling." Hugh, looking over his shoulder, helped him to arrange them in the proper suits. The hand that held the cards was small and thin and bluish brown on the outer side, pink on the inner.

At home, at the supper table, he said, "At the Davises' they — " and his sister Sadie said, "You like it so much at them white folks' house, why don't you go and live with them?"

He and Hugh Davis were friends all through grade school and high school. On Saturdays they went fishing together, and when they were old enough to be allowed to handle a gun they went hunting. Rabbits, mostly.

With a dry throat and weak knees and a whole row of Davises looking up at him solemnly, Hugh embarked upon the opening paragraphs of the high-school commencement address: "The Negro is here through no fault of his own. He came to us unwilling and in chains. He remains through necessity. He inhabits our shores today a test of our moral civili-zation. . . ." This must have been in the spring of 1904. I imagine there was a certain amount of shifting of feet on the part of the audience.

ON his way to school, Billie Dyer had to pass an old house on Eighth Street that I remember mostly because there was a huge bed of violets by the kitchen door. I was never inside it but Billie Dyer was, and in that house his fate was decided. The house belonged to a man named David H. Harts, who was of my grandfather's generation. He had fought in the Civil War on the Union side, and been mustered out of the Army with the rank of captain. Though he had no further military service, he was always spoken of as Captain Harts. He was a member of the local bar association but applied himself energetically to many other things besides the practice of law. He was elected to the State Assembly, served a term as mayor of Lincoln, and ran for governor on the Prohibition ticket. His investments in coal mines, real estate, proprietary medicine, and interurban railroads had made him a wealthy man, but he was not satisfied to go on accumulating money; he wanted the men who worked for him to prosper also. Because coal mining was a seasonal occupation, he started a brick factory, so that the miners would have work during the summer months.

Everybody knew that Billie Dyer got very good grades in school, and Captain Harts's son John, who was four years older, would sometimes stop him on his way home from school. After a visit to the icebox they would sit on the back steps or under the grape arbor or in his room and talk. At some point in his growing up, John Harts had eye trouble sufficiently serious that the family doctor suggested he stop studying for a while and lead a wholly outdoor life. For months he lived all alone in a cabin in the woods. Every three or four days his father would drive out there with provisions. Occasionally he stayed the night. John Harts tried not to count the days between his father's visits or to wonder what time it was. Denied books, his hearing became more acute. He recognized the *swoosh* that meant a squirrel had passed from one tree to another. He heard, or didn't hear, the insects' rising and falling lament. The birds soon stopped paying any attention to him. He made friends with a toad. As he and his father sat looking into the fire his father told one story after another about his boyhood on a farm in Pennsylvania; about the siege of Vicksburg; about how when they were floating past what looked like an uninhabited island in the Mississippi they were fired on by Confederate infantry; about how when they were defending a trestle bridge some fifteen miles south of Jackson, Tennessee, Henry Fox, a sergeant in Company H, ran across the bridge in full view of the enemy and brought relief at the end of the day; how when they were stationed between the White and Arkansas rivers, a large number died of the malaria from the cypress swamp; how he was captured and used the year he spent in a military prison to study mathematics and science. Even though John Harts had heard some of these stories before, he never tired of hearing them. Lying awake, listening to the sound of his father's breathing, he knew there was no one in the world he loved so much. Sometimes his father brought his older brother and came again early the next morning, so that his brother would be in time for school. One Saturday he brought Billie Dyer. With their trousers rolled above the knee, they cleaned out the spring together. When it got dark, John Harts saw that Billie Dyer wished he was home. He talked him out of his fear of the night noises by naming them. There was a thunderstorm toward morning, with huge flashes of lightning, so that for an instant, inside the cabin, they saw each other as in broad daylight.

There is no record of any of this. It is merely what I think happened. I cannot, in fact, imagine it not happening. At any rate, it is known that when John Harts went away to college he wrote to Billie Dyer every week — letters of advice and encouragement that had a lasting effect on his life. At twenty-one, John Harts went to work as an engineer for the Chicago & Alton Railroad, and while he was operating a handcar somewhere on the line an unscheduled fast train sent the handcar flying into the air. People surmised that he didn't hear or see the locomotive until it was suddenly upon him, but in any case the flower of that family was laid to rest in Section A, Block 4, Lot 7 of the Lincoln Cemetery.

From time to time after that, Billie Dyer would put on his best clothes and pay a call on Captain Harts and his wife. When he graduated from high school, Captain Harts said to him, "And what have you decided to do with your life?" At that time, in Lincoln, it was not a question often asked of a Negro. Billie Dyer said, "I would like to become a doctor. But of course it is impossible." Captain Harts spoke to my grandfather and to several other men in Lincoln. How much they contributed toward Billie Dyer's education I have no way of knowing, but it does not appear to have been enough to pay all his expenses. It was thirteen years from the time he finished high school until he completed his internship at the Kansas City General Hospital. This could mean, I think, that he had to drop out of school again and again to earn the money he needed to go on with his studies. On the other hand, given the period, is it wholly beyond the realm of possibility that he should have come up against instructors who felt they were serving the best interests of the medical profession when they gave him failing marks for work that was in fact satisfactory, and forced him to take courses over again? In July 1917 he came home ready to begin the practice of medicine, but America had

declared war on Germany, the country was flooded with recruiting post-
ers ("Uncle Sam Wants YOU!"), and they got to him. He was the first
Negro from Lincoln to be taken into the Army.

2

IN 1975, a Dallas real-estate agent named Jim Wood, wandering through
a flea market in Canton, Texas, bought an Army-issue shaving kit, a
Bible, and a manuscript. He collected shaving memorabilia and they were
a single lot. Nothing is more improbable or subject to chance than the
fate of objects. On the flyleaf of the Bible was written, in an old-fashioned
hand, "To Dr. William H. Dyer from his father and mother." The
manuscript appeared to be a diary kept by Dr. Dyer during the First
World War. Months passed before Wood bothered to look at it. When
he did, he became so interested that he read it three times in one sitting.
He was convinced that Dr. Dyer must have made a significant contribu-
tion to the community he lived in, wherever that might be, and to the
medical profession. So, for several years, with no other information than
the diary contained, he tried to find Dr. Dyer or his heirs. Finally it
occurred to him to write to the Lincoln public library.

The diary is a lined eight-by-twelve-inch copybook with snapshots
and portrait photographs and postcards pasted in wherever they were
appropriate. That it escaped the bonfire is remarkable; that it fell into the
hands of so conscientious a man is also to be wondered at.

What seems most likely is that Dr. Dyer's wife was ill and that someone
not a member of the family broke up the household. But then how did
the diary get to Texas from Kansas City? It is eerie, in any case, and as if
Dr. Dyer had gone on talking after his death, but about a much earlier
part of his life. When the odds are so against something happening, it is
tempting to look around for a supernatural explanation, such as that
William Dyer's spirit, dissatisfied with the life he had led (the unremitting
hard work, the selfless dedication to the sick and to the betterment of his
race), longed for a second chance. Or, if not that, then perhaps wished to
have remembered the eight months he spent in a half-destroyed country,
where the French girls walked arm in arm with the colored soldiers and
ate out of their mess pans with them, and death was everywhere.

On the first page of the diary he wrote, "With thousands of others I
decided to offer my life upon our Nation's altar as a sacrifice that Democracy might reign and Autocracy be forever crushed." In 1917, the age of

public eloquence was not quite over, and when people sat down on a momentous occasion and wrote something it tended to be a foot or two above the ground.

Three hundred friends and neighbors were at the railroad station to see him off, on a Sunday afternoon, and he was kept busy shaking hands with those who promised to remember him in their prayers. Somebody took a snapshot of him standing beside his father and mother. Alfred Dyer's rolled-brim hat and three-piece suit do not look as if they had been bought for someone else to wear and handed on to him when they became shabby. He is a couple of inches taller than his son. Both are fine-looking men.

From the diary: "Mother and Father standing there with tears in their eyes ... when I kissed them and bade them farewell. . . . My eyes too filled with tears, my throat became full, and for miles as the train sped on I was unable to speak or to fix my mind upon a single thought."

His orders were to proceed to Fort Des Moines, a beautiful old Army post, at that time partly used as a boot camp for medical officers. He was disappointed with his quarters (a cold room in a stable) and did not at first see the need for a medical officer to spend four hours a day on the drill field.

After two months he was moved to Camp Funston, in Kansas. It was the headquarters of the 92nd Division, which was made up exclusively of Negro troops — the Army was not integrated until thirty-one years later, by executive order of Harry Truman. The barracks at Camp Funston were still being constructed, and thousands of civilian workmen poured into the camp every day, along with the draftees arriving by train from Kansas, Missouri, Colorado, Arizona, and Texas. He was assigned to the infirmary of the 317th Ammunition Train, and when he was not treating the sick he weeded out recruits who were physically unfit for military service. The year before, he had fallen in love with a young woman named Bessie Bradley, who was teaching in a night school. His free weekends were spent in Kansas City, courting her. In January and February, an epidemic of cerebrospinal meningitis swept through the camp and kept him on his feet night and day until it subsided. In March, he got a ten-day furlough and took Bessie Bradley to Illinois and they were married.

At Camp Funston a bulletin was read to all the soldiers of the 92nd Division: "The Division Commander has repeatedly urged that all colored members of his commands, and especially the officers and noncommissioned officers, should refrain from going where their presence will be resented. In spite of this injunction, one of the Sergeants of the Medical Department has recently . . . entered a theater, as he undoubtedly had a legal right to do, and precipitated trouble by making it possible to allege race discrimination in the seat he was given. . . . Don't go where your presence is not desired."

This bulletin so stuck in his craw that he managed to get his hands on a copy of it, and it is written out in his diary in full, against some ultimate day of judging.

Early in June, the order came for the division to proceed to Camp Upton for embarkment overseas. Lieutenant Dyer tried to call his wife, but the troops were denied access to telegraph and telephone lines. The next day, the trains began pulling out of the camp. When his section drew into the railway station in Kansas City, he saw that there was an immense crowd. Without any hope whatever that his wife would be among them or that he would find her if she were, he put his head out of the train window and heard her calling to him.

The division was hurried from Camp Upton to the embarkation port at Hoboken and onto a magnificent old steamship that until the war had been carrying passengers back and forth across the Atlantic for the Hamburg-American line. It put out to sea with five thousand men on board, and when Lieutenant Dyer went on deck the next morning he saw that they had joined a great convoy of nine transport ships, two battle cruisers, and half a dozen destroyers. His ship was under the command of a colonel of a unit of the National Guard.

From the diary: "From the very start there was that feeling of prejudice brought up between the white and colored officers, for among the first orders issued were those barring colored officers from the same toilets as the whites, also barring them from the barber shop and denying colored officers the use of the ship's gymnasium." The sea was calm. The enlisted men were continually on the lookout for periscopes but saw instead flying fishes and porpoises and a whale that spouted. Lieutenant Dyer was assigned the daily sanitary inspection of certain compartments in the fore part of the ship, and the physical examination of six hundred men. Twice a day he submitted written reports to the ship's surgeon. On June 21st, shots were fired from all the surrounding ships at what proved to be a floating beer keg. A convoy of British destroyers brought them safely into the harbor at Brest. At nine-fifteen in the evening, when the men of his unit began to go ashore, the sun was still above the horizon. He was struck by the fact that the houses were all of stone and closely jammed together and very old, and by the expression of sadness on the faces of the French people. The women young and old all were in black and seemed to be in the deepest mourning. Four little tykes standing by the roadside sang, "Hail, hail, the gang's all here! What the hell do we care now," in perfect English. His unit marched three miles through the gathering darkness to a barracks that had been a prison camp during the time of Napoleon ("a terrible and dirty old place"), and stayed there four days awaiting orders. Twice he got a pass into the city. The French people were friendly when he went into a shop or attempted to converse with them. He sat down on a park bench and children congregated around him. Soon they were sitting on his knees and, pointing, told him the French words for his eyes, nose, ears, and neat mustache.

After three days and nights on a train and a nine-mile hike, his unit ended up in a camp outside a village forty-eight kilometers southeast of Poitiers. It was a beautiful region, untouched by the war. The men pitched their shelter tents in a level field, the officers were billeted in nearby manor houses. They were the first American troops in this region, and the natives fell in love with them and came visiting every day. ("With them there was *No Color Line*.") On Bastille Day, before a great crowd, the troops gave a demonstration of American sports — footraces, three-legged races, boxing, wrestling, and baseball.

On July 22nd, Companies B and C, with Lieutenant Dyer as their medical officer, had orders to proceed to Marseilles, where they were to procure trucks for the 317th Ammunition Train and drive them to the front. The officers rode first class, the enlisted men were crowded in boxcars but happy to be making the trip. It was the height of summer, and everywhere women and old men and children were working in the fields. He saw ox teams but no horses. And no young men. Along the tracks, leaning on their pickaxes and shovels as they waited for the train to pass by, were hundreds of German soldiers with "PG" printed in large white letters on the backs of their green coats. In the railway station of every city they came to he saw trainload after trainload of French soldiers headed for the front, where the last great German offensive was being beaten back in the second Battle of the Marne. His own train went east, through vineyards. At Montluçon there was a stopover of several hours, and an elderly English professor showed Lieutenant Dyer and another officer about the city and then took them to the home of an aristocratic French family to meet a pupil of his, a young lady who was very anxious to hear the English spoken by Americans. After Lyons they turned south, following the Rhône Valley. Every time the train emerged from a tunnel, the men in the boxcars cheered. On the fourth day, after emerging from a tunnel three miles long, he saw the blue water of the Mediterranean.

The population of Marseilles was so mixed that it seemed as if God had transplanted here a sample of His people from all the kingdoms of the earth. Most of the men were in uniform of some sort. The Algerian soldiers (many of them "black as tar") with their little red skullcaps and the Hindus in their turbans and loose garments were the strangest. How in such garments could they fight in the trenches? As the men of his company walked through the streets, people exclaimed, "Ah, Americans!" They were welcome in the best hotels, the best theaters, everywhere. But it was a wicked city. Sitting at a table in a sidewalk café, he saw many beautiful women who were clearly prostitutes.

No ammunition trucks were available, and so they traveled back through the same picturesque scenery until gradually it became less picturesque and the farms less well tended. At Is-sur-Tille, where there was a huge American advance-supply base, they spent the greater part of the day on a siding. That night, no lights were allowed in the railroad cars, and from this they knew they were approaching the front. The 92nd Division headquarters was now at Bourbonne-les-Bains, three hundred kilometers southeast of Paris. As Lieutenant Dyer stepped down onto the station platform, the first officers he saw were from his old Camp Funston unit. He reported to the division surgeon and was put on duty in a camp just outside the city.

During the week that his unit remained here, their lockers were taken from them, their equipment was reduced to fifty pounds, and they were issued pistols and ammunition. On the twelfth of August they left the camp in a long convoy of motortrucks, which traveled all afternoon and night and stopped the next morning in the pretty little village of Bruyères. Here they were quartered in an old barracks that turned out to be comfortable enough when put in sanitary condition. Bruyères was a railroad terminal where American and French divisions and supplies were unloaded for the front. Aside from some humiliating divisional orders, which the diary does not go into, his stay there was pleasant. In the evening he walked out on the hills beyond the town and watched the anti-aircraft guns firing at German bombers. The distant flashes of cannons were like sheet lightning on the horizon.

Toward the end of August, on a night of the full moon — though it was almost totally obscured by clouds — he sat in a crowded truck with a rifle between his knees and his eyes focused on the dim road ahead. The convoy drove without lights, and they kept passing Army vehicles that had broken down or had slid off the road into a ditch, and infantrymen who, because of fatigue and the weight of their packs, had fallen out of the line to rest. He gave up counting the houses with their roofs gone or that were completely destroyed. The whole countryside had a look of desolation. At three o'clock in the morning, the convoy arrived at a silent and largely destroyed town. The truck he was riding in drove up an alley and stopped. He and two other officers lay down in front of a building that appeared to be intact and, using the stone doorstep for a pillow, fell asleep from exhaustion. In the morning, the occupants of the building, leaving for work, stepped over them. He got up and asked where they were and was told that it was Raon-l'Étape, in the Vosges.

For two days the American troops bivouacked in a wood, with German planes lingering high in the air above them in spite of the anti-aircraft guns. Then they were moved back to the town, and that night an enemy bomber dropped four bombs on the place where they had camped, creating terrific explosions. He was billeted at the house of a Mme. Crouvésier, whose two sons were in a prison camp in Germany. Working chiefly at night, because the Germans had occupied this area for three weeks in 1914 and knew the roads perfectly, the 317th moved ammunition of all calibers from the woods where it was hidden to four regiments of American infantry and a French artillery unit that was operating with them. The town was full of graves — in backyards, in gardens, everywhere. While he stood looking at an enemy observation balloon it suddenly went up in a fiery cloud. A German plane was brought down at Raon-l'Étape and the dead aviators were given a military funeral, which he attended.

After nearly a month here, he again found himself in a convoy, which drove all day and at 11 p.m. stopped along the roadside for the night. The truck he was riding in was so crowded that he got out and slept on the ground, wrapped in his blankets, and was awakened two hours later by a downpour. He moved under the truck, but his blankets became so wet that he gave up and moved back into the truck, and with the rain trickling down the back of his neck finished out the night.

Two days later, they reached their destination — the Argonne Forest. There were no accommodations for them, not even water to drink or to cook with, and the mud everywhere was over their shoe tops. They pitched their tents under bushes and trees to keep from being observed by the enemy airplanes constantly flying over. The companies of the 317th were detailed to handle supplies at a nearby railhead and deliver hundreds of horses to units at the front. ("While camped in this wet, filthy woods, many of our boys became ill from the dampness, cold, and exposure, thereby causing me much work and worry, caring for them.") Division headquarters issued a bulletin that Negro soldiers would be used to handle mustard-gas cases, because they were less susceptible than whites. ("Why is the Negro less susceptible to mustard gas than the whites? *No one can answer.*") On September 25th, a very heavy bombardment began, and it kept up for thirty-six hours without a stop. ("The old woods . . . trembled as if by earthquake, the flashes of the cannon lighted up the inside of our tents, and our ears were deafened.") Lieutenant Dyer went several times to the American evacuation hospital, a quarter of a mile away, and saw a continuous stream of ambulances bringing wounded soldiers to it from the front. The dead were also being brought back, on trucks, piled like cordwood and dripping blood.

They moved on, to Sainte-Menehould, forty-seven kilometers west of Verdun, and were billeted on the top floor of a French barracks. From their windows they could see the lines. The area was full of American soldiers plodding along under their heavy packs. Standing on the top of a hill, he could make out the Argonne Forest, with smoke hanging over it. Big guns were belching from all the surrounding hills. The 317th worked round the clock. With no tall trees and only one other building near it, the barracks made a fine target. ("All through the night the fighting kept up and though scared stiff and expecting to be blown to atoms at any moment I finally fell asleep.")

On the seventh of October, Companies B and C left Sainte-Menehould. The trucks drove south and east all day, in a driving rain, with a cold wind. In many places the road was camouflaged with green burlap supported on wire fences sometimes fifteen feet high and thickly interwoven with bushes and small trees. They passed through towns where not one house was standing whole and there was no longer any civilian population. A ruin next to a graveyard meant that there had been a church on this spot. Even the grass was burned up. ("At 5 p.m. we reached the city of Commercy, where we had orders to spend the night. We were taken to a French barracks where there were fairly good quarters for officers and men. We had just gotten comfortably located in the building, quite glad to get out of the inclement weather, and were preparing to eat, when another order came for the ammunition train to move on. . . . The rain fell and the wind blew and I sat on an open truck helping the driver watch the road to prevent running over an embankment, which would probably have meant our death. . . . All night long we traveled on, wondering what our destination would be and why we should be ordered to move on such a night.") At four in the morning, the convoy stopped in the village of Belleville. Cold, wet, and hungry, he got down and stomped on the ground, hoping to generate a little body heat. At daybreak a feed cart came by and the driver pitched them a few steaks left over from the breakfast of a labor battalion.

Belleville was so protected by the surrounding hills that the shells from the enemy guns at Metz almost never reached it. Lieutenant Dyer and another lieutenant were billeted in the ancient, dilapidated house of an elderly French couple. The officers' second-floor room had one small window. On the walls and rafters were a few traces of whitewash. There was a fireplace and two immense wardrobes. Over their heads was a loft full of straw, in which rats, mice, and birds nested. Sometimes their frisking sent chaff down on the faces of the two men. The beds were good. Lying in his, Lieutenant Dyer listened to the sound of the German planes overhead and tried to gauge, by the whine of a falling shell, whether the explosion would be a safe distance away.

He set up his infirmary in a small electrical plant. Because of the constant cold and rainy weather, there was a great deal of sickness among the colored troops. (Not once does he speak of what in America was called "the Spanish flu," but it was that, undoubtedly, that the men in his company were coming down with.)

Companies A, D, E, F, and G and their artillery, in training in the South of France since July, arrived in Belleville. ("Major Howard, my commanding officer from whom I had been separated about four months, called to see me . . . and complimented me on my good work, saying he had seen the Division Surgeon and not one complaint was made against me. During the whole month of October we labored on, hearing much talk of peace and were very anxious for the final drive, which would end forever Autocracy and give Democracy the right to reign. On the morning of November 8th, however, while we were in the midst of our activities, a terrible thing occurred at Belleville. . . . A colored boy who had been convicted of rape in August was hanged or lynched in an open field not far from my infirmary. The execution was a military order, but so openly and poorly carried out that it was rightly termed a lynching.")

The next day, the drive against Metz began, and two days later, while tremendous barrages were being laid down by the artillery in support of the infantry's advances, the news reached them that Germany had signed an armistice. As everywhere else in the Western world, bells rang, whistles blew, people shouted for joy.

On December 6th, he and another officer climbed into a truck and after a two-hour ride through no-man's-land arrived in Metz. He found it untouched by the fighting and the most beautiful city he had seen in France. The buildings were modern; the streets were wide and well paved and lighted with gas or electricity; there were streetcars riding up and down. But the people were cold and unfriendly to them, and spoke German mostly, and it was clear from the way a pack of children followed them in the street that they had never seen a Negro before.

On the night of December 15th, he was awakened by the orderly boy. In a heavy fog, a passenger train from Metz had plowed into a troop train full of happy French soldiers returning home from the front. It was a dreadful sight. The cars were telescoped and splintered, and the bodies of the dead and dying were pinned under the wreckage. The rest of the night he dressed wounds and put splints on broken arms and legs.

Three days later, the 317th began to leave Belleville. Now on foot, now in trucks or trains, they moved westward toward their port of embarkation. Sometimes he slept on straw, in dirty makeshift buildings that had been occupied by other soldiers before them and were infested with lice. For two days and nights he rode in a crowded railway coach with the rain dripping down on him from a leak in the ceiling. On Christmas Eve, in the ancient village of Domfront, in Normandy, the medical unit stood about in the rain and snow until 3 a.m., waiting to be billeted by a captain who, it turned out, had forgotten about them. Shivering in the cold, he remembered the Biblical text: *Foxes have holes and the fowls of the air have nests, but the Son of Man hath not where to lay his head.*

The people of Domfront were extremely hospitable, and the colored troops reciprocated by being on their best behavior. He was kept busy inspecting them daily for vermin and acute infections, but he found time to visit the places of historical interest and had his picture taken at the foot of the castle wall. Then he himself came down with influenza and had to be looked after by the men of his medical corps.

Late in January, his unit was ordered to proceed to the delousing station at Le Mans. The weather was cold, and there was a light snow on the ground. They reached Le Mans at eleven o'clock at night, after a twelve-hour ride. When he climbed down out of the truck, he had difficulty walking. He took off his boots and discovered that his feet were frozen. ("For a week thereafter, my feet were so swollen and blistered that I was unable to wear a shoe or leave my quarters.") During the two weeks he spent at the delousing camp he ran into several boys from Springfield that he knew. They had seen hard service with the 8th Illinois Infantry and showed it.

The unit made its final train journey from Le Mans to Brest, where thousands of soldiers were now crowded into the area around the port. The barracks were long wooden shacks with a hall running through the middle and small rooms opening off it. The only heat came from two stoves, one at either end of the hall. ("The weather was extremely damp and chilly at Brest, the raw wind off the ocean penetrating to the marrow.") There was more sickness.

On the morning of February 22nd, the 317th marched to the port. They had been informed by a bulletin from headquarters that if there was any disorder in the ranks they would be sent back to camp and detained indefinitely. Their packs uniformly rolled, their guns and shoes polished, they moved in utter silence like a funeral procession. The *Aquitania* rode at anchor in the harbor, and they were loaded onto small barges and ferried out to it. Lieutenant Dyer's cabin had mahogany fittings and a private bathroom. There were taps for fresh water and salt water, and the soap did not smell of disinfectant. While he was in the tub soaking, the room began to rock, and he realized that they had put out to sea. There is more, but why not leave him there, as lighthearted as he was probably ever going to be.

3

OF Dr. Dyer's roughly forty years of medical practice in Kansas City there is no record that I know of. The pattern of his days must have been regular and consistent. I picture him with a stethoscope in the pocket of his white coat and a covey of interns crowding around him.

In 1946, Hugh Davis, who was then living in California and an architect, came with his wife to Lincoln for a family visit. While he was there, he got Dr. Dyer's address and wrote to him to say that they would be going through Kansas City with a stopover of several hours and would like to see him. The answer was an invitation to dinner. There had been no communication between them for a good many years. The walls of the Dyers' Kansas City apartment were covered with Bessie Dyer's paintings, which the Davises liked very much. She was self-taught, with the help of a book that she got from the public library. They all sat down to a full Thanksgiving dinner, though actually Thanksgiving was about ten days away. And the friendship simply picked up where it had left off.

Two years later, when the Dyers went out to California, they were entertained at Hugh and Esther Davis's house in Palo Alto, along with a medical acquaintance the Dyers were staying with. My younger brother was also invited. He had just come out of the Army after a tour of duty in Germany, and was enrolled in law school at Stanford. He remembers Dr. Dyer as soft-spoken and very friendly, if a trifle guarded. He seemed to want, and need, to talk about the situation of educated Negroes in America — how they are not always comfortable with members of their own race, with whom they often have little or nothing in common, and are not accepted by white people whose tastes and interests they share. He was neither accusing nor bitter about this, my brother said. My brother mentioned the fact that Dr. Dyer's mother had helped take care of him when he was a baby, and Dr. Dyer was pleased that my brother remembered her. Three or four times he interrupted the conversation to say "I never expected to sit down to dinner with a grandson of Judge Blinn."

Hugh Davis's widow let me see a few of Dr. Dyer's letters to him written between 1955 and 1957. They are about politics (he was an ardent Republican), the hydrogen bomb, various international crises, a projected high-school reunion that never took place, his wife's delicate health, and — as one would expect of any regular correspondence — the weather. They are signed "Your friend, Billie Dyer." In each letter there is some mention of his professional activity — never more than a sentence, as a rule; taken together they give a very good picture of a man working himself to death.

In January 1956, at which time he was seventy years old, he wrote, "I suppose I should apologize for not having written you sooner but believe it or not, I am now working harder and with longer hours than ever before. Silly, you say, well I quite agree but the occasion is this. In the last four months I have been put on the staffs of three of the major hospitals in our city. I thought at first it was an honor but with the increase in activities which such appointments entail, my work has increased twofold. Since it is the first time that one of my race has had such appointments, I have been working diligently to make good, thereby keeping those doors open." He was still acting as a surgeon for the Santa Fe Railroad, and also for the Kansas City, Kansas, police department.

Three months later he wrote, "Since I have taken on new hospital assignments I have been working much too hard. I was in Chicago this week three days attending the Convention of American Association of Railway Surgeons and derived great benefit from the lectures and demonstrations on recent advances in medicine and surgery."

In June he spent a couple of weeks in the wilds of Minnesota fishing and had a glorious time, though the fishing was poor. In August he wrote, "I am still working as hard as ever altho my physical resistance is not what it used to be & I find I must resort to more frequent short periods of rest."

The letter he wrote in November is largely about the suppression of the Hungarian uprising: "My heart goes out to those people. I was in France in the First World War & I saw refugees going down the roads with a little cart pulled by a donkey & all of their earthly possessions piled high on it. They had been driven from their homes by the advancing German Armies & it was a pitiful sight to behold." He also mentions the fact that the vision in his right eye is somewhat impaired because of a small cataract, and adds, "I am still working at a tremendous pace but realize that I must soon slow down."

In March of the following year he wrote, "I hardly have time to breathe. Indeed I know that at my age I should not be trying such a pace but having broken thru a barrier which was denied me so many years . . ."

In July he wrote, "I too am having my troubles with a nervous dermatitis which all of the skin specialists tell me is due to overwork. . . . I am planning on spending a couple of weeks on the lakes in northern Minnesota for I am very tired and need a rest."

And in August: "I will be 71 years old the 29th of this month and am in fairly good health for an old man of my years. I therefore thank the good Lord for His blessings. . . . I thought I would get out to California this summer but I had to buy a new car, so will have to defer my visit another year. . . . I agree with you that Ike has been a little wishy washy since he has been in the White House. It seems that he speaks softly but does not carry the big stick like Teddy Roosevelt once did. Hugh I shall never forget the political rallies and torchlight processions they had in Lincoln when we were boys. We don't see anything like that any more, and when the circuses came to town with their big parades. How I pity the generations of kids today, who are denied such thrills. Remember the old swimming hole in Kickapoo Creek where we used to swim naked and have so much fun. Hugh those were the days."

In January there was a notice in the Lincoln *Evening Courier*: "Dr.

William Dyer, a native of Lincoln, was found dead in his car after an automobile accident at Kansas City, Kan., Tuesday morning. He apparently suffered a heart attack while driving."

THERE have been at least three histories of Logan County. The first was published in 1878 by a firm that went through the state doing one county after another. It has portrait engravings and brief biographies of the leading citizens, for which they must have paid something. The style is a little like First and Second Chronicles: "Michael and Abram Mann, John Jessee and Thomas Sr., Lucas and Samuel Myers were from Ohio and are now in their graves." Many natural wonders that the early settlers remembered found their way into this book — prairie fires so numerous that at night they lighted up the whole circuit of the horizon. And mirages. Also extreme hardships — the ague, caused by hunting their horses in the wet grass, and a drop in the temperature so great and so sudden, on a rainy December afternoon in 1836, that men on horseback were frozen to the saddle. And primitive artifacts, such as a door with wooden hinges, a wooden lock, and a buckskin drawstring.

Another history, published in 1911, was the work of a local man and is overburdened with statistics. The most recent is a large book — nine by twelve — heavy to hold in the hand and bound in red Leatherette. The likeness of Abraham Lincoln is on the cover, embossed in gold, as if somewhere in the afterlife his tall shade had encountered King Midas. There are hundreds of photographs of people I don't know and never heard of, which is not to be wondered at since we moved away from Lincoln in 1923, when I was fourteen years old.

Someone who had never lived there might conclude from this book that the town had no Negroes now or ever. Except for the group pictures of the Lincoln College athletic teams, in which here and there a dark face appears among the lighter ones, there are no photographs of black men and women. And though there are many pictures of white churches of one denomination or another, there is no picture of the African Methodist Episcopal Church — only a column of text, in which the buildings it occupied and the ministers who served it are listed. And these sentences: "Mr. Arian [surely Aaron misremembered?] Dyer and wife Harriet moved here from Springfield, Illinois, in 1874. . . . The sinners in Lincoln found the hope in Christ and joined the church. Among them were Alfred Dyer and wife Laura. . . ."

I go through the book looking for the names that figured so prominently in the conversation of my elders and find almost none. And realize that the place to look for them is the cemetery. The past is always being plowed under. There is a page of pictures of the centennial parade, but nowhere are the names of the Ten Most Distinguished Men called to mind. What is one to think if not that the town, after celebrating its hundredth birthday, was done with history and its past, and ready to live, like the rest of America, in a perpetual present?

In the index I found "Dyer, William, 90, 202." Both references turned out to be concerned with a white man of that name.

Love

MISS *Vera Brown*, she wrote on the blackboard, letter by letter in flawlessly oval Palmer method. Our teacher for the fifth grade. The name might as well have been graven in stone.

As she called the roll, her voice was as gentle as the expression in her beautiful dark-brown eyes. She reminded me of pansies. When she called on Alvin Ahrens to recite and he said, "I know but I can't say," the class snickered but she said, "Try," encouragingly, and waited, to be sure that he didn't know the answer, and then said, to one of the hands waving in the air, "Tell Alvin what one-fifth of three-eighths is." If we arrived late to school, red-faced and out of breath and bursting with the excuse we had thought up on the way, before we could speak she said, "I'm sure you couldn't help it. Close the door, please, and take your seat." If she kept us after school it was not to scold us but to help us past the hard part.

Somebody left a big red apple on her desk for her to find when she came into the classroom, and she smiled and put it in her desk, out of sight. Somebody else left some purple asters, which she put in her drinking glass. After that the presents kept coming. She was the only pretty teacher in the school. She never had to ask us to be quiet or to stop throwing erasers. We would not have dreamed of doing anything that would displease her.

Somebody wormed it out of her when her birthday was. While she was out of the room the class voted to present her with flowers from the greenhouse. Then they took another vote and sweet peas won. When she saw the florist's box waiting on her desk, she said, "Oh?"

"Look inside," we all said.

Her delicate fingers seemed to take forever to remove the ribbon. In the end, she raised the lid of the box and exclaimed.

"Read the card!" we shouted.

Many Happy Returns to Miss Vera Brown, from the Fifth Grade, it said.

She put her nose in the flowers and said, "Thank you all very, very much," and then turned our minds to the spelling lesson for the day.

After school we escorted her downtown in a body to a special matinee of D. W. Griffith's *Hearts of the World*. She was not allowed to buy her ticket. We paid for everything.

We meant to have her for our teacher forever. We intended to pass right up through sixth, seventh, and eighth grades and on into high school taking her with us. But that isn't what happened. One day there was a substitute teacher. We expected our real teacher to be back the next day but she wasn't. Week after week passed and the substitute continued to sit at Miss Brown's desk, calling on us to recite and giving out tests and handing them back with grades on them, and we went on acting the way we had when Miss Brown was there because we didn't want her to come back and find we hadn't been nice to the substitute. One Monday morning she cleared her throat and said that Miss Brown was sick and not coming back for the rest of the term.

In the fall we had passed on into the sixth grade and she was still not back. Benny Irish's mother found out that she was living with an aunt and uncle on a farm a mile or so beyond the edge of town. One afternoon after school Benny and I got on our bikes and rode out to see her. At the place where the road turned off to go to the cemetery and the Chautauqua grounds, there was a red barn with a huge circus poster on it, showing the entire inside of the Sells-Floto Circus tent and everything that was going on in all three rings. In the summertime, riding in the backseat of my father's open Chalmers, I used to crane my neck as we passed that turn, hoping to see every last tiger and flying-trapeze artist, but it was never possible. The poster was weather-beaten now, with loose strips of paper hanging down.

It was getting dark when we wheeled our bikes up the lane of the farmhouse where Miss Brown lived.

"You knock," Benny said as we started up on the porch.

"No, you do it," I said.

We hadn't thought ahead to what it would be like to see her. We wouldn't have been surprised if she had come to the door herself and thrown up her hands in astonishment when she saw who it was, but instead a much older woman opened the door and said, "What do you want?"

"We came to see Miss Brown," I said.

"We're in her class at school," Benny explained.

I could see that the woman was trying to decide whether she should tell us to go away, but she said, "I'll find out if she wants to see you," and left us standing on the porch for what seemed like a long time. Then she appeared again and said, "You can come in now."

As we followed her through the front parlor I could make out in the dim light that there was an old-fashioned organ like the kind you used to see in country churches, and linoleum on the floor, and stiff uncomfortable chairs, and family portraits behind curved glass in big oval frames.

The room beyond it was lighted by a coal-oil lamp but seemed ever so much darker than the unlighted room we had just passed through. Propped up on pillows in a big double bed was our teacher, but so changed. Her arms were like sticks, and all the life in her seemed concentrated in her eyes, which had dark circles around them and were enormous. She managed a flicker of recognition but I was struck dumb by the fact that she didn't seem glad to see us. She didn't belong to us anymore. She belonged to her illness.

Benny said, "I hope you get well soon."

The angel who watches over little boys who know but they can't say it saw to it that we didn't touch anything. And in a minute we were outside, on our bicycles, riding through the dusk toward the turn in the road and town.

A few weeks later I read in the Lincoln *Evening Courier* that Miss Vera Brown, who taught the fifth grade in Central School, had died of tuberculosis, aged twenty-three years and seven months.

SOMETIMES I went with my mother when she put flowers on the graves of my grandparents. The cinder roads wound through the cemetery in ways she understood and I didn't, and I would read the names on the monuments: Brower, Cadwallader, Andrews, Bates, Mitchell. In loving memory of. Infant daughter of. Beloved wife of. The cemetery was so large and so many people were buried there, it would have taken a long time to locate a particular grave if you didn't know where it was already. But I know, the way I sometimes know what is in wrapped packages, that the elderly woman who let us in and who took care of Miss Brown during her last illness went to the cemetery regularly and poured the rancid water out of the tin receptacle that was sunk below the level of the grass at the foot of her grave, and filled it with fresh water from a nearby faucet and arranged the flowers she had brought in such a way as to please the eye of the living and the closed eyes of the dead.

The Man in the Moon

IN the library of the house I grew up in there was a box of photographs that I used to look through when other forms of entertainment failed me. In this jumble there was a postcard of my mother's brother, my Uncle Ted, and a young woman cozying up together in the curve of a crescent moon. I would have liked to believe that it was the real moon they were sitting in, but you could see that the picture was taken in a photographer's studio. Who she was it never occurred to me to ask. Thirty or forty years later, if his name came up in conversation, women who were young at the same time he was would remark how attractive he was. He was thin-faced and slender, and carried himself well, and he had inherited the soft brown eyes of the Kentucky side of the family.

In the small towns of the Middle West at that time — I am speaking of, roughly, the year 1900 — it was unusual for boys to be sent away to school. My uncle was enrolled in a military academy in Gambier, Ohio, and flunked out. How much education he had of a kind that would prepare him for doing well in one occupation or another I have no idea. I would think not much. Like many young men born into a family in comfortable circumstances, he felt that the advantages he enjoyed were part of the natural order of things. What the older generation admired and aspired to was dignity, resting on a firm basis of accomplishment. I think what my uncle had in mind for himself was the life of a classy gent, a spender — someone who gives off the glitter of privilege. And he behaved as if this kind of life was within his reach. Which it wasn't. There was a period — I don't know how long it was, perhaps a few months, perhaps a year or so — when if he was strapped and couldn't think of anybody to put the bite on, he would write out a check to himself and sign it with the name of one of his sisters or of a friend.

I don't think anything on earth would have induced my father to pass a bad check, but then his family was poor when he was a child, and lived on the street directly behind the jail. Under everything he did, and his opinions about human behavior, was the pride of the self-made man. He blamed my uncle's shameless dodges on his upbringing. When my Grandfather Blinn would try to be strict with his son, my father said, my grandmother would go behind his back and give Teddy the money. My grandmother's indulgence, though it may have contributed to my uncle's lapses from financial probity, surely wasn't the only cause of them. In any case, the check forging didn't begin until both my grandparents were dead.

My grandfather was brought up on a cattle farm in Vermont not far from the Canadian border. He left home at sixteen to work as a book-keeper in a pump factory in Cincinnati. Then he began to read law in a law office there. More often than not, he read on an empty stomach, but he mastered Blackstone's *Commentaries* and Chitty's *Pleadings*, and shortly before his twenty-first birthday (nobody thinking to inquire into his age, which would have prevented it) he was admitted to the bar. What made him decide to move farther west to Illinois I don't know. Probably there were already too many lawyers in Ohio. When he was still in his early thirties he tried to run for Congress on the Republican ticket and was nosed out by another candidate. Some years later the nomination was offered to my grandfather at a moment when there was no serious Demo-cratic opposition, and he chose not to run because it would have taken him away from the practice of law. By the time he was forty he had a considerable reputation as a trial lawyer, and eventually he argued cases before the Supreme Court. Lawyers admired him for his ability in the courtroom, and for his powers of close reasoning. People in general saw in him a certain largeness of mind that other men didn't have. From the way my mother spoke of him, it was clear that — to her — there never had been and never could be again a man quite so worthy of veneration. My uncle must often have felt that there was no way for him to stand clear of his father's shadow.

Because my grandfather had served a term on the bench of the Court of Claims, he was mostly spoken of as Judge Blinn. His fees were large but he was not interested in accumulating money and did not own any land except the lot his house stood on. He was not at all pompous, but when he left his office and came home to his family he did not entirely divest himself of the majesty of the law, about which he felt so deeply.

From a large tinted photograph that used to hang over the mantelpiece in my Aunt Annette's living room, I know that he had a fine forehead, calm grey eyes, and a drooping mustache that partly concealed the shape of his mouth.

There were half a dozen imposing houses in Lincoln but my grandfather's house wasn't one of them. It stood on a quiet elm-shaded street, and was a two-story flat-roofed house with a wide porch extending all across the front and around the sides. It was built in the eighteen-seventies and is still there, if I were to drive down Ninth Street. It is well over a hundred years old — what passes for an old house in the Middle West. My father worked for a fire-insurance company and was gone three days out of the middle of the week, drumming up business in small-town agencies all over the state. We lived across the street from my grandfather's house. Though I haven't been in it for sixty years, I can still move around in it in my mind. Sliding doors — which I liked to ease in and out of their recesses — separated the back parlor, where the family tended to congregate around my grandmother's chair, from the front parlor, where nobody ever sat. There it was always twilight because the velvet curtains shut out the sun. If I stood looking into the pier glass between the two front windows I saw the same heavy walnut and mahogany furniture in an even dimmer light. Whether this is an actual memory or an attempt on the part of my mind to adjust the past to my feelings about it I am not altogether sure. The very words "the past" suggest lowered window shades and a withdrawal from brightness of any kind. Orpheus in the Underworld. The end of my grandfather's life — he died horribly, of blood poisoning, from a ferret bite — cast a shadow backward over what had gone before, but in point of fact it was not a gloomy house, and the life that went on in it was not withdrawn or melancholy.

My Aunt Edith was the oldest. Then came my mother. Then Annette. Between Annette and my uncle there was another child, who didn't live very long. My grandmother was morbidly concerned for my uncle's safety when he was little, and Annette was told that she must never let him out of her sight when they were playing together. She was not much older than he was, and used to have nightmares in which something happened to him. They remained more or less in this relationship to each other during the whole of their lives.

My mother and her sisters had a certain pride of family, but it had nothing to do with a feeling of social superiority, and was, actually, so unexamined and metaphysical that I never understood the grounds for it.

It may have been something my grandmother brought with her from Kentucky and passed on to her children. That branch of the family didn't go in for genealogy, and the stories that have come down are vague and improbable.

When I try the name Youtsey on a Southerner, all the response I ever get is a blank look. There appear to have been no statesmen in my grandmother's family, no colonial governors, no men or women of even modest distinction. That leaves money and property. My grandmother's father, John Youtsey, owned a hundred acres of land on the Licking River, where he raised strawberries for the markets of Cincinnati. He was also a United States marshal — that is to say, he had been appointed to carry out the wishes of the judicial district in which he lived, and had duties similar to those of a sheriff. Three of his sons fought in the Civil War, on the side of the North. Shortly before the war broke out, he began to build a new house with bricks fired on the place. I saw it once. I was taken there by one of my mother's cousins. The farm had passed out of the family and was now owned by a German couple. My grandmother used to take her children to Kentucky every summer and when the July term of court was over, my grandfather joined them. My mother told me that the happiest days of her childhood were spent here, playing in the attic and the hayloft and the water meadows, with a multitude of her Kentucky cousins. But as I looked around I saw nothing that I could accept as a possible backdrop for all that excitement and mirth and teasing and tears. There wasn't even a child's swing. The farmer's wife told us to look around as much as we liked, and went back to her canning. We paused in the doorway of a long empty room. I concluded from the parquet floors that it must have been the drawing room. Since my mother's cousin had gone to some trouble to bring me here, I felt that I ought to say something polite, and remarked, "In my great-grandfather's time this must have been a beautiful room," and he said with a smile, "Grandfather kept his wheat in it." My uncle may have inherited his *folie des grandeurs* from some improvident ancestor but it wasn't, in any event, the bewhiskered old gentleman farmer who built and lived in this house.

The lessons that hardship had taught my Grandfather Blinn he was unable to pass on to his son. He must have had many talks with Ted about his future, and the need to apply himself, and what would happen to him if he didn't. Hunger that is only heard about is not very real. My uncle had a perfect understanding of how one should conduct oneself after one has arrived; it was the getting there that didn't much interest him. The most plausible explanation is that he was a changeling.

FROM a history of Logan County published in 1911 I learned that Edward D. Blinn, Jr. — that is, my Uncle Ted — was the superintendent of the Lincoln Electric Street Railway. My grandfather must have put him there, since he was a director and one of the incorporators of this enterprise. One spur of the streetcar tracks went from the courthouse square to the Illinois Central Railroad depot, another to a new subdivision in the northwest part of town, and still another to the cemeteries. In the summertime the cars were open on the sides, and in warm weather pleasanter than walking. Except during the Chautauqua season, they were never crowded. The conductor stomped on a bell in the floor beside him to make pedestrians and farm wagons get out of the way, and from time to time showers of sparks would be emitted by the overhead wires. What did the superintendent have to do? Keep records, make bank deposits, be there if something went wrong, and in an emergency run one of the cars himself (with his mind on the things he would do and the way he would live when he had money). The job was only a stopgap, until something more appropriate offered itself. *But what if nothing ever did?*

When my grandfather's back was turned, Ted went to Chicago and made some arrangements that he hoped would change the course of his life; for a thousand dollars (which, of course, he did not have), a firm in Chicago agreed to supply him with an airplane and, in case my uncle didn't choose to fly it, a pilot. It was to be part of the Fourth of July celebration. The town agreed to pay him two thousand dollars if the plane went up.

Several years ago the contract was found tucked between the pages of a book that had been withdrawn from the Lincoln College library — God knows how it got there. It is dated June 27, 1911 — to my surprise; for it proves that I was a few weeks less than three years old at the time, and I had assumed that to be able to remember the occasion as vividly as I do I must have been at least a year older than that.

The plane stood in a wheat field out beyond the edge of town. The wheat had been harvested and the stubble pricked my bare legs. My father held me by the hand so I would not get lost in the crowd. Very few people there had ever seen an airplane before, and all they asked was to see this one leave the ground and go up into the air like a bird. Several men in mechanic's overalls were clustered around the plane. Now and then my uncle climbed into the cockpit and the place grew still with expectation. The afternoon wore on slowly. The sun beat down out of a brassy sky. Word must have passed through the crowd that the plane was not going to go up, for my father said suddenly, "We're going home now." Looking back over my shoulder I saw the men still tinkering with the airplane engine. My father told me a long time later that while all this was going on my grandfather was pacing the floor in his law office, thinking about the thousand dollars he would have to raise somehow if the plane failed to go up, and that if it did go up there was a very good chance his only son might be killed.

Using what arguments I find it hard to imagine (except that a courtroom is one thing and home is another, and drops of water wear away stone), Ted persuaded my grandfather to buy a motorcar. The distance from my grandfather's house to his law office was less than a mile, and the roads around Lincoln were unpaved, with deep ruts. Even four or five years later, when motorcars were beginning to be more common, an automobile could sink and sink into a mudhole until it was resting on its rear axle. But anyway, there it was, a Rambler, with leather straps holding the top down, brass carriage lamps, and the emergency brake, the gearshift, and the horn all on the outside above the right-hand running board. It stood in front of my grandfather's house more like a monument than a means of locomotion. It is unlikely that anyone but Ted ever drove it, and it must have given a certain dash to his courtship of a charming red-headed girl named Alma Haller. I have pursued her and her family through three county histories and come up with nothing of any substance. Her father served several terms as a city alderman, he was a director of the streetcar company, and he owned a farm west of Lincoln, but there is no biography, presumably because he was not cooperative. Anyway, the soft brown eyes, the understanding of what is pleasing to women, assiduousness, persistence, something, did the trick. They were engaged to be married. And if either family was displeased by the engagement I never heard of it.

My uncle had the reputation in Lincoln of being knowledgeable about motors, and a friend who had arranged to buy an automobile in Chicago asked Ted to go with him when he picked it up. On the way down to Lincoln the car skidded and went out of control and turned over. My uncle was in the seat beside the driver. His left arm was crushed and had to be amputated. My grandmother's premonitions were at last accounted for. What I was kept from knowing about and seeing because I was a small child it does not take very much imagination to reconstruct. He is lying in a hospital bed with his upper chest heavily bandaged. There are bruises on his face. He is drowsy from morphine. Sometimes he complains to the nurse or to Annette, sitting in a chair beside his bed, about the pain he feels in the arm that he has lost. Sometimes he lies there rearranging the circumstances that led up to the accident so that he is at the wheel of the car. Or better still, not in the car at all. When the morphine wore off and his mind was clearer, what can he have thought except that it was somebody else's misfortune that came to him by mistake?

When he left the hospital, and forever afterward, he carried himself stiffly, as if he were corseted. He did not let anyone help him if he could forestall it, and was skillful at slipping his overcoat on in such a way that it did not call attention to the fact that his left arm was immovable and ended in a grey suède glove.

A few years ago, one of Alma Haller's contemporaries told me that she had realized she was not in love with Ted and was on the point of breaking off the engagement but after the accident felt she had to go through with it. They went through with it with style. All church weddings that I have attended since have seemed to me a pale imitation of this one. In a white corduroy suit that my mother had made for me, I walked down the aisle of the Episcopal church beside my Cousin Peg, who was a flower girl. I assume that I didn't drop the ring and that the groom put it on the fourth finger of the bride's left hand, but that part I have no memory of; though the movie camera kept on whirring there was no film in it. What was he thinking about as he watched the bridal procession coming toward him? That there would be no more sitting in the moon with girls who had no reason to expect anything more of him than a good time? That there, in satin and lace, was his heart's desire? That people were surreptitiously deciding which was the real arm and which the artificial one? All these things, perhaps, or none of them. The next thing I remember (the camera now having film in it again) is my mother depositing me on a gilt chair, at the wedding reception, and saying that she would be right back. Her idea of time and mine were quite different. The bride's mother, in a flame-colored velvet dress, interested me briefly; my grandmother always wore black. I had never before seen footmen in knee breeches and powdered wigs passing trays of champagne glasses. Or so many people in one house. And I was afraid I would never see my mother again. Just when I had given up all hope, my Aunt Edith appeared with a plate of ice cream for me.

In the next reel, it is broad daylight and I am standing — again with my father holding my hand — on a curb on College Avenue. But this time it is so I will not step into the street and be run over by the fire engines. As before, there is a crowd. It is several months after the wedding. There is a crackling sound and yellow flames flow out of the upstairs windows and lick the air above the burning roof of the house where the wedding reception took place. The gilt furniture is all over the lawn, and there is talk about defective wiring. The big three-story house is as inflammable as a box of kitchen matches.

In the hit-or-miss way of children's memories, I recall being in a horse and buggy with my aunt and uncle, on a snowy night, as they drove around town delivering Christmas presents. And on my sixth birthday our yard is full of children. All the children I know have come bringing presents, and when London Bridge falls I am caught in the arms of my red-haired aunt, and pleased that this has happened. Then suddenly she was not there anymore. She divorced my uncle and I never saw her again. After a couple of years she remarried and moved away, and she didn't return to Lincoln to live until she was an old woman.

As often happened with elderly couples during that period, my grandmother's funeral followed my grandfather's within the year. In his will he named all four of his children as executors, and Ted quit his job with the streetcar company in order to devote himself to settling the estate. My grandfather did not leave anything like as much as people thought he would. He was in the habit of going on notes with young men who needed to borrow money and had no collateral. When the notes came due, more often than not my grandfather had to make good on them, the co-signer being unable to. He also made personal loans, which his family knew about but which he didn't bother to keep any record of since they were to men he considered his friends, and after his death they denied that there was any such debt. Meanwhile, it became clear to anyone with eyes in his head that my uncle was spending a lot of money that could only have come from the estate. My mother and my aunts grew alarmed, and asked my father to step in and represent their interests. He found that Ted had already spent more than half of the money my grandfather left. Probably he didn't mean to take more than his share. It just slipped through his fingers. He would no doubt have run through everything, and with nothing to show for it, if my father hadn't stopped him. My father was capable of the sort of bluntness that makes people see themselves and their conduct in a light unsoftened by excuses of any kind. I would not have wanted to be my uncle when my father was inquiring into the details of my grandfather's estate, or have had to face his contempt. There was nothing more coming to Ted when the estate was finally settled, and, finding himself backed into a corner, he began forging checks. The fact that it didn't lead to his being arrested and sent to prison suggests that the sums involved were not large. I once heard my mother say to my Aunt Edith (who had stopped having anything to do with him) that when she wrote to Ted she was always careful not to sign her full name. The friends whose names he forged were young, in their twenties like my uncle, and poor as Job's turkey. How he justified doing that to them it would be interesting to know. When it comes to self-deception we are all vaudeville magicians. In any case, forging checks for small amounts of money relieved his immediate embarrassment but did not alter his circumstances.

Children as they pass through one stage of growth after another are a kind of anthology of family faces. At the age of four I looked very much like one of my mother's Kentucky cousins. Holding my chin in her hand, she used to call me by his name. Then for a while I looked like her. At the age of eleven or twelve I suddenly began to look like my Uncle Ted. When people remarked on this, I saw that it made my father uneasy. The idea that if I continued to look like him I would end up forging checks amused me, but faulty logic is not necessarily incompatible with the truth, which in this case was that when, because of Christmas or my birthday, I had ten or fifteen dollars, I could always think of something to spend it on. All my life I have tended to feel that money descends from heaven like raindrops. I also understood that it doesn't rain a good deal of the time, and when I couldn't afford to buy something I wanted I have been fairly content to do without it. My uncle was not willing, is what it amounted to.

When my mother died during the influenza epidemic of 1918–19, I turned to the person who was closest to her, for comfort and understanding. I am not sure whether this made things harder for my Aunt Annette or not. Her marriage was rocky, and more than once appeared to be on the point of breaking up but never did. When my Uncle Will came home he would pass through the living room, leaving behind him a sense of strain between my aunt and him, but as far as I could make out it had nothing to do with my being there. Sometimes I found my Uncle Ted there, too. I didn't know, and didn't ask, where he was living and what he was doing to support himself. I think it was probably the low point of his life. There was no color in his face. His eyes never lit up or looked inquiringly or with affection at any of the people seated around the dining-room table. If he spoke, it was to answer yes or no to a question from my aunt. That when he and Annette were alone he opened his heart to her as freely as I did I have no doubt.

Defeat is a good teacher, Hazlitt said. What it teaches some people is to stop trying.

EXCEPT for the very old, nothing, good or bad, remains the same very long. My father remarried, and was promoted, and we had to move to Chicago. I went to high school there, and my older brother went off to college, at the University of Illinois, in Champaign-Urbana. On the strength of his experience with the streetcar company, my uncle had managed to get a job in Champaign, working for a trolley line that meandered through various counties in central and southern Illinois. Nobody knew him there, or anything about him. He was simply Ed Blinn, the one-armed man at the ticket counter. He kept this job for many years, from which I think it can be inferred that he didn't help himself to the petty cash or falsify the bookkeeping. During the five years that my brother was in college and law school they would occasionally have dinner together. He tried to borrow money from my brother, whose monthly allowance was adequate but not lavish, and my brother stopped seeing him. Once, when Ted came up to Chicago, he invited me to have dinner with him at the Palmer House. Probably he felt that it was something my mother would have wanted him to do, but this idea didn't occur to me; adolescents seldom have any idea why older people are being nice to them. He was about forty and I was fifteen or sixteen, and priggishly aware that, in taking me to a restaurant that was so expensive, he was again doing things in a way he couldn't afford. He had an easier time chatting with the headwaiter than he did in getting any conversation out of me. After we got up from the table he gave me a conducted tour of a long corridor in the hotel that was known as Peacock Alley. I could see that he was in his natural element. I would have enjoyed it more if there had been peacocks. When I followed my brother down to the university I didn't look my uncle up, and he may not even have known I was there.

Some years later, from a thousand miles away, I learned that he had married again. He married a Lincoln woman, the letter from home said. Edna Skinner. He and his wife were running a rental library in Chicago, and she was expecting a baby. Then I heard that the baby died, and they had moved back to Lincoln, and she was working at the library, and somebody had found him a job running the elevator in the courthouse — where (as people observed with a due sense of the irony of it) his father had practiced law.

By that time my father had retired from business and he and my stepmother were living in Lincoln again. When I went back to Illinois on a visit, I saw my Aunt Annette. She was angry at Ted for marrying. Though she did not say so, what she felt, I am sure, was that there were now two children she couldn't let out of her sight. And she disliked his new wife. She said, "Edna only married him because she was impressed with his family." All this, however, didn't prevent my aunt from doing what she could for them. The grocer was given to understand that they could charge things to her account. She did this knowing that my Uncle Will was bound to notice that the grocery bills were padded, and would be angry with her. As he was. She refused to tell the grocer that her brother and his wife were not to charge things anymore, and my Uncle Will, not being sure what the consequences would be if he put a stop to it, allowed it to continue. Also, living in a small town, there is always the question of what people will think. One would not want to have it said that, with the income off several farms and a substantial balance at the bank, one had let one's brother-in-law and his wife go hungry.

I did not meet Edna until I brought my own wife home to Lincoln for the first time. We had only been married three or four months. When we were making the round of family visits, it struck me as not quite decent not to take her to meet Ted and the aunt I had never seen. My father didn't think that this was necessary. Though they all lived in the same small town, my father never had any reason to be in the courthouse or the library, and he hadn't had anything to do with Ted since the days, thirty years before, when he had to step in and straighten out the handling of my grandfather's estate. But I saw no reason I shouldn't follow my own instincts, which were not to leave anybody out. I was thirty-six and so grateful to have escaped from the bachelor's solitary existence that all my feelings were close to the surface. I couldn't call Ted, because they had no telephone, but somebody told me where they were living and we went there on a Sunday morning and knocked on the screen door. As my uncle let us in, I saw that he was pleased we had come. The house looked out across the college grounds and was very small, hardly big enough for two people. Overhanging trees filtered out the sunlight. I found that I had things I wanted to say to him. It was as if we had been under a spell and now it was broken. There was a kind of easy understanding between us that I was not prepared for. I felt the stirring of affection, and I think he may have as well.

Edna I took to on sight. She had dark eyes and a gentle voice. She was simple and open with my wife, and acted as if meeting me was something she had been hoping would happen. Looking around, I could see that they didn't have much money, but neither did we.

I wrote to them when we got home, and heard from her. After my uncle died, she continued to write, and she sent us a small painting that she had done.

Not long ago, by some slippage of the mind, I was presented with a few moments out of my early childhood. My grandfather's house, so long lived in by strangers, is ours again. The dining-room table must have several leaves in it, for there are six or eight people sitting around it. My mother is not in the cemetery but right beside me. She is talking to Granny Blinn about . . . about . . . I don't know what about. If I turn my head I will see my grandfather at the head of the table. The windows are there, and look out on the side yard. The goldfish are swimming through their castle at the bottom of the fishbowl. The door to the back parlor is there. Over the sideboard there is a painting of a watermelon and grapes. No one stops me when I get down from my chair and go out to the kitchen and ask the hired girl for a slice of raw potato. I like the greenish taste. When I come back into the dining room I go and stand beside my uncle. He finishes what he is saying and then notices that I am looking with curiosity at his glass of beer. He holds it out to me, and I take a sip and when I make a face he laughs. His left hand is resting on the white damask tablecloth. He can move his fingers. The catastrophe hasn't happened. I would have liked to linger there with them, but it was like trying to breathe underwater. I came up for air, and lost them.

THE view after seventy is breathtaking. What is lacking is someone, *anyone*, of the older generation to whom you can turn when you want to satisfy your curiosity about some detail of the landscape of the past. There is no longer any older generation. You have become it, while your mind was mostly on other matters.

I wouldn't know anything more about my uncle's life except for a fluke. A boy I used to hang around with when I was a freshman in Lincoln High School — John Deal — had a slightly older sister named Margaret. Many years later I caught up with her again. My wife and I were on Nantucket, and wandered into a shop full of very plain old furniture and beautiful china, and there she was. She was married to a Russian émigré, a bearlike man with one blind eye and huge hands. He was given to patting her affectionately on the behind, and perfectly ready to be fond of anyone who turned up from her past. I learned afterward that he had been wounded in the First World War and had twice been decorated for bravery. Big though his hands were, he made ship's models — the finest I have ever seen. That afternoon, as we were leaving, she invited us to their house for supper. The Russian had made a huge crock of vodka punch, which he warned us against, and as we sat around drinking it, what came out, in the course of catching up on the past, was that Margaret and Edna Blinn were friends.

Remembering this recently, I looked up Margaret's telephone number in my address book. The last letter I had had from her was years ago, and I wasn't sure who would answer. When she did, I said, "I want to know about my Uncle Ted Blinn and Edna. How did you happen to know her?"

"We were both teaching in the public schools," the voice at the other end of the line said. "And we used to go painting together."

"Who was she? I mean, where was she from?"

"I don't know."

"Was she born in Lincoln?"

"I kind of think not," the voice said. "I do know where they met. At your grandfather's farm, Grassmere."

"My grandfather didn't have a farm."

"Well, that's where they met."

"My grandfather had a client, one of the Gilletts, who owned a farm near Elkhart — I think it was near Elkhart. Anyway, she moved East and he managed the farm for her. It was called Gracelands. Could it have been there that they met?"

"No. Grassmere."

Oral history is a tangle of the truth and alterations on it.

"They had a love affair," Margaret said. "And Edna got pregnant and lost her job because of it."

"Even though they got married?"

"Yes. It was more than the school board could countenance, and she was fired. He quit his job in Champaign and they went to Chicago and opened a rental library."

"I know. . . . What did the baby die of?"

"It was born dead."

Looking back on my uncle's life, it seems to me to have been a mixture of having to lie in the bed he had made and the most terrible, undeserved, outrageous misfortune. The baby was born dead. He lost his arm in that automobile accident and no one else was even hurt. They put whatever money they had into that little rental library in Chicago just in time to have it go under in the Depression.

THE oldest county history mentions an early pioneer, Thomas R. Skinner, who came to that part of Illinois in 1827, cleared some land near the town of Mt. Pulaski, and was the first county surveyor and the first county judge. Edna was probably a direct or a collateral descendant. She may also have been the daughter of W. T. Skinner, who was superintendent and principal of the Mt. Pulaski High School. Whatever her background may have been, she was better educated and more cultivated than any of the women in my family, and if she had had money would, I think, have been treated quite differently.

From that telephone call and the letter that followed I learned a good deal that I hadn't known before. Edna worshipped my uncle, Margaret said. She couldn't get over how wonderful, how distinguished, he was. He was under no illusions whatever about himself but loved her. He called her "Baby."

She never spoke about things they lacked, and never seemed to realize how poor they were. She lived in a world of art and music and great literature. He had a drinking problem.

They lived in many different houses — in whatever was vacant at the moment, and cheap. For a while they lived in what had been a one-room Lutheran schoolhouse. They even lived in the country, and Ted drove them into town to work in a beat-up Ford roadster. Whatever house they were living in was always clean and neat. Annette gave them some of my Grandmother Blinn's English bone china, and Edna had some good furniture that had come down in her family — two Victorian chairs and a walnut sofa upholstered in mustard-colored velvet.

Annette and my Uncle Will Bates went to Florida for several months every winter, and while they were away Ted and Edna lived in their house. She loved my Aunt Annette, and was grateful to her for all she had done for them, and didn't know that the affection was not returned.

Margaret found Ted interesting to talk to and kind, but aloof. She had no idea what he was paid for running the elevator in the courthouse. Edna's salary at the library was seventy-five dollars a month. He made a little extra money by selling cigarettes out of the elevator cage, until some town official put a stop to it because he didn't have a license.

My uncle always dressed well. (Clothes of the kind he would have thought fit to put on his back do not wear out, if treated carefully.) Edna had one decent dress, which she washed when she got home from the library, and ironed, and wore the next day. She loved clothes. When she wanted to give herself a treat she would buy a copy of *Harper's Bazaar* and thumb through the pages with intense interest, as if she were dealing with the problem of her spring wardrobe.

She was a Christian Scientist and tended to look on the bright side even of things that didn't have any bright side. She would be taken with sudden enthusiasms for people. When she started in on the remarkable qualities of someone who wasn't in any way remarkable, Ted would poke fun at her. The grade-school and high-school students who came to the library looking for facts for their essays on compulsory arbitration or whales or whatever found her helpful. She encouraged them to develop the habit of reading, and to make something of their lives. Some of them came to think of her as a friend, and remained in touch with her after they left school. At the end of the day, Ted came to the library to pick her up and walk home with her. Margaret didn't think that he had any men friends.

They had a dog, a mutt that had attached himself to them. Whatever Ted asked the dog to do he would try to do, even if it was, for a dog, impossible. Or when he had, in fact, no clear idea of what was wanted of him. He made my uncle laugh. Not much else did.

He must have been in his early sixties when he got pneumonia. He didn't put up much of a fight against it. Edna believed that he willed himself to die.

"Sometimes she would invite me for lunch on Sunday," Margaret said. "Your uncle ate by himself in the other room — probably because there weren't enough knives and forks for three. Having fed him, Edna would get out the card table and spread a clean piece of canvas on it or an old painting, and set two places with the Blinn china. The forks were salad forks, so small that they tended to get lost on the plates. And odd knives and spoons, jelly glasses, and coffee cups from the ten-cent store. Then she would bring on, in an oval silver serving dish, an eggplant casserole, or something she had invented. She was a superb cook, and she did it all on a two-burner electric plate. After the lunch dishes were washed and put away we would go off painting together. There was nothing unusual about her watercolors but her oils were odd in an interesting way. She couldn't afford proper canvas and used unsized canvas or cardboard, and instead of a tube of white lead she had a small can of house paint. She had studied at the Art Institute when they lived in Chicago. I think now that she saw her life as being like that of Modigliani or some other bohemian starving in a garret on the Left Bank. Ted was ashamed of the way they lived. . . . Only once did she ask me for help. She had seen a coat that she longed for, and it was nine dollars. Or it may have been that she needed nine dollars to make up the difference, with what she had. At that time you could buy a Sears, Roebuck coat for that. Anyway, she asked if I would take two paintings in exchange for the money. . . . When I saw her after her heart attack she was lovely and slender — much as she must have looked when she and Ted first knew each other. She spent the last year or so of her life living in what had been a doctor's office. . . . That nine-dollar coat continues to haunt me."

SHE was buried beside Ted, in the Blinn family plot. My grandfather's headstone is no higher than the sod it is embedded in, and therefore casts no shadow over the grave of his son.

With Reference to an Incident at a Bridge

(For Eudora Welty)

WHEN I see ten-year-old boys, walking along the street in New York City or on the crosstown bus, I am struck by how tiny they are. But at the time I am speaking of, I wasn't very big myself. So far as I was concerned, the town of Lincoln was the Earthly Paradise, the apple that Eve prevailed upon Adam to eat being as yet an abstraction, and therefore to all intents and purposes still on the tree. I had an aunt and uncle living in Bloomington, thirty miles away, and for a time I went to Peoria with my mother to have my teeth straightened. Those two towns, and Springfield, the state capital, constituted the outer limits of the known world. The unknown world, the infinitude of unconscious emotions and impulses, didn't come up in ordinary conversation, though I daresay there were some people who were aware of it.

At twelve I was considered old enough to join the Presbyterian church, and did. In Sunday school and church I recited, along with the rest of the congregation, "I believe in the Holy Ghost, the holy catholic church, the communion of saints, the forgiveness of sins, the resurrection of the body, and the life everlasting." That any part of this formal confession was not self-evident did not cross my mind, nor, I think, anyone else's. We said it because it was true, and vice versa.

Twelve was also the age at which I could join the Boy Scouts and I did that, too. There was only one Scout troop in town, and the scoutmaster, Professor C. S. Oglevee, was a man in his early fifties, who taught biology at Lincoln College, and was the official weather observer. He was, as well, an unordained minister and an Elder in the Presbyterian church. The Scouts were all drawn from the Presbyterian Sunday school.

At Scout meeting I said, "A Scout is trustworthy, loyal, helpful, courteous, kind," and so on, with the same fervor that I recited the Apostles'

Creed, and downtown I went out of my way to help elderly people across the street who could have managed perfectly well on their own, for the traffic was negligible. A Model A or a Model T Ford proceeding at the speed of fifteen miles an hour or a farm wagon was what it generally amounted to.

In a short while I passed from second-class to first-class Scout, and kept the silver fleur-de-lys on my hat polished, and looked forward to becoming an Eagle Scout, beyond which there were no further pinnacles to climb. In my imagination the right sleeve of my uniform was covered with merit badges from the cuff to the shoulder, and I did accumulate quite a few.

One day, in quest of specialized information of some sort, I went to see Professor Oglevee at home. He lived in a beautiful old mansion out at the edge of town. It had been built by a pillar of the church, whose widow Professor Oglevee was in the position of a son to. The house was set well back from the street, and painted white, and had a porte cochere, and was shaded by full-grown elm trees. The architect who designed it must have had the antebellum mansions of Georgia and Mississippi in mind. There was no other house in town like it. The white columns along the front had formerly graced the façade of the Lincoln National Bank. In that house I heard the word "whom" for the first time. A woman answering the telephone while a church social was going on outside in the garden said, "To whom do you wish to speak? . . . To *whom?*" — stopping me in my tracks.

On one side of the lawn there was an apple orchard and on the other a pasture with a little stream running through it: Brainerd's Branch. It says something about old Mrs. Brainerd that children could go there without a sense that they were trespassing. In the early spring I used to walk along the stream listening to the musical sound it made, and sometimes stopping to build a dam. Tucked away in a remote corner of the pasture was a one-room clubhouse with a fireplace, which my brother's generation of Boy Scouts had built under Professor Oglevee's direction. Scout meetings were held there, and after the formal business was out of the way we sat around on the floor roasting wienies over the coals and studying the *Scout Manual*.

Professor Oglevee's room was on the ground level of the house, where the floor was paved with uncemented tiles that clanked as you walked over them. To get to his desk by the window we had to thread our way between piles of scientific and nature publications. Afterward he took me outside and explained the mysteries of his rain gauges. He was a walking encyclopedia. With a dozen boys at his heels, all clamoring for his undivided attention, he moved through the woods identifying trees and plants and mosses. He was immensely patient, good-natured, and kind. So clearly so that I felt there was not room in his nature for the unpredictable crankiness and unreasonable severity other grown-ups exhibited from time to time. If anybody said one word against him, even today, I would get excited. Which means, of course, that I didn't allow for the fact that he was a fallible human being. The flaws that as a fallible human being he must have had nobody ever knew about, in any case. But on one occasion he shocked me. Somebody said "Professor? . . . Professor? . . . Professor, what kind of a tree is this the leaf of?" and he glanced at it and said, "A piss-elm." Though he then apologized for his language, the fact remained that he had said it.

WHOSE idea it was to organize the Cub Scouts I don't remember, if I ever knew. A great many things seemingly happened in the air over my head. Cub Scouts had to be between ten and twelve years old, and they did not all go to the Presbyterian Sunday school. It was left to the Boy Scouts to lead them. Among the six or eight little boys who turned up for the first meeting was Max Rabinowitz, whose father had a clothing store on a rather dingy side street facing the interurban tracks and the Chicago & Alton depot, and was a Russian Jew. This distinction would not have meant anything to me if it also had not represented a prejudice of some kind on the part of my elders. I suppose it is why I remember Maxie and not any of the others.

There were a dozen or more old families in town who were German Jewish. The most conspicuous were the Landauers and the Jacobses. Nate Landauer ran a ladies' ready-to-wear shop on the north side of the courthouse square, and his brother-in-law, Julius Jacobs, a men's clothing store on the west side of the square. Once a year my father or my mother took my brother and me downtown and we were fitted out by Mr. Jacobs with a new dark-blue suit to wear to church on Easter Sunday.

The school yard had various forms of unpleasantness, but anti-Semitism was not one of them. In the Presbyterian church, the doctrine of Original Sin was held over our heads, with no easy or certain way to get off the hook. It was hardly to be expected that the Crucifixion was something the Jews could live down. But on the other hand, it was a very long time ago, and the Landauers and the Jacobses were not present. Mrs. Landauer and Mrs. Jacobs both belonged to my mother's bridge club.

At that age, if I thought about social acceptance at all it was as one of the facts of nature. Looking back, I can see that manners entered into it, but so did money. The people my parents considered to be of good families all had, or had had, land, income from property, something beside wages from a job.

The Russian-Jewish family was quite different. They were immigrants, spoke imperfect English, and had only recently passed through Ellis Island. So far as the Lincoln *Evening Courier* was concerned, news that was not local tended to be about a threatened coal strike or calling out the National Guard to quell some disturbance. Very seldom was there any mention of what went on in Europe. I was a grown man before I learned about the pogroms that drove the Rabinowitzes from their homeland. When I try to recall what the inside of Mr. Rabinowitz's store was like, what emerges through the mists of time is an impression of thick-soled shoes, heavy denim, corduroy, and flannel — work clothes of the cheapest kind. The bank held a mortgage on the stock or I don't know Arkansas. The chances are that he held out until the Depression and then went under, along with a great many other people whose financial underpinnings were more substantial.

What made Maxie want to be a Cub Scout? Had he been reading Ernest Thompson Seton and contracted a longing for the wilderness? Or did he, a newcomer, in his loneliness just want to belong to a group, any group, of boys his own age? We taught the Cub Scouts how to tie a clove hitch and a running bowline and how (if you were lucky) to build a fire without any matches and other skills appropriate to the outdoor life. Somebody, after a few weeks, decided that there ought to be an initiation. Into what I don't think we bothered to figure out.

On a Monday night we walked the little boys clear out of town in the moonlight and halted when we came to a bridge. Somebody suggested a footrace with blindfolds on. A handkerchief was included in the official Cub Scout uniform and they all had one. If they had been sent running up the road until we called to them to stop, they might have tripped or bumped into each other and fallen down, but probably nothing worse. I noticed that the bridge we were standing on had low sides that came up about to the little boys' belly buttons. I cannot pretend that I didn't know what was going to happen, but a part of me that I was not sufficiently acquainted with had taken over suddenly, and he/I lined the blindfolded boys up with their backs to one side of the bridge, facing the other, and said, "On your marks, get set, *go!* . . ." and they charged bravely across the bridge and into the opposite railing and knocked the wind out of themselves.

I believe in the forgiveness of sins. Some sins. I also believe that what is done is done and cannot be undone. The reason I didn't throw myself on my knees in the dust and beg them (and God) to forgive me is that I knew He wouldn't, and that even if He did, I wouldn't forgive myself. Sick with shame at the pain I had inflicted, I tore Max Rabinowitz's blindfold off and held him by the shoulders until his gasping subsided.

Considering the multitude of things that happen in any one person's life, it seems fairly unlikely that those little boys remembered the incident for very long. It was an introduction to what was to come. And cruelty could never again take them totally by surprise. But I have remembered it. I have remembered it because it was the moment I learned that I was not to be trusted.

My Father's Friends

MY father died in 1958, a few months after his eightieth — and my fiftieth — birthday. The day after he was buried, my stepmother brought out two heavy winter overcoats for me to try on, and then she and my older brother and I went to the storeroom above the garage, and she showed me a brown leather suitcase of my father's, a much more expensive piece of luggage than I had ever owned. None of this was my idea, but I nevertheless could feel on my face an expression of embarrassment, as if I had been caught out in something. My stepmother was not given to thinking ill of people but when my brother and I were children he had assumed the role of the prosecuting attorney. I glanced at his face now; nothing unkind there. The coats wouldn't have fitted him, or my younger brother, and since I was named after my father, the initials on the suitcase were mine, and who would want a suitcase with somebody else's initials on it? So why did I feel that I had appeared to be showing a too avid interest in the spoils?

Later on that afternoon I started out on foot to call on two of my father's friends who were not well enough to come to the funeral. The first, Dean Hill, was a man my father went fishing with. He was also a cousin of my stepmother. He had inherited a great many acres of Illinois farmland, and he had a beautiful wife. Apart from a trip to Biloxi in the dead of winter, they lived very much as other Lincoln people of moderate means did. I had known him since I was a young boy, and never had a conversation with him. When I go home to Lincoln I tend to put aside whatever in my life I suspect would be of no interest to people there, and sometimes this results in my feeling that I am going around with my head in a brown paper bag. But on this occasion I felt I could be my true self. To my surprise I found that he read books. In Lincoln the women put their names down for best-sellers at the desk of the public library, and the men read the evening newspaper. "What the book is about is a matter of indifference to me," Dean Hill said. "I am interested in the writer — in what he is carefully not saying, or saying and doesn't know that he is. What his real position is, as distinct from the stated one. It keeps me amused. All forms of deception are entertaining to contemplate, don't you find? Particularly self-deception, which is what life is largely made up of."

I found myself telling him about my guilty feelings at accepting my father's things, and he nodded and said, "Once when I was sitting in a jury box the judge said, 'Will the defendant rise,' and I caught myself just in time. If one isn't guilty of one thing one is certainly guilty of another is perhaps the only explanation for this kind of irrational behavior. . . . I'm glad you have the coats and the suitcase, and I'm sure your father would be too. Enjoy them." He then went on to speak affectionately of my father. "I have no other friend like him," he said. "I am already beginning to feel the loss. Most people have a hidden side. Your father was exactly what he appeared to be. It is very rare."

I left the house with a feeling of exhilaration. I couldn't help feeling that my father's part in this old friendship had somehow been handed on to me, like the overcoats and the suitcase. And in fact it had. When Dean Hill and his wife came to New York six months later, he invited me to lunch at the Plaza, and the conversation was easy and intimate. Everything that he had to say interested me because of its originality and wisdom. While living all his life in a very small Middle Western town and keeping his eye on his farms, he had managed to be aware of the world outside in a way that no one else there was. Or at least no one I knew. He was worried about my stepmother. It was a case of the oak and the ivy, he said, and he didn't think she would manage very well without my father. (He was quite right. She was ten years younger than my father, and when he was alive she was perky and energetic and always talking about taking off for somewhere — except that they couldn't, because of his emphysema. After he was gone, the tears she wiped away with her handkerchief were simply followed by more tears. She spent the remaining fifteen years of her life in nursing homes, unable to cope with her sadness.)

I wrote to Dean Hill, and he answered my letters. The last time I saw him, in Lincoln, twenty-eight years ago, I could talk to him but he couldn't talk to me. He had had a stroke. His speech was garbled and unintelligible. He appeared to feel that it was his fault.

M Y second call, the day after the funeral, was on Aaron McIvor, who for ten years was a golfing companion of my father's. They also occasionally did some business together. Mr. McIvor dabbled in a number of things, including local politics, and he must have made a living out of all this or he would have gone to work for somebody else. Now and then my father would be asked to handle an insurance policy personally, and in doing so he used the name of Maxwell, McIvor & Company as agent.

Though it would be accurate to say that Aaron McIvor was not like anybody else in Lincoln, it would also, in a way, be meaningless, since small-town people of that period were so differentiated that the same thing could have been said of nearly everybody. He had sad eyes and a sallow complexion and two deep furrows running down his cheeks. The tips of his fingers were stained with nicotine and the whites of his eyes were yellowish also, in a way more often found in dogs than in human beings. Nothing that he said was ever calculated to make people feel better about themselves, but he could be very funny.

As I zigzagged the five or six blocks between Dean Hill's house and the McIvors' that afternoon, I was struck by how little the older residential part of Lincoln had changed. A house here or there where no house was before. A huge old mansion gone.

Aaron McIvor's daughter-in-law directed me up the stairs to his bedroom. The ashtray on a chair beside his bed was full of cigarette butts. He looked the same, only old. I didn't stay long and I wished I hadn't gone to see him, because he had things to say against my father that, the day after his funeral, I didn't feel like listening to.

"McIvor is eccentric," my father would say, when his name came up in conversation. It was not something my father would have wanted anybody to say about him. But he did not expect people to be perfect, and Mr. McIvor's eccentricities in no way interfered with the friendship. Because he said so many unflattering things, it was assumed that he was a truthful man. I don't think this necessarily follows. But if you wanted him you had to take him as he was. The caustic remarks were brushed aside or forgiven. And people loved to tell how, when he was courting his wife, he never brought her candy or flowers but simply appeared, in the evening after supper, and stretched out in the porch swing with his head in her lap and went to sleep.

His wife, whom I called "Aunt" Beth, was my mother's closest friend. When I shut my eyes now, I see her affectionate smile, and the way her brown eyes lighted up. People loved her because she was so radiant. It cannot have been true that she was never tired or that there was nothing in her life to make her unhappy or depressed or complaining, but that is how I remember her.

When I was a little boy of six I met her on a cinder path at the Chautauqua grounds one day and she opened her purse and took out a dime and gave it to me. "I don't think my father would want me to take it," I said. My father knew a spendthrift when he saw one, and, hoping to teach me the value of money, he had put me on an allowance of ten cents a week, with the understanding that when the ten cents was gone I was not to ask for more. Also, if possible, I was to save part of the ten cents. "It's perfectly all right," Aunt Beth said. "Don't you worry. I'll explain it to him." I took off for the place where they sold Cracker Jack. And she stands forever, on the cinder path at the Chautauqua grounds, smiling at the happiness she has just set free. I long to compare her with something appropriate, and nothing is, quite, except the goodness of being alive.

The thing about my mother and Aunt Beth was that they were always so lighthearted when they were together. Sometimes I understood what they were laughing about, sometimes it would be over my head. My father and mother were both mad about golf. I used to caddie for my father, and if he made a bad approach shot he was inconsolable. He would pick his ball out of the cup and walk toward the next tee still analyzing what he had done that made the ball end up in a bunker instead of on the green near the flag. You felt he felt that if he could only have lived that moment over again and kept his shoulder down and followed through properly, the whole rest of his life might have been different. And that Aaron McIvor mournfully agreed with him. The two women were unfazed by such disasters. My mother would send a fountain of sand into the air and go right on describing a dress pattern or some china she had seen in a house in Kentucky. When she and Aunt Beth had talked their way around nine holes—usually my father and Mr. McIvor played in a foursome of men—they would add up their scores and sit down on the balcony of the clubhouse until their husbands joined them. Then, more often than not, they would come back to our house for Sunday-night supper. When my mother went out to the kitchen, Mr. McIvor would get up from his chair and follow her with the intent to ruffle her feathers. My mother had no use for the family her younger sister had married into. Perched on the kitchen stool, Mr. McIvor said admiring things about them. How well educated they were. How good they were at hanging on to their money. How one of them found a mistake of twenty-seven cents in his monthly bank statement and raised such Cain about it that the president of the bank came to him finally in tears. How no tenant farmer of theirs ever drew a simple breath that they didn't know about. And so on. My mother would emerge from the pantry with a plate of hot baking-powder biscuits in her hand and her face flushed with outrage, and we would sit down to scrambled eggs and bacon.

In my Aunt Annette's sun parlor there was a wicker porch swing that hung on chains from the ceiling. *Creak . . . creak . . .* Just as if you were outdoors, only you weren't. It was a good place from which to survey what went on in Lincoln Avenue. Sitting with her arm resting on the back of the swing, my aunt was alternately there and not there, like cloud shadows. Now her attention would be focused on me (for I was twelve years old and I had lost my mother a couple of years before and my father had sold our house and was on the point of remarrying and I needed her), now on a past that stretched well beyond the confines of my remembering. I didn't mind when she withdrew into her own thoughts; her physical presence was enough. One day I saw, on the sidewalk in front of the house, a very small woman in a big black hat. Not just the brim, the whole hat was big, an elaborate structure of ribbon and straw and jet hatpins that she moved under without disturbing.

"Who is *that*?" I asked.

Turning her head, my aunt said, "Old Mrs. McIvor. Aaron's mother. She was born in England."

"Some hat," I said.

"She's been going by the house for many years and I have never seen her without it."

The things I am curious about now I was not curious about then. Where, in that small town of twelve thousand people, did Aaron McIvor's mother live? Did she live by herself? And if so, on what? And what brought her all the way across the Atlantic? And what happened to his father? And how on earth did she come by that hat? None of these questions will I ever know the answer to.

Pre-adolescent boys, at a certain point, become limp, pale, undemanding, unable to think of anything to do, so saturated with protective coloration that they are hardly distinguishable from the furniture, and not much more aware of what is going on around them. I'm not quite sure when Aunt Beth and Mr. McIvor adopted a baby, but it didn't occur to me that any disappointment or heartache had preceded this decision. If I ever saw the baby, lack of interest prevented me from remembering it.

I must have been thirteen or fourteen when I heard that Aunt Beth had cancer and was in the hospital. I felt I ought to go see her. I thought my mother would want me to. My Aunt Annette was in Florida and there was no one to enlighten me about what to expect. I went from room to room of the hospital, reading the cards on the doors and peering past the white cloth screens, and on the second floor, in the corridor, I ran into her. She was wearing a hospital gown and her hair was in two braids down her back. Her color was ashen. She saw me, but it was as if she were looking at somebody she had never seen before. Since then, I have watched beloved animals dying. The withdrawal, into some part of themselves that only they know about. It is, I think, not unknown to any kind of living creature. A doctor passed, in a white coat, and she turned and called after him urgently. I skittered down the stairs and got on my bicycle and rode away from the hospital feeling I had made a mistake. I had and I hadn't. She was in no condition to receive visitors, but I had acquired an important item of knowledge – dying is something people have to live through, and while they are doing it, unless you are much closer to them than I was to her, you have little or no claim on them.

After she was gone, when I rode past her house, I always thought of her. The house had a flat roof and the living-room windows came almost to the floor of the front porch. The fact that there were so few lights burning on winter evenings may have accounted for the look of sadness. Or it could have been my imagination.

FOR years after we moved to Chicago my stepmother was homesick and we always went down to Lincoln for the holidays so that she could be with her family. One evening, a couple of days after Christmas, I happened to be walking down Keokuk Street, and when I came to the McIvors' house I turned in at the front walk. I don't know what made me do it. Recollection of those Sunday-night suppers when my mother was alive, perhaps, or of my father and Mr. McIvor retiring to my father's den, where he kept the whiskey bottle, for a nightcap. The housekeeper let me in. The little boy – I had almost forgotten about him – who peered at me from behind her skirt must have been six or seven. Mr. McIvor hadn't come home from his office yet, she said, and retired to the kitchen.

I couldn't remember ever having been inside the house before, and I looked around the living room: dark varnished woodwork, Mission furniture, brown wallpaper, brown lampshades. It didn't seem at all likely that after Aunt Beth died Mr. McIvor destroyed all traces of her, but neither did it seem possible that she would have chosen to live with this disheartening furniture. There were brass andirons in the fireplace but no logs on them and no indication that the fireplace was ever used. No books or magazines lying around, not even the *Saturday Evening Post*. The little boy wanted to show me the Christmas tree, in the front window. The tree lights were not on, and he explained that they were broken. The opened presents under the tree — a cowboy suit, a puzzle, a Parcheesi board, and so on — were still in the boxes they had come in. With a screwdriver that the housekeeper produced for me I located the defective bulb, and the colored lights shone on the child's pleased face. The stillness I heard as I stood looking at the lighted tree was beyond my power to do anything about. I said good-bye to the little boy and picked up my hat and coat and left, without waiting for Mr. McIvor to come home.

WHEN I married I took my wife to Lincoln. She was introduced to all the friends of the family, including Aaron McIvor, whom she was charmed by. She told me afterward that at one point in their conversation he turned and looked at me and then said, "He's a nice boy but queer — very queer."

WHEN I went to see Mr. McIvor on the day after my father's funeral, his criticism boiled down to the fact that my father liked women too much, and let them twist him around their little finger.

My father was an indulgent husband, but he hated change and was devoted to his habits, and it took a prolonged campaign and all sorts of stratagems on my stepmother's part to get him to agree to enclose the screened porch or buy a new car. In any case, he was not a skirt chaser. So what did all this mean?

I think even more than by what he said I was upset by his matter-of-fact tone of voice — as if my father's death had aroused no feelings in him whatever. There was no question that my father considered Aaron McIvor his friend. Could it be that he disliked my father, and perhaps always had? Or did he dislike everybody, pretty much?

As I listened to him, I wondered if he had been envious of my father — of his success in business, and of the fact that he was, many people would have said, as fortunate in his second marriage as he was in his first. Because Aaron McIvor had made a decision and stuck to it didn't mean that he never considered the alternative. And even a so-so marriage might have been better than the unshared bed and the unending solitude he came home to day after day for something like forty years.

"I don't agree with you," I said, and "I don't think that's right." And he said with a sniff, "I knew him better than you did."

It crossed my mind, after I had left the house, that he might have been playing with me the game he used to play with my mother. But on those far-off Sunday evenings he had a look of glee in his eyes, where now there was simply animosity. From which it did not appear that I was excluded.

I always assumed he was fond of my mother or he wouldn't have enjoyed teasing her. Was it on her account that he resented the fact that my father had remarried — if he did resent it? If I had had my wits about me, I would have retraced my steps and asked Dean Hill what he thought. He and Aaron McIvor were not, so far as I know, friends, but they had spent a lifetime in the same small town, where everything is known, about everybody. Also, they were direct opposites — the one so even-tempered and observant and responsive to any kind of cordiality, the other so abrasive. And opposites often instinctively understand each other. Whether Dean Hill came up with a believable explanation or not, ambiguity was meat and drink to him, and he would probably have considered the conversation in that bleak upstairs bedroom from angles I hadn't thought of. He might even have suggested, tactfully, that in my being so hot under the collar there just could be something worth looking into. My father and I were of very different temperaments, and he didn't know anything about the kind of life I was blindly feeling my way toward. He had only my best interests at heart, but as an adolescent and in my early twenties I had resented his advice and sometimes taken pleasure in doing the opposite of what he urged me to do.

Instead, I stopped off at my Aunt Annette's. She listened to my account of the visit to Aaron McIvor and did not attempt to explain his behavior, beyond saying he had always been that way. She then told me something

I didn't know: "As Beth lay dying, she said to Aaron, 'You are the dearest husband any woman ever had.'"

In the face of that, nothing I had been thinking seemed worth giving serious consideration to. She was his life. There wasn't the faintest chance of his finding another woman like her, and it was not in his nature to make concessions. So he made do with housekeepers, and brought up his son. When he was stumped by something he went to see the old woman with the big black hat, who knew a thing or two about bringing up children (or so I like to think) and who was not put off by anything he said, being of the opinion that his bark was worse than his bite.

The Front and the Back
Parts of the House

THOUGH it took me a while to realize it, I had a good father. He left the house early Tuesday morning carrying his leather grip, which was heavy with printed forms, and walked downtown to the railroad station. As the Illinois state agent for a small fire and windstorm insurance company he was expected to make his underwriting experience available to local agents in Freeport, Carbondale, Alton, Carthage, Dixon, Quincy, and so on, and to cultivate their friendship in the hope that they would give more business to his company. I believe he was well liked. Three nights out of every week he slept in godforsaken commercial hotels that overlooked the railroad tracks and when he turned over in the dark he heard the sound of the ceiling fan and railway cars being shunted. He knew the state of Illinois the way I knew our house and yard.

He could have had a much better job in the Chicago office but my mother said Chicago was no place to raise children. When the offer came a second time, ten years later, my father accepted it. He was forty-four and ready to give up the hard life of a traveling man. My stepmother wept at the thought of leaving her family and Lincoln but came to like living in Chicago. They lived there for twenty years. With my future in mind — he wasn't just talking — my father assured me solemnly that you get out of life exactly what you put into it. I took this with a grain of salt; a teacher in my high school in Chicago, a woman given to reading Mencken and *The American Mercury*, had explained to me that there are people who have always drawn the short end of the stick and will continue to. But for my father the maxim was true. He reserved a reasonable part of his life for his responsibilities to his family and his golf game, and everything else he put into the fire-insurance business. He ended up Vice-President in Charge of the Western Department, which satisfied his aspirations. When the presidency was offered to him he turned it down. It would have meant moving East, and he foresaw that in the New York office he would be confronted with problems he might not be able to deal with confidently.

A detached retina brought his career to a premature end. They moved back to Lincoln, to the same street, Park Place, but a different house. I was in my early forties and living in the country, just beyond the northern suburbs of New York City, and trying to make a living by writing fiction, when my father wrote me that it was about time I paid them a visit. He met me at the station, and as we drove into Park Place I saw that time is more than an abstract idea: Maple and elm saplings that were staked against the wind when we moved away had become shade trees. I spent the first evening with my father and my stepmother, and next morning after breakfast I walked over to my Aunt Annette's. She was my mother's younger sister, and they were very close. I loved going to her house because nothing ever changed there. When she sold it many years later because the stairs got to be too much for her, I felt the loss, I think, more than she did.

In that house the present had very little resonance. The things my aunt really cared about had all happened in the early years of her life. My Great-Grandfather Youtsey's farm on the Licking River in Kentucky, where she spent every summer of her childhood, had passed out of the family. The Kentucky aunts and uncles she was so fond of she was not free to visit anymore. Her father and mother and my mother were all lying side by side in the cemetery.

In the front hall, under the stairs, there was a large framed engraving of the Colosseum, bought in Rome the year I was born. In the living room there were further reminders: Michelangelo's *Holy Family*, the Bridge of Sighs, and a Louis XV glass cabinet full of curios. Lots of Lincoln people had been to Chicago, and some even to New York, but very few had any firsthand knowledge of what Europe was like — except the coal miners, and they didn't count. The sublime souvenirs kept their importance down through time.

Over the high living-room mantelpiece was a portrait-size tinted photograph of my Grandfather Blinn. I could almost but not quite remember him. When I stood and contemplated it I was defeated by the unseeing look that likenesses of dead people always seem to have. My Aunt Annette was his favorite child. To his boyhood on his father's cattle farm near St. Johnsbury, Vermont, and to the obstacles he surmounted in order to become a lawyer, the photograph offered no clue whatever. Nor did it convey what a warmhearted man he was. What it did suggest, if anybody wanted to look at it that way, was that in my uncle's house a dead man was held in greater esteem than he was.

My aunt had made what other members of the family considered a mistaken marriage, which she had long ago stopped discussing with anyone. If she had really wanted to she could have extricated herself from it. It was as if she believed in the irrevocability of choices, and was simply living with the one she had made as a young woman.

My Uncle Will had graduated from Yale with an engineering degree, and held a license to practice surveying, but he also had inherited several farms, and he was gone from six-thirty in the morning until late afternoon, making sure that his tenant farmers didn't do something that might be to their advantage but not his. I guess he was an intelligent man, but if one of the main elements in your character is suspicion, intelligence is more often than not misused. My aunt was a very beautiful woman and he loved her but her beauty was a torment to him. He did not want her to accept invitations of any kind and they never entertained. It upset him if she even went to the Friday-afternoon bridge club, because what if the hostess's husband were to leave his office early and come home?

Annette was alone in the house all day, with no one to talk to but the colored woman in the kitchen. Lula had a great many children and from time to time she quit in order to have another. Sometimes she just quit. Or my aunt fired her because she had failed to show up for too many mornings in a row. She was always eventually asked to come back, because my aunt needed her in the skirmishing that took place with my Uncle Will. The indignant things Annette didn't feel it was safe to say to him Lula, looking him straight in the eye, said. My uncle seldom took offense, perhaps because she was colored and his servant and not to be taken seriously, or perhaps because she was not afraid of him and so had his grudging respect. When my aunt couldn't find her glasses she borrowed Lula's, which, even though there was only one lens and that had a crack in it, worked well enough. And when she felt like crying, Lula let her cry.

Like the house, my aunt changed very little over the years. Her hair turned grey, and she was heavier than she was when I was a child, but her clear blue eyes were still the eyes of a young woman.

I opened the front door and called out and she answered from the sun porch. My feelings poured out of me, as always when I was with her.

Suddenly she interrupted what I was telling her to say, "I have a surprise for you. Hattie Dyer is in the kitchen."

I got up from my chair and for the length of time it took me to go through the house blindly like a sleepwalker I had the beautiful past in my hand. When I walked into the kitchen I saw a grey-haired colored woman standing at the sink and I said "Hattie!" and went and put my arms around her.

I don't know what I expected. I hadn't thought that far. Or imagined what her response might be.

There was no response. Any more than if I had hugged a wooden post. She did not even look at me. As I backed away from her in embarrassment at my mistake, she did not do or say anything that would make it easier for me to get from the kitchen to the front part of the house where I belonged.

If I had acted differently, I asked myself later — if I had been less concerned with my own feelings and allowed room for hers, if I had put out my hand instead of trying to embrace her, would the truce between the front and the back parts of the house have held? Would she have wiped her hand on her apron and taken my hand? And said (whether it was true or not) that she remembered me? And listened politely to my recollections of the time when she worked in our kitchen? And then perhaps I would have perceived that her memories of that time were vague or nonexistent, so that we very soon ran out of things to say?

I didn't tell my aunt what had happened. I was afraid she would say "Why did you put your arms around her?" and I didn't know why. Also, I thought she might be provoked at Hattie, and I didn't want to have to consider her feelings as well as my own.

The next time I was in Lincoln, a year or two later, Lula was back and saw me coming up the walk and opened the front door to me.

TWICE a day, with dragging footsteps — for he was an old man — Alfred Dyer came up the brick driveway of our house on Ninth Street to clean out the horse's stall and feed and curry him, and shovel coal into the furnace. His daughter Hattie kept house for my Grandmother Blinn at the end of her life when, immobilized by dropsy, she sat beside the cannel-coal fire in the back parlor, unable to arrive at the name of one of her children or grandchildren without running through the entire list of them. I don't remember ever being alone with her, though I expect I was. Or anything she ever said to me. I was five years old when she died. The day after her funeral my mother sat down at the kitchen table with Hattie and when they had finished talking about the situation in that house my mother asked her if she would like to come across the street and work in ours.

Hattie was a good cook when she came to us and she learned effortlessly anything my mother chose to teach her. She was paid five dollars a week — two hundred and sixty dollars a year, the prevailing wage for domestic servants in the second decade of this century. If you take into consideration the fact that it was one-twelfth of my father's annual salary, it doesn't seem so shocking.

The week took its shape from my father's going away and returning, but otherwise every day was a repetition of other days, with, occasionally, an event intruding upon the serenity of the expected. My older brother came down with chicken pox and I caught it from him. Or we had company. Or the sewing woman settled down in an empty bedroom and, with her mouth full of pins, arranged tissue-paper patterns and scraps of dress material on the headless dress form. Sometimes my mother's friends came of an afternoon and the tea cart was wheeled into the living room and they sat drinking tea and talking as if their lives depended on it, and I would go off upstairs to play and come down an hour later to find them gone and Hattie washing the teacups.

Monday mornings two shy children that I knew were hers came to the back door with an express wagon and Hattie gave them our washing, tied up in a sheet, for her mother to do. I knew that old Mrs. Dyer's house was on Elm Street, near the intersection at the foot of Ninth Street hill, and I assumed that when Hattie finished the supper dishes and closed the outside kitchen door behind her, that was where she went. It may or may not have been true. After three or four days Mrs. Dyer sent the washing back, white as snow and folded in such a way that it gave my mother pleasure as she put it away in the upstairs linen closet.

There were places in that house that I went to habitually, the way animals repeat their rounds: the window seat in the library, the triangular space behind a walnut Victorian sofa in the living room, the unfurnished bedroom over the kitchen. And if I was suddenly at loose ends because the life had gone out of the toys I was playing with, I would find my mother and be gathered onto her lap and consoled. If she was not home

I would wander out onto the back porch and listen to the upward-spiraling sound of the locusts.

The dog went to my mother when he wasn't sure we all liked him as much as it is possible for a dog to be liked, and felt better after she had talked to him. My brother, who was four years older than I, had a running argument with her about whether he was eleven or, as he insisted, twelve. If in the dead of winter my father opened his three-tiered metal fishing box and sorted through the flies, he chose the room where she was to do it in. When summer came she packed a picnic hamper, and my father brought the horse and carriage around to the high curbing in front of the house, and against a disapproving background of church bells we drove out into the country to a walnut grove with a stream running through it. My mother sat on a plaid lap rug and pulled in one sunfish after another, while my father tramped upstream casting for bass. We could have been the only people on earth. I think my mother enjoyed those long drowsy fishing expeditions but in any case she did whatever it made him happy to do. How much he loved her I heard in his voice whenever he called to her. And how much she loved him I saw in her face when he arrived on the front porch on Friday afternoon and we all came out of the house to greet him. As my father stood with his arms around us, the dog wormed his way past my legs so that his presence too would be recognized.

The Christmas holly that the first grade had cut out of red and green paper and pasted on the schoolroom windows was replaced by George Washington's hatchet, which turned up again on the scorecard that my mother brought home to me from her bridge club. When we looked at the teacher we also saw the calendar on the wall behind her desk: April 1, 1915: April Fool's Day.

I have learned to read. I can read sentences out of the evening paper. The big black headlines are often about the war between Germany and the Allies. From the window seat in the library I watch as my father stands and holds an opened-out page of the Lincoln *Evening Courier* across the upper part of the fireplace so the chimney won't smoke. (The war between *us* broke out when I was three or four years old. I woke up in the night with a parched throat and called out — it was by no means the first time this had happened — for a drink. And waited for my mother's footsteps and the bathroom glass against my dry lips. Instead, his voice, from across the hall, said, "*Oh*, get it yourself!") The newspaper catches fire and floats up the chimney, and I pull the curtain behind me in order to peer out at the darkness and the piles of snow. In May, where the piles of dirty snow were, the flowering almond is in bloom. It has suckered and spread through the wire fence into the Kiests' yard. Do the flowers on that side belong to them or to us?

D. W. Griffith's *Birth of a Nation* is showing at the movie theater downtown and there are scenes in it that have made all the colored people in Lincoln angry. I am told to stay out of the kitchen.

The sentences we are called on to read out loud in class are longer and more complicated. We have to memorize the forty-eight states and their capitals, and the countries of South America. With a pencil behind his ear, my father goes through an accumulation of inspection slips, making a check mark now and then, and hands them to me to alphabetize. (Spreading them around me on the rug, I am proud to be of help to him.)

Slumped down in her chair, my mother feels with the toe of her shoe for the buzzer that is concealed under the dining-room rug. My brother and I find her searching hilarious. My father wonders why she just doesn't buy a little bell she can ring. In the end she has to give up, and calls out to the kitchen. The pantry door swings open and Hattie appears to clear away the plates and bring the dessert. She too thinks it is funny that the buzzer is never where it is supposed to be.

How many years was she with us? Five, by my calculations. One day I went out to the kitchen for a drink of water and saw her daughter Thelma at the kitchen sink with an apron on. She said she had come to work for us. She was twelve years old but tall for her age. I asked my mother where Hattie was and my mother said, "She's been having trouble with her husband and moved to Chicago." My mother didn't say what the trouble was and I assumed it was one of the things that are not explained to children. But I felt the trouble was serious if Hattie had to go away. And her absence made me aware of an unpleasant possibility: Things could change.

To everything that my mother said to Thelma she answered "Yes, ma'am" and "No, ma'am," but as though she were hearing it from a great distance, and she moved with the slowness of a person whose heart is somewhere else. My mother detected a film of grease on all the dishes and spoke to her about it. When there was no improvement, she decided that Thelma wasn't ever going to be like Hattie, and let her go.

The good-natured farm girl who was in our kitchen after that was taking classes at night so she could pass an examination and work in the post office. My mother was satisfied with her but spoke regretfully of Hattie, who knew what she wanted done without having to be told.

The school calendar has marched straight on to the fall half of the year 1918. We have learned how to do long division. The women who come to our house in the afternoon put their teacups aside and hem diapers as they sit gossiping. They all know what my mother has told me in confidence, that I am going to have a baby brother or a baby sister. They also know — in a small town there was no way for such a thing not to be known — that my mother had a difficult time when my brother was born, and again with me. Only my Aunt Annette knew that at this time she had premonitions of dying.

My mother hopes that the baby will be a girl, and I am sure that what my mother wants to have happen will happen. Nothing turned out the way anybody hoped or expected it to. My younger brother was born in a hospital in Bloomington during the height of the epidemic of Spanish influenza. Toward the end of the first week in January, Alfred Dyer, coming up the driveway to tend the furnace, cannot have failed to see the funeral wreath on the door.

There is no cure but time. One of my mother's friends said that, putting her hand on my father's shoulder as he sat, hardly recognizable, in his chair. I thought about my mother in the cemetery and wondered if she would wake up and try to get out of her coffin and not be able to. But children have to go to school no matter what happens at home. I learned that the square root of sixty-four is eight, and that π is 3.14159 approximately, and represents the ratio of the circumference to the diameter of a circle.

YEARS passed without my thinking about Hattie Dyer at all, and then suddenly there I was backing away from her in confusion. When I told my wife about it she said, "It wasn't Hattie you embraced but the idea of her." Which was clearly true, but didn't explain Hattie's behavior.

Because my mother was fond of her it doesn't necessarily follow that Hattie was fond of my mother. My mother may have been only the white woman she worked for. But if this were true I think I would have sensed it as a child. Perhaps — it was so long ago — she neither remembered nor cared what my mother was like by the time I put my arms around her in my aunt's kitchen.

If I had had the courage to stand my ground and say to her, "Why do you refuse to admit that you knew me when I was a little boy?" I don't think she would have given me any answer. However, people do communicate their feelings helplessly. Jealousy can be felt even in the dark. Lovers charge the surrounding air with their delirium. What I felt as I backed away from that unresponsive figure was anger.

MY Aunt Edith was married to a doctor and lived in Bloomington. They had no children and she wanted to take the baby when my mother died, but my father clung to the belief that my mother would have wanted him to keep the family together and not let my brothers and me grow up in separate households, no matter how loving. We were too young to shift for ourselves while he was away, and what he needed was a woman who knew how to run a house and take care of a baby. Hattie could have managed it with one hand tied behind her. So could Annette's Lula. And they would have brought life into the house with them. I cannot believe that there were no more colored women like them in Lincoln. But he thought (and so did everybody else) that he had to have a white woman. The first housekeeper was hired because she had been a nurse. She had nothing whatever to say, not even about the weather. She had never been around children before, and I felt no inclination to lean against her.

My brother and I struggled against the iron fact that my mother wasn't there anymore. Or ever going to be. Tears did not help. The house was like a person in a state of coma. If Annette had not turned up sometime during every day I think we would all have stopped breathing. Any domestic crisis that arose remained undealt with until my father came home. He never knew when he left the house on Tuesday morning what brand-new trouble he would find when he returned on Friday afternoon. My mother's clothes closet was empty. Her silver-backed comb and brush and hand mirror were still on her dressing table, but without the slight disorder of hairpins, powder, powder puff, cologne, smelling salts, and so on, they were reduced to being merely objects. How endless the nights must have been for him, in the double bed where, when he put out his hand, it encountered only the cold sheets.

The first housekeeper lasted three months. The second took offense no matter which way the wind blew, and it would have been better to have no one. She made mischief between the two sides of the family and was dismissed when she developed erysipelas. The farm girl passed her examination and gave notice. And so it went. Each time my father's arrangements collapsed he turned in desperation to old Mrs. Dyer, and though she was crippled with rheumatism she came and fed us until he found someone to take over from her.

During this period he made an appointment with the local photographer. The result is a very strange picture. My father sits holding the baby on his lap. The baby looks uncomfortable but not about to cry. My father is wearing a starched collar and a dark-blue suit, and looks like what he was, a sad self-made man. My older brother has a fierce expression on his face, as if he means to stare the camera out of countenance. I am standing beside him, a thin little boy of ten, in a Norfolk jacket, knee pants, and long black stockings. The photographer was a man with a good deal of manner, and as he ducked his head under the black cloth and then out again to rearrange the details of our bodies I was threatened with an attack of the giggles, which would not have been appropriate, because my father meant the picture to be a memorial of our bereavement.

Annette and her husband were in the habit of spending the winter in Florida. The first Christmas after my mother's death she sent him and my Cousin Peg down South without her so she could be with us. Shortly after that I became aware of conversations behind closed doors and then somebody forgot to close the door. Out of fury because she had been dismissed, the second housekeeper had written several unsigned poison-pen letters to my Grandmother Maxwell, in which she said that my father was carrying on with my Aunt Annette. My Uncle Will Bates received similar letters. His response was to put a stop to Annette's coming to our house at all.

My brother felt that it would be disloyal to my father if he set foot in my uncle's house. Nothing on earth (and certainly not the awkwardness) could have kept me from being where Annette was. What I didn't tell her about my feelings she seemed to know anyway. She told Lula to put an extra place at the table for me, and made me feel loved. She also got me to accept (as far as I was able at that age to do this) the succession of changes that came about, a year later, when my father's grief wore itself out and he put his life with my mother behind him. Children, with no conception of how life goes on and on, expect a faithfulness that comes at too high a price. Now that I am old enough to be his father I have no trouble saying yes, of course he should have remarried. He had always liked women, and without feminine companionship, without someone sitting at the opposite end of the table whom he could feel tenderly about, he would have turned sour and become a different man. He began to accept invitations, and the matchmakers put their heads together.

There used to be, and probably still is somewhere, a group picture of the guests at my father's wedding, which took place in the house of my stepmother's sister, in 1921. The photographer set up his tripod and camera on the lawn in front of the house, and as the guests assembled in front of him there was a good deal of joking and laughter. I had already passed over the line into puberty but not yet reached the stage of hyper-critical judgments when I would find the loud laughter of a room full of grown people enjoying themselves unbearable.

DURING the years that my father lived in Chicago his heavy leather grip, that my mother had hated the sight of, remained on a closet shelf unless we took the train down to Lincoln. There were several people he felt obliged to call on whenever he went home, and one of them was Mrs. Dyer, who still lived in the little house at the foot of Ninth Street hill. He expected his sons to go with him. The visits went on as long as she lived. Mr. Dyer was never there, and I think must have died. I was not expected to take part in the conversation; only to be there. And so my eyes were free to roam around the front room we sat in. The iron potbel-lied stove, the threadbare carpet, the darkened wallpaper. The calendar, courtesy of the local lumber company. The hard wooden chairs we sat on. Mrs. Dyer and my father talked about her health, about changes in Lincoln, about how fast time goes. And then he made some excuse that got us on our feet. As we were saying good-bye he took out his billfold and extracted a new ten-dollar bill. But not one word did either of them say about the thing that had brought him there, which was that in the time of his greatest trouble, when there was no one else he could have turned to, she didn't fail him.

IN a box of old papers, not long ago, I found an eighty-page history of the town of Lincoln, published by Feldman's Print Shop, in 1953, when Lincoln was celebrating the hundredth anniversary of its founding. Thumbing through it I came upon a picture of Mrs. Dyer, looking just the way I remembered her. She was beautiful as an old woman, and probably always was. In the photograph she is wearing a black silk dress with a lace collar. Her mouth is sunken in with age, but her eyes are as bright as a child's, and from her smile you'd think it had been a privilege to stand over a tub of soapy water doing other people's washing year in and year out. Surrounding the picture there is an interview with Hattie, who had been chosen as "a respected citizen of the community" to give "something of the history of one of our distinguished colored families." The interview is only five hundred words long, and I assume that much of what she said never got into print. For example, what about her brother Dr. William Dyer? Was the interviewer aware that he had succeeded in becoming a doctor when this was exceedingly rare for a Negro and that he was on the surgical staffs of the best hospitals in Kansas City? Or that he was also among those citizens of Lincoln who were especially honored at the centennial celebration? Perhaps the history went to press before this fact was known. In any case, while Dr. Dyer was in town for the honoring he stayed with her. He had managed to put himself in a position where no white man could summon him with the word "Boy!" She must have been immensely proud of him. The interview does quote Hattie as saying that in Alfred Dyer's house "there were no intoxicants allowed, no dancing, no card playing, but how we loved to dance! And we did dance when they were away from home." As long as her father was able to work, Hattie said, he was employed by the B. P. Andrews Lumber Company in town. I suspect he had many jobs, some of them overlapping. It is hard to believe how little people were paid for their labor in those days, but the Dyers managed. They didn't have to walk along the railroad right-of-way picking up pieces of coal. In the interview, Hattie said she was a year old when she was brought to the house on Elm Street.

When her mother first came to Lincoln from Missouri, she worked in a boardinghouse run by a Mrs. Jones, Hattie said. It was on the site of the high school — which, in the twenties, when I went there, was an old building with deep grooves in the stairs worn by generations of adolescent feet. Mrs. Jones's establishment must have ceased to exist a very long time ago. If you have ever eaten in a boardinghouse you know every last one of them. The big oak dining-room table with all the leaves in it, and barely enough room for the thin young colored woman to squeeze between the chair backs and the sideboard. No sooner were the dishes from the midday meal washed and put back on the table and the pots and pans drying upside down in a pyramid on the kitchen range than it was time to start peeling potatoes for supper. Jesus loved her and that got her back on her feet when she was too tired to move. And before long, Alfred Dyer was waiting at the kitchen door to take her to prayer meeting.

"In looking back over the years," Hattie said to the interviewer, "I am proud of my father and mother, who were highly regarded by all who knew them, white as well as black. Their deep religious faith has been my help and strength throughout my life."

During one of those times when my father was searching for a house-keeper and Mrs. Dyer was in our kitchen, she stopped me as we got up from the table at the end of dinner and asked if I'd like to go to church with her to hear a choir from the South. It was a very cold night and there was a white full moon, and walking along beside Mrs. Dyer I saw the shadows of the bare branches laid out on the snow. Our footsteps made a squeaking sound and it hurt to breathe. The church was way downtown on the other side of the courthouse square. As we made our way indoors I saw that it was crammed with people, and overheated, and I was conscious of the fact that I was the only white person there. Nobody made anything of it. The men and women in the choir were of all ages, and dressed in white. For the first time in my life I heard "Swing Low, Sweet Chariot," and "Pharaoh's Army Got Drownded," and "Were You There When They Crucified My Lord?" and "Joshua Fit de Battle of Jericho." Singing "Don't let nobody turn you round," the choir yanked one another around and stamped their feet (in church!). I looked at Mrs. Dyer out of the corner of my eye. She was smiling. "Not my brother, not my sister, but it's me, *O Lord!*" the white-robed singers shouted. The people around me sat listening politely with their hands folded in their laps, and I thought, perhaps mistakenly, that they too were hearing these spirituals for the first time.

I COULD have asked my aunt about Hattie and she would have told me all that a white person would be likely to know, but I didn't. More years passed. I found that I had a nagging curiosity about Hattie — about what her life had been like. Finally it occurred to me that my Cousin Tom Perry, who lives in Lincoln, might be able to learn about her. He wrote back that I had waited too long. Among white people there was nobody left who knew her, and he couldn't get much information from the black people he talked to. He did find out that when she moved back to Lincoln, she lived in the little house on Elm Street. Tom was in high school with her son, who was an athlete, a track star. He became an undertaker and died in middle age, of cancer of the throat. Hattie spent the last years of her life in Springfield with one of her daughters. Her son was born after Hattie came back to Lincoln to live, and his last name was Brummel, so whatever the trouble with her husband was, they stayed together.

In his letter my cousin said that at the time of his death Alfred Dyer owned his own house and the houses on either side of it. This surprised me. He did not look like a property owner. All three houses were torn down recently, Tom said, and the site had not been built on.

I HAVE not been inside our house on Ninth Street since I was twelve years old. It was built in the eighteen-eighties, possibly even earlier. The last time I drove past it, five years ago, I saw that the present owners had put shutters on the front windows. Nothing looks right to me that is not the way I remember it, but it is the work of a moment, of less time than that, to do away with the shutters and bring back into existence the lavender-blue clematis on the side porch and the trellis that supported it, the big tree in the side yard that was killed by the elm blight, the house next door that burned down one night twenty-five or thirty years ago.

Though I know better, I half believe that if the front door to our house were opened to me I would find the umbrella stand by the window in the front hall and the living-room carpet would be moss green. Sometimes I put myself to sleep by going from room to room of that house, taking note of my father's upright piano with the little hand-wound Victrola on it, Guido Reni's *Aurora* over the living-room mantelpiece, the Victorian sofas and chairs. I make my way up the front stairs by the light of the gas night-light in the upstairs hall, and count the four bedroom doors. Or I go through the dining room into the pantry, where, as the door swings shut behind me and before I can push open the door to the brightly lit kitchen, I experience once more the full terror of the dark. Beyond the kitchen is the laundry, where the big iron cookstove is. Opening off this room are two smaller rooms, hardly bigger than closets. One contains jars of preserved fruit and vegetables and a grocery carton full of letters to my mother from my father. The other room is dark and has a musty odor. The dog sleeps here, on a square of old dirty carpet, and there is a toilet of an antiquated kind. Hattie is expected to use this toilet and not the one in the upstairs bathroom that we use. You could argue, I suppose, that some such arrangement would have been found in other old houses in Lincoln, and because it was usual may not have given offense—a proposition I do not find very convincing.

My mother was thirty-seven when she died. When I try to recall what she was like, I remember what a child would remember. How she bent over the bed and kissed me good night and drew the covers around my chin. How she made me hold still while she cut my bangs. If I try to see her as one adult looking at another, I realize how much there is that I don't know. One day I heard her exclaim into the telephone "It won't do!" and wondering what wouldn't do I listened. After a minute or two it became clear that a colored family was on the point of buying a house on the other side of the street from ours, and that my mother was talking to somebody at the bank. This in itself was odd. If my father had been home, she would have got him to do it. She must have believed that the matter wouldn't wait until he got home. "It won't do!" she kept repeating into the telephone. "It just won't do." A few weeks later, when a moving van drew up before the house in question, it was to unload the furniture of a white family.

One of the things I didn't understand when I was a child was the fact that grown people — not my father and mother but people who came to our house or that they stopped to talk to on the street — seemed to think they were excused from taking the feelings of colored people into consideration. When they said something derogatory about Negroes, they didn't bother to lower their voices even though fully aware that there was a colored person within hearing distance. Quite apart from what Hattie may have overheard in Lincoln, what she saw and lived through in Chicago, including race riots, might easily have been enough to make her fear and hate all white men without exception. And so in that case it was the color of my skin — the color of my skin and the physical contact — that accounted for what happened in my Aunt Annette's kitchen. Having arrived at this conclusion I found that I didn't entirely believe it, because at the time I had the feeling that Hattie's anger was not a generalized anger; it had something to do with who I was. Did somebody in our family do something unforgivable to her? My Grandmother Blinn? Not likely. My father always leaned over backward to be fair and just toward anybody who worked for him. Though I cannot bring back the words, I can hear, in a kind of replay, the sound of my mother and Hattie talking. We are in the throes of spring housecleaning. Her black hair bound up in a dish towel, my mother stands in the double doorway between the front hall and the living room and directs Hattie's attention to a corner of the ceiling where a spider has taken refuge. With a dust mop on the end of a very long pole, Hattie dislodges it. There is no sullenness in Hattie's voice and no strain in my mother's. They are simply easy with one another.

In the end I decided that I must be barking up the wrong tree, and that what happened in my aunt's kitchen was simply the collision of two experiences. And I stopped thinking about it until I had a second letter from my cousin. "I don't understand it," he wrote. "The colored people in Lincoln have always been very open. If you asked one of them a question you got the answer. This is different. They don't seem to want to talk about Hattie Dyer." In a P.S. he added that the elderly black man who took care of his yard was reading one of my books. Miss Lucy Jane Purrington, whose yard he also looked after, had lent it to him. And in a flash I realized what the unforgivable thing was and who had done it.

FROM time to time I have published fiction that had as a background a small town very much like Lincoln, or even Lincoln itself. The fact that I had not lived there since I was fourteen years old sealed off my memories of it, and made of it a world I knew no longer existed, that seemed always available for storytelling. Once, I began to write a novel without knowing what was going to happen in it. As the details unfolded before my mind, I went on putting them down, trusting that there was a story and that I would eventually find it. The novel began with an evening party in the year 1912. I didn't bother to make up the house where the party took place because there at hand was our house on Ninth Street and it gave me pleasure to write about it. The two main characters were an overly conscientious young lawyer named Austin King and his wife, Martha, who was pregnant. He had not been able to bring himself to say no to a letter from Mississippi relatives proposing to visit. At the beginning of the novel the relatives have arrived, the party is about to begin, and Martha King is not making things any easier for her husband by lying face down across her bed and refusing to speak to him.

Characters in fiction are seldom made out of whole cloth. A little of this person and something of that one and whatever else the novelist's imagination suggests is how they come into being. The novelist hopes that by avoiding actual appearances and actual names (which are so much more convincing than the names he invents for them), by making tall people short and red-headed people blond, that sort of thing, the sources of the composite character will not be apparent.

We did in fact have a visit of some duration from my Grandmother Maxwell's younger sister, who lived in Greenville, Mississippi, and her husband, their two grown sons, married daughter, son-in-law, and grand-child, a little girl of four. Remembering how their Southern sociability transformed our house, I tried to bring into existence a family with the same ability to charm, but whose ambiguous or destructive natures were partly imagined and partly derived from people not even born at the time of this visit. The little girl crossed over and became the daughter of Austin and Martha King. The young woman of the invented family was unmarried, and an early feminist, and without meaning to she whittled away at the marriage of her Northern cousin, whom she had fallen in love with. Though I did my best to change my Mississippi relatives beyond recognition, many years later my father told me that in one instance I had managed to pin the donkey's tail on the part of the animal where it belonged. But it was wholly by accident. If you turn the imagination loose like a hunting dog, it will often return with the bird in its mouth.

About fifty pages into the writing of the novel I had a dream that revealed to me the direction the story was trying to take and who the characters were stand-ins for. My father was musical, and could play by ear almost any instrument he picked up, and once had the idea of putting on a musical comedy with local talent. The rehearsals took place in our living room. He sat at the piano and played the vocal score for the singers. My mother sat on the davenport listening and I sat beside her. Things did not go well. The cast was erratic about coming to rehearsals, the tenor flagrantly so. One rainy evening only one member of the cast showed up, the pretty young woman who had the soprano lead. She and my father agreed that there was not much point in going on with it. Two and a half years after my mother's death she became my stepmother. It is not the sort of thing that is subject to proof, but I nevertheless believe, on the strength of the dream and of the novel I had blindly embarked on, that I caught something out of the air—a whiff of physical attraction between the young woman and my father. And since it was more than I could deal with I managed not to think about it for the next twenty-seven years.

Austin King's house was clearly our house, to anyone who had ever been in it. In 1912 Hattie was across the street at my Grandmother Blinn's. But during the visit of my Great-Aunt Ina and her family Hattie was working in our kitchen. However, I never had it in mind to write about her. Rachel, the colored woman who worked in the Kings' kitchen, was imaginary. Insofar as she was modeled on anyone, it was the West Indian maid of a family in New York I came to know years later. They lived in a big old-fashioned sunless but cheerful apartment off upper Madison Avenue. The front door was never locked, and I used to open it often when I was a solitary young man. I forget whether Renée came from

Haiti or Guadeloupe. About her private life I knew nothing whatever and I don't think the family she worked for did either.

In a run-down part of Lincoln I once saw a railroad caboose that had come to rest on concrete blocks, in a yard littered with cast-off objects that were picturesque but of no value: a funeral basket, a slab of marble, a broken-down glider, etc. Rachel had to live somewhere, and so why not here? Her five children were not all by the same father but they were all equally beautiful to her. She was easygoing, and perfectly able to be a member of the family one minute and a servant the next, but nobody owned her or ever would. None of this corresponds in any way with the little I know about Hattie Dyer's life and character, but I am afraid that is beside the point. In an earlier, quasi-autobiographical novel, thinking that my father and stepmother would probably not be comfortable reading about themselves, I made the protagonist's father a racetrack tout living far out on the rim of things, and an elderly friend of the family said disapprovingly, "Why did you make your father like that?" So perhaps there is no way to avoid or forestall identifications by a reader bent on making them.

When I was working on the novel about the Kings, it did not occur to me that Hattie would read it or even know it existed. A few women who had known me as a child would put their names on the waiting list at the Lincoln Public Library, one or two at the most might buy it, is what I thought. Men didn't read books. The *Evening Courier* and the Chicago *Tribune* supplied them with all the reading matter they required.

Early on in the writing of the novel the characters took over, and had so much to say to one another that mostly what I did was record their conversation. The difference between this and hallucination is not all that much. One day a new character appeared, and inserted himself retroactively into the novel. He came on a slow freight train from Indianapolis. "Riding in the same boxcar with him, since noon, were an old man and a fifteen-year-old boy, and neither of them ever wanted to see him again. His eyes were bloodshot, his face and hands were gritty, his hair was matted with cinders. His huge, pink-palmed hands hung down out of the sleeves of a corduroy mackinaw that was too small for him and filthy and torn. He had thrown away his only pair of socks two days before. There was a hole in the sole of his right shoe, his belly was empty, and the police were on the lookout for him in St. Louis and Cincinnati."

On the night of the party, while Rachel was still at the Kings', he appeared at her house and frightened all the children, one of whom was his. Rachel was not totally surprised when she walked in on him. She had dreamt about him two nights before. When she realized he was not just after money but meant to settle down with them she took her children and fled. I was frightened of him, too, even as he took life on the page. For a week he stayed blind drunk, and as I described how he lay half undressed on a dirty unmade bed, barely able to lift the bottle to his mouth, I thought *Why not?* and let the fire in the stove go out, and the outside door blew open, and in a little while he died of the cold he had stopped feeling.

I have no reason to think that Hattie's husband, Fred Brummel, was anything but a decent man. My mother's statement that Hattie was having trouble with him possibly amounted to no more than that they were of two minds about moving to Chicago. If Hattie did indeed read my book then what could she think but that I had portrayed her as a loose woman and her husband as a monster of evil? And people in Lincoln, colored people and white, would wonder if I knew things about Fred Brummel that they didn't, and if he was not the person they took him for. I had exposed their married life and blackened his character in order to make a fortune from my writing. I was a thousand miles away, where she couldn't confront me with what I had done. And if she accused me to other people it would only call attention to the book and make more people read it than had already. If all this is true (and my bones tell me that it *is* true) then why, when I walked into my aunt's kitchen, should she be pleased to see me?

I do not feel that it is a light matter.

Any regret for what I may have made Hattie feel is nowhere near enough to have appeased her anger. She was perfectly right not to look at me, not to respond at all, when I put my arms around her. I must have seen Fred Brummel at one time or another or else why does his name conjure up a slight, handsome man whose skin was lighter than Hattie's? If, now, I were to go out to the cemetery in Lincoln and find his grave (which would take some doing) and sit beside it patiently for a good long time, would I learn anything more than that dust does not speak, to anyone, let alone to a stranger? He was once alive. He married Hattie and they had several children. That much is a fact. It does not seem too much to assume that he was happy on the day she told him she would marry him. And again when he held his first child in his arms. And that he was proud of Hattie, as proud as my father was of my mother. Who are now dust also.

The Holy Terror

My older brother and I shared a room when we were children, and he was so good at reading my mind that it left me defenseless against his teasing. When I learned something that the family was holding back from him and hadn't considered it safe to tell me, either, my first thought was *He will see it in my face!* But by that time he and I were living in different parts of the country and seldom saw each other, and from necessity I had acquired, like any other adult, an ability to mask my thoughts and feelings. His life was hard enough as it was, and there was no question but that this piece of information would have made it more so. The older generation are all dead now, and what they didn't want my brother to know would still be locked up inside me if my brother's heart hadn't stopped beating, one day in the summer of 1985.

The firm mouth, the clear ringing voice, the direct gaze. In a family of brown-eyed or blue-eyed people his eyes were hazel.

As a small child — that is to say, when he was five years old — he was strong and healthy and a holy terror. Threats and punishments slid off him like water off a duck's back. My father, with the ideas of his period, believed that children should learn obedience above everything else, but he was new at being a father, and besides, three days a week he wasn't there. My mother was young and pleasure-loving and couldn't say no to an invitation to a card party, and often left my brother with the hired girl, who was no match for him. He was named Edward, after my Grandfather Blinn. My father's sister christened him "Happy Hooligan," after a character in the funny papers, and part of the name stuck. "Look out, Happy, don't do that!" people shrieked, but he had already done it. One afternoon as my mother emerged from the house dressed fit to kill, he turned the garden hose on her. My Aunt Edith, hearing the commotion, opened the screen door and came out to see what was going on, and she too got a soaking. My brother continued to hold the two women at bay until the stream of water abruptly failed: My father had crept around the side of the house to the outdoor faucet. My brother dropped the hose and ran. At that time, my Aunt Annette lived farther down the street and if he got to her he was safe. She was not afraid of anybody and would simply wrap her skirts around him and there he'd be. She was upstairs dressing and heard him calling her, but by the time she got to the front door my father was holding him by the arm, and possession is nine-tenths of the law.

Down through the years, when family stories were being brought out for company, someone was bound to tell the incident of the garden hose, and about how my father's cigars had to be kept under lock and key.

All such outrageous behavior came to an end before Hap had reached his sixth birthday. The year was 1909. My Aunt Annette, driving a horse and buggy, stopped in front of our house. There was something she wanted to tell my mother. As they were talking my brother said, "Take me with you." Annette explained that she couldn't but he seldom took no for an answer, and started climbing up the back wheel of the buggy in order to get in beside her. She finished what she had to say and flicked the horse's rump with her whip. I was a baby at the time and there is no way I could remember my mother's screams, but even so I am haunted by them.

My brother's left leg was amputated well above the knee. At some point in my growing up I was told, probably by my father, that if the surgeon had been able to leave three or four more inches of stump it would have made a considerable difference in my brother's walking.

By the time I was old enough to observe what was going on around me, my brother had an artificial leg — of cork, I believe, painted an unconvincing pink. When I opened my eyes in the morning there it was, leaning against a chair. I had no conscious feelings about it. It was just something my brother had to have so he could walk. Over his stump he wore a sort of sock, of wool, and the weight of the leg was carried by a cloth harness that went around his shoulders. In the evening after supper my father would give him lessons in walking properly: "If you will only lead with your wooden leg instead of dragging it behind you as you walk, it won't be noticeable." This was *almost* true. But when Hap was tired he forgot. It has been more than seventy years since we were boys together in that house, but my shoulder remembers the weight of his hand as we walked home through the dusk. If he saw someone coming toward us, the hand was instantly withdrawn.

IN the earliest picture of my brother that I have ever seen, taken when he was a year old, he is sitting astride Granny Blinn's shoulders. He was her first grandchild and the apple of everybody's eye. As soon as he was old enough to walk he wanted to be with the men, where the air was blue with cigar or pipe smoke and the talk was about horses and hunting dogs, guns and fishing tackle. Between my Grandfather Blinn and my brother there was a deep natural sympathy — the old bear with the cub he liked the smell of. In my mind I see my brother sitting in the front seat of a carriage, studying now the details of the harness on the horse's back and now my grandfather's face for a response to what he is telling my grandfather. And being allowed to hold the reins when they came to a place where the horse was not likely to be startled by any sudden movement from the side of the road. At a very early age he resolved to follow my Grandfather Blinn into the profession of law, and he never deviated from this.

He was nine years old when my grandfather died. My grandmother died that same year, and the house was sold to a family named Irish, from out in the country. They had three boys and a girl, and Mrs. Irish's mother lived with them. I think it is more than likely that before the moving men had finished carrying the Irishes' furniture up the front walk and into the house Hap and Harold Irish had sized each other up and decided it was safe to make the first move. As it turned out, they were friends for life. Harold was a sleepy-eyed boy who noticed things that other people missed. My brother preferred his company to that of any other boy he knew. Harold understood, without having to be told, that my brother could not bear any expression of pity or any offer of help. With intelligence and skill he circumvented his physical handicap. My father and mother never made anything of this, but they cannot have failed to notice that there was very little other boys could do that Hap couldn't do also.

On October afternoons while the maple leaves came floating down from the trees, the boys of the neighborhood played football in a vacant lot on Eleventh Street. The game broke up when they couldn't see the ball anymore. With a smudged face and pieces of dry grass sticking to his clothes, Hap would place himself on the crossbar of Harold's bicycle, which was always waiting for him. He had a bicycle, and could ride it, but to do this with security and élan you need two good legs. Hashing over plays that had miscarried, they rode home to Ninth Street. If other offers of a ride were made, my brother declined them.

In winter when it was still dark I would be wakened by the sound of gravel striking against the window, and Hap would get up from his warm bed and dress and go off with Harold to see if they had caught anything in the traps they had set at intervals along Brainerd's Branch. They had learned from an ad in a boys' magazine that you could get a quarter for a properly stretched and dried muskrat skin, and they meant to become rich. If they waited till daylight they would find their traps sprung and empty. Other boys — coal miners' sons from the north end of town, they believed — also knew about that ad. More often than not it was bitterly cold, and to reach the pasture where the traps were they had to cope with a number of barbed-wire fences half buried in snowdrifts. I am sure, because I used to see it happen on other occasions, that Harold climbed through the barbed wire and walked on, leaving Hap to bend down and hold the wires apart and pull his artificial leg through after him. My mother was forever mending rips in his trousers.

The summer he was fifteen he and I were sent to a Boy Scout camp in Taylorville, Illinois. With the whole camp watching him he climbed up the ladder to the high-diving platform, his cotton bathing suit imperfectly concealing his stump, and hopped out to the end of the board and took off into a jackknife. His life was one long exercise in gallantry. He wanted to make people forget he was crippled — if possible to keep them from even knowing that he was. He wanted to be treated like anyone else but behaved in such a way as to arouse universal admiration. Not leading with his artificial leg but dragging it after him across the clay court, he won the camp tennis singles. It is no wonder so many people loved him.

BEFORE I was old enough to have any recollection of it, my Aunt Edith worked for a time as a nurse in a state asylum for the feeble-minded, out past the edge of town. She met there and eventually married a resident physician named William Young, who soon struck out on his own. As a child I loved to sit on one of his size 12 shoes while he walked back and forth talking to my mother about grown-up matters. A deep attachment existed between our whole family and this big, easygoing, humorous man, whose hands smelled of carbolic acid and who never said "Not now" to anything any child wanted him to do.

It was he who told me the truth about Hap's accident. I was in my late twenties when this happened. One day when we were alone together he spoke in passing of my brother's "affliction" — of what a pity it was. Out of a desire to make the unacceptable appear less so, I mentioned something I had been given to understand — that the leg had been broken in so many places they had no choice but to cut if off. My uncle looked at me a moment and then said, "It was a simple fracture, of a kind that not once in a hundred times would have required an amputation." After which, he went on to tell me what Hap didn't, and mustn't ever, know.

In those days, their fees being small, doctors commonly eked out their income by dispensing medicine themselves instead of writing out prescriptions. The family doctor in Lincoln, with easy access to morphine, had become addicted to it and should have been prevented from practicing. Uncle Doc, not liking the sound of what he was told over the telephone day after day about Hap's condition, got on a train and came to Lincoln. He saw immediately that the broken bone was not set. He also saw the unmistakable signs of gangrene. And taking my father aside, he told him that the leg would have to be cut off to save my brother's life.

"Your Grandfather Blinn called that doctor in and cursed him all the way back to the day he was born," Uncle Doc said to me. "In my whole life I have never witnessed anything like it."

This may have a little relieved my grandfather's feelings but it did not undo what had happened. My Aunt Edith, more sensibly, went to Chicago and came home with the finest set of lead soldiers money could buy. Cavalry officers wearing bearskin busbies and scarlet jackets. On black or white horses. For many years my brother played with them with passionate pleasure. Nothing could really make up for the fact that he was doomed to spend the rest of his life putting on and taking off that artificial limb, and could never again run when he felt like it, as fast as his two legs would carry him.

SINCE I was not a natural athlete like my brother, or an athlete at all, it crossed my mind more than once that having an artificial leg would not have been such a great inconvenience to me, because what I liked to do best was to retire to some out-of-the-way corner of the house and read. I even entertained the fantasy of an exchange with Hap. Along with this idea and rather at odds with it was a superstitious fear that came over me from time to time when I remembered that my mother's only brother lost an arm in an automobile accident when he was in his early twenties. Was there a kind of family destiny that would one day overtake me as well?

There was a period in my life when I lay down on a psychoanalyst's couch four times a week and relived the past. Eventually we arrived at my brother's lead soldiers. I begged to be allowed to play with them and my brother invariably said no. He kept them out of my reach, on top of a high bookcase. One day when Hap was out of the house I put a stool on the seat of a straight chair and climbed up on it. I had just got my hands on the box when I heard the front door burst open and my brother called out, "Anybody home?" In my guilty fright I tried to put the box back, lost my balance, and fell. If my mother had not appeared from the back part of the house at that moment, I don't know what my brother would have done to me. Not one horseman survived intact. I see Hap now, sitting on the floor in the living room, gluing a head back on one of them. The horse already had a matchstick for one of its hind legs, so it would stand up. He never forgave me for what I had done. I didn't expect him to.

The Germanic voice coming from a few feet beyond the crown of my head suggested that my brother's accident had been a great misfortune not only for him but for me also; because I saw what happens to little boys who are incorrigible, I became a more tractable, more even-tempered, milder person than it was my true nature to be. About these thoughts that one is told on good authority one thinks without their ever crossing the threshold of consciousness, what is there to say except "Possibly"? In support of the psychoanalytic conjecture, a submerged memory rose to the surface of my mind. At that Scout camp where Hap won the singles tennis championship I was awarded a baseball glove for Good Conduct.

WHO has that picture of Hap sitting on Granny Blinn's shoulders, I wonder. Or the one of him driving a pony cart. It was a postcard — which means that it was taken by a professional photographer. On the reverse someone had written "Edward, aged seven, at the Asylum." It was an odd choice. Uncle Doc was practicing in Bloomington by that time. Did the family, even so, regard the asylum grounds as home territory? The road to the Lincoln Chautauqua ran alongside them, and driving by with my father and mother I used to stare at the inmates standing with their hands and faces pressed against the high wire netting, their mouths permanently slack and sometimes drooling. Perhaps the photographer wanted the institutional flower beds as a background. In the photograph my brother is wearing a small round cap. The pony and cart were not borrowed for the occasion but his own. He is holding the reins, and the pony is, of course, standing still. My brother's chin is raised and he is facing the camera, and the expression on his face is of a heartbreaking uncertainty.

Most children appear to be born with a feeling that life is fair, that it must be. And only with difficulty accommodate themselves to the fact that it isn't. That look on my brother's face — was it because of his sense of the disproportion between the offenses he had committed and the terrible punishment for them? Was he perhaps bracing himself for a second blow, worse than the first one? Or was it because of what happened to him when he left our front yard to play with other children? A little boy who couldn't run away from his tormentors or use his fists to defend himself because they were needed for his crutches, and who could easily be tripped and toppled, was irresistible. Since Hap refused, even so, to give up playing with them, my father paid a colored boy named Dewey Cecil to be his bodyguard.

I ASSUMED, irrationally, that Hap would die before I did; he was older and when we were growing up together he always did everything first, while I came along after him and tried to imitate him when it was at all possible. During the past few years I have often thought, When he is gone there will be no one who remembers the things I remember. Meaning the conversations that took place in the morning when he and I were dressing for school. The time we had chicken pox together. The way the light from the low-hanging red-and-green glass shade fell on all our faces as we sat around the dining-room table. The grape arbor by the kitchen door. The closet under the stairs. The hole in the living-room carpet made by the rifle he said wasn't loaded. The time I tried to murder him with a golf club.

We were waiting for my father to finish his foursome, and for lack of anything better to do Hap threw my cap up in a tree, higher than I could reach. I picked up a midiron and started after him. With a double hop, a quick swing with his bum leg, and another double hop he could cover the ground quite fast, but not as fast as I could. I meant to lay him out flat, as he so richly deserved. Walter Kennett, the golf coach, grabbed me and held me until I cooled down.

My brother didn't mind that I had tried to kill him. He always liked it when I showed signs of life.

What He Was Like

HE kept a diary, for his own pleasure. Because the days passed by so rapidly, and he found it interesting to go back and see how he had occupied his time, and with whom. He was aware that his remarks were sometimes far from kind, but the person they were about was never going to read them, so what difference did it make? The current diary was usually on his desk, the previous ones on a shelf in his clothes closet, where they were beginning to take up room.

His wife's uncle, in the bar of the Yale Club, said, "I am at the age of funerals." Now, thirty-five years later, it was his turn. In his address book the names of his three oldest friends had lines drawn through them. "Jack is dead," he wrote in his diary. "I didn't think that would happen. I thought he was immortal. . . . Louise is dead. In her sleep. . . . Richard has been dead for over a year and I still do not believe it. So impoverishing."

He himself got older. His wife got older. They advanced deeper into their seventies without any sense of large changes but only of one day's following another, and of the days being full, and pleasant, and worth recording. So he went on doing it. They all got put down in his diary, along with his feelings about old age, his fear of dying, his declining sexual powers, his envy of the children that he saw running down the street. To be able to run like that! He had to restrain himself from saying to young men in their thirties and forties, "You do appreciate, don't you, what you have?" In his diary he wrote, "If I had my life to live over again — but one doesn't. One goes forward instead, dragging a cart piled high with lost opportunities."

Though his wife had never felt the slightest desire to read his diary, she knew when he stopped leaving it around as carelessly as he did his opened mail. Moving the papers on his desk in order to dust it she saw where he had hidden the current volume, was tempted to open it and see what it was he didn't want her to know, and then thought better of it and replaced the papers, exactly as they were before.

"To be able to do in your mind," he wrote, "what it is probably not a good idea to do in actuality is a convenience not always sufficiently appreciated." Though in his daily life he was as cheerful as a cricket, the diaries were more and more given over to dark thoughts, anger, resentment, indecencies, regrets, remorse. And now and then the simple joy in being alive. "If I stopped recognizing that I want things that it is not appropriate for me to want," he wrote, "wouldn't this inevitably lead to my not wanting anything at all — which as people get older is a risk that must be avoided at all costs?" He wrote, "Human beings are not like a clock that is wound up at birth and runs until the mainspring is fully unwound. They live because they want to. And when they stop wanting to, the first thing they know they are in a doctor's office being shown an X ray that puts a different face on everything."

AFTER he died, when the funeral had been got through, and after the number of telephone calls had diminished to a point where it was possible to attend to other things, his wife and and daughter together disposed of the clothes in his closet. His daughter folded and put in a suit box an old, worn corduroy coat that she remembered the feel of when her father had rocked her as a child. His wife kept a blue-green sweater that she was used to seeing him in. As for the rest, he was a common size, and so his shirts and suits were easily disposed of to people who were in straitened circumstances and grateful for a warm overcoat, a dark suit, a pair of pigskin gloves. His shoes were something else again, and his wife dropped them into the Goodwill box, hoping that somebody would turn up who wore size-9A shoes, though it didn't seem very likely. Then the two women were faced with the locked filing cabinet in his study, which contained business papers that they turned over to the executor, and most of the twenty-seven volumes of his diary.

"Those I don't know what to do with, exactly," his wife said. "They're private and he didn't mean anybody to read them."

"Did he say so?" his daughter said.

"No."

"Then how do you know he didn't want anybody to read them?"

"I just know."

"You're not curious?"

"I was married to your father for forty-six years and I know what he was like."

Which could only mean, the younger woman decided, that her mother had, at some time or other, looked into them. But she loved her father, and felt a very real desire to know what he was like as a person and not just as a father. So she put one of the diaries aside and took it home with her.

When her husband got home from his office that night, her eyes were red from weeping. First he made her tell him what the trouble was, and then he went out to the kitchen and made a drink for each of them, and then he sat down beside her on the sofa. Holding his free hand, she began to tell him about the shock of reading the diary.

"He wasn't the person I thought he was. He had all sorts of secret desires. A lot of it is very dirty. And some of it is more unkind than I would have believed possible. And just not like him — except that it *was* him. It makes me feel I can never trust anybody ever again."

"Not even me?" her husband said soberly.

"Least of all, you."

They sat in silence for a while. And then he said, "I was more comfortable with him than I was with my own father. And I think, though I could be mistaken, that he liked me."

"Of course he liked you. He often said so."

"So far as his life is concerned, if you were looking for a model to — "

"I don't see how you can say that."

"I do, actually. In his place, though, I think I would have left instructions that the diaries were to be disposed of unread. . . . We could burn it. Burn all twenty-seven volumes."

"No."

"Then put it back in the locked file where your mother found it," he said.

"And leave it there forever?"

"For a good long while. He may have been looking past our shoulders. It would be like him. If we have a son who doesn't seem to be very much like you or me, or like anybody in your family or mine, we can give him the key to the file — "

"If I had a son the *last* thing in the world I'd want would be for him to read this filth!"

" — and tell him he can read them if he wants to. And if he doesn't want to, he can decide what should be done with them. It might be a help to him to know that there was somebody two generations back who wasn't in every respect what he seemed to be."

"Who was, in fact — "

"Since he didn't know your father, he won't be shocked and upset. You stay right where you are while I make us another of these."

But she didn't. She didn't want to be separated from him, even for the length of time it would take him to go out to the kitchen and come back with a margarita suspended from the fingers of each hand, lest in that brief interval he turn into a stranger.

A SET OF TWENTY-ONE
IMPROVISATIONS

1. A love story

"MADAME MOLE," everyone said, out of respect. For what she was and how she did things. The thick fur and the usually cold eye that saw immediately the disadvantages of a poorly located and badly laid out tunnel. Her own tunnel had never been equaled and indeed the full extent of it, taking both the upper and the lower level into consideration, was only guessed at, for visitors had seen only the first hundred anterooms. She was descended on her mother's side from the Moles of Longview, whose enormous spreading family tree had for its trunk a mole brought over in a cage by one of William the Conqueror's body servants. It escaped during the Battle of Hastings, into a land that had hitherto been happily free of them, and before that fatal moment when Harold glanced up at the sun and received an arrow in his eye, the mole had already established a temporary home under the battlefield. The family was ennobled under William Rufus, for the harassment they had caused the Saxons, and Charles II made the ninetieth baronet an earl in gratitude for the number of Cromwell's horses that had stepped in a tunnel and — but it is better not to go into all that, especially if you like horses. In a time of war, disasters are to be expected, unless you are a mole and can go below into the silence of old roots, and sleeping grubs, and ant chambers, flints, and fossils.

Madame Mole's husband was never called anything but Mole, for she had married beneath her. His family didn't bear thinking of, but he was a large good-natured willing creature, and, though not very many of her acquaintances realized this, she would have been nowhere without him. For she designed the new shafts of her great masterwork and he went to work with the hard end of his socially undistinguished nose and by nightfall there the new shaft was, ready for her to explore, and having reached the end of it, they would settle down cozily together and she would chew his ears by way of showing her love and appreciation. Then she would go about arranging the furniture and putting out pieces of bone china where they would show to advantage. What is the natural life of a mole? I don't actually know, but a good long time, I should think. Mole traps rust immediately and are notoriously inefficient, and what exasperated gardener is willing to stand waiting at twenty minutes after 10 a.m. and twenty minutes after 4 p.m. for the barely perceptible heaving at the end of a run, and start furiously digging with a spade when it begins. Not one mole in a hundred thousand meets with an accident of any kind, and when it does happen you can be sure it was because they had grown careless. What happened to Madame Mole and her husband was something so much larger than a mere accident that they were at a loss to describe it. They were lying in bed one morning and she was comfortably chewing on his ear, when he saw that the bedroom chandelier was swinging. "Stop jiggling the bed," she said, and he said, "I'm not. *It's* doing it." At which point all the fine china plates fell off the wall and broke into smithereens and dirt began raining down on the bedsheets. While he was taking in what was happening, she leapt out of bed and rushed to each of the seven doors in turn. What should have been a shaft, and *was* a shaft when they went to sleep the night before, was blocked with stones, timbers, and rubbish. In places she could see the sky, and it would not have been too difficult to tunnel up into the open, at this stage, but think what would meet them if they did! She took hold of his ear with her teeth and dragged him out of the bed and under it, and while she lay huddled next to him in fright, he put his hard nose to the ground and started tunneling. Straight down, hour after hour, without any plan to guide him or any consideration for how it would look when the furniture was arranged and the china plates hung where they would show to best advantage: The Longview Willow and Spode that had come down to her from the Shaftsburys, and the hand-painted Limoges chocolate set that was a wedding present from Cousin Emma Noseby and I forget what all, but *she* never forgot. An earthquake was what they assumed it must be, and it did bear certain resemblances to an earthquake, for after a period of very difficult going suddenly they would find themselves in a fissure leading straight down toward the center of the earth, and then it was possible to make very good progress with no effort whatsoever. Machines is what it was. Huge yellow machines rented out by an Italian contractor at two, three, and four hundred dollars a day. Weighing many tons. Big enough to lift great trees and fling them aside, with their roots exposed to the shocked gaze of the sky. The arrangements of thousands and thousands of years — roots, stones, fossilized ferns, and fossilized fish from the earliest years of the planet were crushed, scraped up in huge mechanical shovels, poured into trucks, and hauled away to desecrate some other part of the landscape. And if Madame Mole and Mole had emerged from their ruined mansion to see what was happening, they would have been scooped up with the Longview Willow, and the sweet-smelling leaf mold of centuries, the dear green grass, and the murdered trees. There had been nothing to equal it in the way of pure destruction since the Battle of Hastings. If it had been for a housing development Madame Mole would have perhaps accepted it with some degree of philosophic resignation. She could understand homemaking even when it was aboveground and so not very practical. But this was to make an eight-lane highway for cars, a means for more people to get away from their homes faster, because of all the things that had made home unbearable — the polluted air, the noise of jet airplanes and so on. It is just as well they never knew the nature of the disaster that sent them down, down, down to the center of the earth. When they reached it they had no idea. It was dark there, of course, and he had left his wristwatch on the table beside their bed, and so they simply kept on going. When he grew tired or discouraged she chewed on his ear until he felt better. And when she wept thinking of all of her treasures left behind, he curled his fur tightly around her fur and in the shared warmth they fell asleep. And when they woke he commenced digging. Eventually the soil began to be looser, and the grubs more frequent, and finally there were root hairs and then big roots and suddenly without any warning they emerged into broad daylight. They were in a terraced field, on a mountainside, in a country that Madame Mole recognized instantly because there was the blue leaning willow tree, and there was the lake, and the bluebird in the sky, and the blue curlicue clouds, and the houses with eaves that curled up at the corners. It was a view she had seen ever since she could remember, because it was on every single piece of the Longview Willow china. "Oh you clever Mole, how glad I am I married you!" she cried, and they withdrew into the tunnel so that, chewing on his ear, she could plan the layout of their new home.

2. The industrious tailor

ONCE upon a time, in the west of England, there was an industrious tailor who was always sitting cross-legged, plying his needle, when the sun came up over the hill, and all day long he drove himself, as if he were beating a donkey with a stick. "I am almost through cutting out this velvet waistcoat," he would tell himself, "and when I am through cutting the velvet, I will cut the yellow satin lining. And then there is the buck-ram, and the collar and cuffs. The cuffs are to be thirteen inches wide, tapering to ten and a half — his lordship was very particular about that detail — and faced with satin. The basting should take me into the after-noon, and if all goes well, and I don't see why it shouldn't, I ought to be able to do all twenty-seven buttonholes before the light gives out."

When snow lay deep on the ground and the sheep stayed in their pens, the shepherd came down to the tavern and in the conviviality he found there made up for the months of solitude on the moors. During the early part of the summer, when it was not yet time for anybody to be bringing wheat, barley, and rye to the mill to be ground into flour, the miller got out his hook and line and went fishing. In one way or another, everyone had some time that he called his own. On the first of May, lads and lasses went into the wood just before daybreak and came back wearing garlands of flowers and with their arms around each other. From his window the tailor saw them setting up the Maypole, but he did not lay aside his needle and thread to go join in the dancing. It is true that he was no longer young and, with his bald head and his bent back and his solemn manner, would have looked odd dancing around a Maypole, but that did not deter the miller's wife, who weighed seventeen stone and was as light on her feet as a fairy and didn't care who laughed at her as long as she was enjoying herself.

When the industrious tailor came to the end of all the work that he could expect for a while and his worktable was quite bare, he looked around for some lily that needed gilding. Sorting his pins, sharpening his scissors, and rearranging his patterns, he congratulated himself on keeping busy, though he might just as well have been sitting in his doorway enjoying the sun, for his scissors didn't need sharpening, and his patterns were not in disorder, and a pin is a pin, no matter what tray you put it in.

As with all of us, the tailor's upbringing had a good deal to do with the way he behaved. At the age of eight, he was apprenticed to his father, who was a master tailor and not only knew all there is to know about making clothes but also was full of native wisdom. While the boy was learning to sew a straight seam and how to cut cloth on the diagonal and that sort of thing, the father would from time to time raise his right hand, with the needle and thread in it, and, looking at the boy over the top of his spectacles, say "A stitch in time saves nine," or "Waste makes want," or some other bit of advice, which the boy took to his bosom and cherished. And he had never forgotten a wonderful story his father told about an ant and a grasshopper. Of all his father's sayings, the one that made the deepest impression on him was "Never put off till tomorrow what you can do today," though as a rule the industrious tailor had already done it yesterday and was hard at work on something that did not need to be done until the day after.

WHAT is true of the day after tomorrow is equally true of the day after that, and the day after that, and the day after that, and so on, and in time a very curious thing happened. There was the past — there is always the past — and it was full of accomplishment, of things done well before they needed to be done, and the tailor regarded it with satisfaction. And there was the future, when things would have to be done, and bills would have to be made out and respectfully submitted and paid or not paid, as the case might be, and new work would be ordered, and so on. But it was never right now. The present had ceased to exist. When the industrious tailor looked out of the window and saw that it was raining, it was not raining today but on a day in the middle of next week, or the week after that, if he was that far ahead of himself, and he often was. You would have thought that he would sooner or later have realized that the time he was spending so freely was next month's, and that if he had already lived through the days of this month before it was well begun he was living beyond his means. But what is "already"? What is "now"? The words had lost their meaning. And this was not as serious as it sounds, because words are, after all, only words. "I could kill you for doing that," a man says to his wife and then they both cheerfully sit down to dinner. And many people live entirely in the past, without even noticing it. One day the tailor pushed his glasses up on his forehead and saw that he was in the middle of a lonely wood. He rubbed his poor tired eyes, but the trees didn't go away. He looked all around. No scissors and pins, no bolts of material, no patterns, no worktable, no shop. Only the needle and thread he had been sewing with. He listened anxiously. He had never been in a wood before. "Wife?" he called out, but there was no answer.

He knew that it was late afternoon, and that he ought to get out of the wood before dark, so he stuck the needle in his vest and started walking along a path that constantly threatened to disappear, the way paths do in the wood. Sometimes the path divided, and he had to choose between the right and the left fork, without knowing which was the way that led out of the wood. The light began to fail even sooner than he had expected. When it was still daytime in the sky overhead, it was already so dark where he was that he could find the path only by the feel of the ground under his feet.

"I don't see why this should happen to me," he said, and from the depths of the wood a voice said "To *who?*" disconcertingly, but it was only an owl. So he kept on until he saw a light through the trees, and he made his way to it, through the underbrush and around fallen logs, until he came to a house in a clearing. At this time of night they'll be easily frightened, he thought. I must speak carefully or they'll close the door in my face. When the door opened in answer to his knock and a woman stood looking out at him from the lighted doorway, he said politely, "It's all right, ma'am, I'm not a robber."

"No," the woman said, "you're an industrious tailor."

"Now, how did you know that?" he asked in amazement.

The woman did not seem to feel that this question needed answering, and there was something about her that made him uneasy, and so, though he would much rather that she invited him in and gave him a place by the fire and a bit of supper, he said, "If you would be kind enough to show me the way out of the wood — "

"I don't know that I can," the woman said.

"Isn't there a road of some kind?"

"There's a road," the woman said doubtfully, "but it wasn't built in your lifetime."

"I beg pardon?"

"And anyway, you'd soon lose it in the dark. You'll have to wait until morning. How did you happen to — "

At that point a baby began to cry, and the woman said, "I can't stand here talking. Come in."

"Thank you," he said. "That's very kind of you, ma'am," and as he stepped across the threshold there was suddenly no house, no lighted room, no woman. Nothing but a clearing in the wood.

In disappointment so acute that it brought tears to his eyes, he sat down on the ground and tucked his legs under him and tried to get used to the idea that he wasn't going to sit by a warm fire, under a snug roof, with a bit of supper by and by, and a place to lay his head at bedtime.

I will catch my death of pneumonia, he thought. He put his hand to his vest; the needle was still there. He felt his forehead, and then took his glasses off, folded them carefully, and put them in his vest pocket. Then he stretched out on the bare ground and, looking up through the trees, thought about his tailor shop, and about a greatcoat that he was working on. It was of French blue, part true cashmere and part Lincoln wool, with a three-tiered cape, and it wasn't promised until a fortnight, but he would have finished it and have given it to his wife to press if he hadn't suddenly found himself in this lonely wood. Then he thought about his wife, who would be wondering why he didn't come upstairs for his supper. And then about his father, who had a stroke and never recovered the use of his limbs or his speech. In the evening, after the day was over, the industrious tailor used to come and sit by his father's bed, and he would bring whatever he was working on — a waistcoat or a pair of knee breeches, or an embroidered vest — and spread it out on the counterpane, to show his father that the lessons had been well learned and that he needn't worry about the quality of work being turned out by the shop. And instead of being pleased with him, his father would push the work aside impatiently. There seemed to be something on his mind that he very much wanted to say, some final piece of wisdom, but when he tried to speak he could only utter meaningless sounds.

Now, through the tops of the bare trees, the tailor could see the stars, so bright and so far away . . . But how did it get to be autumn, he wondered. And why am I not cold? Why am I not hungry? He fell asleep and dreamed that he had more work to do than he could possibly manage, and woke up with the sun shining in his face.

"Wife?" he called out, before he remembered where he was or what had happened to him.

He sat up and looked around. There was no house in the clearing, and no sign that there ever had been, but there was a path leading off through the woods, and he followed it. At this time, more than half of England was forests, and so he knew that it might be days before he found his way out of the wood. "I must be careful not to walk in a circle," he told himself. "That's what people always do when they are lost." But one fallen tree, one sapling, one patch of dried fern, one bed of moss looked just like another, and he could not tell whether he was walking in a circle or not. Now and then, not far from the path, there would be a sudden dry rustle that made his heart race. Was it a poisonous viper? What was it? The rustle did not explain itself. Oddly enough, he himself, stepping on dry leaves and twigs, did not make a sound.

"I ought to be living on roots and berries," he said to himself, and though there were plenty of both, he did not know which were edible and which were not, and he did not feel inclined to experiment. But when he came to a spring, he thought, I will drink, because this far from any house or pasture it cannot be contaminated. . . . He knelt down and put his face to the water and nothing happened. His throat was as dry as before. The water remained just out of reach. He leaned farther forward and again nothing happened. The water kept receding until his face touched dry gravel. He raised his head in surprise and there was the beautiful spring, glittering, jewel-like in the sunlight, pushing its way under logs and between boulders, murmuring as it went, but not to be drunk from. "Can it be that I am dead?" the tailor asked himself. And then, "If I am dead, why has nobody told me where to go, or what's expected of me?"

As he walked on, he tried to remember if in the old days, before he suddenly found himself in this wood, he had ever got down on his hands and knees to drink from a spring. All he remembered was that when the other boys were roaming the woods and bathing in the river, he was in his father's shop learning to be a master tailor.

"It is possible that I am dreaming," he said to himself. But it did not seem like a dream. In dreams it is always — not twilight exactly, but the light is peculiar, comes from nowhere, and is never very bright. This was a blindingly beautiful sunny day.

"At all events," he said to himself, "I am a much better walker than I had any idea. I have been walking for hours and I don't feel in the least tired. And even if it should turn out that I have been walking in a circle — "

At that moment he saw, ahead of him, what seemed like a thinning out of trees, as if he was coming to the edge of the wood. It proved to be a small clearing with a house in it. Smoke was rising from the chimney, and as the tailor came nearer an unpleasant suspicion crossed his mind.

"Oh, it's you," the woman said, when she opened the door and saw him standing there. She had a baby in her arms, and she didn't look particularly pleased to see him, or concerned that he had passed the whole night on the bare ground and the whole day walking in a circle.

"I'm sorry to trouble you, ma'am," he said, "but if you will be so kind as to show me that road you were speaking of —"

The baby began to fret, and the woman jounced it lightly on her shoulder. "As you can see, I'm busy," she said. "And I don't see how you got here in the first place."

"Neither do I," he said.

"Did you come on a spring anywhere in the wood?"

He nodded.

"And did you drink from it?"

"I couldn't," he said. "When I put my face to the water, there wasn't any."

"I'm afraid there's nothing I can do," the woman said, and he saw that she was about to close the door in his face.

"Please, ma'am," he said, "if you'll just show me where that road begins I won't trouble you any further, I promise you."

"Why you had to come today of all days, when the baby's cutting a tooth, and the fire in the stove has gone out, and I still have to do the churning. . . . You haven't murdered somebody? No, I can see you haven't. If the police are after you —"

"The police are not after me," the tailor said with dignity, "and I haven't committed any crime that I know of."

"Well, that doesn't mean anything," the woman said. "Come, let me show you the road."

He followed her across the clearing, and when she stopped they were standing in front of a clump of white birch trees. Beyond it the tangled underbrush began, and the big trees.

"I don't see any road," the tailor said.

"That's what I mean," the woman said. She stood looking at him and frowning thoughtfully.

"Even if there was only a path —" the tailor began, and the woman said, "Oh, be quiet. If I let you go off into the woods again, you'll only end up here the way you did before. And I can't ask you into the house, because — Have you ever held a baby?"

"Oh, yes," the tailor said. "My children are grown now, but when they were little I often held them while my wife was busy doing something."

As he was speaking, the woman put the baby in his arms. The baby turned its head on its weak neck and looked at him. Though the woman made him uneasy, the baby did not. The baby's face contorted, and he saw that it was about to cry. "Hush-a," he said, and jounced it gently against his shoulder, and felt the head wobble against his neck, and the down on the baby's head, softer than any material in his shop.

"This may not work," the woman said, and started back across the clearing, and he followed her, still holding the baby.

At the door of the house she took a firm grip on the hem of the baby's garment and then she said, "Go in, go in," and after a last look over his shoulder at the clearing in the wood he stepped across the threshold, expecting to find himself outside again, and instead he was in his own shop, sitting cross-legged on his worktable.

HE listened and heard the twittering of birds as they flitted from branch to branch in the elm tree outside, and then the miller's wife, laughing at some joke she had just made. He saw by the quality of the light outside that it was only the middle of the afternoon. A wagon came by, and the miller's wife called to whoever was in the wagon, and a man's voice said, "Whoa, there . . . Whoa . . . Whoa." The tailor listened with rapt attention to the conversation that followed, though he had heard it a hundred times. Or conversations just like it. All around him on the work-table were scraps of French-blue material, and he could see at a glance what was waiting to be stitched to what. Finally the man said, "That's rich! That's a good one. Gee-up . . ." and the wheels turned again, and the slow plodding was resumed and grew fainter and was replaced by the sound of a child beating on a tin pan. The miller's wife went home, but there were other sounds — a dog, a door slamming, a child being scolded. Then it was quiet for a time, and without thinking the tailor put his hand to his vest and found the needle. Two boys went by, saying, "I dare you to do it, I dare you, I double-dare you!" Do what, the tailor wondered, and went on sewing.

The quiet and the outbreaks of sound alternated in a way that was so regular that it almost seemed planned. A loud noise, such as a crow going caw, caw, caw, seemed to produce a deeper silence afterward. He studied the beautiful sound of footsteps approaching and receding, so like a piece of music.

The light began to fail and he hardly noticed it, because as the light went it was accompanied by all the sounds that mean the end of the day: men coming home from the fields, shops being closed, children being called in before dark.

When the tailor could not see any longer, he put his work aside and sat, listening and smiling to himself at what he heard, until his wife called him to supper.

3. The country where nobody ever grew old and died

THERE used to be, until roughly a hundred and fifty years ago, a country where nobody ever grew old and died. The gravestone with its weathered inscription, the wreath on the door, the black arm band, and the friendly reassuring smile of the undertaker were unknown there. This is not as strange as it at first seems. You do not have to look very far to find a woman who does not show her age or a man who intends to live forever. In this country, people did live forever, and nobody thought anything about it, but at some time or other somebody had thought about it, because there were certain restrictions on the freedom of the inhabitants. The country was not large, and there would soon not have been enough land to go around. So, instead of choosing an agreeable site and building a house on it, married couples chose an agreeable house and bought the right to add a story onto it. In this way, gradually, the houses, which were of stone, and square, and without superfluous ornamentation, became towers. The prevailing style of architecture was very much like that of the Italian hill towns. Arriving at the place where you lived, you rang the concierge's bell and sat down in a wicker swing, with your parcels on your lap, and were lifted to your own floor by ropes and pulleys.

A country where there were no children would be sadness incarnate. People didn't stop having them, but they were placed in such a way that the smallest number of children could be enjoyed by the greatest number of adults. If you wanted to raise a family, you applied for a permit and waited your turn. Very often by the time the permit came, the woman was too old to have a child and received instead a permit to help bring up somebody else's child.

Young women who were a pleasure to look at were enjoyed the way flowers are enjoyed, but leaving one's youth behind was not considered to be a catastrophe, and the attitudes and opinions of the young were not anxiously subscribed to. There is, in fact, some question whether the young of that country really were young, as we understand the word. Most people appeared to be on the borderline between maturity and early middle age, as in England in the late eighteenth century, when the bald pate and the head of thick brown hair were both concealed by a powdered wig, and physical deterioration was minimized by the fashions in dress and by what constituted good manners.

All the arts flourished except history. If you wanted to know what things were like in the period of Erasmus or Joan of Arc or Ethelred the Unready, you asked somebody who was alive at the time. People tended to wear the clothes of the period in which they came of age, and so walking down the street was like thumbing through a book on the history of costume. The soldiers, in every conceivable kind of armor and uniform, were a little boy's dream.

As one would expect, that indefatigable traveler Lady Mary Wortley Montagu spent a considerable time in this interesting country before she settled down in Venice, and so did William Beckford. Lady Mary's letters about it were destroyed by her daughter after her death, because they happened to contain assertions of a shocking nature, for which proof was lacking, about a contemporary figure who would have relished a prosecution for libel. For Beckford's experiences, see his *Dreams, Waking Thoughts, and Incidents* (Leipzig, 1832).

One might have supposed that in a country where death was out of the question, morbidity would be unknown. This was true for I have no idea how many centuries and then something very strange happened. The young, until this moment entirely docile and unimaginative, began having scandalous parties at which they pretended that they were holding a funeral. They even went so far as to put together a makeshift pine coffin, and took turns lying in it, with their eyes closed and their hands crossed, and a lighted candle at the head and foot. This occurred during Beckford's stay, and it is just possible that he had something to do with it. Though he could be very amusing, he was a natural mischief-maker and an extremely morbid man.

The mock funerals were the first thing that happened. The second was the trial, *in absentia*, of a gypsy woman who was accused of taking money with intent to defraud. This was not an instance of a poor foolish widow's being persuaded to bring her husband's savings to a fortune-teller in order to have the money doubled. In the first place, there were no widows, and the victim was a young man.

The plaintiff — just turned twenty-one, Beckford says, and exceedingly handsome — stated under oath that he had consulted the gypsy woman in the hope of learning from her the secret of how to commit suicide. For it seems that in this country as everywhere else gypsies were a race apart and a law unto themselves. They did not choose to live forever, so they didn't. When one of them decided that life had no further interest for him, he did something. What, nobody knew. It was assumed that the gypsy bent on terminating his existence sat down under a tree or by a riverbank, some nice quiet place where he wouldn't be disturbed, and in a little while the other gypsies came and disposed of the body.

The plaintiff testified that the gypsy woman studied his hand, and then she looked in her crystal ball, and then she excused herself in order to get something on the other side of a curtain. That was the last anybody had seen of her or of the satchel full of money which the plaintiff had brought with him.

The idea that a personable young man, on the very threshold of life, had actually wanted to die caused a tremendous stir. The public was barred from the trial, but Beckford was on excellent terms with the wife of the Lord Chief Justice and managed to attend the hearing in the guise of a court stenographer. The story is to be found in the Leipzig edition of his book and no other, which suggests that he perhaps did have something to do with the events he describes, and that from feelings of remorse, or shame, wrote about them and then afterward wished to suppress what he had written. At all events we have his very interesting account. The jury found for the plaintiff and against the gypsy woman. After the verdict was read aloud in the court, the attorney for the defense made an impassioned and — in the light of what happened afterward — heartbreaking speech. If only it had been taken seriously! He asked that the verdict stand, but that no effort be made to find his client, and that no other gypsy be questioned or molested in any way by the police. The court saw the matter in a different light, and during the next few days the police set about rounding up every single gypsy in the country. The particular gypsy woman who had victimized the young man with a bent for self-destruction was never found. The others were subjected to the most detailed questioning. When that produced no information, the rack and the thumbscrew were applied, to no purpose. You might as well try to squeeze kindness out of a stone as torture a secret out of a gypsy. But there was living with the gypsies at that time a middle-aged man who had been stolen by them as a child and who had spent his life among them. When he was brought into the courtroom between two bailiffs, the attorney for the defense lowered his head and covered his eyes with his hand. The man was put on the witness stand and, pale and drawn after a night of torture, gave his testimony. Shortly after this, the gravestone, the wreath, the arm band, and the smiling undertaker, so familiar everywhere else in the world, made their appearance here also, and the country was no longer unique.

4. The fisherman who had nobody to go out in his boat with him

ONCE upon a time there was a poor fisherman who had no one to go out in his boat with him. The man he started going out with when he was still a boy was now crippled with rheumatism and sat all day by the fire. The other fishermen were all paired off, and there was nobody for him. Out on the water, without a soul to talk to, the hours between daybreak and late afternoon were very long, and to pass the time he sang. He sang the songs that other people sang, whatever he had heard, and this was of course a good deal in the way of music, because in the olden times people sang more than they do now. But eventually he came to the end of all the songs he knew or had ever heard and wanted to learn some new songs. He knew that they were written down and published, but this was no help to him because he had never been to school and didn't know how to read words, let alone the musical staff. You might as well have presented him with a clay tablet of Egyptian hieroglyphics. But there were ways, and he took advantage of them. At a certain time, on certain days of the week, the children in the schoolhouse had singing, and he managed to be in the vicinity. He brought his boat in earlier those days, on one pretext or another, and stood outside the school building. At first the teacher was mystified, but he saw that the poor fisherman always went away as soon as the singing lesson was over, and putting two and two together he realized why the man was there. So, one day, he went to the door and invited the fisherman in. The fisherman backed away, and then he turned and hurried off down the road to the beach. But the next time they had singing, there he was. The schoolteacher opened a window so the fisherman could hear better and went on with the lesson. While the children were singing "There were three sisters fair and bright," the door opened slowly. The teacher pointed to a desk in the back row, and the fisherman squeezed himself into it, though it was a child's desk and much too small for him. The children waved their hands in the air and asked silly questions and giggled, but, never having been to school, the fisherman thought this was customary and did not realize that he was creating a disturbance. He came again and again.

People manage to believe in magic—of one kind or another. And ghosts. And the influence of the stars. And reincarnation. And a life everlasting. But not enough room is allowed for strangeness: that birds and animals know the way home; that a blind man, having sensed the presence of a wall, knows as well where to walk as you or I; that there have been many recorded instances of conversations between two persons who did not speak the same language but, each speaking his own, nevertheless understood each other perfectly. When the teacher passed out the songbooks, he gave one to the fisherman, well aware that his only contact with the printed page was through his huge, calloused hands. And time after time the fisherman knew, before the children opened their mouths and began to sing, what the first phrase would be, and where the song would go from there.

Naturally, he did not catch as many fish as he had when he was attending to his proper work, and sometimes there was nothing in the house to eat. His wife could not complain, because she was a deaf-mute. She was not ugly, but no one else would have her. Though she had never heard the sound of her own voice, or indeed any sound whatever, she could have made him feel her dissatisfaction, but she saw that what he was doing was important to him, and did not interfere. What the fisherman would have liked would have been to sing with the children when they sang, but his voice was so deep there was no possibility of its blending unnoticeably with theirs, so he sat in silence, and only when he was out in his boat did the songs burst forth from his throat. What with the wind and the seabirds' crying, he had to sing openly or he would not have known he was singing at all. If he had been on shore, in a quiet room, the sound would have seemed tremendous. Out under the sky, it merely seemed like a man singing.

He often thought that if there had only been a child in the house he could have sung the child to sleep, and that would have been pleasant. He would have sung to his wife if she could have heard him, and he did try, on his fingers, to convey the sound of music—the way the sounds fell together, the rising and descending, the sudden changes in tempo, and the pleasure of expecting to hear this note and hearing, instead, a different one, but she only smiled at him uncomprehendingly.

The schoolteacher knew that if it had been curiosity alone that drew the fisherman to the schoolhouse at the time of singing lessons, he would have stopped coming as soon as his curiosity was satisfied, and he didn't stop coming, which must mean that there was a possibility that he was innately musical. So he stopped the fisherman one day when they met by accident, and asked him to sing the scale. The fisherman opened his mouth and no sound came. He and the schoolteacher looked at each other, and then the fisherman colored, and hung his head. The schoolteacher clapped him on the shoulder and walked on, satisfied that what there was here was the love of music rather than a talent for it, and even that seemed to him something hardly short of a miracle.

IN those islands, storms were not uncommon and they were full of peril. Even large sailing ships were washed on the rocks and broken to pieces. As for the little boats the fishermen went out in, one moment they would be bobbing on the waves like a cork, now on the crest and now out of sight in a trough, and then suddenly there wasn't any boat. The sea would have swallowed it, and the men in it, in the blinking of an eye. It was a terrible fact that the islanders had learned to live with. If they had not been fishermen, they would have starved, so they continued to go out in their boats, and to read the sky for warnings, which were usually dependable, but every now and then a storm — and usually the very worst kind — would come up without any warning, or with only a short time between the first alarming change in the odor of the air, the first wisps of storm clouds, and the sudden lashing of the waters. When this happened, the women gathered on the shore and prayed. Sometimes they waited all night, and sometimes they waited in vain.

One evening, the fisherman didn't come home at the usual time. His wife could not hear the wind or the shutters banging, but when the wind blew puffs of smoke down the chimney, she knew that a storm had come up. She put on her cloak, and wrapped a heavy scarf around her head, and started for the strand, to see if the boats were drawn up there. Instead, she found the other women waiting with their faces all stamped with the same frightened look. Usually the seabirds circled above the beach, waiting for the fishing boats to come in and the fishermen to cut open their fish and throw them the guts, but this evening there were no gulls or cormorants. The air was empty. The wind had blown them all inland, just as, by a freak, it had blown the boats all together, out on the water, so close that it took great skill to keep them from knocking against each other and capsizing in the dark. The fishermen called back and forth for a time, and then they fell silent. The wind had grown higher and higher, and the words were blown right out of their mouths, and they could not even hear themselves what they were saying. The wind was so high and the sound so loud that it was like a silence, and out of this silence, suddenly, came the sound of singing. Being poor ignorant fishermen, they did the first thing that occurred to them — they fell on their knees and prayed. The singing went on and on, in a voice that none of them had ever heard, and so powerful and rich and deep it seemed to come from the same place that the storm came from. A flash of lightning revealed that it was not an angel, as they thought, but the fisherman who was married to the deaf-mute. He was standing in his boat, with his head bared, singing, and in their minds this was no stranger or less miraculous than an angel would have been. They crossed themselves and went on praying, and the fisherman went on singing, and in a little while the waves began to grow smaller and the wind to abate, and the storm, which should have taken days to blow itself out, suddenly turned into an intense calm. As suddenly as it had begun, the singing stopped. The boats drew apart as in one boat after another the men took up their oars again, and in a silvery brightness, all in a cluster, the fishing fleet came safely in to shore.

5. The two women friends

THE two women were well along in years, and one lived in a castle and one lived in the largest house in the village that was at the foot of the castle rock. Though picturesque, the castle had bathrooms and central heating, and it would not for very long have withstood a siege, no matter how antiquated the weapons employed. The village was also picturesque, being made up of a single street of thatched Elizabethan cottages. The two women were friends, and if one had weekend guests it was understood that the other would stand by, ready to entertain them. When the conversation threatened to run out, guests at Cleeve Castle were taken to Cleeve House and offered tea and hot buttered scones, under a canopy of apple blossoms or in front of a roaring fire, according to the season. The largest house in the village had been made by joining three of the oldest cottages together, and the catalogue of its inconveniences often made visitors wipe tears of amusement from their eyes. The inconveniences were mostly felt by the servants, who had to carry cans of hot water and breakfast trays up the treacherous stairs, and who, when they were in a hurry, tripped over the uneven doorsills and bumped their heads on low beams. Guests at Cleeve House were taken to the castle and plied with gin and ghost stories.

One would have expected this arrangement, so useful to both women, to be lasting, but the friendship of women seems often to have embedded in it somewhere a fishhook, and as it happened the mistress of Cleeve House was born with a heavier silver spoon in her mouth, and baptized in a longer christening gown, and in numerous other ways was socially more enviable. On the other hand, the money that had originally gone with the social advantages was, alas, rather run out, and it was without the slightest trace of anxiety that the woman in the castle sat down to balance her checkbook. Weekend guests at the castle tended to be more important politically or in the world of the arts — flashy, in short. And the weekend guests at Cleeve House more important to know if it was a question of getting your children into the right schools or yourself into the right clubs. In a word, nobby. But how the woman who lived in the castle could have dreamed for one minute that she could entertain a member of the royal family and not bring him to tea at Cleeve House, to be amused by the catalogue of its inconveniences and the story of how it came to be thrown together out of three dark, cramped little cottages by an architect who was a disciple of William Morris, it is hard to say. Perhaps the friendship had begun to seem burdensome and the duties one-sided. Or perhaps it was the gradual accumulation of tactful silences, which avoided saying that the woman who lived in the village was top drawer and the woman who lived in the castle was not, and careless remarks, such as anybody might be guilty of with a close friend, which frankly admitted it. In any event, one does not go running here, there, and everywhere with a member of the royal family in tow. There is protocol to be observed, secretaries and chauffeurs and valets have to be consulted, and the conversation doesn't threaten to run out because what you have, in these circumstances, isn't conversation in the usual sense of the word. But anyway, the mistress of Cleeve House sat waiting for the telephone to ring, with the wrinkles ironed out of her best tablecloth, and her Spode tea set brought down from the highest shelf of the china closet, and the teaspoons polished till you could see your face in them, and her Fortuny gown taken out of its plastic bag and left to hang from the bedroom chandelier. And, unbelievably, the telephone did not ring. In the middle of the afternoon she had the operator check her phone to see if it was out of order. This was a mistake, because in a village people are very apt to put two and two together. By nightfall it was known all up and down the High Street that her in the castle was entertaining royalty and had left her in the big house to sit and twiddle her thumbs.

Not that the mistress of Cleeve House cared one way or the other about the royal family. No, it was merely the slight to a friendship of very long standing that disturbed her. And for the sake of that friendship, though it cost her a struggle, she was prepared to act as if nothing unusual had happened when the telephone rang on Sunday morning, and to suggest that the mistress of Cleeve Castle bring her guests to tea. The telephone rang on Monday morning instead. To anyone listening in, and several people were, it was clear that she was speaking a little too much as if nothing unusual had happened. However, the invitation — to drive, just the two of them, in the little car, over to the market town and have lunch at the Star and Garter — was accepted. And because one does not entertain royalty and then not mention it, the subject came up finally, in the most natural way, and the mistress of Cleeve House was able to achieve the tone she wanted, which was a mixture of reasonable curiosity and amused indifference. But it was all over between them, and they both knew it.

They continued to see each other, less often and less intimately, for another three or four months, and then the woman who lived in the largest house in the village finished it off in a way that made it possible for her to carry her head high. The husband of the woman who lived in the castle had, unwisely, allowed his name to be put up for a London club that was rather too grand for a man who had made a fortune in wholesale poultry. Even so, with a great deal of help from various quarters or a little help from the right quarter, he might have made it. There were two or three men who could have pulled this off single-handed, and when one of them came down to Cleeve House for the weekend, it was the turn of the mistress of the castle to sit and wait for the telephone to ring. On Monday morning, the nanny of the children of Cleeve House (who were really the woman's grandchildren) took them to play with the children of the castle, as she had been doing every Monday morning all summer, and was told at the castle gate that the children of the castle were otherwise occupied. Though they had not been in any way involved and did not even know the cause of the falling out, the children of the castle and the children of Cleeve House were enemies from that day forth, and so were their nannies. The two husbands, being more worldly, still exchanged curt nods when they met in the High Street or on the railway platform. As for the two women, they very cleverly managed never even to set eyes on one another.

Weekend guests at Cleeve House were taken for a walk, naturally, because it was one of the oldest villages in England, and when they saw the castle, with rooks roosting in the apertures of the keep, they cried out with pleasure at finding a place so picturesque that near London. When the mistress of Cleeve House explained that she was no longer on friendly terms with the castle, their faces betrayed their disappointment. And with a consistency that was really extraordinary, people who were staying at

Cleeve Castle sooner or later came back from a walk saying, "The village is charming, I must say. But who is that fascinating grey-haired woman who walks with a stick and lives in that largish house on the High Street? We're dying to meet her."

CITY people get over their anger, as a rule, but it is different if you live in a village. For one thing, everybody knows that you are angry, and why, and the slightest shift in position is publicly commented on, and this stiffens the antagonism and makes it permanent. Something very large indeed — a fire, a flood, a war, a catastrophe of some sort — is required to bring about a reconciliation and push the injured parties into one another's outstretched arms.

One winter morning, the village learned, via the wireless, that it was in the direct path of a new eight-lane expressway connecting London and the seacoast. The money for it had been appropriated and it was too late to prevent the road from being built, but the political connections of Cleeve Castle working hand in glove with the social connections of Cleeve House could perhaps divert it so that some other village was obliterated. After deliberating for days, the woman who lived in the castle picked up the telephone and called Cleeve House, but while the telephone was still ringing she hung up. The injury to her husband (what a way to repay a thousand kindnesses!) was still too fresh in her mind. There must be some other way of dealing with the problem, she told herself, and sitting down at her desk she wrote a long and affectionate letter to a school friend who was married to a Member of Parliament, imploring his help.

After considering the situation from every angle, the woman who lived in the largest house in the village came to the only sensible conclusion, which was that some things are worth swallowing your pride for, and she put on her hat and coat and walked up to the castle. But when she came to the castle gate, the memory of how her grandchildren had been turned away (the smallness of it!) filled her with anger, and she paid a call on the vicar instead.

In due time the surveyors appeared, with their tripods, sighting instruments, chains, stakes, and red flags, and the path of doom was made clear. The government, moved by humane considerations, did, however, build a new village. The cottages of Upper Cleeve, as it was called, were all exactly alike and as ugly as sin. There was no way on earth that you could join three of them together and produce a house that William Morris would have felt at home in. The castle was saved by its rocky situation, but its owners did not choose to look out on an eight-lane expressway and breathe exhaust fumes and be kept awake all night long by trucks and trailers. So the rooks fell heir to it.

6. The carpenter

ONCE upon a time there was a man of no particular age, a carpenter, whom all kinds of people entrusted with their secrets. Perhaps the smell of glue and sawdust and fresh-cut boards had something to do with it, but in any case he was not a troublemaker, and a secret is nearly always something that, if it became known, would make trouble for somebody. So they came to his shop, closed the door softly behind them, sat down on a pile of lumber, and pretended that they had come because they enjoyed watching him work. Actually, they did enjoy it. Some of them. His big square hands knew what they were doing, and all his movements were relaxed and skillful. The shavings curled up out of his plane as if the idea was to make long, beautiful shavings. He used his carpenter's rule and stubby pencil as if he were applying a moral principle. When he sawed, it seemed to have the even rhythm of his heartbeat. Though the caller might forget for five minutes what brought him here, in the end he stopped being interested in carpentry and said, "I know I can trust you, because you never repeat anything . . . " and there it was, one more secret added to the collection, a piece of information that, if it had got out, would have broken up a friendship or caused a son to be disinherited or ruined a half-happy marriage or cost some man his job or made trouble for somebody.

The carpenter had discovered that the best way to deal with this information that must not be repeated was to forget it as quickly as possible, though sometimes the secret was so strange he could not forget it immediately, and that evening his wife would ask, "Who was in the shop today?" For people with no children have only each other to spy on, and he was an open book to her.

Sometimes the person who had confided in him seemed afterward to have no recollection of having done this, and more than once the carpenter found himself wondering if he had imagined or misremembered something that he knew perfectly well he had not imagined and would remember to his dying day. In the middle of the night, if he had a wakeful period, instead of thrashing around in the bed and disturbing his wife's sleep, he lay quietly with his eyes open in the dark and was a spectator to plays in which honorable men were obliged to tell lies, the kind and good were a prey to lechery, the old acted not merely without wisdom but without common sense, debts were repaid not in kind but in hatred, and the young rode roughshod over everybody. When he had had enough of human nature, he put all these puppets back in their box and fell into a dreamless sleep.

For many years his life was like this, but it is a mistake to assume that people never change. They don't and they do change. Without his being able to say just when it happened and whether the change was sudden or gradual, the carpenter knew that he was no longer trustworthy — that is to say, he no longer cared whether people made trouble for one another or not. His wife saw that he looked tired, that he did not always bother to stand up straight, that he was beginning to show his age. And she tried to make his life easier for him, but he was a man firmly fixed in his habits, and there was not much she could do for him except feed him well and keep small irritations from him.

Out of habit, the carpenter continued not to repeat the things people told him, but while the secret was being handed over to him he marvelled that the other person had no suspicion he was making a mistake. And since the carpenter had not asked, after all, to be the repository of everybody's secret burden, it made him mildly resentful.

One day he tried an experiment. He betrayed a secret that was not very serious — partly to prove to himself that he could do such a thing and partly in the hope that word would get around that he was not to be trusted with secrets. It made a certain amount of trouble, as he knew it would, but it also had the effect of clearing the air for all concerned, and the blame never got back to him because no one could imagine his behaving in so uncharacteristic a fashion. So, after this experiment, he tried another. The butcher came in, closed the door softly, looked around for a pile of lumber to sit on, and then said, "There's something I've got to tell somebody."

"Don't tell me," the carpenter said quickly, "unless you want every Tom, Dick, and Harry to know."

The butcher paused, looked down at his terrible hands, cleared his throat, glanced around the shop, and then suddenly leaned forward and out it came.

"In short, he wanted every Tom, Dick, and Harry to know," the carpenter said to his wife afterward, when he was telling her about the butcher's visit.

"People need to make trouble the way they need to breathe," she said calmly.

"I don't need to make trouble," the carpenter said indignantly.

"I know," she said. "But you mustn't expect everyone to be like you."

The next time somebody closed the door softly and sat down and opened his mouth to speak, the carpenter beat him to it. "I know it isn't fair to tell you this," he said, "but I had to tell somebody . . . " This time he made quite a lot of trouble, but not so much that his wife couldn't deal with it, and he saw that the fear of making trouble can be worse than trouble itself.

After that, he didn't try any more experiments. What happened just happened. The candlemaker was sitting on a pile of lumber watching him saw a chestnut plank, and the carpenter said, "Yesterday the one-eyed fiddler was in here."

"Was he?" the candlemaker said; he wasn't really interested in the fiddler at the moment. There was something on his mind that he had to tell somebody, and he was waiting for the carpenter to stop sawing so he wouldn't have to raise his voice and run the risk of being overheard in the street.

"You know the blacksmith's little boy?" the carpenter said. "The second one? The one he keeps in the shop with him?"

"The apple of his eye," said the candlemaker. "Had him sorting nails when he was no bigger than a flea. Now he tends the bellows."

"That's right," said the carpenter. "Well, you know what the fiddler told me?"

"When it comes to setting everybody's feet a-dancing, there's no one like the one-eyed fiddler," the candlemaker said. "But I don't know what he'd of done without the blacksmith. Always taking him in when he didn't have a roof over his head or a penny in his pocket. Drunk or sober."

"You know what the fiddler told me? He said the blacksmith's little boy isn't his child."

"Whose is he?"

"Who does he look like?"

"Why, come to think of it, he looks like the one-eyed fiddler."

"Spitting image," the carpenter said. And not until that moment did he realize what was happening. It was the change in the candlemaker's face that made him aware of it. First the light of an impending confidence, which had been so clear in his eyes, was dimmed. The candlemaker looked down at his hands, which were as white and soft as a woman's Then he cleared his throat and said, "Strange nobody noticed it."

"You won't tell anybody what I told you?" the carpenter found himself saying.

"No, of course not," the candlemaker said. "I always enjoy watching you work. Is that a new plane you've got there?"

For the rest of the visit he was more friendly than usual, as if some lingering doubt had been disposed of and he could now be wholly at ease with the carpenter. After he had gone, the carpenter started to use his new plane and it jammed. He cleaned the slot and adjusted the screw and blew on it, but it still jammed, so he put it aside, thinking the blade needed to be honed, and picked up a crosscut saw. Halfway through the plank he stopped. The saw was not following the pencil line. He gave up and sat down on a pile of lumber. The fiddler had better clear out now and never show his face in the village again, because if the blacksmith ever found out, he'd kill him. And what about the blacksmith's wife? She had no business doing what she did, but neither did the blacksmith have any business marrying someone young enough to be his daughter. She was a slight woman with a cough, and she wouldn't last a year if she had to follow the fiddler in and out of taverns and sleep under hedgerows. And what about the little boy who so proudly tended the bellows? Each question the carpenter asked himself was worse than the one before. His head felt heavy with shame. He sighed and then sighed again, deep heavy sighs forced out of him by the weight on his heart. How could he tell his wife what he had done? And what would make her want to go on living with him when she knew? And how could he live with himself? At last he got up and untied the strings of his apron and locked the door of his shop behind him and went off down the street, looking everywhere for the one-eyed fiddler.

7. The man who had no friends and didn't want any

THERE was a man who had no enemies — only friends. He had a gift for friendship. When he met someone for the first time, he would look into the man or the woman or the child's eyes, and he never afterward mistook them for someone else. He was as kind as the day is long, and no one imposed on his kindness. He had a beautiful wife, who loved him. He had a comfortable, quiet apartment in town and a beautiful little house by the sea. He had enough money. All summer he taught children to sail boats on the salt water and on winter afternoons he sat in his club and helped old men with one foot in the grave to remember names, so they could get on with their recollecting. If necessary, he even helped them to remember the point of the recollection, which he had usually heard before. In the club he was never alone for a minute. If he sat down by the magazine table, the other members gathered around him like fruit flies — the young, uneasy new members as well as his bald-headed contemporaries. The places he had lived in stretched halfway around the world, and he was a natural-born storyteller. His conversation went to the head, like wine. At the same time, it went straight to the heart. He was a lovely man, and there aren't any more like him.

But there was also in the same club a man who had no friends — and, of course, not a single enemy either. He was always alone. He had never married. Though he had too much money, no one had ever successfully put the finger on him. He did not drink, and if someone who had been drinking maybe a little too much nodded to him on the way upstairs to the dining room, he did not respond, lest it turn out that he had been mistaken for somebody else. He tried sitting at the common table, in the hope that it would broaden his mind, but it was not the way he had been given to understand it would be, so he moved to a table by the window, a table for two, and for company he had an empty plate that did not contradict itself, a clean napkin that lived wholly in the present, a glittering glass tumbler that had its facts and figures straight, an unprejudiced knife, an unsentimental fork, and two logical spoons. Actually, his belonging to this particular club at all was due to a mistake on the part of the secretary of the committee on admissions, who had been instructed to notify another man of the same name that he had been elected to membership.

The man who had no friends did not want any, but he was observant, and from his table by the window he saw something no one else saw: The man who had no enemies, only friends, did not look well. It could be nothing more than one of those sudden jerks by which people grow older, but there was a late-afternoon light in his eye, and also his color was not good. Joking, he made use of the elevator when the others moved toward the stairs. And more and more he seemed like a man who is listening to two conversations at once. Sometimes for a week or ten days he would not appear at the club at all, and then he would be there again, moving through the stately, high-ceilinged rooms like a ship under full sail — but a ship whose rigging is frayed and whose oak timbers have grown lighter and lighter with time, and whose seaworthiness is now entirely a matter of the excellence of the builder's design.

The first stroke was slight. The doctor kept him in bed for a while, but he was able to spend the summer in his house by the sea, as usual. During the period of his convalescence, his wife informed the doorman at the club that he would be happy to see his friends. Naturally, they came — came often, came in droves, and found the invalid sitting up in bed, in good spirits, though not quite his old self yet. They were concerned lest they stay too long, and at the same time found it difficult to leave until they had blurted out, while it was still possible, how much he meant to them. These statements he was somehow able to dispose of with humor, so that they didn't hang heavy in the air afterward.

The man who had no friends also inquired about him, and the doorman, after some hesitation, gave him the message too, thinking that since this was the first time in fourteen years that he had ever asked about anybody, he must be a friend. But he didn't pay a call on the sick man. He had asked only out of curiosity. When he returned to town in September, he saw on the club bulletin board an announcement of a memorial service for the man who had a gift for friendship. He had died about a month before, in his sleep, in the house by the sea. The man who had no friends had reached the age where it is not unusual to spend a considerable part of one's time going to funerals, but no one had died whose obsequies required his presence, and again he was curious. He marked the date in the little memorandum book he always carried with him, and when the day came he got in a taxi and went to the service.

THE small stone chapel filled up quickly, for of course they all came, all the friends of the man who had no enemies. They came bringing their entire stock of memories of him, which in one or two instances went back to their early youth. And in many cases there was something about their dress, some small mark of color — the degree of red or bright blue that is permitted in the ties of elderly men, the *Légion d'honneur* in a lapel — because it had seemed to them that the occasion ought not to be wholly solemn, since the man himself had been so impatient of solemnity. The exception was the man who had no friends. He wore a dark-grey business suit and a black-and-white striped tie, and sat alone in the back of the chapel. To his surprise, the funeral service was completely impersonal. Far from eulogizing the dead man or explaining his character to people who already knew all there was to know about it, the officiating clergyman did not even mention his name. There was a longish prayer, and then quotations from the Scriptures — mostly from the Psalms. The chapel had a bad echo, but the idea of the finality of death came through the garbled phrases, even so. The idea of farewell. The idea of a funeral on the water, and mourners peering, through torchlight, at a barque that is fast disappearing from sight. The man who had no friends sat observing, with his inward eye, his own funeral, in an empty undertaking parlor. The church was cold. He felt a draft on his ankles.

The young minister raised his voice to that pitch that is customary when the prayers of clergymen are meant to carry not only to the congregation but also to the ear of Heaven. There was a last brief exhortation to the Deity, and then the service was over. But during the emptying of the chapel something odd happened. The people there had not expected to derive such comfort from the presence of one another, and when their eyes met, their faces lit up, and they kept reaching out their hands to each other, over the pews. The man who had no friends saw what was happening and hurriedly put on his overcoat, but before he could slip out of the church, he felt his arm being taken in a friendly manner, and a man he knew only by sight said, "Ah yes, he belonged to you too, didn't he? Yes, of course." And no sooner had he extricated himself from this person than someone else said, "You're not going off by yourself? Come with us. Come on, come on, stop making a fuss!" And though he could hardly believe it, he found himself sitting on the jump seat of a taxi, with four other men, who took out their handkerchiefs and unashamedly wiped the tears away, blew their noses, and then sat back and began to tell funny stories about the dead man. When he got out of the cab, he tried to pay for his share, but they wouldn't hear of it, so he thanked them stiffly, and they called good-bye to him as if they were all his friends, which was too absurd — except that it didn't end there. The next day at the club they went right on acting as if they had a right to consider themselves his friends, and nothing he said or didn't say made any difference. They had got it into their heads he was a friend of the man who died, and so one of them. Shortly after the beginning of the new year, what should he find but a letter, on club stationery, informing him that he had been elected to the Board of Governors. He sat right down and wrote a letter explaining why he could not serve, but he saw at once that the letter was too revealing, so he tore it up. For the next three years he went faithfully, but with no pleasure, to the monthly dinners, and cast his vote with the others during the business meeting that followed the dinner. At the very last meeting of his term, just when he thought he was escaping, the secretary read off the names of the members who were to serve on the House Committee, and his name was among them. It seemed neither the time nor the place to protest, and afterward, when he did protest, he was told that it was customary for the members of the Board of Governors to serve on one committee or another after their term was finished. If he refused, the matter would be placed before the Board of Governors at their next meeting. He didn't want to call that much attention to himself, so he gave in. He served on the House Committee for two years, and at these meetings found that he was in sympathy with the prevailing atmosphere, which was of sharp candor and common sense. Inevitably he became better acquainted with his fellow committee members, and when they spoke to him on the stairs he couldn't very well not respond. For a while he continued to sit at his table by the window, but someone almost always came and joined him, so in the end he decided he might as well move over to the common table with the others. Later he served on the Rules Committee, the Archives Committee, the Art Committee, the Library Committee, the Music Committee, and the Committee on Admissions. Finally, when there were no more committees for him to serve on, someone dropped a remark in his presence and he saw the pit yawning before him. He took a solemn vow that he would never permit his name to be put up for president of the club, but it was put up; they did it without asking his permission, for it was an honor that had never been refused and they couldn't imagine anyone's wanting to refuse it.

He made an ideal president. He understood facts and figures, being a man of means, and since he had no family life, he was free to give all his time to the affairs of the club. A curmudgeon with a heart of gold is what they all said about him. Sometimes they even said it to his face. Fuming, he was made to sit for his portrait, shortly before he died, at the age of eighty-four, of pneumonia. As so often happens, the portrait was a failure. There was a bleak look in the eyes that wasn't at all like him, the members said, shaking their heads, and the one man who really understood him — who had never once tried to be his friend — was not there no contradict them.

8. A fable begotten of an echo of a line of verse by W. B. Yeats

ONCE upon a time there was an old man who made his living telling stories. In the middle of the afternoon he took his position on the steps of the monument to Unaging Intellect, in a somewhat out-of-the-way corner of the marketplace. And people who were not in a hurry would stop, and sometimes those who were in a hurry would hear a phrase that caught their attention, such as "in the moonlight" or "covered with blood," and would pause for a second and then be spellbound. It was generally agreed that he was better than some storytellers and not as good as others. And his wife would wait for him to come home, because what they had for supper depended on what he brought home in his pockets. She couldn't ask him to stop at this or that stall in the market-place and buy what they needed. Being old, he was forgetful and would bring part of what she needed but not all. Standing on the marble steps of the monument, with his voice pitched so that it would carry over the shoulders of those who made a ring around him, he never forgot and he never repeated himself. That is to say, if it was a familiar story he was telling, he added new embellishments, new twists, and again it would be something he had never told before and didn't himself know until the words came out of his mouth, so that he was as astonished as his listeners, but didn't show it. He wanted them to believe what was in fact true, that the stories didn't come from him but through him, were not memorized, and would never be told quite that same way again.

Forgetfulness is the shadow that lies across the path of all old men. The statesman delivering an oration from the steps of the Temple of Zeus at times hesitated because he didn't know what came next. And the storyteller's wife worried for fear that this would happen to him, and of course one day it did. Kneeling in front of the executioner's block, the innocent prince traveling incognito waited for the charioteer who was going to force his way through the crowd and save him from the axe, and nothing happened. That is to say, there was a pause that grew longer and longer until the listeners shifted their feet, and the storyteller took up in a different part of the story, and then suddenly swooped back to the prince and saved him, but leaving the audience with the impression that something was not right, that there was something they had not been told. There was. But could the storyteller simply have said at that point, "I don't remember what happened next"? They would have lost all faith in him and in his stories.

"I think you were just tired," his wife said when he told her what had happened. "It could happen to anybody." But in her heart she foresaw that it was going to happen again, and more seriously. "Once upon a time there was a younger son of the Prince of Syracuse who had one blue eye and one brown, and a charm of manner that made anyone who talked to him believe that — " This had to be left hanging because he who had always known everything about his characters, as God knows everything about human beings, didn't know, and tried to pretend that he meant this to be left hanging; but of course the listeners knew, and word got around that his memory was failing, his stories were not as good as they used to be, and fewer and fewer people stopped to listen to him, and those who did had to be content with fragments of stories, more interesting sometimes than the perfectly told stories had been, but unsatisfactory and incomplete.

Knowing that this was going to happen, his wife had been putting a little by to tide them over in their old age, and so they didn't starve. But he stayed home from the marketplace because it was an embarrassment to him that he couldn't tell stories anymore, and sometimes he sat in the sun and sometimes he followed his wife around and while she was digging a spider out of a corner of the ceiling he would say, "Once upon a time there was a girl of such beauty and delicacy of feeling that she could not possibly have been the child of the hardworking but obtuse couple who raised her from infancy, and although they seemed not to realize this, she had an air of expectancy that — " Here he stopped, unable to go on, and although his wife would have given anything to know what it was that the girl was expecting and if it really came about and how, she said nothing, because, poor man, his head was like a pot with a hole in it. Sometimes when her work was done she sat in the sun with him, in silence. They had been together for a very long time and did not always need to be saying something. But she would have liked it if he knew how much she did for him; instead, he seemed to take it for granted that when he was hungry there would be food, and when he was tired there was the bed, with clean sheets on it smelling of sunshine. She realized that it was not in his nature to be aware of small, ordinary things of this kind — that his mind trafficked in wonders and surprises. And it was something that she lived with the beginnings of so many wonderful stories she could think about as she went about her work: The story of the flute player's daughter, who picked up his instrument one day and played — although she had never to his knowledge touched it before or been given any instruction in the fingering or in breathing across the hole — better than any flute player he had ever heard. When he asked her how she was able to do this, she said, "I don't know. It just came to me that I knew how to do it." And when he asked her to do it again she couldn't, and this troubled her so much that she became melancholy and — and what? The storyteller didn't know. The thread of invention had given way at that point. . . . The story of the African warrior who was turned into a black cat, who at night wanted to be outdoors so that he could search for the huge moon of Africa that he remembered — the only thing that he remembered — from before his transformation. . . . The story of the old woman with a secret supply of hummingbirds. . . . The story of the brother and sister who in some previous incarnation had been man and wife. . . . With all these unfinished stories to occupy her mind, the story-teller's wife did not lack for things to think about. She wished that he could finish them for his sake, but she had come to prefer the fragments to the finished stories he used to tell. And in time she came to see that they couldn't be finished because they were so interesting there was no way for the story to go on.

The old man felt differently. "I would like just once before I die," he said to himself often, "to finish a story and see the look of thoughtfulness that a perfect story arouses in the faces of the people listening to me in the marketplace." Now, when he took his stand on the steps of the monument, the passersby hesitated, remembered that there was no use listening to him, because he always lost the thread of the story, and so passed on, saying to one another, "What wonderful tales he used to tell!"

Some vandal had chipped off the nose and two fingers of the statue to Unaging Intellect, and it had never been much admired, but he had told so many stories with the recognition that the monument was at his back that he had come to have an affection for it. What he had no way of knowing was that the monument had come to have an affection for him. What would otherwise have been an eternity of marble monumentality was made bearable by his once-upon-a-times. But why all these princes and talking parrots, these three wishes that land the guesser into a royal palace which is more marble, and uninhabitable, these babies switched in their cradle for no reason but to make a strange story, these wonders that are so much less wonderful than the things that are close to home? And because it is part of the storyteller's instinct to know what his audience wants to hear, one day when there was nobody around, the storyteller began: "Once upon a time there was an old man whose wits were slipping, and although he knew he didn't deserve it, he was well taken care of by his wife, who loved him. They had children but the children grew up and went away." Here the statue took on a look of attentiveness which the old man did not see because his back was turned to it. "The old couple had only each other, but that was a lot because with every year of their lives they had a greater sense of the unbreakable connection that held them. It was a miracle and they knew it, but they were afraid to talk about it lest something happen. Lest they be separated . . ." On and on the story went, with the monument rooted to its place by interest in what the old man was saying. Monuments do not have anyone who loves them. They exist in solitude and are always lonely, especially at night when there is no one around. The thought that human beings could undress and get into bed and sleep all night side by side was more beautiful than the monument could bear. The fact that she cooked for him because he was hungry and that his hunger was for what she cooked because it was cooked with love. That he was under the impression that, old and scatterbrained as he was, he was the one who took care of her and that she would not be safe without him . . . When the storyteller said, "From living together they had come to look alike," the monument said, "Oh, it's too much!" For there is no loneliness like the loneliness of Unaging Intellect.

9. The blue finch of Arabia

ON the evening of the twenty-fourth of December, an old woman and an old man got off the train at a little wayside station on the Trans-Siberian Railroad and hurried across the snow to the only lighted shop in the village, which was a pet shop. In their excitement they left the door open, which annoyed the proprietor, who was deaf, and they had a hard time making him understand what they wanted. They had come from Venice, they said, on the strength of a rumor that he had a pair of blue finches. The proprietor shook his head. He had had *one* blue finch, not a pair, and he had sold it that morning.

"Tell us who you sold it to!" the old woman cried.

"We'll give you a thousand dollars," the old man said, "if you'll just tell us his name."

"I didn't ask him."

"But how could you *not* ask him his name?" the old man and the old woman cried.

"Did I ask yours when you came in just now and left the door wide open?" the proprietor said. "Besides, it was the common blue finch of Africa, and not the one you are looking for."

"You know about the blue finch of Arabia?" the old man shouted.

"Certainly," said the pet-shop proprietor.

"But I daresay you have never seen one?" said the old woman slyly, in a normal tone of voice, hoping to test the pet-shop proprietor's hearing.

"A pair only," the proprietor said, turning off his hearing aid. "Never just one."

"We'll give you two thousand dollars," said the old man, dancing up and down, "if you'll just tell us where you saw them."

"Very well," said the pet-shop proprietor. "Where is the two thousand?"

"What's that?" asked the old man.

"I say where is the two thousand dollars?" the pet-shop proprietor shouted. "This is a very good hearing aid I am wearing. Here — try it, why don't you?"

The old man looked at the old woman, who nodded, and then he reached in his pocket and took out his checkbook, and she opened her purse and took out her pen, and then he turned to the pet-shop proprietor. "Name?" he shouted.

"Make it out to cash," the pet-shop proprietor said.

When the old man had finished writing out the check for two thousand dollars, he put it on the counter between the pet-shop proprietor and him, and he and the old woman leaned forward with their eyes bright and their mouths open and said, "Now, tell us where you saw them. They're worth half a million dollars."

"The pair of blue finches?"

"Are we talking about canaries?" asked the old man, drumming his nails on the counter.

"I saw them —" the pet-shop proprietor said, closing his eyes, "I saw them —" he repeated, looking tired and ill, and older than he had looked when they first came into the shop; "I saw them —" he said, suddenly opening his eyes and looking happier than the old man and the old woman had ever seen anybody look, "*in a forest in Arabia.*"

The old man shrieked with anger and disappointment, and the old woman reached for the check for two thousand dollars, which was already in the pet-shop proprietor's wallet in his inside coat pocket, though nobody saw him pick it up, fold it, and put it there.

The old man and the old woman ran out into the deep snow, crying police, crying help, and leaving the door wide open behind them. As it happened, there were no police at that wayside station on the Trans-Siberian Railroad. They rattled the door of the railway station but it was locked. On the outside, the schedule of trains was posted, and they lit matches, which they shielded with their hands and then with the old man's hat, trying to make out how long they would have to wait in the cold before another train came along that would take them back to Venice. When they did see, finally, they couldn't believe it, and went on lighting more matches and looking at the timetable in despair. The next train going in either direction was due in nine days. In the end, since all the other houses were closed and dark, they had to go back to the pet shop, and this time the old man pulled the door to after him. The pet-shop proprietor, seeing that they were about to speak, adjusted his hearing aid; but though they opened their mouths again and again, no sound came out, and after shaking the apparatus several times, the pet-shop proprietor put it in his pocket and said in a normal tone of voice, "If you don't mind the conversation of birds, and if fish don't make you restless, and if you like cats and don't have fleas, there is no reason why you can't stay here until your train comes."

So they did. They stayed nine days, there in the pet shop, among the birds of every size and color, and the cats of all description, the monkeys and the dogs, the long-tailed goldfish, and the tame raccoons. At first they were restless, but they had promised not to be, and gradually, because whatever the pet-shop proprietor did was interesting and whatever he had in his shop was living and beautiful, they forgot about themselves, about the passing of time, about Venice, where they had a number of important appointments that it would cost them money not to keep, and even about the blue finch of Arabia, which they had never seen but only heard about. What they had heard was how rare and valuable it was, not that its song is more delicate than gold wire and its least movement like the reflections of water on a wall. The old woman helped the pet-shop proprietor clean out the cages, and the old man brushed and curried the cats, who soon grew very attached to him, and when the pet-shop proprietor said suddenly, "You have just time to walk from here to the railway station at a reasonable pace before your train pulls in," they were shocked and horrified.

"But can't we stay?" the old woman cried. "We've been so happy here these last nine days."

The pet-shop proprietor shrugged his shoulders. "It's all right with me if you want to spend the rest of your life in a wayside station on the Trans-Siberian Railroad," he said, "but what about the appointments you have in Venice?"

The old woman looked at the old man, who nodded sadly.

"Before you go," said the pet-shop proprietor, "I would like to present you with a souvenir of the establishment." He opened a door just large enough to put his hand through, and reached into a huge cage that went all the way up to the ceiling and the whole length of the room and was full of birds of every size and color, and took out two small ones, both of them blue as the beginning of the night when there is deep snow on the ground. "Here," he said, thrusting the birds into a little wire cage and closing the door on them.

"But won't they get cold?" the old woman asked. "Won't they die on that long train ride?"

"Why should they?" asked the pet-shop proprietor. "They came all the way from — "

At that moment they heard the train whistle, the train that was taking them back to Venice, and so the old man rushed for the door, and the old woman picked up the cage with the blue birds in it and put it under her coat, and they floundered through the snow to the railway station, and the conductor pulled them up onto the train, which was already moving, and it was just as the pet-shop proprietor said: The birds stood the journey better than the old man and the old woman.

At the border the customs inspector boarded the train, and went through everybody's luggage until he came to the old man and the old woman, who were dozing. He shook first one and then the other, and pointing to the bird cage he said, "What kind of birds are those?"

"Bluebirds," the old man said, and shut his eyes.

"They look to me like the blue finch of Arabia," the customs inspector said. "Are you sure they're bluebirds?"

"Positive," the old woman said. "A man who has a pet shop in a way-side station of the Trans-Siberian Railroad gave them to us, so we don't have to pay duty on them. The week before, he sold somebody a blue finch, but it was the common blue finch of Africa."

"We had all that long trip there," the old man said, opening one eye, "and this long trip back, for nothing. When do we get to Venice?"

"If they had been the blue finch of Arabia," the customs inspector said, "you would have been allowed to keep them. Ordinary birds can't cross the border."

"But they do all the time," the old woman said, "in the sky."

"I know," the customs inspector said, "but not on the Trans-Siberian Railroad. Hand me the cage, please."

The old man looked at the old woman, who stood up stiffly, from having been in one position so long, and together they got off the train, missing their appointments in Venice, and spent the remaining years of their life in a country where they didn't speak the language and there was no Commodities Exchange, rather than part with a pair of birds that they had grown attached to on a long train journey, because of their color, which was as blue as the beginning of night when there is deep snow on the ground, and their song, which was more delicate than gold wire, and their movements, which were like the reflections of water on a wall.

10. The sound of waves

ONCE upon a time there was a man who took his family to the seashore. They had a cottage on the ocean, and it was everything that a house by the ocean should be — sagging wicker furniture, faded detective stories, blue china, grass rugs, other people's belongings to reflect upon, and other people's pots and pans to cook with. The first evening, after the children were in bed, the man and his wife sat on the porch and watched the waves come in as if they had never seen this sight before. It was a remarkably beautiful evening, no wind, and a calm sea. Far out on the broad back of the ocean a hump would begin to gather slowly, moving toward the shore, and at a certain point the hump would rise in a dark wall and spill over. A sandpiper went skittering along the newly wetted, shining sand, the beach grass all leaned one way, the moon was riding high and white in the evening sky, and wave after wave broke just before it reached the shore. The woman said to the man, "What are you thinking about?"

"I was thinking about how many waves there are," he said, which made her laugh.

"Thousands upon thousands," he said solemnly. "Millions . . . Billions . . ."

He had been brought up far inland, where the only water was a pond or a creek winding its way through marshes and pastures, and though this was not his first time at the ocean, he could not get over it. No duck pond has ever yet gathered itself into a dark wall of water. Creeks gurgle and swirl between their muddy banks, but never succeed in producing anything like the ocean's lisp and roar. There was nothing to compare it to except itself.

The next morning he went for a swim before breakfast. The waves were high, but he waited, and the moment came when he could run in and swim out into deep water. He swam until he was tired, and then rode in on a wave, and dried himself, and went back to the house with a huge appetite.

There was no newspaper to remind him that it was now Sunday the twentieth, and that tomorrow would be Monday the twenty-first. There was a clock in the kitchen, but he seldom looked at it, and his watch lay in his bureau drawer with the hands resting at one-fifteen. The only thing that kept him from feeling that time was standing still was the sound that came through the open windows: *Sish . . . sish . . . sish . . . sish . . . a-wish . . . sish. . . .*

As always when people are at the ocean, the years fell away. The crow's-feet around the man's eyes remained white longer than the rest of his face, and then all the wrinkles were smoothed away during the nights of deep sleep and the days of idleness. He and his wife were neither of them young, and nothing could bring back the look of really being young, but five, ten, fifteen years fell off them. When they made love their bodies tasted of the salt sea, and when the wave of lovemaking had spent itself, they lay in one another's arms, and heard the sound of the waves. This year, and next year, and last year, and the year before that, and the year after next, and before they came, and after they had gone. . . .

The woman was afraid of the surf, and would not go past a certain point, though he coaxed her to join him. She stood timidly, this side of the breaking waves, and he left her after a while and went out past the sandy foam, to where he could stand and dive through the incoming wall of water. There was always the moment of decision, and this was what she dreaded, and why she remained on the shore — because the moment came when you had to decide and she couldn't decide. Years ago she had been rolled, and the fright had never left her. So had he, of course. He remembered what it had been like, and knew that if he wasn't careful diving through the waves he would be whipped around and lose control of what happened to him, and his face would be ground into the sharp gravel at the water's edge, his bathing trunks would be filled with sand, and, floundering and frightened, he would barely be able to struggle to his feet in time to keep it from happening all over again. But he was careful. He kept his eyes always on the incoming wave, and, swimming hard for a few seconds, he suddenly found himself safe on the other side. As he came out of the water, his face was transformed with happiness. He took the towel his wife held out to him and, hopping on one leg, to shake the water out of his ears, he said, "This is the way I remember feeling when I was seventeen years old."

While she was shopping for food he went into the post office and waited while a girl with sun-bleached hair sorted through a pile of envelopes. He came away with several, including a bank statement, which he looked at, out of habit — debits and credits, the brief but furious struggle between incoming salary and outgoing expenses — and then put in the same drawer with his watch.

ALL through sunny days, and cloudy days, and days when it rained, and days when the fog rolled in from the ocean and shut out the sight of the neighboring houses, the waves broke, and broke, and broke, always with the same drawn-out sound, and silently the days dropped from the calendar. The vacation was half over. Then there were only ten more days. Then it was the last Sunday, the last Monday. . . . Sitting up in bed, the man saw that there was a path of bright moonlight across the water, which the incoming waves passed through, and the moonlight made it seem as if you could actually see the earth's curve.

During the final week there were two days in a row when the sky was racked with storm clouds, and it rained intermittently, and the red flag flew from the pole by the lifeguard's stand, and only the young dared go in. Like dolphins sporting, the man thought as he stood on the beach, fully dressed, with a windbreaker on, and watched the teen-agers diving through the cliffs of water. The waves went *crash!* and then *crash!* and again *crash!* all night long.

This stormy period was followed by a day when the ocean was like a millpond, and the waves were so small they hardly got up enough hump to spill over, but spill over they did. *Sish . . . sish . . . a-wish . . .* Since the world began, he thought, stretched out on his beach towel. The I.B.M. machine had not been invented that could enumerate them. It would be like counting the grains of sand all up and down the miles and miles of beach. It would take forever. He could not stop thinking about it, and he decided that in a way it was worse than being rolled.

It was what reconciled him, in the end, to the packing and the last time for this and the last time for that, and getting dressed in city clothes, and the melancholy ritual of departure. It was too much. The whole idea was more than the mind could manage. Outside the human scale. Rather than think about the true number of the waves, he gave up his claim to the shore they broke upon, and the beach grass all leaning one way, and the moon's path across the water, and the illusion that he could actually see the earth's curve.

From the deck of the ferryboat that took them across the bay to the mainland, he watched the island grow smaller and smaller. And in two weeks' time he had forgotten all about what it was like, *this year . . . next year . . . last year . . . and before we came . . . and after we've gone . . .*

11. The woman who never drew breath except to complain

In a country near Finland dwelt a woman who never drew breath except to complain. There was in that country much to complain of — the long cold winters, the scarcity of food, and robber bands that descended on poor farmers at night and left their fields and barns blazing. But these things the woman had by an inequality of fate been spared. Her husband was young and strong and worked hard and was kind to her. And they had a child, a three-year-old boy, who was healthy and happy, obedient and good. The roof never leaked, there was always food in the larder and peat moss piled high outside the door for the fireplace she cooked by. But still the woman complained, morning, noon, and night.

One day when she was out feeding her hens, she heard a great beating of wings and looked up anxiously, thinking it was a hawk come to raid her hencoop, and saw a big white gander, which sailed once around the house and then settled at her feet and began to peck at the grain she had scattered for her hens. While she was wondering how she could catch the wild bird without the help of her husband, who was away in the fields, it flapped its great soft wings and said, "So far as I can see, you have less than any woman in this country to complain about."

"That's true enough," the woman said.

"Then why do you do it?" asked the bird.

"Because there is so much injustice in the world," the woman said. "In the village yesterday a woman in her sleep rolled over on her child and smothered it, and an old man starved to death last month, within three miles of here. Wherever I look, I see human misery, and here there is none, and I am afraid."

"Of what?" asked the bird.

"I am afraid lest they look down from the sky and see how blessed I am, compared to my neighbors, and decide to even things up a bit. This way, if they do look down, they will also hear me complaining, and think, 'That poor woman has lots to contend with,' and go on about their business."

"Very clever of you," the bird said, cleaning the underside of its wing with its beak. "But in the sky anything but the truth has a hollow ring. One more word of complaint out of you and all the misfortunes of all your neighbors will be visited on you and on your husband and child." The bird flapped its wings slowly, rose above her, sailed once around the chimney, and then, flying higher and higher, was lost in the clouds. While the woman stood peering after it, the bread that she had left in the oven burned to a cinder.

THE bread was the beginning of many small misfortunes, which occurred more and more frequently as time went on. The horse went lame, the hens stopped laying, and after too long a season of rain the hay all rotted in the fields. The cow went dry but produced no calf. The roof began to leak, and when the woman's husband went up to fix it, he fell and broke his leg and was laid up for months, with winter coming on. And while the woman was outside, trying to do his work for him, the child pulled a kettle of boiling water off the stove and was badly scalded.

And still no word of complaint crossed the woman's lips. In her heart she knew that worse things could happen, and in time worse things did. A day came when there was nothing to eat in the larder and the woman had to go the rounds of her neighbors and beg for food, and those she had never turned hungry from her door refused her, on the ground that anyone so continually visited by misfortune must at some time have had sexual intercourse with the Devil. The man's leg did not heal, and the child grew sickly and pale. The woman searched for edible roots and berries, and set snares for rabbits and small birds, and so kept her family from starving, until one day, when she was far away in the marshes, some drunken soldiers happened by and wantonly set fire to the barns, and went on their way, reeling and tittering. The heat of the burning barns made a downdraft, and a shower of sparks landed on the thatched roof of the farmhouse, and that, too, caught on fire. In a very few minutes, while the neighbors stood around in a big circle, not daring to come nearer because of the heat of the flames, the house burned to the ground, and the man and the child both perished. When the woman came running across the fields, crying and wringing her hands, people who had known her all their lives and were moved at last by her misfortunes tried to intercept her and lead her away, but she would have none of them. At nightfall they left her there, and she did not even see them go. She sat with her head on her knees and listened for the sound of wings.

At midnight the great bird sailed once around the blackened chimney and settled on the ground before her, its feathers rosy with the glow from the embers. The bird seemed to be waiting for her to speak, and when she said nothing it stretched its neck and arched its back and finally said, in a voice much kinder than the last time, "This is a great pity. All the misfortunes of all your neighbors have been visited on you, without a word of complaint from you to bring them on. But the gods can't be everywhere at once, you know, and sometimes they get the cart before the horse. If you'd like to complain now, you may." The wind blew a shower of sparks upward and the bird fanned them away with its wings. The woman did not speak. "This much I can do for you," the bird said, "and I wish it was more."

When the woman raised her head, she saw a young man whose face, even in the dying firelight, she recognized. There before her stood her child, her little son, but grown now, in the pride of manhood. All power of speech left her. She put out her arms and in that instant, brought on by such a violent beating of wings as few men have ever dreamed of, the air turned white. What the woman at first took to be tiny feathers proved to be snow. It melted against her cheek, and turned her hair white, and soon put the fire out.

The snow came down all night, and all the next day, and for many days thereafter, and was so deep that it lasted all winter, and in the spring grass grew up in what had once been the rooms of the farmhouse, but of the woman there was no trace whatever.

12. The masks

ONCE upon a time there was a country where everyone wore masks. They were born wearing them. About twelve months they lasted, and were shed the way a snake sheds its skin, and for the same reason, and under the old mask there was a new one, at times all but undistinguishable from the old one, at times startlingly different. The first warning was a loosening of the skin next to the hairline, and as soon as he noticed it the person would retire for two days, and food would be left on a tray outside his door, and when he emerged with an entirely new mask his friends and family were careful not to stare openly at him until he had got used to it. The masks were not what we think of masks as being — for purposes of disguise, say, at a fancy-dress ball, or for purposes of concealment. In that fortunate country people had no need to conceal their feelings, and the masks let anger come through, as an ordinary face does, and joy, and sadness, and triumph. That is to say, the mask was their true face but they could not keep it for more than twelve months, and if you had said what a pity, they would have said, "Yes, but so is it a pity that my little granddaughter cannot always stay five years old. Never to change one's mask is not in the nature of things." When that same little granddaughter, who had been wearing the mask of a strong and healthy child, emerged from her room with the mask of a child who is wan, tires easily, and is sickly, it struck terror to the old woman's heart, for the masks were sometimes prophetic.

People were fond of their masks and did not discard them when they were no longer of any use. Parents saved the masks of their children until they were old enough to take care of them themselves and realize their value. In the privacy of his own room, the person would go to the closet where the masks were kept and take out the mask of the period when he had been most happy, or sometimes the opposite of it, and try it on in front of the mirror, remembering old emotions. Sometimes they even went so far as to wear them in public, fastened on over their current mask, with an elastic under the chin, and the hair down to conceal the line where it had peeled from the face. And their friends would affectionately smile, remembering how they were at that period, and understanding why they chose to return to it for a brief moment. Ministers of the Gospel, professors, politicians and statesmen, official heroes of all kinds were obliged to wear the same mask year after year, no matter what new mask had formed under the old one, or how ragged the original mask had become with constant wear. When a great artist died, or a king, or a President, or a general who had changed the course of history, his masks, all of them, were hung in a museum that had been built for that purpose, and the idea was that they would hang there in perpetuity, for the edification of posterity. No doubt they would have if there had been such a thing as posterity. Or perpetuity. Instead, the masks of the great and famous were forever being shifted around — from the most conspicuous place in the main hall to some obscure alcove, and vice versa. Or even to a storeroom in the basement, where they were to be seen only on written request. When an ordinary person died, his masks were gathered up, usually by someone whose own mask was bathed in tears, and put away in a pine box. From time to time the box would be opened and the masks looked at longingly or with new understanding. They did not deteriorate, or suffer the slightest change. As year after year passed, the box would be opened less frequently, and sometimes when it was opened it would be by a person who had never actually seen any of the masks before, though he had of course heard of the person they belonged to. Or it might be someone who had the name and even the facts wrong, and, studying the masks, would arrive at all sorts of interesting conclusions that were occasionally taken seriously, and so muddied the stream of history.

The living masks of saints grew less distinct in outline the closer they came to the knowledge of God. Lovers, especially at the beginning of their rapturous exploration of one another's natures and bodies, would sometimes childishly exchange masks — as if it made the slightest difference to a heart overflowing with feeling. The masks of husbands and wives long married and deeply connected by subterranean knowledge of one kind and another grew to look more and more alike, so that if they had changed masks with each other it would hardly have been noticed. The discarded masks took up more and more room, inevitably, and people with imagination sometimes felt that it was hardly worth their while to grow a new mask every twelve months when there were so many of them in pine boxes in storeroom after storeroom stretching back and back into the distant past. They didn't expect anyone to take their carping seriously, but on the other hand change would never come about if people did not, for one reason or another, accept it as a possibility. In the case of the fortunate kingdom where everyone wore masks, it began with the young. Whereas people in their forties and fifties and upward continued to retire into their bedrooms at the appointed time and to emerge with a new face, it was said that fourteen- and fifteen-year-olds were passing the time when this should happen, and rejoiced in the thought that in failing to produce a new mask they were defying their parents. When several years passed and they still had not changed their masks, they knew they were part of a New Movement. "It's a fad," people said. "And like every other fad it will pass." But they saw nervously that the younger children had taken the idea up too, and finally it spread to children too young to know what it meant not to change one's mask ever. And, not wanting to appear peculiar, the older people did not retire when the twelve-month period was up, and, instead, kept their old mask, and so it became clear at last that Nature, not Fashion, was at work.

After that the discarded masks were taken out of the pine boxes and thrown out on the dustheap, and with time they became extremely rare, like authentic Chippendale and Chinese Export and gold coins from the reign of the Emperor Hadrian. They were studied by the historian and the moral philosopher. As for people in general, they seemed to grow old much faster than formerly, because having no mask they had to create one with the play of facial muscles, and this gave rise to crow's-feet, and wrinkles across the forehead, and deep lines etched from the corners of the nose to the corners of the mouth, and sagging flesh, which fooled nobody, of course, because the heart of the person underneath this simulated mask was either always young or never had been.

13. The man who lost his father

ONCE upon a time there was a man who lost his father.

His father died of natural causes — that is to say, illness and old age — and it was time for him to go, but nevertheless the man was affected by it, more than he had expected. He misplaced things: his keys, his reading glasses, a communication from the bank. And he imagined things. He imagined that his father's spirit walked the streets of the city where he lived, was within touching distance of him, could not for a certain time leave this world for the world of spirits, and was trying to communicate with him. When he picked up the mail that was lying on the marble floor outside the door of his apartment, he expected to find a letter from his father telling him . . . telling him what?

The secret of the afterlife is nothing at all — or rather, it is only one secret, compared to the infinite number of secrets having to do with this life that the dead take with them when they go.

"Why didn't I ask him when I had a chance?" the man said, addressing the troubled face in the bathroom mirror, a face made prematurely old by a white beard of shaving lather. And from that other mirror, his mind, the answer came: *Because you thought there was still time. You expected him to live forever . . . because you expect to live forever yourself.* The razor stopped in mid-stroke. This time what came was a question. *Do you or don't you? You do expect to live forever? You don't expect to live forever?* The man plunged his hands in soapy water and rinsed the lather from his face. And as he was drying his hands on a towel, he glanced down four stories at the empty street corner and for a split second he thought he saw his father, standing in front of the drugstore window.

His father's body was in a coffin, and the coffin was in the ground, in a cemetery, but that he never thought about. Authority is not buried in a wooden box. Nor safety (mixed with the smell of cigar smoke). Nor the firm handwriting. Nor the sound of his voice. Nor the right to ask questions that are painful to answer.

So long as his father was alive, he figured persistently in the man's conversation. Almost any remark was likely to evoke him. Although the point of the remark was mildly amusing and the tone intended to be affectionate, there was something about it that was not amusing and not entirely affectionate — as if an old grievance was still being nourished, a deep disagreement, a deprivation, something raked up out of the past that should have been allowed to lie forgotten. It was, actually, rather tiresome, but even after he perceived what he was doing the man could not stop. It made no difference whether he was with friends or with people he had never seen before. In the space of five minutes, his father would pop up in the conversation. And you didn't have to be very acute to understand that what he was really saying was "Though I am a grown man and not a little boy, I still feel the weight of my father's hand on me, and I tell this story to lighten the weight. . . ."

Now that his father was gone, he almost never spoke of him, but he thought about him. At my age was his hair this thin, the man wondered, holding his comb under the bathroom faucet.

Why, when he never went to church, did he change, the man wondered, dropping a letter in the corner mailbox. Why, when he had been an atheist, or if not an atheist then an agnostic, all his life, was he so pleased to see the Episcopal minister during his last illness?

Hanging in the hall closet was his father's overcoat, which by a curious accident now fit him. Authority had shrunk. And safety? There was no such thing as safety. It was only an idea that children have. As they think that with the help of an umbrella they can fly, so they feel that their parents stand between them and all that is dangerous. Meanwhile, the cleaning establishment had disposed of the smell of cigar smoke; the overcoat smelled like any overcoat. The handwriting on the envelopes he picked up in the morning outside his door was never that handwriting. And along with certain stock certificates that had been turned over to him when his father's estate was settled, he had received the right to ask questions that are painful to answer, such as "Why did you not value your youth?"

He wore the overcoat, which was of the very best quality but double-breasted and long and a dark charcoal grey — an old man's coat — only in very cold weather, and it kept him warm. . . . From the funeral home they went to the cemetery, and the coffin was already there, in a tent, suspended above the open grave. After the minister had spoken the last words, it still was not lowered. Instead, the mourners raised their heads, got up from their folding chairs, and went out into the icy wind of a January day. And to the man's surprise, the outlines of the bare trees were blurred. He had not expected tears, and neither had he expected to see, in a small group of people waiting some distance from the tent, a man and a woman, not related to each other and not married to each other, but both related to him: his first playmates. They stepped forward and took his hand and spoke to him, looking deeply into his eyes. The only possible conclusion was that they were there waiting for him, in the cold, because they were worried about him. . . . In his father's end was his own beginning, the mirror in his mind pointed out. And it was true, in more ways than one. But it took time.

HE let go of the ghost in front of the corner drugstore.

The questions grew less and less painful to have to answer. The stories he told his children about their grandfather did not have to do with a disagreement, a deprivation, or something raked up out of the distant past that might better have been forgotten. When he was abrupt with them and they ran crying from the room, he thought, *But my voice wasn't all that harsh*. Then he thought, *To them it must have been*. And he got up from his chair and went after them, to lighten the weight of his father's irritability, making itself felt in some mysterious way through him. They forgave him, and he forgave his father, who surely hadn't meant to sound severe and unloving. And when he took his wife and children home — to the place that in his childhood was home — on a family visit, one of his cousins, smiling, said, "How much like your father you are."

"That's because I am wearing his overcoat," the man said — or rather, the child that survived in the man. The man himself was pleased, accepted the compliment (surprising though it was), and at the first opportunity looked in the mirror to see if it was true.

14. The old woman whose house was beside a running stream

THERE was an old woman whose house was beside a bend in a running stream. Sometimes the eddying current sounded almost like words, like a message: *Rill, you will, you will, sill, rillable, syllable, billable.* . . . Sometimes when she woke in the night it was to the sound of a fountain plashing, though there wasn't, of course, any fountain. Or sometimes it sounded like rain, though the sky was clear and full of stars.

Around her cottage Canada lilies grew, and wild peppermint, and lupins, Queen Anne's lace taller than her head, and wild roses that were half the ordinary size, and the wind brought with it across somebody else's pasture the smell of pine trees, which she could see from her kitchen window. Here she lived, all by herself, and since she had no one to cook and care for but herself, you might think that time was heavy on her hands. It was just the contrary. The light woke her in the morning, and the first thing she heard was the sound of the running stream. It was the sound of hurry, and she said to herself, "I must get up and get breakfast and make the bed and sweep, or I'll be late setting the bread to rise." And when the bread was out of the way, there was the laundry. And when the laundry was hanging on the line, there was something else that urgently needed doing. The stream also never stopped hurrying and worrying on to some place she had never thought about and did not try to imagine. So great was its eagerness that it cut away at its banks until every so often it broke through to some bend farther on, leaving a winding bog that soon filled up with wild flowers. But this the old woman had no way of knowing, for when she left the house it was to buy groceries in the store at the crossroads, or call on a sick friend. She was not much of a walker. She suffered from shortness of breath, and her knees bothered her a good deal. "The truth is," she kept telling herself, as if it was an idea she had not yet completely accepted, "I am an old woman, and I don't have forever to do the things that need to be done." Looking in the mirror, she could not help seeing the wrinkles. And her hair, which had once been thick and shining, was not only grey but so thin she could see her scalp. Even the texture of her hair had changed. It was frizzy, and the hair of a stranger. "So long ago," she said to herself as she read through old letters before destroying them. "And it seems like yesterday." And as she wrote out labels, which she pasted on the undersides of tables and chairs, telling whom they were to go to after her death, she said, "I don't see how I could have accumulated so much. Where did it all come from?" And one morning she woke up with the realization that if she died that day, she would have done all she could do. Her dresser drawers were tidied, the cupboards in order. It was a Tuesday, and she did not bake until Thursday, and the marketing she had done the day before. The house was clean, the ironing put away, and if she threw the covers off and hurried into her clothes, it would be to do something that didn't really need doing. So she lay there thinking, and gradually the thoughts in her mind, which were threadbare with repetition, were replaced by the sound of conversation that came to her from outside — *rill, you will? You will, still. But fill, but fill* — and the chittering conversation of the birds. Suddenly she knew what she was going to do, though there was no hurry about it. She was going to follow the stream and see what happened to it after it passed her house.

She ate a leisurely breakfast, washed the dishes, and put a sugar sandwich and an orange in a brown paper bag. Then, wearing a black straw hat in case it should turn warm and an old grey sweater in case it should turn cold, she locked the house up, and put the key to the front door under the mat, and started off.

THE first thing she came to was a rustic footbridge, which seemed to lead to an island, but the island turned out to be merely the other side of the stream. Here there were paths everywhere, made by the horses in the pasture coming down to drink. She followed now one, now another, stepping over fallen tree trunks, and pausing when her dress caught on a briar. Sometimes the path led her to the brink of the stream at a place where there was no way to cross, and she had to retrace her steps and choose some other path. Sometimes it led her through a cool glade, or a meadow where the grass grew up to her knees. When she came to a barbed-wire fence with a stile over it, she knew she was following a path made by human beings.

First she was on one side of the stream and then, when a big log or a bridge invited her to cross over, she was on the other. She saw a house, but it was closed and shuttered, and so, though she knew she was trespassing, she felt no alarm. When the path left the stream, she decided to continue on it, assuming that the stream would quickly wind back upon itself and rejoin her. The path led her to a road, and the road led her to a gate with a sign on it: KEEP THIS GATE CLOSED. It was standing open. She went on, following the road as before, and came to another gate, with a padlock and chain on it, but right beside the gate was an opening in the fence just large enough for her to crawl through. The road was deep in dust and lined with tall trees that cast a dense shade. She saw a deer, which stopped grazing and raised its head to look at her, and then went bounding off. The road brought her to more houses — summer cottages, not places where people lived the year round. To avoid them she cut through the trees, in the direction that she assumed the running stream must be, and saw still another house. Here, for the first time, there was somebody — a man who did not immediately see her, for he was bent over, sharpening a scythe.

"I'm looking for the little running stream," she said to him.

"You left that a long way back," the man said. "The river is just on the other side of those big pine trees."

"Is there a bridge?"

"Half a mile upstream."

"What happens if I follow the river downstream on this side?"

"You can't," the man said. "There's no way. You have to go upstream to the bridge."

Should she turn around and go home, she wondered. The sun was not yet overhead, so she walked on, toward the trees the man had pointed to, thinking that he might be mistaken and that it might be the running stream that went past her house, but it wasn't. It was three times as broad, and clearly a little river. It too was lined with wild flowers, and in places they had leaped over the flowing water and were growing out of a log in midstream. The river was almost as clear as the air, and she could see the bottom, and schools of fish darting this way and that. Rainbow trout, they were. Half a mile upstream and half a mile down made a mile, and she thought of her poor knees. The water, though swift, was apparently quite shallow. She could take off her shoes and stockings and wade across.

Holding her skirts up, she went slowly out into the river. The bottom was all smooth, rounded stones, precarious to walk on, and she was careful to place her feet firmly. When she was halfway across she stepped into a deep hole, lost her balance, and fell. She tried to stand up, but the current was too swift, and she was hampered by her wet clothing. Gasping and swallowing water, she was tumbled over and over as things are that float downstream in a rushing current. "I did not think my life would end like this," she said to herself, and gave up and let the current take her.

When she opened her eyes, she was lying on the farther bank of the river. She must have been lying there for hours, because her hair and her clothing were dry. In the middle of the river there was a young man, who turned his head and smiled at her. He had blond hair and he was not more than twenty, and he had waders on which came up to his waist, and his chest and shoulders were bare, and she could see right through him; she could see the river and the wild flowers on the other bank. Had he pulled her out? You can't see through living people. He must be dead. But he was not a corpse, he was the most angelic young man she had ever seen, and radiantly happy as he whipped his line back and forth over the shining water. And so, for that matter, was she. She tried to speak to him but could not. It was too strange.

He waded downstream slowly, casting as he went, and she watched him until he was out of sight. She saw that there was a path that followed the river downstream. I'll just go a little farther, she thought, and started on. She wanted to have another look at the beautiful young man, who must be just around the next bend of the river. Instead, when she got there, she saw a heavy, middle-aged man with a bald head. He also was standing in the middle of the river, casting, and a shaft of sunlight passed right through him. She went on. The path was only a few feet from the water, and it curved around the roots of old trees to avoid a clump of bushes. She saw two horses standing by the mouth of a little stream that might be the stream that went past her house — there was no way of telling — and she could see right through them, too, as if they were made of glass. Soon after this she began to overtake people on the path — for her knees no longer bothered her, and she walked quite fast, for the pleasure of it, and because she had such a feeling of lightness. She saw, sitting on the bank, a boy with a great many freckles, who caught a good-sized trout while she stood watching him. He smiled at her and she smiled back at him, and went on. She met a very friendly dog, who stayed with her, and a young woman with a baby carriage, and an old man. They both smiled at her, the way the young man and the boy had, but said nothing. The feeling of lightness persisted, as if a burden larger than she had realized had been taken off her shoulders. If I keep on much farther, I'll never find my way home, she thought. But nevertheless she went on, as if she had no choice, meeting more people, and suddenly she looked down at her hands and saw that they too were transparent. Then she knew. But without any fear or regret. So it was there all the time, an hour's walk from the house, she thought. And with a light heart she walked on, enjoying the day and the sunlight on the river, which seemed almost alive, and from time to time meeting more people all going the same way she was, all going the same way as the river.

15. The pessimistic fortune-teller

ONCE upon a time there was a girl who told fortunes by the roadside. She did not need to do this for a living. Her father was an entrepreneur who had made a great deal of money and was on the board of directors of so many companies and charities that only his secretary knew the full extent of them, but one day when he came home from his office there his daughter was, with a silk scarf tied around her head, and large earrings, and a long skirt, and looking in every way like a gypsy except her pale, pinched face.

At first people thought it was a game, and were suspicious, and either hurried past her or crossed to the other side of the street, but women cannot resist lifting the curtain of the future just a tiny bit, and so, pretending not to take it seriously, but actually with an open mind, some-body sat down at the card table and offered her open palm. Not for long, though. What she heard was nothing she wanted to hear, and nothing like so comforting as the prognostications of ordinary gypsy fortune-tellers: no tall dark handsome man, no sea voyage, no business ventures that must not be acted upon in the early part of the month, but instead a threat to the thing she held nearest and dearest. With a pale, pinched face she hurried home and shut herself in her room and began restlessly to clean out her bureau drawers in an effort to get what she had been told out of her mind.

Many combinations of circumstances can be reasonably dismissed as the result of coincidence, but not all. At some point the combination is so remarkable that it could not occur except by design, by some ultimate cause or Prime Mover. Though the woman made every effort to forestall the thing that the girl told her might happen, the events unrolled exactly as she had predicted, and the steps that were taken to prevent the calamity seemed, in the end, to have actually helped to bring it about.

Meanwhile other women stopped on their way home from the market or from the church or a call on a sick friend — never with their husbands, because they did not care to waste the energy it would require to defend their action, and because, also, a woman who has no secrets from her husband is not a woman but a child.

And what did they hear, sitting at the card table in front of the rich merchant's house, with their hand lying palm upward in the hand of the merchant's thin-faced daughter? Miscarriages, misfortunes, death in the family, financial reverses, ill health, ill will on the part of those who were nearest and dearest to them. One would have thought that one experience with so pessimistic a fortune-teller would have been enough, and perhaps it would have been if the miscarriage had not actually occurred, and the misfortune, and the death in the family, and all the rest, exactly as predicted. And thinking always that if they knew what was going to happen they could do something to forestall it, the women went back. They told their friends, in strictest confidence, and the friends came, looking woebegone even as they sat down and before they had heard a word of the fate that was in store for them.

The girl's father was not able to stop her from putting a scarf on her head and dressing up in earrings and a long Roman-striped skirt and sitting at the card table on the front lawn with a pack of cards ready to be turned up one at a time, in a sequence that was never meaningless and never optimistic. She was of age, and had an inheritance from her grandmother, and was sufficiently strong-minded, as he had every reason to know, that she would simply have set up her fortune-telling in some other place where he wouldn't even be in a position to know what was going on, or to help her if she needed help. And of course before very long she did. No one can consistently and successfully foretell disaster without being held in some way responsible for it, no matter how much reason argues that it is not the case. The feelings know better. And in time the women who sat down at the card table pressed their lips in a thin line, clutched their purses tightly to their stomachs, and the hand that they extended was not relaxed but tense and in some cases trembled. Or the eyes beseeched a softer, kinder interpretation of what was to come, and when the women did not get it, they fished through their purse for a handkerchief, wiped the tears away furtively, and blew their nose, and heaved a sigh as if their misfortune, the death in the family, the financial reverse had already taken place. As indeed it might just as well have, because take place it did, exactly as foretold, and whether you shed tears before or after an event in no way changes the event or how it affects you.

It speaks a great deal for the superior rationality of men over women that no husband succumbed to the temptation to have his fortune told, but if the entrepreneur's daughter had had any understanding whatever of business affairs, or of the stock market, or of real-estate values, who knows what might have happened? But she didn't. The only losses she understood were emotional. So the men were free to consider what to do about her. Social ostracism was considered and rejected. She had never been popular at parties and had reached the point where she refused all social invitations. They could have ruined her father financially, and seriously considered doing this, and decided against it, on the ground that it would not get at the root of the matter, or affect the income from the trust that had been set up for her by her grandmother. Clearly she had powers that people ought not to have, and clearly in earlier times she would have been regarded as a witch and burned. They got to her through her mother, with the help of their wives. And the girl, turning the cards over, foresaw what would happen as a result of her visit to the famous psychiatrist, and what the psychological tests would show, and kept the appointment and took the tests and allowed herself to be shut up in a hospital and treated with drugs that temporarily invoked such complete confusion of mind that for days she lost sight of even her own identity, let alone what was going to happen to the doctors and nurses who, with the best intentions, were doing this to her. Before being led away for her first shock treatment she asked to be allowed to use a deck of cards, but that was the last time. When she came home, cured of her melancholy and also of her talent for divining the future, there was a general feeling of relief, as if they had, by taking appropriate measures, indeed got at the root of the trouble and they could expect a long happy prosperous life, without a single serious misfortune or so much as a cloud in the sky. The young married couple who lost their first child did not know that it was going to happen, and so in the suddenness of their grief did not think to blame anybody except themselves, and since this was not reasonable, and similar sorrows could be pointed out to them and are clearly part of the pattern of human life, they came in time to accept the disaster, and were not surprised it did not repeat itself, but merely bent over their newborn child with loving and thankful hearts. Men suffered financial reverses and either shot themselves or went off to South America, depending on their temperament. The ill will of those who were close, people learned to live with, recognizing that an element of this could be found in a remote corner of their own hearts, and when a gypsy fortune-teller set up shop in an empty building on a back street at the edge of the business district, the women — in pairs, clutching their purses, and with an eye for roaches and bedbugs — sat down to have the curtain of the future lifted a tiny bit. The gypsy was a professional and knew her trade, and the fact that no tall dark handsome man came along and swept the stout middle-aged woman off her feet, that a business venture acted upon in the beginning of the month was as fortunate or as unfortunate as one postponed till the end of the month, that they did not go on a long sea voyage — all this didn't matter in the least. They paid what they were asked and went off in pleased expectation of good luck they were too old or too ill or too set in their ways ever to have.

16. The printing office

IN a certain large city, on a side street that was only two blocks long, there was a two-story building with a neon sign that read R. H. GILROY ◆ PRINTING. This sign, which was strongly colored with orchid and blue and flickered anxiously, was the crowning achievement of thirty years of night work and staying open on Saturdays and Sundays. R. H. Gilroy was a short, irascible man with a green eyeshade, a pencil behind his ear, and a cigar butt in the corner of his mouth. The sign didn't mention the printer's wife, though it should have. She answered the telephone and did the bookkeeping and wrote out bills in a large, placid, motherly handwriting, and knew where everything was and how to pacify her husband when he got excited.

From her desk by the radiator, Maria Gilroy looked out on the Apex Party Favors Company and A. & J. Kertock Plumbing and Heating, directly across the street. She could also see the upper stories of the Universal Moving and Storage Company, two blocks north. At odd times of the day, birds swooped down out of the air and settled on the iron ladder that led from the roof of the storage company to the cone-shaped roof of a water tank. The people of the neighborhood — boys lolling on the steps of the vocational high school, the policeman who stood under the marquee of Number 210 when it was raining, and others — took these birds to be pigeons. The printer's wife, who was born and brought up in Italy, knew they were not pigeons but doves. When her eyes demanded some relief from the strain of balancing figures that were, at the same time, too close to her face and too far from her heart, she would get up from her desk by the radiator, and go outdoors and stand looking up, shielding her eyes with her hand and straining for the sound that she remembered from her far-off childhood, and that she could sometimes almost hear, and might indeed have heard if a truck hadn't shifted into low gear or a bus hadn't backfired or if the children who lived over the Apex Party Favors Company and whose only place to play was the street had ever stopped yelling at each other. The silence that was always on the point of settling down on that not very busy street never actually did, and the birds circling through the silence of the upper air never settled on any perch lower than the iron ladder of the water tank of the Universal Moving and Storage Company.

The printer's wife tried various ways of coaxing them down. She bought a china dove in Woolworth's and set it in her window. She tried thought transference. She bought breadcrumbs at the delicatessen and scattered them on the sidewalk. But pigeons flying to and from the marble eaves of the post office saw the breadcrumbs and swooped down and strutted about on the sidewalk, picking and choosing and making sounds that were egotistical and monotonous, and of course they kept the doves away. When it rained, the breadcrumbs made a soggy mess on the sidewalk and the policeman left the shelter of the marquee and crossed the street and told the printer he was violating a city ordinance, which made him terribly excited. So she gave up trying to lure the birds closer and merely watched them. There was sometimes only one on the ladder, and there were never more than three. The business was open on Christmas Day, as usual, and on New Year's, and the birds were either on the ladder or in the air above it, but on the second of January she didn't see them all day, and when they weren't there the next morning, she said, "I wonder if something has happened to my birds."

The printer, who was reading proof for the sixth edition of a third-rate dictionary, bit into his damp, defeated cigar and reached for the pencil behind his ear. "Eeyah!" he exclaimed bitterly, and restored a missing cedilla. On the margin of the proof he wrote a sarcastic note for the typesetter, who was quick as lightning but not, unfortunately, a perfectionist. The printer's wife glanced over her shoulder and saw that the page he was correcting began with the word "doubt" and ended with "downfall." Her eyes traveled down the column of type until they stopped at "dove (duv)." In mounting excitement — for it must be a sign, it couldn't be just an accident — she read on hastily, through the derivation [ME. *douve*, akin to OS. *dūba*, D. *duif*, OHG. *tùba*, G. *taube*, ON. *dūfa*, Sw. *dufva*, Dan. *due*, Goth. *dūbo*, and prob. to OIr. *dub* black. See DEAF] and the first and second meanings, and arrived at the third. The words "emblem of the Holy Spirit" flickered on the page, though the harsh white fluorescent light did not alter, and she felt a moment of fright. Turning her eyes to the window, she saw the orchid faces of A. and J. Kertock, who had just padlocked the door of their shop and were about to go home to their dinner, content and happy with using brass fitting when solid copper was specified and the thousand and one opportunities for padding a plumbing and heating bill. She nodded, and they — quite ready to admit that it takes all kinds to make a world and even though honesty is not the best policy there was no reason why the printer and his wife shouldn't pursue it if it gave them any pleasure — nodded in return. She wanted to throw open the window and ask them if they had seen the doves, but it wasn't that kind of a window.

The next morning, while she was tearing January 3 off her desk calendar, the doves settled down on their perch. It was a very cold day, and she was concerned for them. If they only had a little house they could go into, out of the wind, she kept thinking, and she was tempted to pick up the phone and call the Universal Moving and Storage Company. By the next morning, the wind had dropped and the air was milder, and that evening orchid-and-blue snow drifted gently down on the sidewalk and on the stone window ledge, and on the tarred rooftops across the street. By eleven o'clock, when the neon sign was turned off, the street was like a stage setting.

AT noon on the sixth of January, the printer's wife put on her coat and her plastic boots and trudged through the snow to the delicatessen and came back with three chicken sandwiches on white, three dill pickles, and a paper container of cranberries. Leaning against the garbage cans of Number 210, where it certainly hadn't been a few minutes before, was a Christmas tree with some of the tinsel still on it. It had seen better days, but even so, in a landscape made up entirely of brick, stone, concrete, and plate glass, it was a pleasure to look at, and all afternoon the printer's wife kept getting up from her chair and glancing up the street to see if the tree was still there. At four o'clock she put on her coat and her plastic boots and went out into the street. The policeman saw her pick up the Christmas tree and carry it into the fish market, but he took no notice. When she walked into the printing shop a few minutes later with her arms full of green branches which the fishman had kindly chopped off for her, the printer saw her and didn't see her. Words and printer's symbols were the only things he ever saw and saw. She took the container of cranberries from the top drawer of the filing cabinet and then picked up the branches and went to the back of the shop and climbed the stairway to the second floor, where the back files and the office supplies were kept and where there was an iron stairs leading to a trapdoor that opened onto the roof. The roof of R. H. Gilroy ♦ Printing was flat and tarred, and it had a false front with an ornamental coping. In a corner where the wind would not reach it, the printer's wife made a shelter and sprinkled crumbs (she had eaten the slice of chicken but not the bread) and cranberries in among the green, forest-smelling boughs. The wind whipped at her coat, but she did not feel the cold. And all around her the rooftops were unfamiliar because of the snow, with here a pavilion and there an archway or a garden house or a grotto. The falling snow softened the sound of the trucks in the street, and the children who lived over the Apex Party Favors Company were indoors at that moment, playing under their Christmas tree, which sometimes stayed up until Easter, and was decorated with soiled paper hats, serpentines, crackers without any fortune in them, and papier-mâché champagne bottles. The street grew quieter and quieter and quieter and quieter, and at last, out of a sky as soft and as silent as the snow, three doves descended. They alighted on the ornamental coping and from the ornamental coping they flew to the chimney pots, and from there straight into the corner where the pine boughs had been prepared for them.

Aware that his wife had been standing behind his chair for some time, the printer looked up impatiently. Something in her face, an expression that he recognized as related in some remote way to printer's signs and symbols, made him take off his green eyeshade and place his cigar stub on the edge of the desk and follow her. As they passed the typesetter, she motioned to him, and he stopped his frantic machine and came too. At the top of the iron stair she turned and warned them not to speak. Then she pushed the trap door open slowly. The silence that had been coming and coming had arrived while she was downstairs, and as the two men stepped out onto the roof, bareheaded and surprised by the snow alighting on their faces, they heard first the silence and then the sound that came from the pine boughs.

"*Zenadoura macroura carolinensis*, the mourning dove," the printer whispered, quoting from the great unabridged dictionary that it was his life's dream to set up in type and print. His ink-stained, highly skilled, nervous hand sought and found his wife's soft hand. The typesetter crossed himself. The doves, aware of their presence but not frightened by it, moved among the boughs, seeking out the breadcrumbs, and with a slight movement of their feathered throats making sounds softer than snow, making signs and symbols of sounds, softer and more caressing than lŭv and dŭv, kinder than good, deeper than pēs.

17. The lamplighter

JUST before dark, when it was already dark inside the cottages and barns and outbuildings, the lamplighter came riding up one street and down the next, on his bicycle, with his igniting rod. He did not answer when people called a greeting to him, and so, long ago, they had stopped doing this — not, however, out of any feeling of unfriendliness. "There goes the lamplighter," they said, in exactly the same tone of voice that they said, "Why, there's the moon." Through the dusk he went, leaving a trail of lighted lamps behind him. And as if he had given them the idea, one by one the houses began to show a light in the kitchen, or the parlor, or upstairs in some low-ceilinged bedroom. Men coming home from the fields with their team and their dog, children coming home from their play, were so used to the sight of the lamplighter's bicycle spinning off into the dusk that it never occurred to them to wonder how the lamps he was now lighting got put out.

No two mornings are ever quite the same. Some are cold and dark and rainy, and some — a great many, in fact — are like the beginning of the world. First the idea of morning comes, and then, though it is still utterly dark and you can't see your hand in front of your face, a rooster crows, and you'd swear it was a mistake, because it is another twenty minutes before the first light, when the rooster crows again and again, and soon after that the birds begin, praising the feathered god who made them. With their whole hearts, every single bird in creation. And then comes the grand climax. The sky turns red, and the great fiery ball comes up over the eastern horizon. After which there is a coda. The birds repeat their praise, one bird at a time, and the rooster gives one last, thoughtful crow, and the beginning of things comes to an end. While all this was happening, the villagers were fast asleep in their beds, but the lamplighter was hurrying along on his bicycle, and when he came to a lamp, he would reach up with his rod and put it out.

The lamplighter was not young, and he lived all alone, in a small cottage at the far end of the village, and cooked his own meals, and swept his own floor, and made his own bed, and had a little vegetable garden and a grape arbor but no dog or cat for company, and the rooster that wakened him every morning before daybreak belonged to somebody else. It was an orderly, regular life that varied only in that everything the lamplighter did he did a few minutes earlier or a few minutes later than the day before, depending on whether the sky was clear or cloudy, and whether the sun was approaching the summer or the winter solstice. And since at dusk he was in too great a hurry to stop and speak to anyone, and in the morning there was never anyone to speak to, he lived almost entirely inside his own mind. There, over and over again, he relived the happiness that would never come again, or corrected some mistake that made his face wince with shame as he reached up with his rod and snuffed out one more lamp. The dead came back to life, just so he could tell them what he had failed to tell them when they were alive. Sometimes he married, and the house at the edge of the village rang with the sound of children's excited voices, and in the evening friends whose faces he could almost but not quite see came and sat with him under the grape arbor.

The comings and goings of his neighbors were never as real to him as his own thoughts, and so the first time he saw the woman in the long grey cloak walking along the path that went through the water meadows, at an hour when nobody was ever abroad, it was as if an idea had crossed his mind. She was a good distance away, walking with her back to him, and then the rising sun came between them and he couldn't see her anymore, though he continued to peer over his shoulder in the direction in which he had last seen her.

He told himself that he needn't expect to see her ever again, because he knew every woman in the village and they none of them wore a long grey cloak, so it must be a stranger who had happened to pass this way, very early one morning, on some errand. He looked for her, even so, and the next time he saw her it was from such a great distance that he was not even sure it was the same person, but the beating of his heart told him that it was the woman he had seen crossing the water meadow. After that, he continued to see her — not often, and never at regular intervals, but always at some moment when he was not reliving the happiness that would never come again, or undoing old mistakes, or placating the dead, or peopling his solitary life with phantoms. Only when he wasn't thinking at all would he suddenly see her, and he realized that the distance between them was steadily diminishing. One morning he thought he saw her beckon to him, and he was so startled that he almost fell off his bicycle. He wanted to ride after her and overtake her, but something stopped him. What stopped him was the thought that he might have imagined it. While he was standing there debating what he ought to do and trying to decide whether she really had raised her arm and beckoned to him, suddenly she was no longer there. The early morning mists had hidden her. And in that moment his mind was made up.

Morning after morning, he peered into the distance and saw, through the mist, the familiar shape of a thatch-roofed cottage or a cow standing in a field, or a pollarded willow that had been there ever since he was a small boy. Or he saw a screen of poplars and the glint of water in the ditch that ran in a straight line through the meadows. But not what he was looking for. And as dusk came on and he got out his bicycle and his rod, there was a look of purpose on his face. If anybody had spoken to him as he rode past, stopping only when he came to a lamp that needed lighting, he would not have heard them.

And who said incontrovertibly that things are what they seem? That there is only this one life and no little door that you can step through into — into something altogether different.

One beautiful evening, when the warmth of the summer day lingered long past the going down of the sun, and the women stayed outside past their usual time, talking and not wanting to interrupt their conversation or the children's games, and one kind of half-light succeeded another, and the men came home from the fields and sat down to a glass of cold beer, and the dogs frolicked together, and finally there wasn't any more light in the sky, and in fact you could hardly see your hand in front of your face, suddenly a babble of voices arose all over the village, all saying the same thing: "Where is the lamplighter?"

People groped their way into their houses, muttering, "I don't understand it. This sort of thing has never happened before," and in one house after another a light came on, but the streets remained as dark as pitch. "If this happens again, we'll have to get somebody else to light the lamps," the village fathers said, standing about in groups, each with a lanthorn in his hand, and then, chattering indignantly among themselves, they set off in a body for the lamplighter's cottage, intending to have it out with him. A lot of good it did them.

18. The kingdom where straightforward, logical thinking was admired over every other kind

IN a kingdom somewhere between China and the Caucasus, it became so much the fashion to admire straightforward, logical thinking over every other kind that the inhabitants would not tolerate any angle except a right angle or any line that was not the shortest distance between two points. All the pleasant meandering roads were straightened, which meant that a great many comfortable old houses had to be demolished and people were often obliged to drive miles out of their way to get to their destination. Fruit trees were pruned so that their branches went straight out or up, and stopped bearing fruit. Babies were made to walk at nine months — with braces, if necessary. Elderly persons could not be bent with age. All anybody has to do is look around to see that Nature is partial to curves and irregularities, but it was considered vulgar to look anywhere but straight ahead. The laws of the land reflected the universal prejudice. An accused person was quickly found to be innocent or guilty, and if there were any extenuating circumstances, the judge did not want to hear about them.

In the fiftieth year of his reign the old king, who was much loved, met with an accident. Looking straight ahead instead of where he was putting his feet, he walked into a charcoal burner's pit and broke his neck. The new king was every bit as inflexible as his father, and after he ascended the throne things should have gone exactly as before, only they never do. The king had only one child. The Princess Horizon was as beautiful as the first hour of a summer day, and the common people believed that fairies had attended her christening. Her manner with the greatest lord of the land and with the poorest peasant was the same — graceful, simple, and direct. She was intelligent but not too intelligent, proud but not haughty, and skillful at terminating conversations. She was everything a princess should be. But she was also something a princess should not be.

Or to put it differently, there was a flaw in her character, though it would not have been considered a flaw in yours or mine. Because of the royal blood in her veins, it wasn't suitable for her to be alone, from the moment she woke, in a room full of expectant courtiers, until it was time for her to close her eyes to all the flattery around her and go to sleep. But when the Princess's ladies-in-waiting had finished grouping themselves about her chair and were ready to take up their embroidery, they would discover that the chair was empty. How she had managed to elude them they could not imagine and the chair did not say. Or they would precede her, in the order of their rank, down some long, mirrored gallery, only to find when they reached the end of it that there was no one behind them. When she should have been opening a charity bazaar she was exercising her pony; someone else had to judge the footraces and award the blue ribbon for the largest vegetable and the smallest stitches. When she should have been laying a cornerstone she was climbing some remote tower of the palace, hoping to find an old woman with a spindle. When she should have been sitting in the royal box at the opera, showing off the crown jewels and encouraging the arts, she was in some empty maid's room reading a book. And when the royal family appeared on a balcony reserved for historical occasions and bowed graciously to the cheering multitudes, the Princess Horizon was conspicuously absent. All this was duly reported in the sealed letters the foreign ambassadors sent home to their respective monarchs, and it no doubt explains why there were no offers for her hand in marriage, though she was beautiful and accomplished and everything a Princess should be.

One summer afternoon, the ladies-in-waiting, having searched everywhere for her, departed in a string of carriages, and shortly after the Princess let herself out by a side door and hurried off to the English garden. She was in a doleful mood, and felt like reciting poetry. Everywhere else in the world at the time, English gardens were by careful cultivation made to look wild, romantic, and uncultivated. This English garden was laid out according to the cardinal points of the compass. Even so, it was more informal than the French and Italian gardens, which were like nothing so much as a lesson in plane geometry. Addressing the empty afternoon, the Princess began:

> The wind blows out; the bubble dies;
> The spring entombed in autumn dies;
> The dew dries up; the star is shot;
> The flight is past; and man —

At that moment she observed something so strange she thought she must be dreaming. A small white rosebush named after the Queen of Denmark was out of line with all the other small white rosebushes.

The Princess spent the rest of the afternoon searching carefully through garden after garden. A viburnum was also not quite where it should be. The same thing was true of a white lilac in the Grand Parterre, and a lemon tree in the big round wooden tub in the Carrefour de la Reine. So many deviations could hardly be put down to accident; one of the gardeners was deliberately creating disorder. It was her duty to report this to her father, who would straightway have the gardener, and perhaps all the other gardeners, beheaded. But he would also have the white rosebush and the virburnum and the lilac and the lemon tree moved back to where they belonged, and this she was not sure she wanted to have happen. It stands to reason, the Princess said to herself, that the guilty person must work after dark, for to spread disorder through the palace gardens in broad daylight would be far too dangerous.

That night, instead of dancing all the figures of a cotillion, she sent her partner for an ice and slipped unnoticed through one of the ballroom windows. There was a full moon. The gardens were entrancing, and at this hour not open to the public. Walking through a topiary arch, the Princess came upon a gardener's boy in the very act of transplanting a snowball bush. Instead of calling out for the palace guards, she stood measuring with her eyes exactly how much this particular snowball bush in its new position was out of line with the other snowball bushes.

The gardener's boy got up from his knees and knocked the dirt off his spade. "The deviation is no more than exists between the North Pole and the North Magnetic Pole," he said, "but it serves to restore the balance of Nature." And then softly, so softly that she barely heard him, "I did not know there was anyone like you."

"Didn't you?" the Princess said, and turned to look at him. After a moment she turned away. For once she found it not easy to be gracious, simple, and direct. She said — not rudely, but as she would have to a friend if she had had one — "I have the greatest difficulty in managing to be alone for five minutes."

"I don't wonder," he said. Their eyes met, full of inquiry. "When I look at you, I feel like sighing," he said. "My mouth is dry and there is a strange weakness in my legs. I don't ever remember feeling like this before."

"I know that when Papa and Mama and Aunt Royal and the others come out on the balcony and bow to the cheering multitudes, I ought to be there with them, and that I embarrass Papa by my absence, but I do not feel that appearing in public from time to time is enough. There are other things that a ruling family could do. For example, one could learn to play some musical instrument — the cello, or the contrabassoon. Or get to know every single person in the kingdom, and if they are in trouble help them."

"Your every move and gesture is sudden and free, like the orioles," the gardener's boy said.

"Also, I am very tired of wearing the same emeralds to the same operas year after year," the Princess said. "Isn't it nice about the birds. One says 'as the crow flies,' meaning in a straight line, but when you stand and watch them, it turns out that they often fly in big circles."

"If I had known I would find you here," the gardener's boy said, "I would have come straight here in the first place."

"Or they fly every which way," the Princess said. "And nothing can be done about it."

"I cannot tell you," the gardener's boy said, "how I regret the year I spent wandering through China, and the six months I spent in the Caucasus, and those two years in Persia, and that four months and seventeen days in Baluchistan."

By this time they were sitting on an antique marble bench some distance away. They could hear the music of violins, and the slightest stirring of the air brought with it the perfume of white lilacs.

"What made you take up gardening?" the Princess asked. "One can see at a glance that you are of royal blood. Was it to get away from people?"

"No, it was not that, really. At my father's court it is impossible to get away from people. There is no court calendar and no time of the day or night that anybody is supposed to be anywhere in particular, and so they are everywhere. I long ago gave up trying to get away from them."

"How sad!"

"Until I set off on my travels, I didn't know the meaning of solitude. In my country it is the fashion to admire any form of deviation. The streets of the capital start out impressively in one direction and then suddenly swerve off in quite another, or come to an end when you least expect it. To go straight from one engagement to another is considered impolite. It is also not possible. In school, children aren't taught how to add and subtract, but, instead, the basic principles of numerology. As you can imagine, the fiscal arrangements are extraordinary. People do not attempt to balance their checkbooks, and neither does the bank. No tree or bush is ever pruned, and the public gardens are a jungle where it is out of the question for a human being to walk, though I believe wild animals like it. About a decade ago, the musicians decided that the interval between, say, C and C sharp didn't always have to be a half tone — that sometimes it could be a whole tone and sometimes a whole octave. So there is no longer any music, though there are many interesting experiments with sound. The police do not bother men who like to dress up in women's clothing and vice versa, and the birth rate is declining. In a country where no thought is ever carried to its logical conclusion and everybody maunders, my father is noted for the discursiveness of his public statements. Even in private he cannot make a simple remark. It always turns out to be a remark within a remark that has already interrupted an observation that was itself of a parenthetical nature. As it happens, I am a throwback to a previous generation and a thorn in the flesh of everybody."

"How nice that there is someone you take after," the Princess murmured. "I am said to resemble no one."

"As a baby I cried when I was hungry," the Prince said, caught up in the pleasure of talking about himself, "and sucked my thumb in preference to a jeweled pacifier. Applying myself to my studies, I got through my schooling in one-third the time it took my carefully selected classmates to finish their education, and this did not make me popular on the playing field. Also I was neat in my appearance, and naturally quick, and taciturn — and this was felt as being in some oblique way directed against my father. From his reading of history he decided that the only way to make a troublesome crown prince happy was to abdicate in his favor, and he actually started to do this. But the offer was set in a larger framework of noble thoughts and fatherly admonitions, some of which did perhaps have an indirect bearing on the situation, if one could only have sorted them out from the rest, which had no bearing whatever and took him farther and farther afield, so that he lost sight of his original intention, and when we all sat down to dinner the crown was still on his head . . . I have never talked to anyone the way I am talking to you now. Are you cold sitting here in the moonlight? You look like a marble statue, but I don't want you to become chilled."

She was not cold, but she got up and walked because he suggested it.

"Two days later," he continued, "I saddled my favorite Arabian horse and rode off alone to see the world. When I first came here, walking in a straight line through streets that were at right angles to each other, I felt I had found a second home. After a few weeks, as I got to know the country better — "

Seeing his hesitation, she said, "You do not need to be tactful with me. Say it."

"My impressions are no doubt dulled from too much traveling," he began tactfully, "but it does seem to me that there are things that cannot be said except in a roundabout way. And things that cannot be done until you have first done something else. A wide avenue that you can see from one end to the other is a splendid sight, but when every street is like this, the effect is of monotony." Then, with a smile that was quite dazzling with happiness, the Prince went on, "Would you like to know my name? I am called Arqué. Before setting off on the Grand Tour, I should have supplied myself with letters of introduction, but I was in too much of a hurry, and so here, as in the other countries I visited, I knew no one. I could not present myself at the palace on visiting day because I was traveling incognito. I was free to pack my bags and go, but I lingered, unable to make up my mind what country to visit next, and one morning as I was out walking, an idea occurred to me. I hurried back to the inn and persuaded a stableboy to change clothes with me. Fifteen minutes later I was at the back door of the palace asking to speak to the head gardener. Shortly after that I was on my hands and knees, pulling weeds. The rest you know."

They were now standing beside a fountain. Looking deep into her eyes, he said, "In my father's kingdom there is a bird called the nightingale that sings most beautifully."

"A generation ago there were still a few nightingales here," the Princess said, "but now there aren't any. It seems they do not like quite so much order. This is the first time I have ever walked in the gardens at night. I didn't know that this plashing water would be full of moonlight."

"Your eyes are full of moonlight also," the Prince said.

"I feel I can tell you anything," the Princess said.

"Tomorrow," Prince Arqué said, glancing in the direction of the rose-bush that was named after the Queen of Denmark, "I will move them all back."

"Oh, no!" the Princess cried. "Oh, don't do that! They are perfect just the way they are."

"Would you like to be alone now?" the Prince inquired wistfully. "I cannot bear the thought of leaving you, but I know that you like to have some time to yourself."

"I cannot bear to leave you either," the Princess said.

SINCE they had both been brought up on fairy tales, they proposed to be married amid great rejoicing and live happily ever after, but the Minister of State had other plans, and did not favor an alliance with a country whose foreign policy was so lacking in straightforwardness. The Princess Horizon was locked in her room, Prince Arqué was informed that his visa had expired, and they never saw each other again. According to the most interesting and least reliable of the historians of the period, Prince Arqué succeeded his father to the throne, and left the royal palace, which was as confusing as a rabbit warren, for a new one that he designed himself and that set the fashion for straight lines and right angles in architecture. From architecture it spread to city planning, and so on. King Arqué had a son who was terribly long-winded, and a thorn in his flesh.

As for the Princess Horizon, it seems she found a new and rather dreadful way of disappearing. From the day she was told she could not marry Prince Arqué, she never smiled again, and no one knew what was on her mind or in her heart. When her sympathetic ladies-in-waiting had finished grouping themselves around her chair, to their dismay she was sitting in it. When the royal family appeared on a balcony that was reserved for moments of history, the Princess was with them and bowed graciously to the cheering multitudes. She opened bazaars, laid cornerstones, distributed medals, and went to the opera. When the exiled King of Poland asked for her hand in marriage, the offer was considered eminently suitable and accepted. The exiled King of Poland turned out to have a flaw in his character also, but of a more ordinary kind; he had a passion for gambling. Ace of hearts, faro, baccarat, hazard, roulette — he played them all feverishly, and feverishly the courtiers imitated him, mortgaging their castles and laying waste their patrimony so they could go on gambling. The trees in their neglected orchards soon took on a more natural shape, and sorrowing elders grew bent with age. The common people aped the nobility as usual. New roads were carelessly built and therefore less straight than the old ones, the law of the land became full of loopholes, and only now and then did someone indulge in straightforward, logical thinking.

19. The old man at the railroad crossing

"REJOICE," said the old man at the railroad crossing, to every person who came that way. He was very old, and his life had been full of troubles, but he was still able to lower the gates when a train was expected, and raise them again when it had passed by in a whirl of dust and diminishing noise. It was just a matter of time before he would be not only old but bedridden, and so, meanwhile, people were patient with him and excused his habit of saying "Rejoice," on the ground that when you are that old not enough oxygen gets to the brain.

But it was curious how differently different people reacted to that one remark. Those who were bent on accumulating money, or entertaining dreams of power, or just busy, didn't even hear it. The watchman was somebody who was supposed to guard the railroad crossing, not to tell people how they ought to feel, and if there had been such a thing as a wooden or mechanical watchman, they would have been just as satisfied.

Those who cared about good manners were embarrassed for the poor old fellow, and thought it kinder to ignore his affliction.

And those who were really kind, but not old, and not particularly well acquainted with trouble, said "Thank you" politely, and passed on, without in the least having understood what he meant. Or perhaps it was merely that they were convinced he didn't mean anything, since he said the same thing day in and day out, regardless of the occasion or who he said it to. "Rejoice," he said solemnly, looking into their faces. "Rejoice."

The children, of course, were not embarrassed, and did not attempt to be kind. They snickered and said "Why?" and got no answer, and so they asked another question: "Are you crazy?" And — as so often happened when they asked a question they really wanted to know the answer to—he put his hand on their head and smiled, and they were none the wiser.

But one day a woman came along, a nice-looking woman with grey hair and lines in her face and no interest in power or money or politeness that was merely politeness and didn't come from the heart, and no desire to be kind for the sake of being kind, either, and when the old man said "Rejoice," she stopped and looked at him thoughtfully and then she said, "I don't know what at." But not crossly. It was just a statement.

When the train had gone by and the old man had raised the gates, instead of walking on like the others, she stood there, as if she had something more to say and didn't know how to say it. Finally she said, "This has been the worst year and a half of my entire life. I think I'm getting through it, finally. But it's been very hard."

"Rejoice," the old man said.

"Even so?" the woman asked. And then she said, "Well, perhaps you're right. I'll try. You've given me something to think about. Thank you very much." And she went on down the road.

ONE morning shortly after this, there was a new watchman at the crossing, a smart-looking young man who tipped his hat to those who had accumulated power or money, and bowed politely to those who valued good manners, and thanked the kind for their kindness, and to the children he said, "If you hang around my crossing, you'll wish you hadn't." So they all liked him, and felt that there had been a change for the better. What had happened was that the old man couldn't get up out of bed. Though he felt just as well as before, there was no strength in his legs. So there he lay, having to be fed and shaved and turned over in bed and cared for like a baby. He lived with his daughter, who was a slatternly housekeeper and had more children than she could care for and a husband who drank and beat her, and the one thing that had made her life possible was that her old father was out of the house all day, watching the railroad crossing. So when she brought him some gruel for his breakfast that morning and he said "Rejoice," she set her mouth in a grim line and said nothing. When she brought him some more of the same gruel for his lunch she was ready to deal with the situation. Standing over him, so that she seemed very tall, she said, "Father, I don't want to hear that word again. If you can't say anything but 'Rejoice,' don't say anything, do you hear?" And she thought he seemed to understand. But when she brought him his supper, he said it again, and in her fury she slapped him. Her own father. The tears rolled down his furrowed cheeks into his beard, and they looked at each other as they hadn't looked at each other since he was a young man and she was a little girl skipping along at his side. For a moment, her heart melted, but then she thought of how hard her life was, and that he was making it even harder by living on like this when it was time for him to die. And so she turned and went out of the room, without saying that she was sorry. And after that the old man avoided her eyes and said nothing whatever.

One day she put her head in the door and said, "There's somebody to see you."

It was the grey-haired woman. "I heard you were not feeling up to par," she said, and when the old man didn't say anything, she went on, "I made this soup for my family, and I thought you might like some. It's very nourishing." She looked around and saw that the old man's daughter had left them, so she sat down on the edge of the bed and fed the soup to him. She could tell by the way he ate it, and the way the color came into his face, that he was hungry. The dark little room looked as if it hadn't been swept in a month of Sundays, but she knew better than to start cleaning another woman's house. She contented herself with tucking the sheets in properly and straightening the covers and adjusting the pillow behind the old man's head — for which he seemed grateful, though he didn't say anything.

"Now I must go," she said. But she didn't go. Instead she looked at him and said, "Things aren't any better, they're worse. Much worse. I really don't know what I'm going to do." And when he didn't say what she expected him to say, she stopped thinking about herself and thought about him. "I don't care for the new watchman at the crossing," she said. "He stands talking to the girls when he ought to be letting the gates down, and I'm afraid some child will be run over."

But this seemed to be of no interest to him, and she quickly saw why. Death was what was on his mind, not the railroad crossing. His own death, and how to meet it. And she saw that he was feeling terribly alone.

She took his frail old hand in hers and said, "If I can just get through this day, maybe things will be better tomorrow, but in any case, I'll come to see you, to see how you are." And then, without knowing that she was going to say it but only thinking that he didn't have much longer to wait, she said what he used to say at the railroad crossing, to every person who came that way.

20. A mean and spiteful toad

A TOAD sat under a dead leaf that was the same color it was. Most toads are nice harmless creatures, full of fears, and with good reason, but this toad was mean and spiteful. For no reason. It was born that way. One day a little girl on her way home from school saw him and nudged him gently with the sole of her shoe to see him hop. Which he did, helplessly. But the bile churned in his ice-cold veins and he said — though not so she could hear it — *You will turn against the people who love you the most.* And for the whole rest of the day, under the leaf that was the same color he was, he was pleased. Of all the curses he had ever put on people and other toads, this struck him as the most original.

When the little girl got home, her father was sitting in the big chair that was sacred to him, reading the Sports section of the evening paper. He lowered his newspaper and said, "Did you have a nice time in school today?"

No answer.

"I see," he said, and went on reading the paper. He was an even-tempered man, and it is a fact widely acknowledged that little girls sometimes get up on the wrong side of the bed.

At bedtime, as she was having her bath, her mother started to go in and inquire whether she had taken a washcloth to her ears, and found that the door was locked. She started to call out and then thought better of it. "A new stage," she said to herself and went into the little girl's room and picked up her clothes and opened the window and turned the covers down. She had only this one child and her heart was wholly wrapped up in her.

This made it not exactly easy for the little girl to turn against her, but she knew all about Cinderella and the other little girls whose mother died and whose father presented them with a wicked stepmother, so by a careful reinterpretation and rearrangement of whatever was said at the family dinner table and at other times, she convinced herself that *they* were not her true mother and father but just some people who were taking care of her until her rightful parents came to get her. When her father picked her up and sat her on his lap, as he was given to doing, she squirmed and got down. He waited for her to come and kiss him good night and she didn't.

Later, he said to his wife, "What's with Alice?"

"She's going through a stage. I think it makes her uncomfortable if we show any affection."

Once in a while she would lean against her father, but when he responded by putting his arm around her she was gone. It was all the work of the toad.

"What did I do?" the woman asked over and over again.

And over and over and over again the man responded, "Nothing."

The other toads in the neighborhood knew, of course, about the toad who was mean and spiteful, and they were careful not to sit under or on the leaf he considered his property. Their lives were full of dangers. People sometimes stepped on them without meaning to. Bad boys pulled their legs off. Cars ran over them and left them flat as a pancake in the middle of the highway. In the place where everything is known and recorded, there is a list of the human beings who have been kind to toads, and left a saucer of milk where they could find it, and carefully avoided stepping on them, and been distressed at the sound of the toads' cry as they were about to be hurt. It is not a very long list.

Sometimes the little girl broke down and allowed herself to treat her mother and father as she had before the mean and spiteful toad put a curse on her, but these periods were brief. There was hardly time for her mother to remark to her father, "Have you noticed how happy Alice is these days?" before they saw once more the closed look that meant *Don't touch me.*

One day the woman was on her hands and knees in the garden weeding a flower bed when a tiny voice said, "It isn't any of your doing. It's the mean and spiteful toad who sits under a leaf that is the same color he is."

At first the woman thought she had imagined this, but on reflection she realized that she couldn't have, and looked around to see where the voice had come from, and spotted a toad sitting under a big foxglove. "I didn't know toads could talk," she said.

"Oh yes," the toad said. "But they don't talk to people. At least not very often. It's just that we — the toads who live in this part of the world — have noticed how much you and your husband love that child and we can't bear the way you are being treated."

"It's true that she isn't very affectionate these days," the woman said. "It seems to be a stage she's going through."

"She hates you," the toad said.

"Really?" the woman said, trying not to show how the words had struck her to the heart.

"Both of you," the toad said. "She nudged the mean and spiteful toad with her shoe and he put a curse on her."

If I tell George, the woman thought, he will never believe me. He will think I have gone crazy. . . .

"What's to be done?" she asked.

"By you, nothing," the toad said. "Something has to happen."

"To Alice?"

"No. To the spiteful toad. Wait. Be patient. Hope for the best."

So the woman did. And in the place where each thing that happens to every form of animal, vegetable, and mineral life is recorded, it was recorded that a mean and spiteful toad, with only a small provocation, had made a little girl turn against her mother and father who loved her. Immediately afterward, into the atmosphere was released a small drop of mystery, which during a heavy downpour was absorbed into a drop of rainwater that by a — you might say — miracle fell on the mean and spiteful toad. Feeling a pang of remorse he said to himself, *It's only what they deserve*, and tried to put the matter out of his mind. And couldn't. *If I remove the curse*, he said to himself, *I will be just like every other toad and somebody will step on me. Or my leaf will blow away. Or something. So I won't. I won't, I won't, I won't. I just won't. . . .*

Ordinarily the woman was careful not to touch the little girl but this day the little girl looked so strange and lost that she put her hand on her forehead, thinking she must have a fever. The little girl closed her eyes and shuddered, and then she burst into a storm of tears and threw her arms around her mother and said, "Oh, Mama, I really do love you!"

All the kindhearted toads sitting under leaves here and there in the garden set up a humming in their throats. "Watch out," they said to each other. "I never thought he would do it, but now that he has, he's bound to do something especially mean and spiteful to make up for it."

The leaf that the mean and spiteful toad was hiding under gave forth a faint glow, but that was because of the mystery.

21. All the days and nights

ONCE upon a time there was a man who asked himself, "Where have all the days and nights of my life gone?" He was not a young man, or the thought would never have crossed his mind, but neither was he white-haired and bent and dependent on a walker or a cane, and by any reasonable standards one would have to say that his life had been more fortunate than most. He was in excellent health, he had a loving wife, and children and friends, and no financial worries, and an old dog who never failed to welcome him when he came home. But something had taken him by surprise, and it was this: Without actually thinking about it, he had meant to live each day to the full — as he had — and still not let go of it. This was not as foolish as it sounds, because he didn't feel his age. Or rather, he felt seventeen sometimes, and sometimes seven or eight, and some-times sixty-four, which is what he actually was, and sometimes forty, and sometimes a hundred, depending on whether he was tired or had had enough sleep or on the company he was in or if the place he was in was a place he had been in before, and so on. He could think about the past, and did, more than most people, through much of his adult life, and until recently this had sufficed. But now he had a sense of the departure from him not merely of the major events of his life, his marriage, the birth of his children, the death of his mother and father, but of an endless succes-sion of days that were only different from one another insofar as they were subject to accident or chance. And what it felt like was that he had overdrawn his account at the bank or been spending his capital, instead of living comfortably on the income from it.

He found himself doing things that, if he hadn't had the excuse of absentmindedness, would have been simply without rational explanation: for example, he would stand and look around at the clutter in the attic, not with any idea of introducing order but merely taking in what was there; or opening closet doors in rooms that he himself did not ordinarily ever go into. Finally he spoke to his wife about it, for he wondered if she felt the same way.

"No," she said.

"When you go to sleep at night you let go of the day completely?"

"Yes."

As a rule, he fell asleep immediately and she had to read a while, and even after the light was out she turned and turned and sometimes he knew, even though she didn't move, that she was not asleep yet. If he had taken longer to fall asleep would he also have been able to let go of the — but he knew in his heart that the answer was no, he wouldn't. And even now when he felt that he was about to leave a large part of his life (and therefore a large part of himself) behind, he couldn't accept it as inevitable and a part of growing old. What you do not accept you do not allow to happen, even if you have to have recourse to magic. And so one afternoon he set out, without a word to anybody, to find all the days and nights of his life. When he did not come home by dinnertime, his wife grew worried, telephoned to friends, and finally to the police, who referred her to the Missing Persons Bureau. A description of him — height, color of eyes, color of hair, clothing, scar on the back of his right hand, etc. — was broadcast on the local radio station and the state police were alerted. What began as a counting of days became a counting of weeks. Six months passed, and the family lawyer urged that, because of one financial problem and another, the man's wife consider taking steps to have him pronounced legally dead. This she refused to do, and a year from the day he disappeared, he walked into the house, looking much older, and his first words were "I'm too tired to talk about it." He made them a drink, and ate a good dinner, and went to bed at the usual time, without having asked a single question about her, about how she had managed without him, or offering a word of apology to her for the suffering he had caused her. He fell asleep immediately, as usual, and she put the light out.

I will never forgive him, she said to herself, *as long as I live*. And when he curled around her, she moved away from him without waking him and lay on the far side of the bed. And tried to go to sleep and couldn't, and so when he spoke, even though it was hardly louder than a whisper, she heard what he said. What he said was "They're all there. All the days and all the nights of our life. I don't expect you to believe me," he went on, "but — "

To his surprise she turned over and said, "I do believe you," and so he was able to tell her about it.

"Think of it as being like a starry night, where every single star is itself a night with its own stars. Or like a book with pages you can turn, and that you can go back and read over again, and also skip ahead to see what's coming. Only it isn't a book. Or a starry night. Think of it as a house with an infinite number of rooms that you can wander through, one after another after another. And each room is a whole day from morning till evening, with everything that happened, and each day is connected to the one before and the one that comes after, like bars of music. Think of it as a string quartet. And as none of those things. And as nowhere. And right here. And right now."

A tear ran down the side of her face and he knew it, in the dark, and took her in his arms. "The reason I didn't miss you," he said, "is that we were never separated. You were there. And the children. And this house. And the dog and the cats and the neighbors, and all our friends, and even what was happening yesterday when I wasn't here. What I can't describe is how it happened. I went out for a walk and left the road and cut across Ned Blackburn's field, and suddenly the light seemed strange — and when I looked up, the sky wasn't just air, it was of a brilliance that seemed to come from thousands and thousands of little mirrors and I felt lightheaded and my heart began to pound and — "

She waited for him to go on and when he didn't, she thought he was trying to say something that was too difficult to put into words. And then she heard his soft regular breathing and realized he was asleep.

In the morning I will hear the rest of it, she thought, and fell asleep herself, much sooner than she usually did. But in the morning he didn't remember a thing he had told her, and she had great trouble making him understand that he had ever been away.

William Maxwell was born in 1908, in Lincoln, Illinois. When he was fourteen his family moved to Chicago and he continued his education there and at the University of Illinois. After a year of graduate work at Harvard he went back to Urbana and taught freshman composition, and then turned to writing. He has published six novels, three collections of short fiction, an autobiographical memoir, a collection of literary essays and reviews, and two books for children. For forty years he was a fiction editor at *The New Yorker*. From 1969 to 1972 he was president of the National Institute of Arts and Letters. He has received the Brandeis Creative Arts Award Medal and, for his novel *So Long, See You Tomorrow*, the American Book Award and the Howells Medal of the American Academy of Arts and Letters. He lives with his wife in New York City.

A NOTE ON THE TYPE

This book was set in Janson, a redrawing of type cast from matrices long thought to have been made by the Dutchman Anton Janson, who was a practicing type founder in Leipzig during the years 1668–87. However, it has been conclusively demonstrated that these types are actually the work of Nicholas Kis (1650–1702), a Hungarian, who most probably learned his trade from the master Dutch type founder Dirk Voskens. The type is an excellent example of the influential and sturdy Dutch types that prevailed in England up to the time William Caslon developed his own incomparable designs from them.

Composed by DIX, Syracuse, New York
Printed and bound by R. R. Donnelly & Sons,
Harrisonburg, Virginia
Typography and binding design by
Dorothy Schmiderer Baker